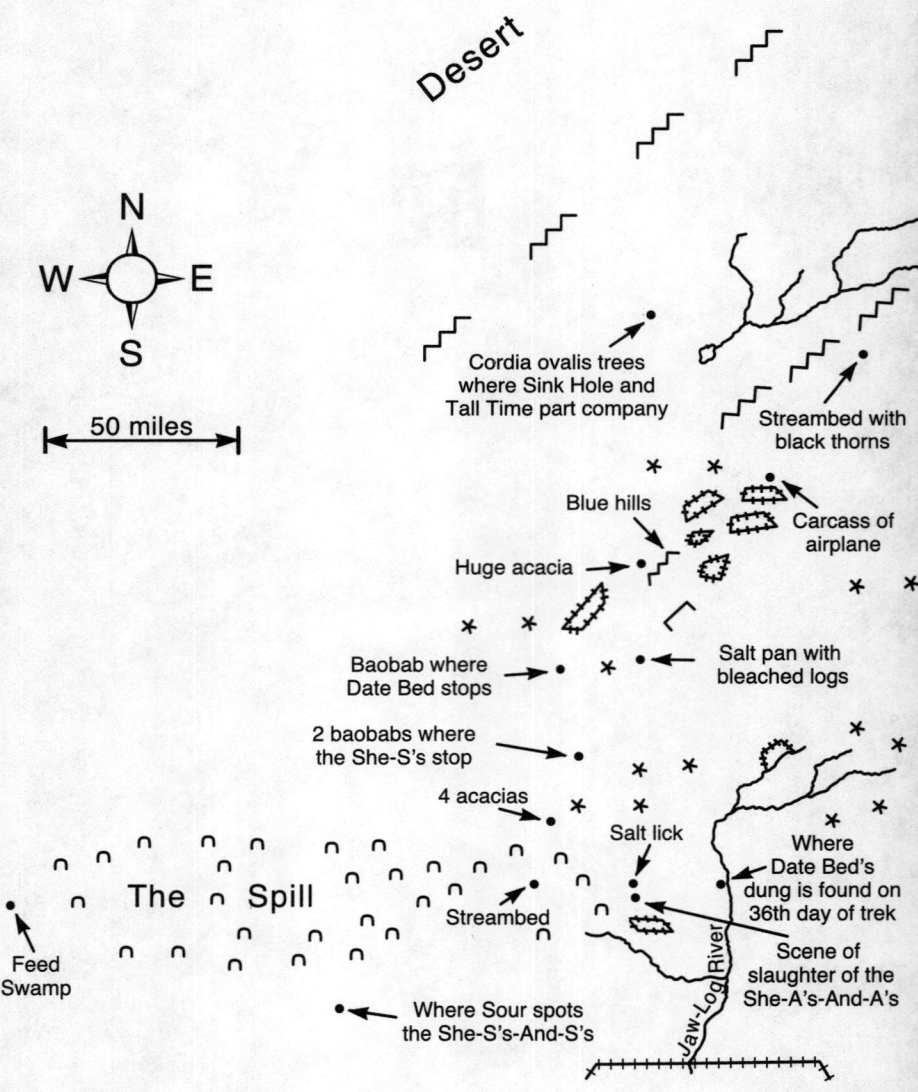

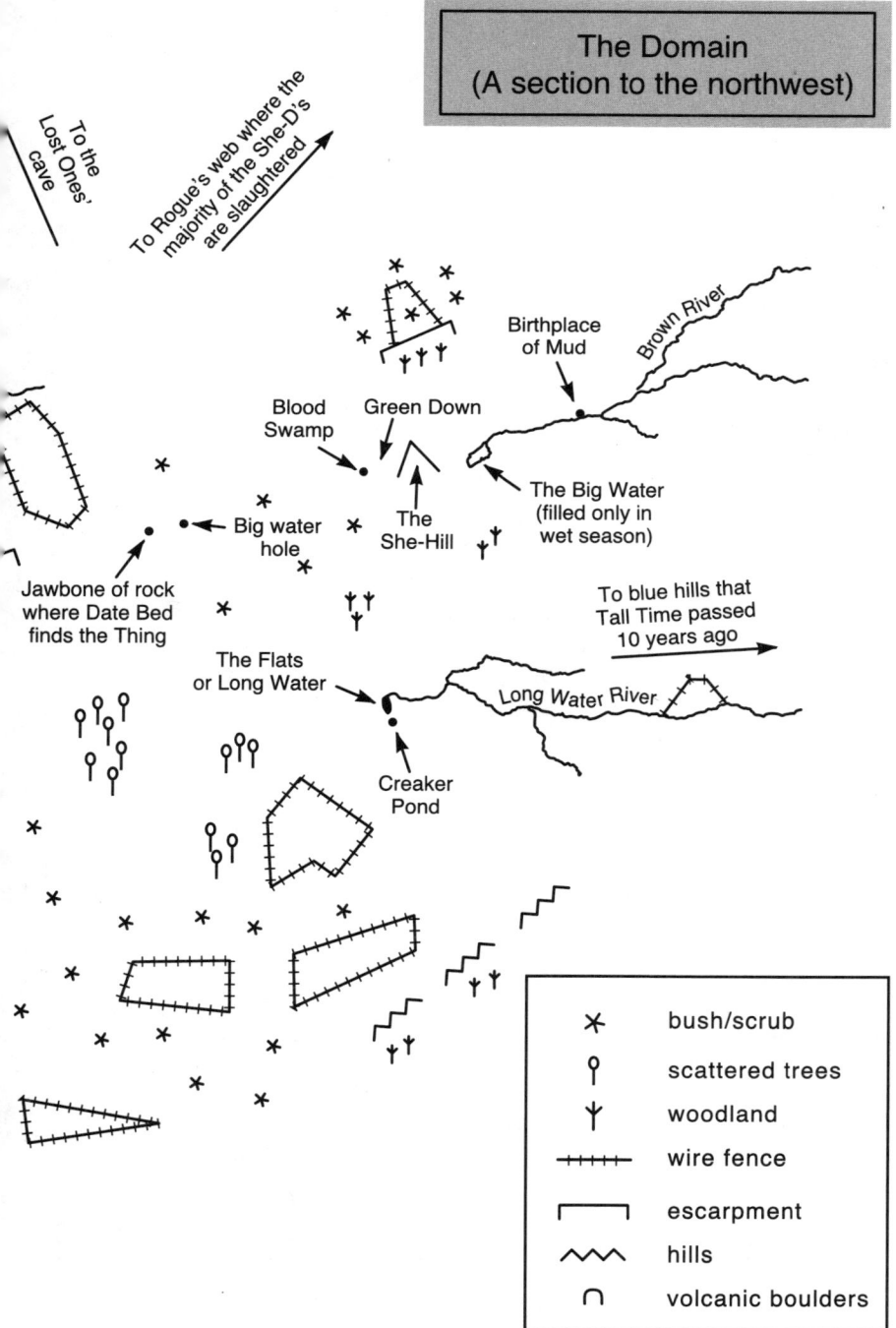

Also by Barbara Gowdy

Mister Sandman

We So Seldom Look on Love

Falling Angels

Through the Green Valley

The Rabbit and the Hare
(published under the name Barbara Purchase)

The White Bone

A Novel

Barbara Gowdy

Metropolitan Books
Henry Holt and Company   New York

Metropolitan Books
Henry Holt and Company, Inc.
Publishers since 1866
115 West 18th Street
New York, New York 10011

Metropolitan Books® is a registered trademark
of Henry Holt and Company, Inc.

Copyright © 1998 by Barbara Gowdy
All rights reserved.

Library of Congress Cataloging-in-Publication Data
Gowdy, Barbara.
The white bone : a novel / Barbara Gowdy.—1st Metropolitan Books ed.
p. cm.
ISBN 0-8050-6036-7
1. African elephant—Fiction. 2. Elephants—Fiction. I. Title.
PR9199.3.G658W47 1999 98-33769
813'.54—dc21 CIP

Henry Holt books are available for special promotions and
premiums. For details contact: Director, Special Markets.

First published in 1998 by HarperCollins Canada

First American Edition 1999

Printed in the United States of America
All first editions are printed on acid-free paper. ∞

3 5 7 9 8 6 4 2

For Chris Kirkwood
and
Rob Kirkwood

and in memory of my father,
Robert Gowdy

Yet in the alert, warm animal there lies
the pain and burden of an enormous sadness.
For it too feels the presence of what often
overwhelms us: a memory, as if
the element we keep pressing toward was once
more intimate, more true, and our communion
infinitely tender.

>—from The Eighth Elegy,
> *Duino Elegies*, Rainer Maria Rilke,
> translated by Stephen Mitchell

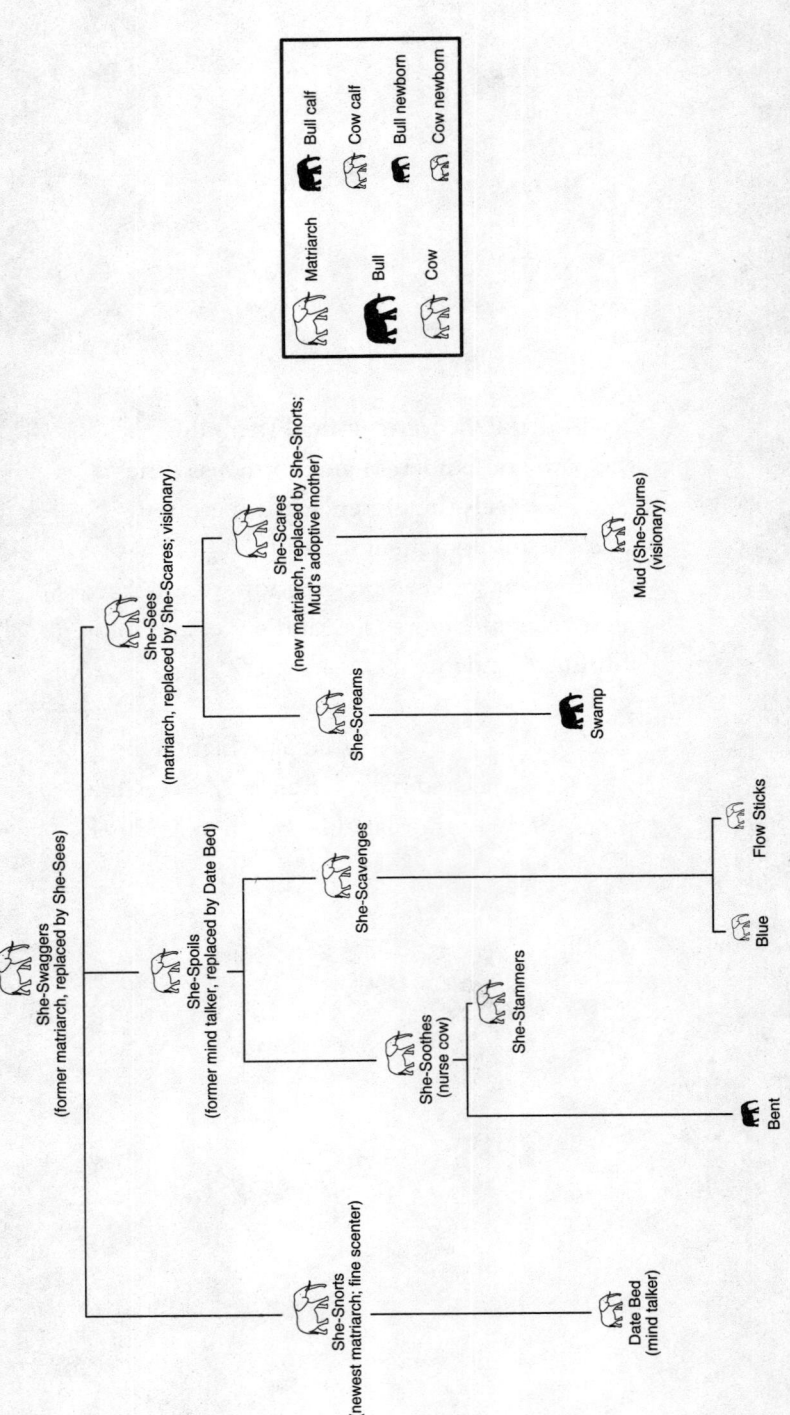

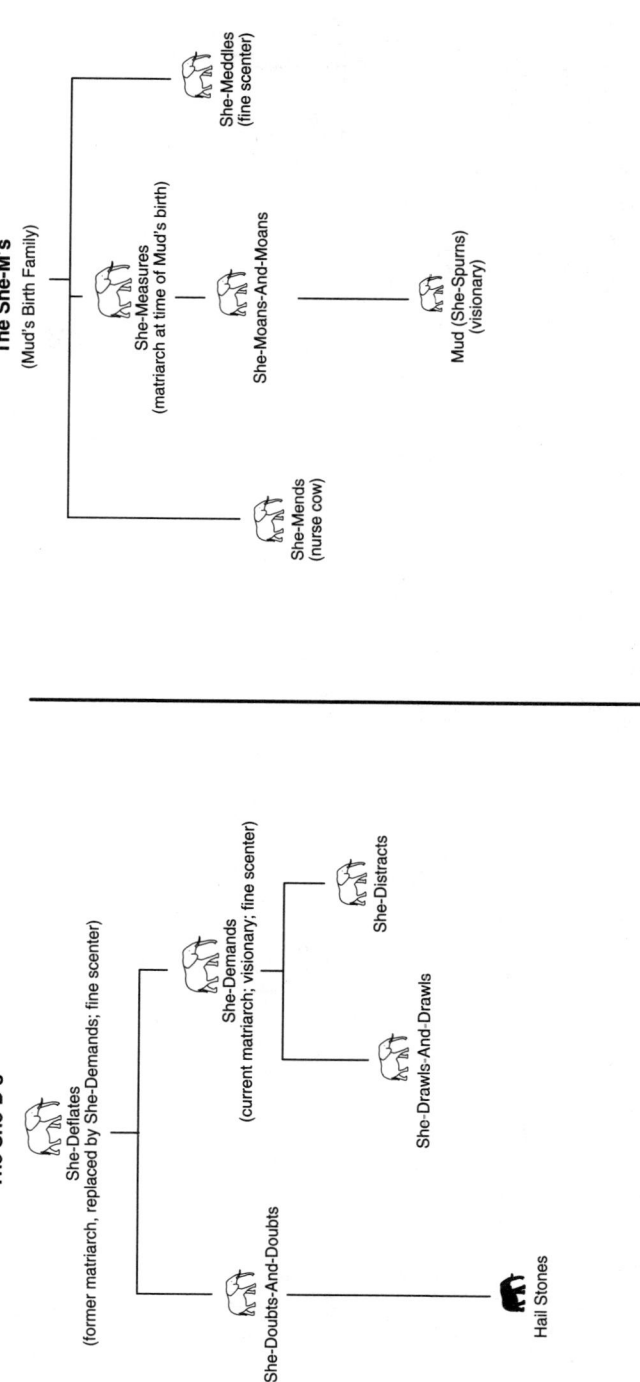

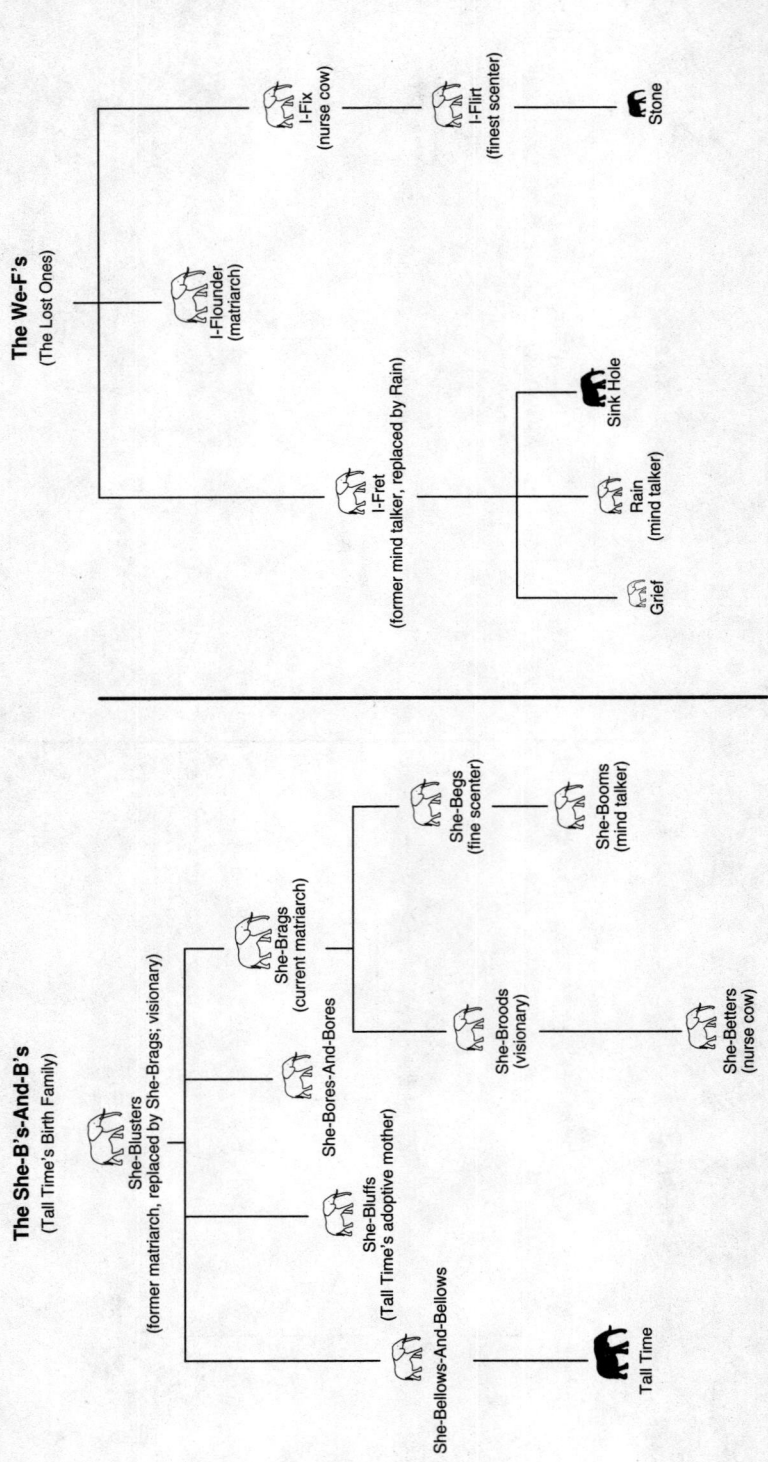

Glossary

All-throat	Gerenuk (it has a long neck)
Away vision	A vision of a distant place in the present moment
Bad tree	Euphorbia candelabrum tree (its latex is toxic)
Big fly	Ostrich
Big grass	Bamboo
Bluff odour	A scent disposed to coating itself with whatever other frail and agreeable scents are in the vicinity
Burr fly	Flappet lark (it produces a high *brrrr, brrrr, brrrr, brrrr* sound during its mating display)
Carrion plant	A foul-smelling parasitic plant found growing on the roots of acacias
Creaker	Cricket
Delirium	Oestrus
Descent	The advent of human beings

Domain	Planet Earth
Drought fruit	The dung of other creatures (crude)
Early milk	The milk secreted by a cow just before she gives birth
Endless song	A song exceeding five hundred verses
Eternal Shoreless Water	Oblivion; the place where the spirits of deceased bulls, calves and tuskless cows go
Feast tree	Acacia tortilis tree (its bark, buds and flowers are all edible and delicious)
Fine scenter	Anybody who possesses exceptional scenting ability (usually only one per family unit)
Fire clearing	A place where humans smoke the flesh of their kills
Fissure	The place of perdition under the Earth where deceased human beings go
Flesh-eater	Carnivore
Flow-stick	Snake
Fly	Bird
Fruits	Testicles (crude)
Formal timbre	A respectful form of address characterized by exaggerated enunciation
Ghastly	Rhinoceros, black or white (it has short unsightly legs, and its "tusks," or horns, are arranged one on top of the other rather than side by side)

Green	Musth
Grounder	Infrasonic call
Grouping	A method of rapidly calculating the passage of time (a group is roughly equivalent to a month) invented by Date Bed
Grunt	Warthog
Hack	Chain saw
Head drool	Temporin
Heat sleep	Heat stroke
Hide-browser	Oxpecker
Hindlegger	Human being
Hind-trunk	Penis (crude)
Honker	Goose
Howler	Jackal
Hump	Termite mound
Jaw-log	Crocodile
Kick fly	Secretary bird (it kicks out backwards as it walks)
Later vision	A vision of the future
Links	Omens, signs and superstitions
Little smoke	Cigarette smoke
Longbody	Cheetah
Long Rains Massive Gathering	Annual congregation of elephants
Lunatic	Wildebeest (it is noisy, chaotic and prone to unpredictable fits of springing and bucking)
Master tracker	Anybody who possesses exceptional tracking ability

Memory night	A particularly starry night
Mind talker	A telepathic cow or cow calf
Mock head drool	The black lines on a cheetah's face
Musth	An annual period of heightened sexual and aggressive activity among bulls lasting anywhere from three days to four months (during this time the penis turns green and dribbles urine)
Other Domain	The place where the spirits of all deceased creatures except for human beings and elephants go
Peak-headed sex	Cows, who have an almost triangular forehead in profile (the forehead of a bull is more rounded)
Radiance	Those few hours during oestrus when a cow is most fertile
Ribs	Zebra (in an earlier incarnation its skeleton covered its flesh)
Roar fly	Helicopter or airplane
Rogue	Son of the She; creator of all creatures except human beings and elephants
Rogue's night	A night when the moon is full
Rogue's web	Wire fence
Shadow memory	An imperfect memory (similar to a human memory)
The She	The first elephant and the mother of all elephants
The She-eye	Sun

She-he	Spotted hyena (both sexes appear to have male genitalia)
She-ones	Elephants of either sex (comparable to "mankind")
Skin	Paint on vehicles
Sky-diver	Eagle or hawk
Slider	Vehicle, specifically truck or jeep
Small time	High noon (shadows are short)
Speck	Insect
Spike weed	Castor oil plant (it has spiky flowers)
Sting	Bullet
Stink tree	Sausage tree (its flowers smell unpleasant)
Strong tusk	The favoured tusk (one tusk is always favoured over another, in the same way that people are either right- or left-handed)
Tail grass	Papyrus
Tall time	Dawn or dusk (shadows are long)
Temporin	A viscous secretion that oozes from a gland behind the eye during states of excitation
Third eye	Visionary capacity (metaphoric)
Trunk	Soulfulness; depth of spirit
Trunk-neck	Vulture, most species (it is believed that sections of a dead elephant's trunk, when incubated by a vulture, become the necks from which the rest of the baby vultures generate)

Underscents	The powerful, ponderous odours heaved up by the earth at night
Visionary	A cow or cow calf who is capable of seeing both the future and the distant present
Water-boulder	Hippopotamus
Water-glory	Water lily
Water tree	Fever tree (it grows along the shores of rivers and lakes)
Wattle	Cow bell
Zeal	A cow's lascivious babble during oestrus

The White Bone

Prologue

If they live long enough they forget everything.

Most of them don't live that long. Nine out of ten are slaughtered in their prime, decades before their memories have started to drain. I speak of the majority, then, when I say it is true what you've heard: they never forget.

They themselves think this accounts for their size. Some go so far as to claim that under that thunderhead of flesh and those huge rolling bones they *are* memory. They contain memory, yes, but what may not be so well known is that they are doomed without it. When their memories begin to drain, their bodies go into decline, as if from a slow leakage of blood.

Before then, every odour they have ever sucked into their trunks, every flicker of sunlight they have ever doused with their tremendous shadows is preserved inside them as a perfect and instantly retrievable moment. They rarely ask, Do you remember? The remembering is taken for granted. It is the noticing they question: Did you smell that? Did you see it?

They see better than you may imagine. Don't believe the stories about their being half blind. They gaze at the horizon, make out what's there, and unlike the carnivores are never dazzled by a herd of moving zebras. If the herd is close enough they can pick out individuals, knowing them by their stripes alone and from a brief look years earlier. The precise tenor of the wind that lowed in the acacias that day, how the sun slammed down through the foliage—these accompany the memory and are re-experienced, and what was scarcely noticed at the time can now be dwelt on.

Suppose, off to one side, waves of salt dust had swirled up from the pan. In memory, they can turn their gaze on the waves and ponder this phenomenon of a lake bed dreaming its lost lake.

Which may start them weeping. To a degree that we would call maudlin they are sentimental; even the big bulls are. Any kind of loss or yearning breaks their hearts.

Chapter One

All day there are glaring omens that go undetected.

Never will this failure of perception be admitted to. Into every precisely remembered hour, foreknowledge will be inserted, voices haunted with conviction saying, "I smelled it coming." Because how is it possible they didn't?

Granted, they are absorbed in deciding Mud's name, but not all of them are, only the five biggest cows. And not completely absorbed either. At intervals they enter the swamp to browse and drink, and the matriarch even dozes and has to be nudged awake late in the afternoon when they summon Mud and announce in a chorus: "From this day forward and forevermore Mud shall be She-Spurns!"

"No," Mud says, stricken.

"She-Spurns!" the cows trumpet. "She-Spurns!"

Mud slaps her ears against her neck. "No."

The cows thud into each other, enraptured by their clamour. They slice their trunks through bolts of sunlight falling between the fever trees and roar, "She-Spurns!" and since nothing happens—no abrupt change in the weather, nobody dropping dead—the sun is deemed to have given consent.

Mud turns and walks toward the swamp. Halfway down the bank her withered leg gives out as if to demonstrate the aptness of the name she had been braced for. Not this one. "She-Spurns!"—their voices have taken on a surprised quality. They are calling her back, either that or marvelling at how, already, she corroborates their decision. She gets herself upright and walks along the foot of the bank. A baboon runs before her snatching up bones. Countless bones are here, grey and shattered most of them, honeycombed with beetle holes. She picks up a slice of skull and holds it against her throat. It is not worth thinking about, all the names they might have given her. Even She-Stumbles—the name she had so dreaded—would have been better, would have been, at least, appropriate.

Why did she let Tall Time mount her? She knew that she would eventually lose her birth name if he did. A kind of derangement overtook her, it seems to her now—the same derangement that overtook him, but what was he risking? A bull can mount a hundred cows and still be entitled to keep his birth name forever.

"That is because bulls are calves forever," She-Snorts said in her customary deadpan when Mud first started to question the practice of renaming females. This was the day after Mud recovered her senses and Tall Time went back to his hermit's life.

"My dear Mud," said She-Sees, swivelling her enormous head in Mud's direction, "the reason a bull does not change his name is that a bull is not changed."

She-Sees is the She-S family matriarch. She is the biggest cow this side of The Big Water, but she is ancient and showing it. In the middle of her sermons she will fall into a memory of some affront she once suffered, and the sermon then dwindles into huffs of outrage, demands for an apology, the uprooting of shrubs, which she cannot even eat, her molars are so worn. Her senses are worn. Everyone, including the youngest calves, will scan toward a strange noise, and there she'll be, scenting the wrong way. Out of the blue she trumpets, "Who?" and "Speak up!" addressing nobody. She introduces herself to members of her own family. "I don't believe I've had the pleasure," she says. She says, "Your reputation precedes you."

"A bull," she went on now—and for the moment she was lucid and imperious—"is merely the digger. You are the dug. You are the altered one. And do you know *how* you are altered?"

"I have a calf tunnel inside me." This murmured in the formal timbre* but dully. Of course Mud knew, and "altered" was not what she was. Nothing so unmutilated as that.

"Which makes you—" She-Sees prompted.

"Hollow."

"Hallowed!" the matriarch trumpeted. She looked exultantly at the other big cows as if Mud had fallen for the bait and then, suddenly grave again, said, "On the entire Domain there is nothing more sacred than a calf tunnel." She eyed Mud over her spectacular tusks. "Declare yourself!" she commanded.

"Mud," Mud said, lowering her head. Displays of feeblemindedness made her shy. "I am Mud."

---

* A respectful form of address characterized by exaggerated enunciation.

Chapter Two

It is a perfect circle surrounded by bands of water. In the old songs and poems it is called The Place, or The Island. The Domain, everyone says these days and has said for hundreds of years.

The first or inner band is saline and thousands of miles wide. The second band is wider still, but this water—known as The Eternal Shoreless Water—is fresh. Where the two bands meet a luminous margin, fine as a hair, precludes leakage. And then, beyond The Eternal Shoreless Water, comes The Mystery, which might be anything. Land or water or fire.

Only the dead have any acquaintance with The Eternal Shoreless Water. As for the band of salt water, nobody now alive has ever seen it, but a few ancient cows whose memories have not entirely drained recall heroic bulls returning white from salt spray and forever subdued by what they had beheld. In the last half century none of the bulls who has ventured out to The Domain's edge has succeeded in getting that far, because, they say, of the profusion of humans and the need to make constant detours around their habitations. The big cows shake their heads. "There have always been hindleggers,"* they mutter, something to that effect. If the big cows are to be believed, no bull today (with the possible exception of Torrent) can match even the least worthy of bulls from the old times.

The She-S family lives in the vast bushland of The Domain's northwest. Here humans are relatively scarce, and why this should be is not known. The grasses are high in the wet seasons, there are streams and underground aquifers. And plenty of creatures for the slaughtering. Perhaps the proximity of The She-Hill is a deterrent (it is big and sacred; humans are small and profane), although no one really believes this, given how humans seem to fear nothing.

Human dwellings dot the region's outskirts, however, and consequently the families of the northwest tend to stay within their small ranges, which occasionally overlap, especially if the matriarchs are closely tied by friendship or blood. Otherwise, families meet only when the sweet fruits lure

---

* An exaggeration. There have been humans since the Descent, which took place ten thousand years ago, during the first long drought, when a starving bull and cow killed and ate a gazelle and in so doing broke the first and most sacred law: "You shall eat no creature, living or dead." Even before the two miscreants had finished their meal they began to shrink. As their bodies grew smaller and thinner, their trunks receded to stubs, their ears contracted and fur sprouted on top of their heads. They rose up on their hind legs to protest but only a weak howl came from their throats. Furious and defiant they declared themselves carnivores, free to prey on any creature who did not walk upright (as they, in their ceaseless rage, now did).

everyone to the escarpment woodlands, or when the rains revive the grasses on Green Down. In a typical year there are two seasons of rain: the short rains, lasting approximately six weeks, and the long rains, lasting up to three months. During the middle weeks of the long rains, on the paradise that Green Down has become, the Long Rains Massive Gathering takes place. This is the great annual celebration to which upwards of forty families journey to feast together and hear the news and sing the endless songs (those exceeding five hundred verses). Since so many cows go into oestrus during the Long Rains Massive Gatherings, it is also a time of mating and of spectacular confrontations between the big bulls. So much is bound to happen, in fact, that cows arriving at a gathering customarily greet each other by declaring their chief intention (next to eating, of course): "I come to seduce." "I come to gossip." "I come to enlighten."

All the other reasons why a matriarch would take her family away from its home are unhappy ones. Drought. Fire. Sickness. Humans. It is this last reason, specifically a rumour of humans abducting newborn calves, that accounts for Mud being born on the banks of a river miles from her birth family's range at Long Water.

◆ ◆ ◆

Mud's birth family is not the She-S's, it is the She-M's. And the She-M's did not know her as Mud but as Tiny. A cow calf who comes into the world at the unusual hour of high noon— the hour when all things have become so diminutive that they fail to throw a shadow—is called either Tiny or Speck. (Bull calves are given the slightly more consequential-sounding name of Small Time.)

Back then the She-M matriarch was still She-Measures, and she had already achieved a degree of fame, both for the symmetry of her tusks and ears (each ear bearing a deep notch in precisely the same place) and for her ability to calculate the likelihood of something happening . . . of rainfall, for instance, or of a lioness bringing down a wildebeest. Mud's mother, She-Moans-And-Moans, was the matriarch's youngest sister. She became somewhat famous in her own right but only after, and as a result of, her death and Mud's birth, events that happened more or less simultaneously. At the outset of her labour she was bitten by a cobra, and yet she managed to stay alive long enough to get Mud born, and not only that but on her feet and even named.

"Tiny," she sang. And then she began to careen.

"You're going to fall!" She-Measures trumpeted.

"She shall be Tiny!" Mud's mother sang.

"The probability of your falling on the newborn is exceedingly high!" She-Measures trumpeted.

They were beside a gutted baobab, and there was also a risk of the baobab itself toppling if Mud's mother leaned against it. She swayed. From Mud's perspective the world was a low grey sky and grey shifting pillars. And particles of red dirt . . . even then, in her first hours, her eyesight had the visionary's exceptional clarity. She felt nothing of fear. When the sky fell, that was simply the next event. Miraculously she wasn't hurt. Her hind legs were trapped under her mother, but they were nestled, beneath her mother's belly and breasts, in a mucky depression.

For some moments the dust continued to rise, accelerated by the force of the death fetor, which had burst out of the body on impact. Now, from the other cows, came an uproar of trumpeting, growling, urinating and defecating, weeping in deep gurgles that jostled the ground.* A cow nudged Mud with one foot until shoved aside by another, larger cow, who lowered herself to her knees, wrapped her trunk around Mud's neck and pulled.

"No!" bellowed the nurse cow. "You'll crack her spine!"

She-Measures and a cow named She-Meddles tried to lift the corpse. The other cows slapped it as if they could rouse it back to life. "Spare the newborn!" they appealed to the sun. They poked their trunks into Mud's mouth, and Mud sucked the tips in vicious fits of craving. Boluses of dung tumbled around her, urine rained down, forming pools. She sucked at the pools.

The hours passed and the distress stayed at a high pitch as She-Measures and She-Meddles kept trying to lift the body. One of them would get down on her knees, slide her tusks under the torso and heave, and the hindquarters or the head would come a few inches off the ground and then thud back down. A little later the other cow would take her turn. She-Measures, who had a young calf of her own, smelled of milk, but whenever Mud squealed to drink, a trunk was thrust into her mouth. Behind her, the heaving and grunting continued. It might have carried on all night had She-Meddles' left tusk not broken off.

---

* They can also weep silently and without tears. Sometimes they do so wilfully but more often "weeping to oneself" is an involuntary reaction dictated by circumstances, such as the need for quiet.

The White Bone

The snap, like a gunshot, had cows and calves bolting out onto the plain. She-Meddles bellowed and hurled herself around like a wildebeest, and She-Measures' calf ran in circles bawling. Mud bawled, thinking that *she* was that calf, its pink ears, its frenzy. A young bull picked up the severed tusk and held it up to his eye. He rotated it and examined it from every angle and then dropped it next to Mud, so close that she could sniff the bloodied root.

By now She-Meddles' roars had dwindled to agonized groans. "Make way!" She-Measures trumpeted, and everyone surrounding Mud stepped back. As the other cow had done, She-Measures got down on her knees, wrapped her trunk around Mud's ears, and tugged.

Mud would remember her first hours of life second for second, both as the coherent sequence of events into which her older mind would gradually translate them and as the blare of images, sounds and smells they were at the time, when everything outside of herself seemed to be the incarnation of everything she sensed. The pain of She-Measures pulling at her, and a spear of sunlight kicking out from between the bodies of the cows, these were the same, one precipitating the other. Fear was the shape of the big cows' feet; craving was the odour of dung. Off and on throughout the day the air shuddered with thunder, and this was the sound of her entrapment.

"Your heart is beating two and a half times as fast as it should be," She-Measures said. She repositioned herself, and Mud mouthed for the breast, and She-Measures then became the taste of milk and the falling night. The scent of the calf that Mud took to be herself was what spawned the fireflies, which themselves were mysterious pricks of yearning and an apprehension of perfect bliss existing elsewhere.

✦ ✦ ✦

The lionesses arrived ahead of the rain. They tore at Mud's mother quietly. Mud, too, was quiet, warned by their furtiveness. The whole of the night rocked in an urgent silence until She-Measures came roaring from the plain.

While the other big cows wept, She-Measures studied the damage to the corpse, muttering how many gashes there were, calculating the trunk-length of them: half a trunk, a third of a trunk. Everybody tossed dirt on the tributaries of blood, and within that barricade of legs Mud had her first vision.* It so exhausted and frightened her that before she fully emerged from it she fell into a sleep not even the thunderstorm disturbed.

The night was over by the time she awoke. In the vision she had watched the family walk away singing, and yet here they were, somewhere behind her. Before her, planted in the rain-and-blood-filled ponds that had been their footprints, were columns of yellow light. The stench of the corpse she assigned to the flies, which she thought had hatched from the tree's bark. She thought the vultures were branches, even when they dived down squawking.

She-Measures was there at once. The vultures hopped backwards but not far. "It would be more merciful to kill you

---

* Visionaries experience two kinds of visions: visions of the future (occasionally referred to as "later visions") and visions of things more or less current in time but far away in space ("away visions").

now," She-Measures murmured, swinging a forefoot close to Mud's head. She allowed Mud to suckle and then said, "There are hindleggers in the vicinity. We cannot stay." She wept. There had been so much weeping that it was familiar to Mud, a comfort, and she fell back asleep.

She awoke to She-Measures groaning, "Mourning order," and the big cows forming another circle, this one outward-facing. "Sing," She-Measures groaned, and each cow passed a hind foot just above the corpse and joined in singing a hymn whose first verse was:

> Let thy blood, here pooled and caking,
> Let thy tusks, thy trunk, thy womb
> Rise to join the She. Her aching
> Love for thee didst will thy doom.

It was a long hymn, three hundred and ninety verses, and at the second-to-last verse She-Measures turned and walked out onto the plain and the rest of the family followed, none of them looking at Mud, none of them lingering. Having envisioned their retreat, Mud knew that they would disappear within a nebula of red dust. She screamed, and one of the larger bull calves came running back to charge the vultures. At a trumpet from She-Measures, however, he wheeled around and raced off again.

The vultures dropped back to the ground. Hissing and shrieking, wings slapping the back of Mud's head, they jumped onto the corpse.

There was the pop of gas, the slosh of innards tumbling out. Rock-sized chunks of gore swilled down Mud's face and into her eyes. She vomited, and the smaller of two birds who were trolling the intestines across the ground hobbled closer and lapped up the pool and then began to pluck at Mud's trunk. In a seizure of panic Mud drummed her forelegs, catching her left heel on a root unearthed during last night's downpour. The rain had loosened the muck that trapped her legs so that this time, when she strained to pull herself free, she succeeded.

She jerked herself to her feet. Considering all the hours that her legs had been under the corpse, she should have collapsed a dozen times before standing, if she stood at all, but after two attempts she was up. She made a wobbly charge at her tormentor, who hopped back onto the carcass.

Her mother's gore had glued her left eye shut, but out of her right she discerned, a quarter of a mile in the distance, a pearly flash. The river. She staggered toward it in what for her was a great migration. Every few steps she fell, and less than twenty yards from her destination she sank into a stupor. When she opened her eyes it was dusk. She worked herself upright and started off again.

The bank of the river was cool and soft underfoot. She dropped onto her left side with the tip of her trunk in the water, her good eye taking in an eagle as it rocked down through laminations of colour in the darkening sky.

◆ ◆ ◆

She was startled awake by a hippo cow and calf as they emerged from the water not ten feet away. She got to her feet and approached the silvery, strange-scented mounds, knowing only that they were the contour of safety. They moved downriver. She started to follow but they picked up their pace. Confused, she stopped. They retreated farther into the night noises: the chirping of crickets, the hoots that incited all the bruises on her legs. Now and then a barking sound clawed down her body, and there was a faraway roar she imagined came from the depression of muck where she had been trapped. She pointed her trunk in that direction and inhaled the death fetor, which still contained flecks of her mother's living scent. In a trance of need, she started to go back.

A Goliath heron glided by in ghostly whispers, and terrified afresh she fell and lay panting as a panorama of barks, grunts, howls, whoops and cackles reared up around her. Out of her right eye she gazed at the perfect circle that was the full moon. She slept, awakening near dawn to her hindquarters being snuffled and nudged. Before she could bring herself to her feet the first nip caught her under her tail. She kicked out with her right hind leg and stumbled to her knees but was quickly up again and whirling to face this new misery.

It was half her size. Four-legged. Hide spiked out in the shape of a scream, backside sloping down. Mouth a crescent banded to the snout, and shining eyes like holes shot through the head, offering a peep of the river. Now that she was standing, it trotted around her and marked a ring in the centre of which she revolved.

A lassitude started to overtake her as a shuddering in the earth drew her attention downward. She could lie here. She lurched a few steps to the side and saw the blossom that her feet had made in the wet sand. Every place of pain lifted off her body in a white flock.

The hyena grunted. She peered at it through her gummed-up left eye. The percussion in the earth intensified, and the hyena growled. Seeing now the teats that trembled from its belly, she tottered forward to suckle but was startled to a standstill when it giggled.

It was staring downriver in the direction of the booming. She twisted her head to look there with her good eye.

Right away she knew what she was seeing, except that she mistook them for her birth family coming back. The sight of those massive grey boulders tumbling out of the vaporous brink of night snapped her out of her langour, and bawling so furiously that her trunk and tail shot out, she swaggered past the hyena and tripped over her feet and fell head-first into the water.

She got up and made it to shore and took a few more steps and fell again.

The herd caught sight of her, eased its pace. She straightened her front legs, but her hind legs folded and she collapsed in a puddle of muck.

"Who is this?" the lead cow said. She wrapped her trunk around Mud's chest and pulled her to her feet.

"Smell how new she is," a second cow said in a flat, insinuating voice that, because it was so unperturbed, Mud found tremendously alluring.

"Where is your mother, my dear?" the lead cow said.

Mud sniffed the leg belonging to this voice. The odour was familiar but not known.

"I smell corpse," the alluring voice said.

A stutter of gasps, and all the trunks lifting.

The White Bone

"The air is theirs,"* a fierce voice said.

The lead cow pointed. "That way," she said. "A she-he."

Through the palisade of legs Mud saw the hyena skulk through the mist.

"Is it a massacre?" a shrill, quavering voice asked.

The alluring voice said, "I'm picking up only one death fetor. It's from a cow, I believe."

More gasps, and weeping now.

"She-Snorts," the lead cow said, "can you smell hindleggers?"

"The faintest stink," the alluring voice said. "They are no longer in the vicinity."

"We'd better leave, anyway," the shrill voice said. Nut-sized tears dripped from her trunk. "They may come back and slaughter us all. If you ask me, and of course nobody will, but in my opinion the best thing to do is to leave this newborn here. That cow may not be related to her at all, and if her family comes searching, they won't know where to look."

She-Snorts blew out a derisive breath.

"I'm not saying we shouldn't mourn the cow," the shrill voice said. "But we don't have to do that right this moment. I'm short of breath. Where's Swamp? Swamp!"

"Calm yourself," the lead cow rumbled. "Wave your ears."

"Wave my ears. Yes, all right, Mother. Swamp. Stay by me, son. I'm having one of my spells."

"I would like to go to the corpse," the fierce voice said.

"No, She-Scares," the lead cow rumbled. "It's not safe.

---

* This is what they say when they are upwind of an odour. When they are downwind and can catch the odour they say, "The air is ours."

She-Screams is right, the hindleggers may not be far. Poor cow. I wonder who she was."

"The newborn has a She-M odour," She-Snorts said.

A throng of trunks descended to Mud. When one slipped into her mouth she sucked the tip, although she anticipated the disappointment of drawing no milk from that source. And yet she smelled milk. Where? She turned in a circle and spotted full breasts under She-Snorts and rushed toward her. A tiny calf was in her way. She thought that the calf was herself, and she halted to be investigated by her own trunk and to gulp in her own milk perfume until, reminded by that smell of where she was headed, she pulled away and tried to go between the forelegs of She-Snorts.

She-Snorts' foot gently nudged her away.

Mud tried again. The foot nudged more forcefully. Mud shrieked.

"Silence," growled the lead cow in a penetrating tone that gonged through the earth.

"One of the She-M's!" She-Screams wailed. "I am especially fond of that family. But I still don't think—"

"Silence!"

Mud leaned against a leg, and its pleated skin was her weariness, its knee her frustration. The trunks all rose again, and by that sudden and unified movement Mud presumed the dawn was raised and the night sounds banished, both.

Chapter Three

In another hour the eye of the She will close, and Her son, Rogue, will assume the watch.*

He is already climbing the sky. A third of the way to the summit He will halt and stare at His mother's Domain with the wide-open eye that should make the carnivores wary but in these calamitous times will make them reckless. They are His beloved creations, the carnivores. The lions, as the most beloved of the beloved, will have their pick of the starving zebras, wildebeests and Thomson's gazelles grazing on the stubble above Blood Swamp. When the lions are so bloated that their stomachs brush the ground, they will collapse, moaning tunes of self-infatuation that, after several more nights, will weary Rogue, and His eye will start its long shutting.

Now, in the lull before the slaughter, Mud holds her trunk aloft and scents her adoptive family, who bathe alongside the hippos in the shallows. The naming ceremony has been over

---

* The She is the mother of elephants. Rogue created all other creatures, with the exception of human beings. He is untrustworthy, mischievous and often malevolent.

for more than an hour but if she goes back the screams will start up again—"She-Spurns! She-Spurns!"—and it will be not a welcoming but a battering. What the big cows do (she knows from when Echo became She-Scavenges) is assail you with your cow name until you accept it.

She lowers her trunk, pinches a wad of sand and throws it over her back. From across the swamp comes the liquid call of doves. Over there, the vegetation is long gone, but on this side the papyrus and sedge grasses still grow and up on the bank are eight standing fever trees. Beyond the swamp is scorched plain, for hundreds of miles and in all directions. It is the worst drought in the matriarch's memory; the worst, therefore, in at least sixty-five years. Just after sunrise, before the wind starts kicking up the dust, Mud will sometimes climb the bank and look around and be astonished by the bleakness: the scattered grazers, their angular wavering shapes . . . the rocks and stumps, the blasted acacia bush to which her family retires each evening.

"Perhaps I'll spend the night here" is her bitter thought now as she watches coils of steam ignite along the swamp's surface.

"Mud," says a voice behind her in a tone of gentle reproach.

Only Date Bed can suddenly appear like that.* Her step is as silent as a master tracker's and she has that rarity known as

---

* Date Bed, daughter of She-Snorts, was born on a bed of ripe desert dates that had been shaken from a tree by Torrent, who is probably her father. ("Father," however, is neither a concept nor a word since bulls are not thought to be co-conceivers of life. A bull digs the calf tunnel, that is all. Sometimes it is necessary for a cow to be mounted by several bulls in succession before she feels she has been "truly dug," and it is the bull credited with having given her this feeling who is also credited with having provided a tunnel spacious enough for a calf to sprout in.)

a "bluff odour," which is a scent disposed to coating itself with whatever other frail and agreeable scents are in the vicinity. She leans into Mud's flank and, when Mud turns around, reaches out her little trunk. Like Mud, she is in her twelfth year, but she is small . . . so small she has yet to go into oestrus.

"Did you have any idea?" Mud thinks. (With Date Bed it is her habit to think, rather than speak, most of her end of a conversation.)

Date Bed gives her narrow head the quick nod that those who don't know her mistake for a twitch. "I was fairly sure," she says, "that it would have to do with your aloofness."

"I am not aloof!" Mud thinks, wounded and outraged, and uncertain.

"I have been devoting some thought to how the big cows arrive at a name," Date Bed says earnestly, "and it seems to me that unless they regard you as a future nurse cow, they choose a name that will antagonize you."

"Antagonize?"

Date Bed blinks. "Irritate," she says.

"I know what the word means," Mud says out loud.

"Provoke," Date Bed says anyway. "They hope that by provoking you, you'll eventually prove them wrong. A misguided strategy, in my opinion. More often than not, cows surrender to their names."

"What about names like She-Sees? She-Measures? Those names flatter."

"Yes," Date Bed says, unfazed. "There are certain exceptions. When my day comes I am hoping for She-Soothes-And-Soothes. Whereas I suspect they will call me She-Squints."

"You *do* squint."

"You spurn," Date Bed says as if it were a harmless fact.

"I don't."

"But you do. At least, you give the impression of spurning, which amounts to the same thing."

"I don't spurn you. I didn't spurn Tall Time."

"No cow is ever named for how she conducts herself in her delirium. Were that the case, every cow in this family would be called She-Seduces."

Mud snorts, grudgingly amused.

Date Bed's expression relaxes. "I can't imagine calling you anything but Mud. I wonder whose idea She-Spurns was. Not your mother's, surely."

"She-Scares isn't my mother," Mud thinks sourly. She looks toward the family. "Why don't you find out?" she thinks, a suggestion that Date Bed listen to the big cows' minds, which Date Bed has taken a vow never to do on the day of a naming ceremony. Date Bed doesn't respond, and Mud is faintly ashamed. "It was She-Screams' idea," she rumbles. "Who else? She-Screams has always resented me."

"No," Date Bed says.

Does she mean no, She-Screams has not always resented her? Or no, She-Screams didn't come up with the name? Either prospect has Mud almost softening toward the big cow when Date Bed says, "She would have submitted something far more offensive."

"Ha!" Mud says, startling a pair of Abyssinian ground-hornbills, who flap up onto the bank, where they turn and begin to roar like lions. Ears tensed, Date Bed steps toward them.

In all but a few families there is a mind talker, only one. She is either a cow or a cow calf, never a bull, and when she dies some other member of the family assumes her gift, first hearing the thoughts of her own kind and then finding that she not only understands the language of most other creatures (insects, humans and snakes are the exceptions) but is able to converse with them, from her end simply by thinking hard. For three years the She-S mind talker was She-Spoils. As she lay dying she said that she felt her heir would be Mud. She was wrong. The vultures hadn't even cleaned her bones before Date Bed started hearing voices. Why Date Bed? "Thus spake the She" is why. Ask the big cows to account for any mystery and they will answer, "Thus spake the She."

"What an irritable pair," Date Bed says now, rejoining her. She is speaking of the hornbills, who have diverted their booming toward a log on which five hooded vultures perch in a formation (every other one facing backwards) that is an especially sensational omen. But today, like the rest of the She-S's, Date Bed and Mud are unaware of the omens. Glancing at the vultures, all Date Bed says is, "Mud, don't you find it curious that trunk-necks refrain from eating each other?"

"You'll have to start calling me She-Spurns," Mud says out loud. She thinks how she has always delighted in the sound of her birth name on Date Bed's tongue, in Date Bed's antiquated and reverent pronunciation of words such as "mud," "dust," "rock," any of the earth-associated words that, generations ago, were held sacred.

"She-Spurns," Date Bed says. "She-Spurns"—lightly, trying to toss it off. And then she lowers her head, as if conceding the name's unpleasantness, and pokes her trunk among a pile of stones that throb pink in the waning light.

Mud scents toward the water.

"I'll come in a minute,"* Date Bed rumbles. She has begun to turn the stones and to bring certain ones up to her dim eyes.

"She-Studies," Mud thinks. "That's what they should call you."

For generations it had been the custom of the She-S's to sojourn near Blood Swamp from the middle of the long dry season until the rains. The swamp is now blood-red in the low sun, but that is not what inspired the name. It was Stay Swamp—and home to three other herds—until humans slaughtered eighteen cows and a newborn here within hours of the newborn's birth. She-Swaggers was the She-S matriarch then, and five years later she led her family back to the swamp because she alone of the former resident matriarchs sensed that the place was safe again. In the twenty years since, although there have been no further slaughters in the vicinity, other families turn up only if sources of water are scarce elsewhere. That none has arrived this season is good news, Mud supposes, and yet considering the drought it is surprising.

Splashing through the warm shallows—or what were the shallows when there were still depths—she stumbles from a

---

* They calculate the passage of time using a complicated method that takes into account the phases of the moon, the position of the sun, the cycles of rain and dryness and, most important, their diet—whether the grass is green or gold or long or short, whether they are eating primarily swamp vegetation or tree vegetation and so on. This method recognizes seasons and exact twenty-four-hour cycles as well as the breakdown of such cycles into smaller units, which are not hours or minutes. For the sake of simplicity, however, "hour," "minute," "moment" and "second" are resorted to throughout this narrative, as are "day" and "year."

cramp in her withered leg. All these seizures in one afternoon are an omen, another powerful one, and yet she thinks only that her leg is buckling under the weight of her disappointment. When the water touches her belly she turns and faces her family in time to see She-Scares charge a flock of geese. Her resentment eases a little. She-Scares adopted her when no other nursing cow was willing to. Twenty days earlier her own calf had died from a fall and until Mud's appearance there seemed to be no explanation for the rivers of milk she continued to leak. Right from the start she was ferociously protective. For Mud as a small calf, carnivores were creatures you saw only from the rear as they fled your charging mother, and your mother's right tusk was like a snake head, all the more deadly for being tiny.

She-Scares' left tusk never grew at all. Cows who don't know her will say, "Such a pity," something to that effect, and when Mud was younger she didn't understand what they meant. There is nothing pitiable about She-Scares. "I have been spared," she herself says, as if tusks were a burden. When a stranger tells her that she looks more like an adolescent calf than a grown cow, she preens, and she may then mention that she has borne just the one calf (rather than the three or four any other cow would crave) and that this "blessing" also accounts for her youthful appearance. Carrying a newborn loosens the skin, she maintains, settles the bones, and worse than that it dulls the perceptions, and it is true that she is extraordinarily alert, especially to sounds. The creakings of a newborn in the belly she can hear days before the mother feels movement, and by these creakings she knows the sex.

She heard Mud's newborn within hours of Mud's oestrus

subsiding. A cow calf, she declared, but Mud insisted, then, that she was mistaken, there was no newborn. Now, apparently, the creakings are earsplitting, and Mud's breasts and belly are fat, and yet she has no sense of harbouring a life, and she doesn't cherish what might be inside her any more than she cherishes her intestines. She prays that she has not been "truly dug," but everybody says that Tall Time is a true digger and She-Scares says that come the rains she will drop a cow calf. The other dug cows, She-Snorts and She-Stammers, will drop bull calves. *They* feel their newborns rolling, and She-Stammers is hearing the dreams of hers.

"B-b-b-bad dreams," she tells everyone with her usual terrorized fluster. "Loud n-n-n-noises, com-commotion," and she has taken to standing protectively over her little brother, Bent, as if he were the dreamer.*

She stands over him now. A hippo tries to enter the water close to her, and she beseeches with her trunk toward She-Scares, who charges it, trumpeting.

But it is the rest of the hippos who suddenly move away. The whole mob swells out of the water and lumbers to the shore, spraying up the geese, whose see-saw honks bore through the air in front of them. Beyond the hippos, clopping down from the plain and setting off explosions of dust, a pair of giraffes appears at the edge of a small group of zebras and wildebeests. The members of this group look starved and unnerved. In some collective dazzlement they stare toward the setting sun (and

---

* Bent was born with his foreknees tucked under his belly. For the first two days of his life he was unable to stand, and the only way he could reach the nipples of his mother, She-Soothes, was to sit on his hind legs directly under her breasts.

that they all face the same way is one more omen that goes unnoticed).

By comparison, the giraffes, who can browse the high foliage—and near the swamp enough of that remains—look indecently hale. They glide through the grazers but suddenly stop a few feet from the shore and rotate their heads so that they, too, are gazing at the sun.

Mud lifts her trunk and swivels it behind herself. Opens her ears. No strange scents that way, no sounds. And still the giraffes continue to stare, and now the oxpeckers that ride the hippos take flight.

Mud turns around.

Above the sun, down through spindles of light, a vulture lounges in silhouette. Mud scans the fever trees. The black shape of a leopard reclines on a limb of the tallest, but it threatens no one, not yet.

Where Mud's family is, the bank is lower, offering an unobstructed view of whatever has arrested the giraffes. Except for She-Sees, everybody is scenting. She-Scares flaps her ears and rumbles a few inaudible words in Mud's direction.

"What is it?" Mud calls, but She-Scares is heading for shore now. As she passes She-Sees, She-Scares nudges her to come along, and like a submissive calf She-Sees obeys.

"It is done," Mud murmurs, surprised. Although she has always known that as the second-biggest and second-oldest cow She-Scares would one day assume command from She-Sees, she is so taken aback by witnessing the actual transition of power that she wades to shore unaware that she is on the verge of a vision. She is in the midst of it, her third eye wide open, before she recovers herself.

The vision is of a web of silver twigs. A "Rogue's web," it must be. (Mud has never seen one but she knows of them, everyone does—their length and their impregnability, the magically regular pattern of their weave and their tendency to form closures within which bewildered cattle often find themselves.) Her third eye slides down. She has no idea what she will see, and so for a few seconds it is incomprehensible. An embankment, boulders. No. Carcasses.

Dozens, hundreds, all wildebeests and zebras. Her third eye tracks along the base of the fence, and the debacle goes on and on. And then her eye veers away and she is looking at another debacle.

The remains of her own kind.

All the faces are hacked off, the trunks tossed aside, the tusks gone and some of the feet as well. Marabou storks step daintily among the wreckage, they seem to lean away from her third eye as it races over the bodies. On a certain cow her eye settles, and by the line of the jaw she recognizes She-Doubts-And-Doubts. So these are the She-D's. Twenty-three bodies she counts before her eye dims.

She starts splashing to shore. Date Bed waits at the water's edge, but Mud races past her to the bank. Halfway up, her bad leg crumples and she slips down, and Date Bed moves behind her and pushes her hindquarters until she gains the lip.

About a hundred yards away, out on the plain, three wraith-like cows and a bull calf drag themselves through the powdery red light. After every spastic step the bull calf flings his head to one side. The biggest cow carries something between her lower jaw and shoulder. She drops it on the ground, producing a high bloom of dust. While she scoops it up with her tusks the others wait.

"What is that?" Date Bed says, sniffing.

"A newborn," Mud says. "A dead newborn."

The reek is that of a corpse at least five days old. It masks the scent of the family, but as they come closer Mud recognizes them. "The She-D's," she says, hurrying forward.

Date Bed falls in beside her. "No," she says, incredulous. The She-D's were one of the largest families.

Mud adds these four to the twenty-three in her vision and says, "Four left out of twenty-seven."

Their own family has reached the travellers. She-Screams shrieks in alarm and is swatted by her mother, She-Sees, who then trumpets, "Declare yourselves!"

Mud lifts her mouth to She-Sees' slotted old ear. "It's the She-D's," she says. "The last of them."

"Oh, dear," says She-Sees. Her trunk plummets.

Mud moves up beside She-Scares and the nurse cow, She-Soothes.

"It's bad," She-Scares says softly.

She-Soothes says, not so softly but toned down from her usual bellow, "A mixture of water-tree bark and grunt piss ought to do it. She-Soothes will need pools of piss."*

She-Soothes and She-Scares are consulting about a poultice for the bull calf. He is Hail Stones, Mud realizes after a moment of puzzlement. . . . It has been two years since she last saw him, at a Massive Gathering, and his odour is masked by

---

* So fond is She-Soothes of her cow name that since the day it was given to her she uses it when speaking of herself, refusing to reduce it to a pronoun.

the stench of his right forefoot. Looking closer she sees that above the middle toenail is a hole in which maggots, livid in the twilight, squirm.

"How will you carry it?" She-Scares asks She-Soothes.

"Carry what?"

"The urine."

"She-Soothes will ask the grunts to piss on the bark itself. She-Soothes will tear off a strip, munch it up, then spit it out, right there where the grunts are."

"Do what you can," She-Scares says. So that the warthogs can be appealed to in their own language she adds, "Take Date Bed."

When the two of them are gone She-Scares approaches the She-D matriarch. "She-Demands," she says, using the formal timbre.

She-Demands rocks from foot to foot.

"We did not cross paths at last year's Massive Gathering," says She-Scares, and as she extends her trunk the air erupts with the gunshot rattle of a flappet lark beating its wings.

The She-D's rear back in terror.

"It's a burr fly!" She-Scares trumpets. "It's only a burr fly!"

The She-D's calm down quickly, as if panic is so familiar to them that it fails to hold their interest. She-Demands shifts the fetid bundle under her chin and regards She-Scares through half-closed, glistening eyes. The cows on either side of her are her eldest daughters: She-Drawls-And-Drawls and She-Distracts.

"What did you name her?" She-Scares asks. She snakes out her trunk to the dead newborn but She-Demands turns her head away, and She-Scares withdraws the trunk and says, "You have reached the water. It is safe here."

The White Bone

✦ ✦ ✦

A nightjar has told Date Bed that the stars are falling. "Are you able to see them?" Date Bed whispers to Mud.

Mud cocks one eye skyward. It is a Rogue's night and she sees only the gaping moon. "Did he say how many?"

"Countless."

"At least the She-D dead are spared *that* atrocity," Mud thinks.

"How do you know?"

"In my vision all the tusks were hacked off."

"But you don't know when that happened."

"There was something so desolate about them."

"Well," Date Bed breathes, "a slaughter—"

"It was more than the slaughter. I can't describe it . . . a hopelessness. I don't think any of them became sky cows."

Sky cows are dead cows who have ascended to the sky to join the family of the She. A star is the shine of a sky cow's tusk. When stars fall it is because sky cows are dropping out of the family of the She and into The Eternal Shoreless Water, where they will bloat and drift insensible among the calves and dead bulls, all of whom fall into The Eternal Shoreless Water directly from this life, the hard truth being that not even newborn calves are granted a spell of bliss in the company of the She. Stars falling in great numbers means that a dead human has slunk out from under the crush of The Domain* and, since he is flat now, easily airborne, has wafted up to the sky, where he is hacking off as many tusks as he can

---

* Dead humans are banished to a place beneath the earth known as The Fissure.

before the She awakens. To have your tusks hacked off in paradise is painless, there is that consolation. To have your tusks hacked off while you are on earth is an incomparable physical anguish regardless of whether you are still alive (the notion that pain ends at the instant of death is not taken for granted). It also denies cows entrance into the family of the She, since for a cow to become a sky cow, at least one tusk, or the stump of a tusk, must remain attached to her skull for a full day and night following her last intake of breath. Like bulls and calves, tuskless cows will never know even a second of paradise.

"Listen," Mud thinks, spreading her ears. The pathetic honking of a wildebeest carries above the rabble of night sounds. The wildebeest is injured. Not by a lioness or leopard, whose choke-hold kills are virtually soundless. By jackals, or wild dogs. Or hyenas. "Do you hear?" she says out loud. "Do you hear?"

"You'll alarm the She-D's," Date Bed whispers. She pulls on Mud's trunk.

But Mud has fallen into a memory of the hyena that circled her on the night of her birth, and she herself is circling as she attempts to keep the hyena in her sights. At the outskirts of the memory she senses Date Bed tugging her, and gradually the hyena gives way to the silver shaft of moonlight agitating across the surface of the swamp and she comes to a stop. The shaft is the reflected strong tusk of the She. It is meant to be a comfort, but how can it be tonight? "I have such dread," Mud thinks.

Date Bed is silent.

"So do you," Mud thinks. "I smell your dread."

"I cannot tell if the dread is my own," Date Bed concedes, "or if I have absorbed the dread of those around me. Your dread." She looks toward the plain. "Theirs."

Earlier she told the family about talking to one of the wildebeest bulls—an unusually approachable and intelligent patriarch—when she went off with She-Soothes to collect warthog urine. Sixty days ago, in a herd of thousands of wildebeests and zebras, the bull arrived at the wire fence of Mud's vision. There was a pond less than a mile away, on the far side of this apparently endless barrier, and the bull said that the smell of water is what kept the herd galloping up and down the fence's length until they succumbed to exhaustion. All of the bull's cows perished from thirst, all the calves perished. How the She-D's died, he couldn't say. He never saw them, which makes sense to Mud. According to her vision, their deaths were more recent.

Mud looks at the She-D's. They seem beyond dread. They huddle together, removed from Mud's family, most of whom sleep now, the cows on their feet, the small calves lying in a clump. Normally the She-S's would have left the swamp at sunset to return to the relatively safe shelter of the acacia bush, but there was no question of abandoning the She-D's, or of waking them. Even Hail Stones appears to be asleep, one ear draped over his eye and his bad right foot resting on his left forefoot. Galled by urine, the worms have fallen from his wound. Some were still convulsing on the ground hours after the poultice was applied, but a few moments ago She-Demands stepped on them. And then returned to guarding the corpse of her newborn. It lies between her forelegs. Behind her, She-Distracts and She-Drawls-And-Drawls doze leaning against each other. All four of them have drunk and bathed and eaten, but they have yet to speak. Even their thoughts are mute. Apart from a bleak cavernous whistling, Date Bed says she hears nothing.

✦ ✦ ✦

The night slides through itself. That avalanche down the bank is the hippos returning. At the shore the two lead hippos stop and crack open their jaws and a dull light flaunts their canines. When She-Scares charges after them, their jaws clamp shut and the whole pack turns and trundles to the end of the swamp where crocodiles throng under a froth of mist.

The giraffes come next. Passing the two families, they dip their necks and look down at the tiny corpse. Giraffes She-Scares tolerates, although barely.

"She-Soothes is as dry as an old teat," She-Soothes roars, and She-Scares jolts around, startled, it seems, by this call to matriarchal duty, and trumpets, "Drink! Eat! Bathe!"

It is not for She-Scares to direct the She-D's, but they, too, head for the water, She-Demands leading them downshore from the She-S's. Hail Stones limps behind the cows, and She-Soothes rumbles to him, "Try not to soak that foot! She-Soothes will bring you all the tail grass you can eat!"

"Let's not overdo it!" cries She-Screams. "What little food there is left is going to have to last us until who knows when!"

"That hasn't stopped you from feasting like a bull," She-Snorts rumbles.

"Or you!" She-Screams shrieks. She tosses her trunk.

She-Screams is an ugly cow. Her face bubbles with warts, her tusks are blunt and chipped, and yet she carries herself with the arrogance of a beauty. Like She-Snorts (a true beauty), she sways her rump and tosses her trunk, except that in her case the intent is not always clear, especially to strangers, who have been known to back away in alarm from her haughty greeting gestures.

"I have my suitors to consider," says She-Snorts. She lolls her trunk at Swamp, who—an odd thing for a fourteen-year-old bull calf, especially such a handsome one—shows no interest in the females. Far from attempting to mount them he scarcely sniffs them, and it is this unnatural but welcome passivity that has allowed him to remain in the family well past the age of expulsion. "Oh, don't rebuff me," She-Snorts says as he ducks away from her, and although pretending to pine for him is a relentless amusement of hers, to which he has never paid any attention, there is, today, a note of melancholy in her voice, and he looks around at her and rumbles, "I am not rebuffing you. I am withdrawing from you."

"Hurry up, son," brays She-Screams. "I feel a spell coming on." She grabs the end of his tail but he pulls free and enters the water on his own, with his customary torpor.

Most of the She-S cows make their way toward the sedge grasses. She-Sees has given up trying to chew the coarse browse, and she stays in the shallows to feed on the thinner grasses and creepers. With her are She-Soothes, She-Scavenges (named for her habit of eating whatever falls from anyone else's mouth) and the three small calves. The She-D's keep to the shallows as well, She-Demands frequently lifting her trunk in the direction of her dead calf, where She-Stammers lingers as if she would like to stand over the body. Eventually She-Stammers moves into the water and contents herself with standing over her brother, Bent, and after that She-Demands appears less fretful.

For an hour or so the two families bathe and feed. The She-D's lean into each other and caress each other with their trunks but still maintain their strange silence, and consequently when She-Demands trumpets, although it is a thin and rattled sound, the She-S's are so alarmed that they start up a chorus of "Help!" and "Beware!" before they know what the danger is.

It's a spotted hyena. Up on the bank, trotting back and forth above the corpse of the newborn. She-Scares sloshes to shore. By the time she reaches it, She-Demands has chased the hyena onto the plain, but for good measure She-Scares chases it farther.

Back on the beach She-Demands walks over to the corpse. She turns and raises a hind foot. Looking off to one side she brings the foot down on the torso.

The whoosh of impact carries out onto the swamp. She lifts her foot again. Whoosh!

Four times she steps on her dead newborn. She kicks sand over the remains, walks to where the sand is dryer and blows two trunkfuls over herself. Her daughters and Hail Stones go to her as the rest of the She-S cows start moving out of the swamp, and She-Scares—who watched the spectacle from up on the bank—slides on her haunches down to the shore and herself kicks sand over the body.

"Mud," She-Demands says.

Mud is coming out of the water a little behind her family, who now surround and sniff the corpse. Surprised at being singled out, she nudges her way through the big cows until she is in front of the She-D matriarch. She-Demands used to be one of the more forbidding cows, famous for her spiritual sermons and the wideness of her head. Now her head slings forward from her shoulders and is so deflated that Mud wonders how it is possible she scented the hyena. Temporin leaks down her face, and respectfully Mud touches the exudate and then slips her trunk into the old cow's mouth but quickly withdraws at the stench of despair and decaying molars. She-Demands dips her head to look at her. In those milky eyes, behind whatever accretions of misery have killed all expression, Mud sees the glitter of a cow alight with visions.

"My newborn I named Mud." Her voice is grainy and soft, as if she has suffered damage to her throat. "Scratch would have been the more appropriate name; there was no mud in the vicinity. However, I prefer the ring of Mud, and I had been dreaming of wallows."

Mud can't think how to respond. Next to her, She-Scares rumbles, "Our Mud just acquired her cow name. She is now She-Spurns."

She-Demands seems not to hear this. To Mud she says, "You have the third eye."

"Yes."

"It will not show you your mother's death or the death of any of your calves. Did you know that?"

Mud did not. That she is unlikely to be shown *herself* is the only prohibition she has ever heard. She turns to look at She-Sees, who also has the third eye, and the old cow looks back at her and mutters, "Knowing things is only a dream of having known them."

Again She-Demands seems not to hear. "You might foresee the deaths of your sisters and aunts," she continues, "your adoptive mother. I foresaw all these deaths in my own family. But you will not foresee the death of the one who gave you life or of the ones to whom you will give life, although you might be offered a glimpse of whatever it is that kills them. Two hundred and ten days ago I foresaw the Rogue's web and the hindleggers dropping out of the belly of the roar fly. I said to myself, we must steer clear of webs. But this web was not known to me. And, in any event, it was not the web that shot us."

"Oh, you were shot," Mud says. "I couldn't see any sting holes."

"You envisioned the slaughter?"

"Just as you were arriving here. I saw the lunatics and ribs, hundreds and hundreds of corpses, and then . . . your family. I counted twenty-three."

"Did you return?" She-Scares asks the She-D matriarch. Not all survivors of a slaughter return to mourn their dead.

"The ne . . . xt a . . . fter . . . noon." This from She-Drawls-And-Drawls, whose peculiar habit of stretching out each word makes it sound as if she is calling from far away. "The tusks we . . . re go . . . ne, and so . . . me of the fe . . . et."

She-Screams begins to weep out loud, and then all the She-S's, even She-Snorts, even Swamp, are weeping out loud, urinating and defecating, streaming temporin. The She-D's step aside from the commotion and are silent until She-Scares recovers herself enough to ask, "How is it that you were spared?"

"We ran," She-Demands says simply.

"We ran and ran," She-Distracts sing-songs.

It is She-Distracts' first utterance. There is a silence as everyone waits in case she has more to say. Instead she breaks into a mad little running-on-the-spot dance, a parody of flight, ears wide, tail out, kicking up her legs.

"Don't," Hail Stones says. "Please." He lays his trunk across her haunches, and she lowers her head and goes still. "Matriarch, I think she is overheated," he says to She-Demands in the formal timbre.

His voice is the musical rumble of a courteous old bull. That beautiful, that unfitting. The She-S's now turn their attention to him, and despite the reek of his wound Mud picks up his savoury odour of fresh dung and fermenting fruit. He is eleven years old. Far too young to properly mount a cow, she thinks, and she looks at his poor foot to account for her sudden desolation.

"Let us get ourselves under the trees," She-Scares says.

Both families move slowly to keep pace with Hail Stones, and in an unusual display of exertion and solicitude Swamp gives him a boost up the bank. When they reach the fever trees, She-Scares pulls down the highest branches so that everybody can browse on the bark and shrivelled leaves, and She-Demands turns to Mud again and says, "We met your birth family."

"The She-M's?" She-Scares says, spreading her ears. The She-M's have become the most secretive of herds, rarely encountered. Mud has not seen them since they left her under the gutted baobab the day after her birth. "Where?" She-Scares says.

"At The She-Hill, coming out of the salt-lick cave. Three cows and two calves."

"Where were the rest?"

She-Demands starts to peel a strip of bark. "Slaughtered," she says.

"Ah!" She-Scares says. She stabs her tiny tusk as if fending off humans.

She-Demands chews and watches her.

"Was She-Measures spared?" Mud asks anxiously.

"She-Measures is no longer the matriarch," She-Demands says. "She has gone dreamy." And as if to demonstrate she shuts her eyes and seems to fall asleep. A pair of cattle egrets lands on her back, and Mud is about to speak when her eyes open and she says, "She has a message for you, Mud. *Two* messages. The first is, forgive her for abandoning you to your doom, but there was only one chance in four hundred and six that the muck would release you. That is the first message. The second is, indulge Me-Me the longbody. She may know where The Safe Place is."

"When did you meet them?" Mud asks, weeping now.

"Fif . . . ty-five days a . . . go," answers She-Drawls-And-Drawls.

She-Scares says, "We are not acquainted with any longbody."

"Nor are we, Matriarch," says Hail Stones. Again he uses the formal timbre.

She-Scares looks at him. " 'She may know where The Safe Place is'? What could that mean? What safe place?"

He dips his head deferentially, as few bull calves do these days when responding to a direct question from another family's matriarch. "The only Safe Place," he says. He limps over to She-Demands and runs his trunk down her flank and says, "Matriarch, might I tell them?"

The White Bone

An airplane passes high overhead, somewhere to the southeast, and She-Demands twists around and squints at the low sun. The plane is too far away even for Mud to see, but a haunted expression grips the matriarch's features. Still, She-Demands has heard Hail Stones and she nods.

"Thank you," he says. He turns to the She-S's. Despite the stench of his foot they move closer. "This story," he says, "was told to us by Rancid of the She-D's-And-D's,* cousin to our matriarch. It concerns a magical bone called the white bone, which we call the white prize because whenever somebody speaks of it by name it loses a small portion of its power. Rancid was so worried about the white prize becoming entirely powerless that he asked us to keep the story to ourselves. But it seems to me that this is no longer the time for secrecy."

"You can trust in our discretion," She-Scares says.

"Rancid is very big and fearsome," She-Snorts says, "is he not?" Her eyes glitter.

"He is dead," rumbles She-Demands, who continues to nod and look terrified.

---

* When a family grows overly large, one of the older cows may break away— taking her calves, grandcalves and younger sisters with her—to start a new branch of the family. In order to name itself, this branch will double the family sound. A breakaway family splitting off from a family that is already double-sounded will call itself (for example) the Second She-D's-And-D's. Individual cow names are occasionally doubled within a family unit if it is deemed appropriate for a young cow to be named after an older, still-living relative.

"Ah," She-Scares says and tosses her head.

"No, Matriarch," Hail Stones says with another slight bow in her direction, "he was not slaughtered. He died two hundred days ago of a tired heart. We had heard his death rumble and found him lying in the tail grass on the banks of Long Water River. As soon as he saw our matriarch he started telling the story. He knew he was living his final hour, and as he was always very fond of our matriarch he wanted to bequeath her something that might one day be her salvation."

Here Hail Stones grimaces and lifts his bad foot. "Matriarch," he says to She-Scares, "with your permission I would like to lie down."

"Of course," She-Scares says.

"I will clear a bed," says Swamp, and in a second surprising fit of activity he kicks several stones and twigs out of the way.

Hail Stones eases himself onto his side. Everybody forms a circle around him, and he is drenched in shade. He looks up at She-Scares. Using the formal diction he tells them this:

The emergence of humans did not, as is widely assumed, initiate a time of darkness. On the contrary, in the first generations following the Descent, The Domain was a glorious place, and this is partly because humans back then were nothing like today's breed. They ate flesh, yes, and they were unrepentant and wrathful, but they killed only to eat, and very few of them had a taste for she-ones. There weren't any massacres or mutilations. There was plenitude and ease, and between she-ones and other creatures was a rare communion, for (here is another little-known fact) all she-ones were mind talkers, and the minds of all creatures were intelligible.

When the darkness did arrive, however, it was especially catastrophic. No rain fell for six hundred days and six hundred nights. The winds were ceaseless, and the air was thick with black dust. As water and grazing disappeared, the various species grew wary of each other, and the minds of humans, snakes and insects became impenetrable. From the minds of snakes and insects could be heard only a faint chiming. From the minds of humans came a silence so absolute and menacing that many of those who heard it forswore mind talking altogether.

What provoked that terrible silence? It was the darkness... the darkness had entered the humans and was corrupting their already corrupt spirits. Soon they were slaughtering whole families. After devouring the flesh of their kills, they were burning the hides and pulverizing the bones and tusks. They seemed bent on annihilation, and the surviving she-ones fled to the edges of The Domain without any thought of returning to mourn their dead, since they believed that no trace of the dead remained.

They were wrong. In the centre of a circle of boulders the rib of a newborn remained. None of the humans who passed the boulders ever spotted it, even though, over the years, it bleached to a blinding whiteness. Meanwhile it radiated toward all living creatures a quality of forgiveness and hope. But the hearts of humans were hard, and would not be pierced. Not then.

The darkness finally lifted, the massacres eased off, and

the she-ones went back to their old ranges. Released from the miseries of the black dust, a small number of humans felt the power of the white bone. They set out to discover a place of tranquillity and permanent green browse and, when they did, declared it a safe vicinity for every creature on The Domain, including the carnivores, although they themselves were no longer of that order.

Since then, there have been rumours of this refuge among all species, but only she-ones can be led there. What guides them is the white bone, which, in times of darkness, surfaces in various regions of The Domain, always within a circle of boulders or termite mounds to the west of whatever hills are in the region. It constantly moves about. For exactly two days and two nights (long enough for any good tracker to set a course) it stays in a family's or individual's possession and then vanishes to reappear within another circle of boulders or termite mounds. The deeper the darkness, the whiter it is to the eyes of she-ones. (To the eyes of other creatures it is drab and unremarkable.) Any she-one lucky enough to find it should throw it into the air, mark how it lands and be directed by its pointed end. But whoever throws it must believe in its power.

"Otherwise," Hail Stones says, "it will only lead the thrower in circles." He comes to his feet.

The She-S's nearest him step back . . . awkwardly, blinking. They are dazed by what they have heard.

"We never did learn how Rancid came by the legend," Hail Stones says. "He died before we could ask. But we did not doubt him. With his last breath he told us that the short rains would fail to arrive and that Long Water River would migrate in its entirety, and he was right about that as well.* How he could have known is another mystery."

"Rancid never spoke a false word," says She-Demands rather forcefully. Her head still nods.

"He was truth itself," Hail Stones says. He reaches for the old matriarch's trunk and gently pulls on it until she stops moving.

"Well," She-Scares rumbles, "if Rancid predicted this drought when nobody else, not even Tall Time, smelled it coming, then I, for one, believe his story."

There is a rumble of agreement from the other She-S cows.

"Although," says She-Snorts, "it is difficult to imagine a breed of humans pierced by goodness."

"Even the blackest crevices have known a moment of sunlight," observes Swamp . . . who occasionally makes such enticing but unfounded pronouncements.

---

* Inland bodies of water migrate, drop by drop, to sleep caves beyond the edge of the earth. Eventually the water awakens and leaves the caves to drift back over the earth in the form of thunderclouds. When a cloud is near the depression from which it arose, it breaks apart and spills down. (The horizon migrates inversely. During the dry season, as the air becomes increasingly dusty and the distance blurs, the horizon is sluggishly closing in. After the first rains the reinvigorated horizon departs so quickly that within two or three days the distance is once again visible.)

Chapter Four

Ten minutes later the same airplane that disturbed She-Demands dips low over a region of desiccated palm woodland where Tall Time has run for cover. Only when the roar has evaporated does it occur to him that he is facing the escarpment and that, as a result of this blunder, all of his bull relations will fall over. Sickened to think that he could have overlooked such a common superstition, he rumbles a series of infrasonic apologies.* He does so despite the fact that none of his bull relations is within hearing range.

He would have known if they were, there would have been

---

* Infrasonic rumbles, or "grounders," are long-distance body messages. To reach a specific individual the sender rumbles at that individual's unique body frequency. The rumble originates in the belly rather than in the throat and goes down the feet and legs into the ground where it radiates until it enters the feet and legs of the receiver, provided that he or she is within transmission radius. Infrasonic rumbles have the advantage of travelling long distances at great speeds but are prone to interference from earth upheavals, such as stampedes and minor quakes.

some communication. At the very least there would have been a scent, however stale. But in a hundred and ninety days he hasn't come across a single sign or word of any member of his birth family, who are the She-B's-And-B's. He fears for their lives as he fears for the lives of everyone precious to him. With a terrible sense of helplessness—and without reason, since she is safe at Blood Swamp and since he is well aware that all the omens regarding her are favourable—he fears for Mud, imagining her as she was when he first laid eyes on her, timid and homely, or imagining her trying to flee a gang of humans, her withered leg slowing her down.

It is mostly for Mud's sake that he is not at Blood Swamp himself but fifty miles north of it looking for a certain white bone.

During a drought the land is not wanting for bones, and to make matters worse the very existence of the white bone is in question. And yet he has undertaken the search with what some might call his characteristic ardour. He has heard himself described as an ardent bull, prone to excessive enthusiasms and anxieties (and to singular desires and to ridiculous, archaic turns of phrase).

Well, as his old matriarch was fond of saying, "the long-legged go to lengths."

He stomps his left hind foot three times, circles to the left one full revolution, stomps his left forefoot three times, and meanwhile he sings:

> "Flies in the firmament,
> Creakers in the grass,
> Evil creeping close, but
> None shall let it pass,"

a song and dance that has the effect of safeguarding far-flung relations. The song alone can be of assistance to a cow of your intimate acquaintance who happens to be giving birth, although Tall Time doubts that any cow anywhere, of his acquaintance or not, is giving birth right now. Calves don't drop from cows during droughts. . . .

Tall Time himself being an exception, having arrived in the world toward the end of the last bad drought. Dry Time he might have been called, but he was born shortly after sunrise, when the shadows proclaim giants, and his mother decided upon the more imposing name. His mother was the famous singing cow, She-Bellows-And-Bellows. Even her labour cries were tuneful, even her death cries. She died only six hours after Tall Time's birth, at "small time," or high noon. She died for no reason, because "Thus spake the She," so Tall Time was told and so he believed until, while still a calf, he learned of the obscure superstition that if a three-legged hyena crosses the path of a cow within a day and a night of her giving birth, that cow will be dead by the following sunrise.

Had a three-legged hyena crossed his mother's path?

"No," said his adoptive mother, She-Bluffs.

But she often said no for yes, and he didn't believe her. Down on his knees he begged for the truth.

"Three-legged?" she said then. "As it happens there *was* a three-legged one slinking around that day."

He told her about the superstition. "Didn't anybody know about it?" he asked.

"Certainly we knew."

"You *knew?*" He began to weep at even the possibility that no one kept his mother out of harm's way.

"What exactly do you mean by 'know'?" she hedged.

It was a comfort for him to discover that his birth mother had died as a result of a specific circumstance—that, with vigilance, such deaths could be avoided. He became a student of signs, omens and superstitions, or "links," as all three are more often referred to. The common links—tell a fib, maim a "rib"; a "hide-browser" on your left tusk brings good luck—he knew, of course. It was the unsung ones that he was anxious to acquaint himself with. He grilled the cows in his birth family. At Massive Gatherings he would stand next to some ancient matriarch for all the hours it took her to recite every link that had ever entered, and had not yet drained, irredeemably, from her body.* In this way he became an expert of the uncanny, a famous one by the time he quit his family at the precocious age of ten years.

Normally a bull leaves when he is twelve or thirteen, but rarely does he do so, as Tall Time did, for reasons of his own. Any bull will admit that he would have stayed with his family forever had the big cows not driven him off. It is a hard affair, expulsion, and Tall Time has known young bulls to linger near their families for years, tragically optimistic that they will be forgiven their mounting games, their charging games—whatever it was that turned the cows against them. Even these diehards eventually drift away, though, and either they wander on their own or they try (almost always without success) to ingratiate themselves into some other family. In the end they usually take up with a small herd of bachelors

---

* Most of the early leaks from the first several years of drainage are recoverable, as they tend to linger close enough to the body to be reabsorbed.

whose oldest member is a leader of sorts, if he is not decrepit.

That is one course, the more favoured one. The other is to become a hermit . . . seek out cows when the urge to mate overwhelms, but otherwise keep your own counsel. Be your own patriarch.

Tall Time considers himself a hermit, despite a deep and sentimental love of family and friends, and despite the fact that right from the start he was rarely on his own for long. Cow families, lone bulls and often bachelor herds (who are prone to inciting each other into fits of apprehension) visited him whenever an upset in their lives could not be accounted for. Why has my milk dried up? Why do I twitch? Although Tall Time rued the invasion of privacy, he was happy to solve the mysteries, if he could. It flattered him to be consulted, and here were opportunities to confirm or discount the power of certain superstitions and thereby refine his inventory of determinants.

Within fifteen years he knew every link there was, but by then being a celebrity was oppressing him. He became evasive. He dissipated his odour by urinating and defecating in water. He camouflaged his footprints by walking backwards or, whenever possible, on rock. He sang softly. Many of the good-luck rhymes are more potent if sung, and sung with gusto, and he loved to sing, he had his birth mother's tremolo and enough volume to initiate wildebeest stampedes. But when he belted out a tune he risked attracting appreciative audiences of his own kind and so he took to singing under his breath or in his head, except at Massive Gatherings, where he allowed himself to be coaxed into roaring a verse of "Recollections."

None of these precautions would have been onerous had he not also been at the mercy of a thousand superstitions. Defecating in a river is frowned upon but is not apt to harm you. The same is true of defecating in a swamp after dark or under cloud cover. But, "Void in a swamp in the sight of the She and your hind legs will itch from your groin to your knee." And walking in the footprints of a musth bull is courting a gut ache. And so on. Still, he managed to find his way around most injunctions and, when it suited him, to shun his kind—except for Torrent, a master tracker who turned up as he chose and who, in any case, was a welcome source of news.

It was from Torrent that Tall Time learned, in the short dry season of his twenty-seventh year, about another calf whose mother had died hours after the birth and who—a more pitiful story than his—was abandoned by her family as she lay trapped beneath the mother's body. At the brink of death she was rescued by the She-S's.

Her fate moved him, it was so much like his own, and he was curious to find out what had precipitated the mother's ill luck. But it was something else, some uneasy yearning he could not account for, that drove him to seek out the She-S's (whose matriarch he had once, unsuccessfully, tried to mount). Understandably they were wary of his approach. When he was still a long way away, She-Sees spotted him and issued an infrasonic warning that he advance downwind, and even after he had explained himself, only She-Snorts was openly welcoming. She walked a few feet in front of him and swayed her haunches so that the cow calf who trotted under her belly was obliged to sidestep. Since the calf appeared to be the right age—just shy of two years—he assumed she was Mud.

"What do you have to say for yourself?" She-Snorts rumbled in that voice of hers, which was somehow both witheringly sardonic and extraordinarily lascivious. She smiled over her shoulder and flicked a twig in her trunk.

"That you are very beautiful," he answered. She was, he thought she was, but he told her so only because he found her expectation of praise to be like an obstruction that grows larger and more impassable with every second that you refuse to acknowledge it.

"What's more, I bring luck," she said.

"Indeed?" She had his attention.

She released the twig and turned to face him. In precise little steps the calf also turned, and he noticed how narrow her head was and thought that he was seeing what the weight of a cow could do to a newborn's skull.

"Any bull who mounts me is guaranteed a season of excellent health," She-Snorts said.

He rifled his memory for any similar superstition. There was none. "Are you quite sure?"

"Climb on." She shimmied around, offering him her backside. "Find out for yourself."

He smelled her vulva. She was not about to enter oestrus and so he shook his head. "But thank you, nevertheless," he said, baffled by her useless offer.

"Ha!" She tossed up her trunk.

He looked down at her as if from a cliff. For his age he was extremely tall, "the fit of his name," as the saying goes. He was too lean for handsomeness but his tusks were a fair size, and the length of his legs appeared to have an intoxicating effect on cows who really were in oestrus. And yet being so high off the ground was not all to the good, he had found. There were occasions, such as this one, when he felt that what was apparent to everybody else failed to reach him at his altitude, as if he were another creature entirely. A giraffe. A bird.

"You do amuse me," She-Snorts said, scratching her hide on a termite mound. "You mannerly young bachelors."

Oh. He understood now. He was being teased, something he had no stomach for after enduring the deceptions and trickery of his adoptive mother, She-Bluffs. He felt the temporin sliding down his cheeks and he waved his ears to calm himself, and as he did the calf moved out from beneath She-Snorts and so he curled the end of his trunk under her tiny trunk and said, "Mud, is it not?"

The calf gave her head a single decisive shake. "No, I am Date Bed," she said in the formal timbre, "daughter of She-Snorts. I know who you are. You are Tall Time the Link Bull. I am delighted to make your acquaintance."

So taken aback was he by her gravity and old-fashioned eloquence . . . and her courtesy—how could this calf be the blood daughter of She-Snorts?—that he laughed (now *he* was the one laughing), which had the effect of sobering She-Snorts, who sauntered away, and of encouraging the other big cows, who hurried up to him and began to talk all at once:

"My trunk aches, is that from stepping on a flow-stick?"

"Two nights ago in my right ear I heard water."

Above the other voices bleated the voice of She-Screams: "I have borne only one calf! Why should that be? What is the matter, what have I done?"

Addressing all of them, he said, "Eat newborn dung," because doing so generally altered one's fortunes, and then he tensed his ears and raised his trunk to lend himself girth and authority, and bellowed, "Where is the calf named Mud?"

Except for She-Screams, who carried on with her lament, the cows shut up. However mannerly and young he might be, he was still a grown bull, more powerful than any of them.

"Mud is here," a voice said. Low, ferocious, coming from behind him. She-Scares.

He turned and looked down at the calf by her side, and the Earth tilted, the sun flashed, his sense of smell bristled, assaulting him with a thousand queer scents. He was no longer aware of where he was. He knew what was happening to him, though. Six days earlier, at the forks of Brown River, he had come upon a pair of male kudu carcasses whose locked horns indicated that they had died in combat, and the coincidence of those horns at that location was a sign that he should prepare himself for an exceptional encounter of his own.

Mud seemed oddly unmoved. She stepped back and stumbled and was hauled upright by She-Scares, and he saw her withered hind leg and thought, "She is sturdy enough but no beauty." With She-Scares looking on, ears perked, he sniffed her head.

For a moment he inhaled only her calf sweetness. Then he caught a sliver of her nascent cow odour and his penis shot out under his stomach, and Mud squealed and ducked beneath She-Scares.

She-Screams stopped her wailing. She-Soothes, with nursely bravado, scented his mouth. There was a silence, broken finally by She-Sees, who said, "My dear, you are a marvellous length. A shame, really, that none of us is in our delirium."

"But thank you, nevertheless," She-Snorts called.

She-Soothes asked if he had been eating ebony-tree bark. "Enough of that crap," she roared, "and your hind-trunk will lash out like a big fly's leg!"

"It's Mud," he said. "I am aroused by Mud."

"That is ridiculous!" She-Sees trumpeted.

"Unheard of, Matriarch." He extended his trunk to where Mud cowered under She-Scares. Already he craved another draught of her scent. But Mud tottered backwards, out of his reach.

"When she comes into her first delirium I will be the one who digs her calf tunnel," he said. "By my troth." He sniffed the air and cast around for some favourable sign to guarantee his vow. There wasn't any, except for chips of fallen sky in the form of blue flowers, and their power applied more to matters of vitality and digestion. He tossed his trunk. He really felt no need of a sign, he had his will. Although it was puzzling having a will that was not dictated by some link, unless the link that had ordained his seduction by a crippled little calf was still at work, giving him the impression of will.

"You will have competition," She-Scares growled.

"I will be the one."

He walked off, his penis lurching under his belly, until he was out of sound and scent of the entire herd, by which time it was dawning on him that he had not asked Mud about her birth mother. He had not spoken to her at all.

✦ ✦ ✦

He hears another airplane and makes for the thorn bush, which, fortunately, is in the direction opposite the escarpment.

That the escarpment is no longer visible doesn't make any difference. You must not face it when a plane is overhead. Even if you are a hundred miles away, you must not face it.

He cocks his head at the sky, and the plane's shadow sweeps over him. There are two breeds of plane: the small plump breed, which has a single twirling wing on its skull, and this breed, with its stiff wings that never flap or fold and its smooth featherless skin.

In the guts of both are humans. Slaughterers—a new and stunningly voracious generation. It's the tusks they want, sometimes the feet. Almost always they abandon the torso but once in a while they smoke the flesh at fire clearings and then carry it elsewhere, strewing the bones. From the skulls Tall Time can tell whether he has come upon an acquaintance. During the past two hundred days he has discovered twelve acquaintances, one of them his drab, kindly aunt, She-Bores-And-Bores, the cow who unwittingly inspired him to learn the art of sleeping with his eyes open and ears spread, as if he were still listening.

At the fire clearings the humans leave behind the rough wooden skeletons upon which they draped the flesh and hide of the creature they had just torn from its own perfect skeleton. Tall Time stomps these fraudulent skeletons to splinters. He gathers the bones and passes one hind foot a few inches above them in order to release the spirit to the oblivion of The Eternal Shoreless Water, and then he carries them from the clearing, covers them with leaves and dirt and sings a hymn. The skull of She-Bores-And-Bores he took the time to pulverize, and when the pieces were small enough he blew a trunkful at the sun. A plane was passing then, too, cutting between the sun and that flock of bone.

This plane tilts, disappears from view.

Tall Time flings dirt over his back, uneasy now over his alarm. A male cheetah perched eastward on a termite mound guarantees your safety until sunset the following day, and this morning he saw two such cheetahs. He is safe. All afternoon he has been safe. Why did he even bother running for cover?

Because he is losing faith in the links.

No. No, he isn't. He looks up at the sun. "I am not," he swears. If nothing foretold this murderous drought, let alone that the humans would launch an era of unprecedented slaughter, it is because, as Torrent warned, "The links may well be infinite."

But Tall Time isn't comfortable with that either. When Torrent first said it, Tall Time thought the old bull was trying to goad him or was in the midst of some musth delusion. He replied, and he believed it absolutely, "I know every link there is."

This was more than a year ago, at the Long Rains Massive Gathering. It was the last time that the two bulls had laid eyes on each other, and their meeting, although brief, was portentous (it turns out) because Torrent also confided a great secret, despite being deep in musth, in "green," and even more belligerent and crazed than he usually is during that period, what with She-Snorts having come into oestrus.

Scores of cows were in oestrus back then. Unlike now it was a glorious season. The fresh growth high enough to swipe your belly, and all the ponds and swamps returned, the mud revived. You could inhale whole miles of sky without drawing in a speck of dust.

As it has always been, the Massive Gathering took place on Green Down, and because the grass was so unusually lush, families who had not shown up in decades arrived, some having travelled a hundred and fifty miles. Tall Time estimated a crowd of more than four hundred, but She-Reckons put the number precisely at three hundred and eighty-six. Thin-scented and scornful, She-Reckons was hardly the most fetching oestrus female present. She was easily the least flirtatious. Even as Tall Time mounted her she enumerated the oxpeckers, bellowing (to *them*, he assumed), "Keep still!" But Tall Time was not particular. He was desperate to mate and yet obliged to leave the best cows to all the heftier and older musth bulls, of which there were a half dozen in that throng.

The heftiest and oldest and most renowned being Torrent, or the Trunk Bull as many call him in recognition of his valour and depth of spirit and because he is the last of that grand herd of six bachelors who, in their youth, scoured the land searching for abducted calves. At that time in parts of the world where populations of white humans were densest, calves were being enslaved and trained to stand on their hind legs while throwing colossal bubbles back and forth. Without killing a single human or causing any injury to themselves, the bulls rescued eighteen calves by stealing into the sleeping grounds and ripping open or simply lifting the flimsy skin walls of the shelters in which the calves were imprisoned. Noiselessly the bulls walked among the shelters and chewed or yanked apart the restraints.

Torrent still moves noiselessly, even over pebbles and dead leaves, and he still has the sensitive trunk that once sniffed out calves from twenty miles away. Only She-Demands and She-Snorts (both of whom he has mated so often that they have adopted certain of his faculties) can rival his sense of smell.

At every Long Rains Massive Gathering, Torrent is in musth, and all of the other musth bulls stay out of his way. In musth, a bull has no use for any bull of any description, but a bull who also happens to be in musth is especially unwelcome. Regardless of the affection that two bulls may otherwise feel for each other, the larger bull is driven to charge the smaller one and to call him twig-tusk, twig-trunk, cow-bull. Musth bulls of similar size and age get into fights. These fights are a kind of lunacy. They go on for hours, and during most of that time the opponents do nothing except size each other up. The fragrant oestrus cows are still there, beyond the horizon of their enthralment. The bushes and tree stumps are there, looming. Incensed, one of the bulls may attack *them* for a spell. Eventually he'll whirl back on his enemy, but then, out of the corner of his eye, he may spot more bushes, so he'll yank these up by their roots. Meanwhile the other bull is doing the same, both carrying on in this fashion until one craves food more than a cow and walks away.

Tall Time's spell of musth normally starts thirty days before the Massive Gathering and peters out midway through it. At this last gathering he was in musth until the final days, by which time he had weathered (and conceded) two fights, and all the clans were breaking up into their family groupings. Calves who had run wild now leaned into the legs of their mothers, and their mothers—who themselves might have gone a bit wild—were back to their sedate and watchful selves. At the fringes of the dispersing multitude, lone bulls positioned themselves and wondered at a mania that only days before had driven them to mount cows of the ilk of She-Screams. Of She-Wilts.

Tall Time, once he was "ungreen," was unusual in that he always loitered near the She-S's. Stealing a whiff of Mud was never easy, however. She tended to keep apart from everyone except for Date Bed. Whenever she did mingle with her family, it seemed to him that she was always on the far side of a big cow. As for his renown and authority, they were lost on her. Unusual for a female, unique in fact, she had no curiosity about the links.

"I demand to smell you!" he would end up roaring.

She would either move closer to She-Scares, who would threaten him with her deadly little tusk, or she would run in her awkward fashion, her withered leg kicking out sideways, and he would take pity on her and resort to watching her from a distance while smelling her in memory. Sometimes, when She-Scares was between the two of them, she would tell him to go away. He laughed at her spunk. He was charmed.

True to his pledge, he had dug her inaugural calf tunnel on the same morning (more than a year and a half ago now) that she came into her first oestrus. His immediate assumption was that from then on she would understand his attachment to her and occasionally indulge it. But the moment her oestrus passed she went back to dodging him, and every time he met with the She-S's he was more and more vexed by this. There was something so odd about what he felt for her that he had come to believe it must be divine, and that, furthermore, to describe it was to violate it. At this last Massive Gathering he was driven to try. Across foothills of She-S rumps, he called to her, "We are alike!"

"We have mated only once," she called without turning.

"You are not *becoming* like me," he said. "I am trying to tell you that I think of you as I think of myself. Orphaned and self-contained. But smaller . . . and female, needless to say—" From under the young bull who was mounting her She-Snorts laughed, and Tall Time stopped, feeling ludicrous. He browsed on white flowers for a spell and then gathered himself up and said with some emotion, "It was ordained. It was ordained that I would have an unnatural attachment to you from the day of our first meeting until the day of your death." He paused, flustered. "Which is not to say that you will die before me," he said.

Mud peered at him from behind She-Scares. "What day will that be?" she said. Her eyes were the green of the visionaries and when they glittered, as they did now, you could see the gleam fifty yards away.

"What day will what be?" he said, entranced.

"The day I die."

"I dare say I have no idea. You misunderstand."

She lowered her trunk.

"Let me smell you."

"No."

"Why not?"

Date Bed raised her lean little head. "She is not at all like you," she said shyly, in the formal timbre.

He walked away, skimming his trunk over the ground for a whiff of Mud's urine. He felt pitiable and sickened . . . and alarmed, more so than seemed called for, as if any second he would collide with a herd of humans.

It was Torrent he collided with.

"Cow-bull!" Torrent roared.

Tall Time bolted to one side. "Forgive me," he said in the formal timbre.

"Flat-footed twig-stick," Torrent muttered.

Tall Time flattened his ears against his neck. "Quite right," he said.

This was not excessive courtesy, this was terror. In musth, Torrent had been known to gore bulls who were careless enough to catch his eye, let alone bump into him, and Torrent was still deep in musth, his temporin glands swollen, the temporin itself pouring down his face, and his enormous green penis dribbling egg-sized drops that smoked as they hit the stubble and discharged an odour so sharp Tall Time couldn't fathom how the big bull had taken him by surprise. "Very clumsy of me," he murmured. "Entirely my fault."

He turned away but Torrent bellowed, "I've been wanting to talk to you!"

Tall Time looked over his shoulder. The big bull folded his ears and rumbled something menacing and then threw up his great head in which his eyes flew, mad and murderous. Tall Time ran.

"Stop!" Torrent roared.

Tall Time slowed down and looked over his shoulder again, past nervous cows trotting away in all directions and a flock of grouse splashing up like muck.

Torrent rocked from foot to foot. He was evidently making

a terrible effort to calm himself. "Come back here," he said, "you little . . . you scrawny little. . . . Come back here . . . son."

"I haven't been speaking with She-Snorts," Tall Time said. In oestrus, She-Snorts was always pursued by a host of young bulls, the bull who was currently mounting her being only the mightiest of the smallest. But she had yet to enter her "radiance," those few hours during which a cow's scent is at its most delectable and for which Torrent reserved himself.

"I know that," Torrent growled.

"It was the calf Mud I was speaking with."

"Yes, yes, yes. Get over here."

Almost certainly, Tall Time could have outrun Torrent, but he was now curious about whatever was obliging Torrent to subdue his musth mood. More than that he felt sorry for the old bull. He knew what it was like to find yourself persecuting a smaller bull whom a thin current of reason proclaimed a friend.

"I must tell you something," Torrent rumbled. "Several things. Vital . . . vital things. The first of them is, do not imagine that your grasp of the links is infallible. There are links you know nothing of."

"Which links are these?" Tall Time said, affronted. Unconsciously he had dropped the formal timbre.

Torrent jerked his head toward the She-S's. Trunk up, he took a long inhalation. "Any number of them," he rumbled.

"Indeed?" Tall Time said coolly.

Torrent turned back around. "I have only recently come to appreciate, as a result of a remarkable meeting, that the links may well be infinite."

"I know every link there is."

Torrent glowered over the rim of one of his splendid tusks. Frightened afresh, Tall Time took small steps backwards.

"Would that were true," Torrent said.

Tall Time hesitated, struck by something beaten in Torrent's tone. Torrent flapped his torn ears and yanked at the grass. Suddenly he snapped his head around. He closed his eyes, an indication that any moment now She-Snorts would enter her radiance. Torrent's sense of smell being what it was, he would pick up the tell-tale odour even before the bull who was mounting her did. That bull had better be fast on his feet, Tall Time thought.

"I don't suppose you are interested in learning *whom* I met," Torrent said, still sniffing.

"On the contrary," Tall Time said, "I am exceedingly interested."

Torrent looked at him, the expression in his bloodshot eyes at once percipient and deranged. He curled his trunk around a swatch of grass, cut the swatch with his forefoot but instead of eating it he pitched it over his hide, a pointless, calf-like thing to do. "The Lost Ones," he said.

"The Lost Ones?" Tall Time said, astounded.

"You heard me."

Nobody Tall Time knew had ever actually sighted, smelled or caught rumblings of—let alone spoken to—the Lost Ones, or the Forest Dwellers, as they were sometimes called. Always it was a distant acquaintance of a distant acquaintance who was rumoured to have had dealings with them. Despite which, descriptions of them never varied. The abnormally long narrow tusks, the small ears, sleek skin, luminous green eyes. A strong race, though diminutive, beautiful despite their size.

And gifted. All of them visionaries, all of them nimble and capable of scenting seven-day-old dung from twenty miles away. They were glorious singers, what's more. Moving in single file through the forest, trunks grasping tails, they roared like hurricanes, but in melodious harmonies and complex rhythms. "You possess Lost blood," it is said of anyone who sings often and pleasingly, as Tall Time does, but to his thinking that has always been a mere figure of speech. "Lost ears" for tiny ears, "Lost-footed" for sure-footed, "Lost green eyes"—all figures of speech, unless you believed, and many did, that the Lost Ones existed.

Torrent believed. He had never come across any sign of them (until, if he was speaking the truth, recently) but he had always believed. He had even claimed a blood connection. It was Torrent who had originally told Tall Time how the Lost Ones were no different from other she-ones before being driven by humans into an immense forest where they disappeared for centuries and the She Herself declared them vanished while, beneath the thick canopy that denied them the watch and warmth of Her eye, they continued to worship Her. When at last they were found (either by a She-V or a She-G matriarch, members of the two families argue the point to this day), the She was so moved by their steadfast devotion to Her that She granted each of them, and all of their descendants of both sexes, the third eye. As for their stealth and keen trunks, these are attributed to the clear forest water. The reason for their marvellous voices is not so easily explained, although Torrent leans to the theory that they eat the eggs of songbirds. They are capable, he admits, of heartless conduct, such as slaying their deranged elders.

"You met them?" Tall Time asked now.

"I did," Torrent said. His tone was conjectural, as if questioning the event himself.

"When?"

"At the outset of the drought, those first torrid days. I had a sense that the short rains weren't going to arrive, and I was looking for fresh sources of water. Where the big burn is, to the west of it, I came upon a Rogue's web and had to detour north, fifty miles out of my way. I continued to walk north-northwest, in and out of two riverbeds. Then came a cluster of hindlegger nests, and then a desert, a four-day trek that was. At the end of it all were hills. East and west and north, range upon range, and at the base of the hills were forests." His voice rose in a kind of indignation. "Huge feast trees. The leaves still green! I ate until my gut groaned. By the She, I did!"

"I dare say," Tall Time rumbled.

"By the She!" Torrent bellowed. He made another test of the air. Shut his eyes. But he stayed where he was.

"I'm surprised you didn't remain," Tall Time said.

"*Are* you, son?" An insane shine in his eyes.

"With all that lush food—"

"On the seventh day," Torrent roared, "I heard the singing of the Lost Ones! And do you know *what* they were singing?"

Tall Time carefully shook his head.

"It was not a glad song," Torrent said, infuriated, sarcastic. "It was not a welcoming song." And in his tuneless bass he thundered:

"We, survivors of the slaughter,
Mourning sister, son and daughter,
Warn all Lost Ones close by High Hill,
Hide at once or end up gut swill.

"Brutal hindleggers seek big feet,
Tusks and tails; your flesh they then eat.
Heed us, Lost Ones, of your own will
Hide at once or end up gut swill."

"Gut swill!" Tall Time said, appalled by the butchery, of course, but also that a song would contain such uncouth lyrics.

"You doubt me?" Torrent trumpeted.

"No, no, not at all!" Which wasn't quite sincere. Yet even with the gut swill there was nothing addled or suspect about the story, and Tall Time was beginning to entertain the staggering notion that Torrent had indeed met the Lost Ones.

"I found them in a big-grass grove," Torrent said. "A family of eight, which is large by their standards, but they had been near to twice that number before hindleggers massacred seven of them in a pit. A dreadful way to go is a pit slaughter. Dreadful. Have you ever witnessed it?"

"I've heard stories—"

"Not the same thing. Cows dropping out of sight ahead of you. They're running on the path and then they're gone, you think they've dropped over the edge of The Domain. You stop just in time, at the very brink, you almost fall in yourself, you don't see because . . . because. . . ." He broke off, agog.

"The hindleggers camouflage the pits with branches and leaves," Tall Time offered softly.

"You're all running, your mother in the lead. She falls in first. Your newborn sister falls on top of her. Your mother screams. You see that one of the sticks has pierced her through the neck. Those sticks that they plant in the bottom of the pit, the sharp ends pointing upwards. Do you know about them?"

Tall Time nodded.

Torrent nodded. "She is still alive," he said in wonder. "Your mother. Pierced through but still alive. She screams. Your sister"—he started to weep—"screams. Blood shoots up. You have to save them. How? Nobody knows what to do. Your mother is the matriarch, she's the one who knows what to do but she's down in the pit, and the hindleggers, you can hear them, they're right behind you."

Tall Time was now weeping, all of his uncertainty about Torrent's having met the Lost Ones transformed into wrath and grief that seven of them perished in the same way that Torrent's mother did. "I didn't know you had a sister," he sobbed.

Torrent blinked.

"Did she also die?" Tall Time sobbed.

"Quit your blubbering!" Torrent bellowed. He tossed his head, and Tall Time cringed—here came the tusking—but Torrent threw his trunk behind himself and went still. He shut his eyes, inhaled with rapturous concentration. His penis flung urine, which in this late-afternoon light twinkled orange, and then his trunk swung to the front and took on a gentle undulation while he regarded Tall Time with a demented look of friendly interest. "It is true what you've heard," he said conversationally. "The Lost Ones *are* calf-like, except for the length of their tusks. A bull your age would have tusks twice as long as yours, that's no exaggeration. Not nearly as thick, though. And they all have those green eyes but brighter than our visionaries' eyes by a hundred times. Like little green suns, they are, beaming light."

"Extraordinary."

"So they are. So they are. They call themselves We's, as you've no doubt heard. We-B's, We-S's. Individuals prefix their names with 'I.' "

He hadn't heard this. "Why?" he said.

"Well, for one thing, cow calves choose their own cow names. Out of a number of names offered by the big cows."

"That is a terrible responsibility to place upon a young mind."

"It panders to the calf's vanity. They think very highly of themselves, the Lost Ones do, every one of them, even the newborns. The family I am speaking of now, the We-F's, they may be exceptional, but I got the sense that self-importance is a trait common to the whole breed. It tried my patience, as you might imagine, all that preening and talking-down. As if I were a suckling calf! But the matriarch, I-Flounder, she was cordial enough, despite her sorrow and my being so gigantic, compared to them especially, and here I was a bull, sneaking up on them in the middle of nowhere, the first of our kind they'd ever encountered. Naturally, one of them had had a vision of me. It's hard to surprise that lot." His expression became one of amused remembrance. "I said to I-Flounder, 'With a name like that I don't hold out much hope of your finding what you're searching for, not straight away, anyhow.' But she has her talents." As if reminded of She-Snorts he lifted his trunk her way and his penis elongated and shot urine everywhere, and then he backed into a termite mound and gave his rump a vicious scratching.

"What were they searching for?" Tall Time asked.

"The white bone," Torrent said agreeably.

"Whose white bone?"

"Let me ask you this. Have you ever heard of a race of white she-ones? By which I mean *all* white."

"No. Never."

"Nor had I. But according to the We-F's such a race lived on The Domain up until twenty generations ago."

"Is that so?" Tall Time murmured, becoming doubtful again.

"The White Ones, they were called," Torrent said.

Tall Time waited.

"At any rate," the old bull continued, "they are long gone. Long gone." He sighed. He might have been weeping. "Their bones, too," he said. "Their bones are dust. Except—"

The pause continued until Tall Time realized that he was supposed to speak. "Except what?"

"Except for one bone. The magical white bone."

"It survived," Tall Time ventured.

"Perfectly intact, not a mark on it after all this time, not a hole. And it never dulled. On the contrary, it bleaches whiter all the time. By now it would be the whitest thing you've ever seen. That's how you'll know it. It's not big, mind you. It's only a rib, and a newborn's, what's more."

"Have the We-F's seen it?"

"No, not them. Their ancestors." He twined his trunk around a clump of grass and pulled it out by its mucky roots. Absently he knocked the clump against his leg, a wistful look on his face.

"When you say magical—" Tall Time prompted.

Torrent peered at him sidelong. "The Link Bull perks up when magic is mentioned," he said. "The Link Bull is greedy for magic."

Tall Time braced himself.

"The Link Bull!" Torrent roared. He stopped. Shook his head as if struck by an extraordinary notion. He turned in circles, rumbling incoherently. Sniffed the ground, the air, uprooted a poisonous angel's trumpet shrub and hurled it over his head, wove back and forth twirling his trunk, and at last collected himself and in a measured voice said, "The white bone has the power to direct you to The Safe Place. The Safe Place is a paradise. No droughts there, ever. No perils. To be accurate, it is The Second Safe Place, but as I've never known a First Safe Place, I'm thinking of it as *The* Safe Place. At any rate, you throw the white bone, and when it lands it points you in the right direction. For two nights and two days, which is how long the newborn lived, it is in your possession. After that, it disappears, gets scooped up by a sky-diver or a trunkneck who takes it somewhere else and drops it in order to lead others to The Safe Place. So you'd better have figured out your route in those two days and nights." He blew out a contemptuous breath. "By the She," he bellowed, "if you can't hold to a true course by then you don't deserve to find The Safe Place to begin with!"

"I dare say," Tall Time rumbled. He was being won over again by Torrent's conviction.

Scowling, the old bull kicked at the earth. "This very bone is what saved the Lost Ones from the hindleggers generations ago. It was not by accident that the Lost Ones disappeared. They were directed into that forest, The First Safe Place, as they call it, which accounts for all this first and second business. As soon as they arrived there, the white bone disappeared, but they weren't too distressed, not then, because they thought that there were no hindleggers in their new territory. And there weren't for centuries, not until a hundred and eighty days ago."

"Which end of the white bone points you—?"

"The end of the white bone that points you—!" Each word an overenunciated explosion. He paused. "That points you in the right direction," he continued calmly, "is, naturally, the pointed end. But without the white bone, there can be no throwing and no pointing. So the search is on everywhere, all the Lost Ones—not only the We-F's, all of them—searching. I myself am searching, or I was before this . . . before this"—he flailed his trunk at his temporin, his flagellating penis—"madness," he said miserably.

"But why are you searching?"

"The hindleggers have renewed the slaughters!" Torrent roared.

"In the hills where you say the Lost One are, yes, I understand, but not here."

"Are you a visionary, then? Are you prescient?"

"Of course I'm not," Tall Time murmured.

"Then stop interrupting and listen. I-Flounder said to go to the hills and the most barren places and to look for an extremely large standing feast tree. The white bone is invariably dropped near an extremely large standing feast tree. So here's the plan: I go to the hills, you go to the most barren places."

"I?"

"Why do you imagine I am taking this risk?" Torrent roared.

The White Bone

Inches in front of Tall Time's face Torrent's monstrous trunk writhed.

"What risk?" Tall Time asked finally.

Torrent's trunk drooped. "Every time the white bone is spoken of directly it loses some of its power." He was back to his conversational voice. "That is why I-Flounder says it is better to refer to it as the that-way bone." He looked uncomfortable, as if he should have taken this into account before now.

"The that-way bone," Tall Time said.

"Tell nobody," Torrent said. "Not yet, at any rate. If we have this cow whispering to that cow, the power of the thing will be gone before we know it. I myself have told only three other bulls. Master trackers."

"Who?"

"What does it matter who?" Torrent trumpeted. "Now you," he said gruffly, "you're no master tracker but you wander far afield and you generally keep your mouth shut. If we fail to find the that-way bone over the course of the next year, then we'll be obliged to tell others. Widen the search. Bear in mind that there's always the possibility of one of us stumbling upon The Safe Place itself, with or without the that-way bone."

"Are there no hindleggers there?"

"There are, but they are of a different breed entirely. Peaceful. Entranced."

"They don't covet our tusks?"

"They don't covet our tusks, our feet or our flesh." He beamed a maniacal smile.

"I can't believe it," Tall Time said without thinking.

"*You* can't believe it!" Torrent trumpeted, but almost immediately his trunk sank, his eyes extinguished. "It *is* hard to believe," he muttered. "I hardly believe it myself, come to that. And yet there's something familiar about the whole story. As if I'd dreamt it. The entranced hindleggers." He looked at Tall Time. "Do you know what they do all day? Gape at the she-ones. All day long. Some sit in mighty sliders, it makes no difference, they're as quiet as rocks."

"Whatever for?"

"Well, I-Flounder believes they have recovered their memory from before the Descent, suddenly recollected that they used to be she-ones. And they've got it into their furry little heads that if they stare at us hard enough, they'll inflate back to what they were. Grow their ears and so on."

"Who told the We-F's of this Second Safe Place?"

"It was *fore*told," Torrent muttered.

"By a link?"

"No doubt."

"Was it the Lost Ones who said that the links may be infinite?"

But Torrent's trunk was up and sniffing. He flung his head at the low sun and rumbled, "The darkness is coming," and then he was stomping through a line of sweet-scented shrubs from which brown rabbits squirted and zigzagged across the shadows, one soaring over the back of a warthog who was the largest of a tribe of warthogs fanning out of Torrent's way, tails skyward, and the sky itself suddenly a flickering purple corridor of locusts whose thin crackle sounded like the aftermath of the big bull's earth-quaking passage, like the shattering of everything fragile. But within seconds the corridor had swollen across the sky and the crackle was a solid din.

The White Bone

Tall Time was exquisitely conscious of the She-S's greeting Torrent, their delighted, frenzied bawls breaking through the din. He was conscious of the soft earth and the runnels of water and plump roots underfoot.

Suppose there was a place where humans left you alone. Why look for it now, when no sign predicted drought or massacre? Even the locusts, high up as they were and flying northeast on their way to somewhere else, were no threat. Paradise was here. Why abandon it to travel to the most barren places in search of a bone? If the bone even existed. How could Torrent know for certain?

He had somehow known about the locusts. Or so Tall Time imagined.

✦ ✦ ✦

More than a year has passed since that day, and only recently has it dawned on Tall Time that when Torrent said, "The darkness is coming," he had not meant that a flood of locusts was about to wash across the sky and create a sudden twilight.

He had meant this. This landscape of corpses and dust above which the roar of planes pours down from an illimitable emptiness.

He had meant these quailing acacias. . . . Tall Time brushes them with his trunk. "Nothing left alive," he finds himself thinking as if it were an omen.

Another plane passes high overhead. As the sound of it shudders through his skull, his craving for a safe place flames to a certainty that there *is* a Safe Place. And therefore a white bone. He asks himself, Who is he to doubt the legends of a race prescient enough to have foreseen the devastation none of his kind even suspected? That the Lost Ones trusted Torrent with the secret of the white bone and that Torrent, in turn, trusted him . . . this alone, he thinks, is reason enough to believe.

He decides to head south toward a treeless waste overrun with wire fences. It is a region that, until now, he hasn't had the heart to explore.

Chapter Five

In the wake of Hail Stones' story there is another spell of silence, broken finally by Hail Stones himself announcing that in three days he hopes to be strong enough that he and the She-D's can resume their search for the white bone. He says that despite the water and browse, She-Demands is not at ease here.

"Is it an odour?" She-Scares asks, because the fine scenters are sometimes able to smell danger several days before anybody else does.

"Not an odour," Hail Stones says, answering for his matriarch. "Not a premonition either."

"It's a fee . . . ling be . . . hind her eyes," says She-Drawls-And-Drawls.

At which She-Snorts, the other fine scenter in the group, says, "I know that feeling. I have it myself occasionally."

She-Scares whirls on her. "Do you have it now?"

"I don't think so, but I'll make certain." She bats her long eyelashes. "No, it's not there."

"Still," She-Scares rumbles, "if She-Demands is not easy. . . ." She swings her trunk and jabs her little tusk. A flock of ibises circles Blood Swamp and lands in eerie silence before She-Scares faces Hail Stones again. "We shall join you!" she trumpets, and all of the She-S's (except for She-Screams, who wails that her constitution is too delicate to undertake a journey) bellow, "We shall join you!"

By now it is mid-morning, and once the commotion has died, both families begin moving out from under the fever trees and down the bank to the swamp. The She-D cows wade in deeper this time, up to their bellies. Hail Stones lingers at the shore and holds his injured foot above the water until Swamp ambles back to the shallows and says in his listless manner, "It appears you have been abandoned," and then Hail Stones plunges in, not toward Swamp but in the direction of the She-D's.

She-Soothes watches Hail Stones' laboured slog and says nothing. On land he risks "heat sleep," which could kill him, frail as he is. She lifts her trunk toward the plain, and Mud guesses that she is scenting out the warthogs and wondering whether they can be persuaded a second time to donate urine for a new poultice. Or, now that the worms have dropped from the wound, perhaps she has another sort of poultice in mind, one calling for vulture dung or zebra entrails, Mud wouldn't be surprised. She-Soothes is a good nurse cow, zealous and devoted if not shrewd, but in Mud's opinion she is overly fond of the vulgar cures.

"Trunk-neck dung relieves loose bowels, believe it or not," says Date Bed, who is feeding next to Mud.

"I'd prefer loose bowels," Mud thinks, and then glances at She-Screams, but the big cow is facing the other way.

Lately She-Screams has been scolding Mud for thinking, rather than speaking, her end of a conversation with Date Bed. "I know what you're doing!" she shrieked two days ago when Mud was silently responding to Date Bed's explanation of how she classifies plants (edible and inedible, the edible broken down to scrumptious and tolerable, these each broken down to regional and seasonal availability and then to texture and chewability). "You're slandering us!" She-Screams cried.

"Slandering?" Mud said.

"Warty and evil-smelling," She-Screams said, parodying Date Bed's antiquated inflections. She swept a raving glance past the other big cows and shrieked, "Whose ears might those be, I wonder."

"We were discussing the carrion plant," Mud said.

"I scent deception!" She-Screams cried.

"The calf is no liar," She-Scares said severely.

"A thought worth thinking is worth speaking!" She-Screams cried. "It's the rule of tongue! A thought worth thinking!"

Reliving this exchange, Mud now wades farther from the big cows, walking on the bone-strewn swamp bottom. Date Bed follows her. Both of them feed for a while and then Mud thinks, "I wonder if he told us about the white prize out of gratitude or because he knows that your mother is a fine scenter."

"Both, I would imagine. The She-D's benefit as much as we do if we find it."

"They benefit only if the two families stay together."

"We'll stay together. Matriarch just now vowed that we would."

Mud glances at She-Scares. "What is she thinking?"

Date Bed blinks. It is forbidden for a family's mind talker to listen to the mind of the matriarch.

"Go on," Mud urges.

Turning toward She-Scares but squinting beyond her as if interested in the calves playing in the shallows, Date Bed splays her small ears. A moment later she leans into Mud and rumbles in a surprised tone, "She is less inclined to leave than she was a moment ago. She is reluctant to abandon a certain source of water and green food."

"She is wrong," Mud thinks.

"You don't want to be parted from Hail Stones," Date Bed says.

Mud snorts, but then considers whether this is at least partly true. She pivots her trunk in Hail Stones' direction and picks up his wonderful scent, and something in her seems to creak open and breathe and she even has a brief notion of what it is Tall Time experiences when he scents her, but she shakes her head.

"There isn't anything untoward about wanting to remain with him," Date Bed says primly. "He is still only a calf."

"I am aware of that."

"If I should be killed, whom would you talk to?"

"If you should be killed?"

"One day I might be. It is not an impossibility."

"I want us to leave with the She-D's because I have dread," Mud thinks crossly. "I don't know why, but I do. So do you. So does She-Demands." She churns her trunk in the water and her withered leg gives out and she falls and goes under. When she resurfaces, she thinks, "I wish we could leave right now."

"What I wish," says Date Bed, "is that Tall Time was here."

"Why?" Mud thinks, annoyed. Her attention descends to her bloated belly, the newborn there.

"It would help us all to have him translating the landscape." She squints across to the far shore. "There may be links everywhere advising us to stay here until the swamp goes." Delicately she sniffs the air. "You can appreciate why Matriarch would be having second thoughts."

"My leg was seizing up constantly yesterday," Mud thinks. She has suddenly apprehended what a bad omen this is.

"So it was," Date Bed says quietly, turning to look at her.

"If it didn't mean I would have to part with you," Mud thinks, "I would leave on my own."

"Mud!" Date Bed cries, and She-Scares and She-Screams raise their heads.

"Date Bed!" She-Screams trumpets. "Date Bed, you had better start calling her She-Spurns! Do you hear me?"

"Leave your family," Date Bed rumbles, scandalized.

Mud thinks, "The bulls leave."

"Have you ever heard of a cow leaving?"

Mud hasn't.

"What about . . ." Date Bed says, and Mud can tell she is thinking about hyenas but is afraid to speak of them in case Mud falls into her birth memory again and becomes terrorized.

Mud looks at her steadily.

Date Bed looks back, blinking. Eventually she closes her eyes, lifts her trunk and scents a place between Mud's eyes.

Mud doesn't question the oddness of this. It occurs to her that Date Bed may be trying to listen beyond what she, Mud, is thinking. To the source of the visions, perhaps, the pulse or clot that allows Mud to see into the distance. She finds herself remembering something Torrent said, years ago, about nothing wanting substance until it is envisioned—"Once envisioned," he said, "it is obliged to transpire"—and she wonders whether, by staring at Date Bed and imagining the two of them leaving Blood Swamp together, she is forcing substance upon her, fixing her in some way that removes possible futures. She thinks this, knowing that Date Bed hears. Knowing that Date Bed hears, she thinks that she will not leave Blood Swamp without her, and yet she feels as if the two of them have already become separated. She is nostalgic for Date Bed, nostalgic for right now. She feels remotely observed, which almost certainly means that she is living a moment seen by some other visionary (and that the moment is of consequence), but it is also possible that she herself is the observer of the moment. That she is an old, old cow returning to this moment in her mind and that she has already returned to it so many times it ripples with the memories of those previous visits.

And at its frontiers, in visit after visit, is the question of hyenas. Even within the sanctuary of the moment the thought of them starts her quaking.

"I would still leave," she says out loud.

Date Bed opens her eyes.

"That is how great my dread is."

◆ ◆ ◆

Late morning Mud notices that She-Demands has left Hail Stones and her daughters and is wading toward the She-S cows. In water She-Demands moves with the grace of a hippo, her huge wizened head scarcely bobbing. Why isn't her family following her? Mud wonders, and then as She-Demands goes past the She-S's she realizes that the big cow must be coming to see her.

"She-Demands," Mud greets her, and in the formal timbre Date Bed says, "Matriarch." Both of them extend their trunks toward the big cow, who turns away and begins to feed.

Date Bed glances at Mud, inviting a silent response, but Mud suspects that She-Demands has become the She-D's mind talker and so she tries to conceal her perplexity. She resumes feeding, as does Date Bed. The sun is at its meridian before She-Demands speaks.

"*Every* moment is a memory," she says.

Mud and Date Bed look at each other, astounded. The big cow is responding to Mud's thoughts of several hours ago, which means that not only has she become the She-D's mind talker, she heard Mud's mind from fifty yards away.

"Everything has been ordained by the She," she goes on in her soft, battered voice. "Therefore everything must already have been imagined by the She. We live only because we live in Her imagination. Your life, as you experience it, is the She recollecting what She has already imagined. We *are* memory. We are living memory." Her glittering eyes fall on Mud. "Do you understand?"

"Yes," Mud says, although she doesn't, not entirely. It sounds so reconciled, so hard-won, the sermon of a matriarch who has lost twenty-three members of her family.

"What's that?" She-Demands growls suddenly. She swings up her trunk.

Mud and Date Bed do likewise.

The three of them spread their ears. The absence of bird call is wrong. Mud's withered leg starts to tremble and she looks to her right and sees that She-Snorts is also scenting. And now She-Scares, taking her cue from She-Snorts, lifts her trunk. Up go the trunks of the other big cows, the trunks of Hail Stones and She-Distracts and She-Drawls-And-Drawls rising seconds later.

From the shore the odour of anxiety washes out in concentrated waves. The zebras buck their muzzles into the breeze. The giraffes gaze over the plain, their small heads high and fixed. A pair of patas monkeys scrambles up the trunk of the tallest fever tree, and the little calves nervously flop their trunks and crowd around She-Soothes and She-Scavenges, who of all the big cows are nearest to the source of the troubling smell that so far only She-Demands and She-Snorts seem to have homed in on. She-Sees continues to feed, apparently unaware. Unaware of what? Mud wonders but doesn't ask. Nobody does, nobody speaks, even the little calves knowing better than to interrupt tracking concentration. Mud sweeps her eyes along the bank, cocks her head and scans the sky. She looks back at her family and sees that the ears of her adoptive mother are perked forward: She-Scares has heard something. Mud shifts her trunk a few inches to the right, and now she smells it.

The stench of a vehicle.

Within seconds everybody has gone still, everybody has caught the sound or smell. Trunks pivot toward She-Scares and She-Demands, either of whom will signal the next move. There is a good chance that the vehicle isn't headed directly here—vehicles don't drink at the watering places and none have been seen at Blood Swamp in twenty-five years. At this point it would be madness to run out onto the plain and show themselves to the enemy, who are not even the vehicles themselves but the humans riding in their bellies. On their own, vehicles prefer to sleep, but whenever a human burrows inside them they race and roar and discharge a foul odour.

That odour, even the faintest whiff, burns the insides of Mud's trunk. It is all she can do to hold herself still, with her scalding trunk and her shaking leg. Her vision is weirdly sharp. She watches the hippos bloat out of the water, the crocodiles slither into it.

Only the giraffes do not move, and they are the ones who can see the vehicle, if it is visible. Its roar is so close now. The piping of a bird starts up and the stench thickens and finally the giraffes begin to lope away.

"Now," She-Demands rumbles, starting for shore.

By the time they reach the shallows the V formation has already begun, with the two matriarchs at its apex, facing shoreward, flanked by the next biggest cows, who are She-Snorts and She-Scavenges, and then beside and slightly behind each of them, the two next biggest cows, She-Screams and She-Distracts, and so on until Mud and Date Bed, Mud at one tip of the V behind Hail Stones, and Date Bed at the other behind She-Sees, who only yesterday would have been at the apex. Between the arms of the V, the three little calves huddle close to Swamp. He should be part of the formation but nobody says so, not then, everyone is focused on the bank, and except for She-Sees muttering, "Who? Who?" and a trembling whine from She-Screams, everyone is quiet. Even now, there is a possibility that the vehicle may veer off.

It doesn't. It bellows over the bank in a swell of dust as though, despite being upwind, it scented them from the plain. Before it fully stops, the humans leap out. She-Scares gives a dreadful roar. She-Screams and the calves start screaming. There is the rattle of gunshot and She-Scares falls onto She-Demands. With hyena-like yells the humans gallop into the swamp, knees capering above the water, guns firing. She-Scavenges rotates and sinks. The V formation crumbles.

Shoving past the big cows, Mud reaches her adoptive mother. Pink blood froths from She-Scares' throat, red blood jets from a hole in her trunk. Mud tries to stanch the hole with her foot but She-Scares gives her head a toss, and Mud accidentally kicks her in the jaw. Blood loops through the air. Horrified, Mud sinks to her knees, pushes her tusks under She-Scares' torso and heaves. It is useless. Mud is too small, her tusks too short. She comes to her feet. Across from her, She-Distracts is trying to lift She-Demands, who somehow got herself out from under She-Scares but cannot seem to stand.

The little calves squeal and hunker beneath the big cows, who themselves are loath to abandon the fallen matriarchs. More gunshot. The head of She-Distracts flips back, flips forward, a gushing hole between her eyes. Like somebody peering for a closer look, she tips in Mud's direction, then pitches face-first onto her trumpeting mother.

Another round of gunshot. She-Scares is hit again, above her left temple, and is instantly dead. Wildly, Mud looks about. She-Demands has been hit in the torso, she is dead. Everyone else, everyone who is still alive, is either on land or heading for it now, fanning out from the two humans. Bent, the smallest calf, is trying to climb the bank. She-Soothes has already reached the top and she roars at him to hurry. When his knees give out she reaches down, grabs his trunk and hoists him up as if he were weightless. "She-Stammers!" she roars, calling now for her daughter, who runs along the edge of the swamp. Behind She-Stammers are She-Scavenges' newborns, Blue and Flow Sticks. Blue stumbles, and She-Stammers wheels around and takes a shot in the belly. The force of the shot lifts her onto her toes before she drops hard on her side, the sound of impact like the woof of a lion.

Blue gets to her feet. She rushes to She-Stammers and in her terror presses her throat against the cow's flank as if gazing up in wonder at the red mist venting from the topmost bullet holes. The human that shot She-Stammers flings a rope over Blue's head. Where his gun is slung across his back, there is a blinding shine. He yanks on the rope, and Blue thrashes and squalls. Her twin sister, Flow Sticks, rushes back to her. The human jumps astride Blue and kicks her so brutally her forelegs buckle. He goes on kicking until she bolts. Her brief, bird-like screams alternate with her sister's quivering screams, and the human riding her kicks and whoops and holds one hand high. The other human howls. Alongside Blue and the riding human, Flow Sticks keeps pace, turning this way and that as her sister turns. When Blue slows, the human reaches behind himself, grabs his gun, takes aim at Flow Sticks and shoots. The little calf flies sideways and lands on her back, her legs stiff and skyward.

Blue stops. The human kicks her. He thumps her between the eyes with the butt of his gun. Finally she reels in a stunned fashion over to her dead sister. She twines her trunk around one of the upraised legs, and Flow Sticks falls onto her side. The human slides off Blue's back. He walks away. Keeps walking as he turns and lifts his gun. Points the gun at Blue. Shoots.

A horrific wail starts up. Mud has never before seen or heard a chain saw but she knows that this is the sound of one. The human that cradles it is racing in Mud's direction.

By now her bad leg cannot take her weight, and she runs along the shore at a suicidally slow pace. The human, however, is not chasing her. She stops and looks around. The wail of the chain saw rises in pitch. Guided by the human, the saw slices off the front of She-Demands' head in the time it would take Mud to bite through a stick, and yet everything seems to have slowed down, and so the slicing is maliciously prolonged.

"Monster!" Mud trumpets, for this is the real atrocity. Without at least one tusk attached to her skull, even the great She-Demands cannot ascend to the sky herd of the She. "Monster!" She keeps trumpeting it, she cannot help herself. In her ears it sounds as distant and drawn out as if it came from the trunk of She-Drawls-And-Drawls.

The human that shot the calf twins is now about a hundred feet downshore, heading toward She-Sees. He revolves and aims his gun, and after an incalculable pause there is the stutter of the blasts. Mud senses many tight shafts of wind clawing past her right side. An eternity later she hears the bullets pinging off rock, or shattering it, or penetrating in muted gobbles the earthen bank.

Her eyesight is once again phenomenally sharp, and as she runs she glances at the red shallows where the chain-saw human now bends over She-Scavenges. He straightens, a slender tusk in his hand. He pitches it shoreward and it twirls gracefully, end over end—pointed end, bloodied end, pointed end—twice halting in midair, or so it seems to Mud, before it lands on the heap that is the fallen newborn twins. The human whoops and staggers over to She-Scares as a volley of shots explodes downshore.

Mud stops. She-Sees has been hit. On her deeply fissured torso, five holes describe a circle. Vapour puffs from the holes, there is no blood, and the ancient cow remains standing. The human strolls over and raises his gun again. "I don't believe I've had the pleasure!" She-Sees trumpets, extending her trunk in the greeting gesture. When the human is close enough she wraps her trunk around the barrel. The human fires, then prances back from the red spray. Still, She-Sees does not fall. The chain-saw human shouts, and Mud looks toward the shallows. The chain-saw human holds the tiny tusk of She-Scares between his legs. He pumps his hips. More shots from downshore, and then a tremendous shuddering underfoot as She-Sees drops to the ground.

Dimly it occurs to Mud that she should make for the bank. Off she goes, through channels of gunshot, past the corpse of She-Drawls-And-Drawls, whose entire head has been severed . . . blood still bubbles from the flaming gristle of the neck. She steps on smoking gore and spent shells and parings of skin, and when she reaches the bank it is slick with blood so that her ascent is dream-like as she slides down, wins the brink, slides down.

Little by little the earth breaks away under her grappling forefeet until a small gorge is created, out of which she is able to haul herself. She sways inches from the edge, obscurely conscious that she is an easy target for the humans, and takes account of herself. Her palsied leg, her magically keen vision. Her intactness, as if this were a memory, not even her own, into which she has helplessly fallen. Behind her the chain saw brays. To the east, barely visible, is the hump of The She-Hill.

She will go to The She-Hill, she thinks with hypnotic resolve. She starts walking. The stunted bushes and trees glide out of the dust, a ghostly emergence. As she walks she sends infrasonic alarms to each member of her family who may still be alive, but gets no response. If there are signs of her own kind here, she cannot locate them. She has not the acuteness of scent to penetrate the slaughter and dust, and she is unwilling to deviate from the straight path she has set upon, even when she finds herself treading between the fretted bands that are the tracks of the vehicle.

Chapter Six

The landscape that Mud now travels through is known to her, but as a wet season oasis, not as this depleted place. There is nothing green here and nothing in flower and nothing not withered. Almost every tree is black with vultures, the earth a pandemonium of bones poking through drifts of red dust or, where the ground has been burned, through black ash.

The skeletons belong to the grazers, but it is those zebras and wildebeests and gazelles still standing who seem more dead, less lucky, than their fallen relations. The living haven't any young among them, and even the carnivores seem to find this hard to believe. The jackals trotting among the Thomson's gazelles hold their muzzles up and scout over their shoulders as if searching for something more sprightly and delectable than the wretches whose trembling legs they look through.

With the grass cropped right down, and despite the blowing dust, Mud can spot lion prides early enough to avoid them. And yet she takes no detours and they, in their glutted stupor, don't even lift their heads as she goes by. She passes close to the bizarre pairing of a cheetah and a lappet-faced vulture as they rip apart a still-thrashing zebra whose eye finds Mud's an instant before the vulture plucks it out. Farther along, near a cordia ovalis shrub, a patas monkey shakes her dead infant by the foot. When Mud is within a few yards of her she starts jumping and chittering and striking the infant on the ground and then she tosses it and it lands in a flourish of dust at Mud's feet.

Mud halts. The dust funnels off, and Mud takes this to be a manifestation of the spirit flying to that crowded mysterious place (The Other Domain) where all deceased creatures, aside from her own kind and humans, end up. Already, so many flies encase the corpse that it seems alive again. A quivering, nappy-coated, buzzing little horror. Mud snorts a space through the flies, and the odour of newborn, which can be detected through the death fetor, stirs her to kick dirt over the pathetic creature before moving on.

She has been walking for many hours now. Her shadow pools ahead of her, grit clogs her trunk and cakes the corners of her mouth and eyes, and she is thirsty. All of a sudden she is desperately thirsty.

She lifts her trunk, and a host of memories return to her, each a particular and different blossoming of this place and each fraught with its own atmosphere of feeling. What remains invariable, from memory to memory, is the smell of water behind the outcrop of rock. She quits her straight course, but not without apprehension. To deviate is to solicit more ill fortune, so she feels, and yet she races around the outcrop to the depression where water wells up in the fruitful seasons but that smells now only of the powdery impala dung nestled within it.

She digs at the depression with her right forefoot. The ground is petrified, and her toes soon ache from the powerful kicks required to break the earth down. Beneath its layer of dust her foot is black with the dried blood of the slaughtered, and it seems dismally fitting to her that she does not bleed but wears the blood of her adoptive family, as if this were the mark of her connection with them: the undeniable distance, the inescapable attachment. She should have left the swamp the moment Hail Stones said that She-Demands was uneasy, they all should have left, but at least she should have gone and persuaded Date Bed to go with her. Thinking this, her kicks become savage. Clods tumble into the hole she is making, and she retrieves them with her trunk and hurls them at the outcrop, something humanly barbarous fermenting within her.

Eventually, too exhausted to go on, she lets her trunk droop to the hole's bottom. The cool earth down there exhales a wonderful smell that, in her dazed state, takes her a moment to identify. So close is she to the aquifer that she can scrape away the last layer of earth with one final kick.

The water is silty and cold. She bores more deeply until a clear seepage gurgles up. She drinks, showers and dusts herself, then stands there feeling strangely consoled by the wobble of her withered leg, which is at least a known and reliable thing.

"Date Bed!" she trumpets, although trumpeting is useless if nobody has heard her infrasonic calls. Nevertheless she listens, eyes downcast, ears spread, waiting for the shudder underfoot that heralds a far-off rumble. What finally reaches her are the screams of the calves, and by the time she understands that the screams come from memory, she is reliving the slaughter.

She trumpets and runs in circles. At the part where she climbed up and slid down the bank, she climbs up and slides down the rocks and scrapes her leg badly enough to arouse her to the present.

She finds herself on her knees at the bottom of the outcrop. From overhead comes the roar of a plane, and she sinks onto her right side and weeps, for how long she has no idea, but when she is breathing evenly again the shadow of the outcrop leans over her, and an impala drinks at the hole she dug. Inches from her eyes, balanced magically on its end, a flat blue stone holds its colour against the falling light. The stone puts her in mind of one of Tall Time's link songs:

> Except in the cases of berries and specks
> Blue blesses calves and the peak-headed sex.
> Eat a blue stone and for two days and nights
> Those who would harm you are thwarted, by rights.

And so she swallows the stone, gathers up her limbs and sets off back the way she came.

Her mind is suddenly clear, out of its thrall. She knows now that the purpose of her pilgrimage wasn't to go to The She-Hill, it was to stumble upon the blue stone. In the stone's safekeeping she can return to Blood Swamp and mourn the slaughtered members of her family, as it is her sacred obligation to do. The vehicle and its humans will have retreated, and (this didn't dawn on her until now) the She-S survivors will either be at the swamp already or arriving there before morning. Date Bed will be there, if she is still alive. "Let her be alive," Mud prays out loud. She is certain that she saw the bodies of everybody who died at the swamp, both during the slaughter and during her reliving of it, but she didn't see who, if anyone, was wounded, and she didn't see whether the survivors all fled in the same direction once they were up on the plain. Had she been in her right mind she would have immediately searched for dung and drops of blood and gone where they led her, but had she been in her right mind she wouldn't have been granted the blue stone's protection.

It is her own tracks she now follows, placing her feet in any depression that has not been obliterated by dust. The dust has died down with the dying of the wind and even though her bad leg wobbles she moves fast and is soon upon the sad little mess of hide and bone and vulture droppings that was the infant monkey. She keeps walking, into the summits of the plunging shadows and straight down their lengths. As it always is following the death of a matriarch—and if you include She-Sees, three matriarchs died this day—the sunset is gory. Mud cannot look at it, its ecstatic red streams. She fixes her eyes on the ground, where occasionally she tusks out a root stock to eat. She counts her steps, a thing she is able to do while her thoughts are elsewhere, and after every two hundred lets out infrasonic rumbles. Twice, mistakenly, she believes herself to be on the verge of a vision. Her bad leg aches. Her skin, sensing the exhalation of shadows,* twitches uneasily. For all that

---

* This is how darkness spreads.

she is protected by the blue stone from the perils around her, she is not protected from her own mind, and every once in a while she has to shake her head, both to stave off another wholesale reliving of the butchery and to grasp the fact of it. When she passes the remains of the zebra who looked at her before its eye was plucked out, she wonders how far down the vulture's gullet the zebra's eyeball preserved her image.

✦ ✦ ✦

She has come across no she-one dung other than her own from when she set out, and she hasn't heard a single rumble. But this doesn't mean anything one way or another. If her family retreated in another direction, as they clearly did, their dung would be elsewhere, and if they aren't calling it may well be that they have already entered silent mourning. She herself stopped sending calls hours ago out of an unreasonable fear that she would attract hyenas. It isn't until she sees the hyenas prowling the bank of the swamp that she knows she can't be the first to arrive. For so many hyenas to be on the plain when there are corpses all over the shore means that at least two big cows must be down there.

She stops. She could trumpet for help but her fear humiliates her. It wearies her even, some new part of herself that feels ruthless, and she starts walking again with the thought that she will move through the hyenas' ranks as she moved through the bullets and humans, like an invincible visitor in someone else's memory.

The breeze wafts up from the swamp and carries the sweet odour of rot. By the time the hyenas glance over their shoulders she is quite close to them. A pulse flutters in her throat. "Those who would harm you are thwarted," she rumbles to herself, and the hyenas skulk away.

She goes to the bank and looks down. There they are, dispersed among the steaming heaps that are the dead. As silent as the dead. A ponderous elation stirs in her belly, but instead of hurrying to greet them she stays where she is to sort out, in the moonlight, who is who.

Hail Stones—that is Hail Stones in the shallows at the carcass of She-Demands. And Swamp is beside him. A few feet from the two bull calves, where She-Scares fell, is . . . who? She-Screams? No, She-Snorts. And the calf on the shore would be Bent, the only surviving calf. And so the cow next to him must be She-Soothes. Yes, that makes sense, because they are standing over the body of She-Stammers. Behind them, passing one hind foot above the head of She-Sees, is She-Screams.

That's the lot. Is it? Hail Stones, Swamp, She-Snorts, She-Soothes, Bent, She-Screams. She moves along the bank and peers through the dark with rising alarm, and her withered leg buckles and she starts sliding down to the shore.

She-Soothes gets to her first and, trumpeting incoherently, pulls her to her feet. Mud touches the sticky line of temporin under the older cow's left eye, which is missing, the socket stuffed with something that smells of blood and hyena dung. "Your eye," she says, but her voice is lost in the clamour. She-Snorts roars, "Mud!" (not "She-Spurns," as Mud will later appreciate) and, "Jubilation!" Between Mud's forelegs Bent shuffles on his knees and whips his trunk, and She-Screams tosses her head and in the moonlight the whites of her eyes give her a demented look.

And then all at once everybody goes still, as if there is a round of gunshot. But that's not what it is, it is nothing out there. It is a thought they all have. An awareness of the dead.

No one speaks or moves, but when the vultures begin to grunt, a beautiful voice says, "They have fallen into The Eternal Shoreless Water."

It is Hail Stones, who—Mud only now realizes—hasn't left the swamp. She also realizes that he is the last of the She-D's. And that he is right: the descent of the dead is exactly what she sensed. Their vertigo, and the splash.

"Your family is all together now," She-Snorts says in a kindly tone Mud has never before heard her use, and Mud sees that she is the biggest of the three big cows. And therefore the new matriarch. Nonchalant, irreverent, lustful She-Snorts—suddenly the matriarch!

She-Snorts turns her attention back to Mud. When she doesn't speak Mud says, "I had hoped she was with you."

"How did you know what I was thinking?" She-Snorts says, and Mud understands that she is asking, Did Mud hear her mind? Because if she did—if anybody, for that matter, is hearing anybody else's mind—then Date Bed, the family's mind talker, is dead.

Mud swallows around what feels like gravel in her throat. "Matriarch, I didn't know."

"Oh, I really can't bear it!" She-Screams cries. "After everything we've been through, and now to think that Date Bed might be lying somewhere—"

"Piss on that!" roars She-Soothes. "Date Bed will be here before morning." She looks around in her hearty fashion. She is a burly cow with thick bullish tusks and an appalling resilience. When her firstborn bull calf died, shortly after his birth, she dropped a few fronds over the body and bellowed at everyone else to quit their bawling. "What's done is done!" she trumpeted. "She-Soothes wants her browse!" And now, only hours ago, her daughter, She-Stammers, was slaughtered, and her left eye is gone, and yet she stomps her foot and roars, "Why imagine the worst?"

When nobody responds, she bellows, "Date Bed is no fool!"

Normally she can arouse at least one of them to her optimistic way of thinking. Not tonight. Date Bed is far from a fool, but she is so small.

Up on the plain the hyenas cackle. Vultures spiral, the occasional soft flap of their wings so like the flapping of their own ears. Mud and She-Snorts continue to look at each other, and it is just as well that Mud's thoughts can't be heard because what she is thinking is, "I'm the one who loves her. None of you loves her as I do," and the uselessness of her love arouses her to such a pitch of anguish that she thinks of returning to the plain and searching for Date Bed on her own. Which is lunacy, she knows. She splashes into the water, backwards, striding clumsily backwards, and when she hits the body of She-Scares she passes one hind foot over the skull as if to release the spirit to oblivion, where it already is. But Mud isn't yet prepared to see her adoptive mother—a hole where her face was.

Chapter Seven

A bullet from the same round of shots that killed She-Distracts hit Date Bed above her right eye. Instead of the piercing sensation she was braced for, there was a hard smack. She had been struck by a stone, she thought. She touched the wound and felt the hole as a bump. She ran across the shore and up onto the bank, where, blinking through blood, she mistook retreating dust clouds for her family in flight. She chased them for miles, for hours, trumpeting their names and begging them to slow down. They called back, or so she hallucinated, and yet they would not wait. They all ran extraordinarily fast and they took sharp turns in perfect unison, like a flock of birds. The dust buried their tracks, swallowed their scent. By the time she dropped to her knees, on the dazzling white sands of an arid lake, her shadow was streaming out behind her.

◆ ◆ ◆

She awakens at dawn, famished and parched. A terrible pain pulses through the right side of her skull. Out of her left eye she sees the blurred silhouettes of vultures eddying above her. She throws herself to her feet, and the pain in her head rolls like a boulder. The skin on her back and left flank is sunburned. Touching her wound, she now feels the hole as a hole, and she smells the gunpowder. She smells her blood, the sweet wet blood in the hole and the sour crust of blood on her face.

A low mist fumes across the pan. Sunward and some distance apart she spies two dark masses that she suspects are lone male wildebeests guarding their territories until their females return. But they could be hyenas who, because these are abnormal times, have come out to hunt during the day. Or they could be nothing, places where the mist has congested. How abjectly she depends on Mud's keen eyes she has never appreciated until now.

She walks to the edge of the pan and lifts her forefeet onto a low stone table. Since the onset of the drought she has been conducting experiments into infrasonic rumbles and has come up with two theories. One is that standing on rock improves transmission quality. The other is that during severe droughts the ground dries out so thoroughly that the rumbles get blocked behind walls of impenetrable earth.

In either event she has no choice except to try to communicate. She calls to Mud and to her mother. When no answer comes she calls to each of the She-S's in turn. Still no answer. Either the rumbles aren't getting through or. . . .

Or everybody is dead. In which case she spent all those hours yesterday pursuing a mirage.

She reminds herself that she saw She-Scares and She-Scavenges go down, nobody else. Who knows how many others survived? All of them might have, she tells herself as she weeps for the two certain deaths (weeps without tears because she must not waste fluid). All the rest might have survived.

But where are they? Where is *she*? Nothing about this place is familiar, no combination of scents or sounds. She can't smell water. Even at the sunken centre of the pan where she slept she couldn't smell it. She will have to ask for help from somebody. Not from the vultures, those sadistic liars. She starts walking toward the nearest dark shape, sniffing the scoured ground as she goes. If it is a hyena, it won't advise her but it won't attack her either, now that the sun has risen and she is approaching it in this fearless manner.

While it is still a shimmering obscurity it comes to its feet and snorts, thus revealing itself, and she stops where she is, at that respectful distance, and thinks, "Hello, bull ideal."*

No response.

"I apologize for disturbing you," she thinks, walking closer, "but I wonder if you might tell me where we are in relation to The She-Hill."

He lifts his snout.

"The *Ideal* Hill," she amends.

Silence.

She decides to appeal to his sympathy, if he has any. "I am very thirsty," she thinks. "Could you direct me to the nearest source of water?"

He shakes his head, which she takes to be a warning rather than a refusal, although it is possible that he has no idea where

---

* When addressing a species other than her own, a mind talker employs the deferential "bull" or "cow" title (comparable to Mr. or Mrs.) followed by that creature's name for its own kind.

water is, considering that wildebeests can go for hundreds of days without drinking.

"I am wounded," she thinks. Her smell will have conveyed as much, but she wants him to understand that she has no intention of challenging him over his patch of scrub. "I have become separated from my family," she thinks, and her throat constricts in self-pity.

He sweeps his stubby horns. And then he charges her with that awkward, stiff-legged gait they have.

She holds her ground. He is no match for her. When he is close enough that she can feel the gust of his stagnant breath, he stops and looks her up and down and she knows he is gauging her vanity. Wildebeests are under the impression that each species determines its own relative size. Bigness in comparison to other creatures is, they believe, conceit. Whereas smallness is excessive humility and therefore no less prideful. The perfect size, the "ideal" size, is wildebeest size.

"Big and ugly," he concludes. Like the lunatic he is, he starts bounding on the spot, tossing his head, slinging saliva. "Ugly," he grunts. "Ugly, ugly. . . ."

Her wound throbs. Half-blinded by the pain she turns and walks away. She takes care not to step in his dung and she lets out a desperate laugh because she knows fastidiousness to be mad under the circumstances. Mad she may be, but he and his entire species are demented. Most fallen species are, if you ask her. Humans, who are fallen she-ones. Snakes, who are fallen mongooses. Wildebeests are fallen warthogs, hence their slab heads and preoccupation with size.

Through the pearly mist the stones and bones flash with a counterfeit whiteness. She thinks of the white bone, how tragic it would be if one of these countless gleams was her salvation and she passed it by. Not that there is much likelihood of that. Hail Stones said the white bone is almost always dropped within a circle of boulders or termite mounds to the west of whatever hills may be in the region, and there are no hills or boulders here, at least none that she can see. Neither are the bones she picks up very white. Close up they are dull. And cool ... the day is not yet as torrid as her burned back would suggest.

She kicks dirt into the end of her trunk and flings it over her back and between her legs. It is the longest drought in at least sixty-five years. We are being punished, she thinks. Either that, or tested. And then, recalling She-Demands' final sermon, she thinks, "We are being remembered," and this strikes her as a more terrible prospect than the other two because it is unassailable, and she says out loud (appealing to the She, who knows she'll say it, who is recollecting—perhaps with regret—what in some frivolous or barbarous state of mind She once imagined), "I must find water."

But the morning is half over before she finds even another creature. A secretary bird it smells like. For all that they have a reputation for pomposity and standoffishness, the two secretary birds that she has ever spoken with were cordial, although difficult to draw out, it's true.

She hurries toward it. She is still too far away to scent its sex when she detects it turning to look at her.

"Hello, majestic," she thinks.

The bird high-steps in a circle.

"I wonder if you might help me," she thinks.

If the bird thinks something in reply, she doesn't hear. A creature who is not speaking must be looking roughly in her direction for her to hear its mind. She keeps walking, slowly now, until she is near enough that she could touch its stunningly long tail feathers. It is male.

"Hello, bull majestic," she thinks.

He is fixed upon a pile of stones. She refrains from sniffing the pile but believes that she smells rodent dung. She is in terrific pain and her throat is so dry it feels embedded with thorns and yet pleasure leaps up in her because she has never before been this close to a secretary bird. He *is* majestic, she thinks (thinks it hard enough for him to hear). "The fit of his name," as the saying goes. She herself would not have called such creatures "kick flies." (This she thinks privately.) Her kind take it for granted that the backward kick is a strut, a disdainful gesture, whereas she suspects that it is a way of scraping the ground for insects.

The bird's right claw swipes down and comes up clutching a brown snake, which he begins to bash on the stones. After a good dozen blows the snake finally stops writhing, and the bird inclines his head so that he is looking up at Date Bed. "I very nearly failed, thanks to you," he thinks.

"I beg your pardon," Date Bed thinks. The snake is the same breed of puff adder that, over the years, has killed two She-S calves. "Would you know," she thinks, "where there is water in the vicinity?"

"I would." He stretches his neck imperiously.

"Where?"

"Where is what?"

"The water."

"The water is where it is."

"I do not know this region."

"Which fact does not alter the location of the water." He opens his wings and runs in a zigzag, dragging the adder through the dirt and producing a sinuous tube of brown dust whose resemblance to the adder itself is not lost on her.

She heads off in the opposite direction. Sweeping her trunk across the ground, she inhales the discouraging odours of old dung, old urine, old bones, dead flesh. The wind is up. Every time she sprays herself with dust, most of it blows away before it hits her skin, and soon the heat will be unbearable. Already the egrets alighting on her back feel like licks of flame. Where will she shelter? For the first time in her life her memory has failed her. Somehow she got herself here, and ordinarily all she would have to do is picture that journey in her mind's eye and retrace her steps, but yesterday is a haze, as deteriorated as her eyesight.

She walks aimlessly, since no scent guides her. The dung is that of ostriches, hyenas, leopards, warthogs, giraffes, golden jackals. Vultures, naturally. Her own boluses, when she comes across them, lead nowhere. Instead of marking a trail they mark loops, as if she defecated careening. Not all the dung of the other creatures is old, and sometimes she catches whiffs of life—hyenas and wildebeests mostly—amid the carcasses. Whenever she comes to rocky ground she sends out infrasonic calls to Mud and her mother, and where there are dried streams she digs for water. During one of these excavations she discovers a glut of tubers whose juicy pulp takes the desperation off her thirst. It is a day as hot as any she remembers. She hasn't the will to stop herself from reliving all the most torrid days of her life, and so she imagines shade where there is none or attempts to drink at pools that aren't there. Skirting the flaming ground of a memory, she just misses stepping on real flames that, in places where there is still enough dead grass to fuel them, ruffle under whirlwinds of smoke. Black kites hover above the smoke and pretend not to hear her asking for help. Once, she sees what she thinks is a range of low hills but they turn out to be dust clouds created by a flock of vulturine guineafowl who cock their tiny heads at various angles and cackle "Scat!" and she finds herself absurdly frightened.

Her skull throbs ceaselessly now and it is becoming clear to her that she will have to tend to the wound or risk infection. A poultice is required, made either from warthog urine and fever-tree bark (similar to the one She-Soothes applied to Hail Stones' foot) or from hyena dung and fever-tree bark. There are only these two remedies for bullet wounds, as every nurse cow knows.

As Date Bed knows. For her, the momentous times at the Long Rains Massive Gatherings are when somebody falls sick or is injured and the nurse cows from every family—She-Soothes, She-Heals-And-Heals, She-Restores, She-Cures and all the rest—gather around the patient and debate how to proceed. Before she learned not to, she would ask the cows why one treatment was chosen over another, why the ingredients deviated from the standard mixture, and the answer was always a variation of "That's what works," which even as a small calf Date Bed heard as a variation of "Thus spake the She." To her frustration nobody, not even the eminent She-Purges, was interested in the logic behind the remedy.

Date Bed is supremely interested. As early as her second Massive Gathering she would suggest possible explanations:

the dung suffocates the pus; the hollow sticks swallow the fever. The nurse cows would listen with apparent interest but never did their eyes light up, and eventually Date Bed began to understand that they were afraid. You don't wonder about the cures, you don't look too hard at them. To do that is to tamper with their power and offend the She. Offend Her how? Date Bed has never asked, appreciating, as she does, that the nurse cows' fear is itself a breach of faith, which none of them would like to think about, let alone admit to.

In any event, she knows what she needs for her wound. But where in this forsaken territory will she find a fever tree?

She sniffs the air and turns in a circle. So that her eyes will water and temporarily clear her vision, she refrains from blinking. (She wishes there was a remedy for poor vision. A liquid that, unlike tears, did not wash away. A transparent jelly or mucus you daubed on your eyeballs.)

Anywhere is as unprofitable as anywhere else. Bush, stones, fire.

Fire.

Warthog urine or hyena dung scald the wound, that is their therapeutic function. Why scalding should help, Date Bed doesn't know, unless, as she used to hypothesize to the nurse cows, it "burns the badness." Would an ignited stick, then, or a hot stone, not do the same job?

She hurries toward the river of black smoke and low flames. No sticks are there, none that she can see. Plenty of stones and rocks are strewn about, but how can she pick one up without singeing her trunk? If there was a green leaf, a palm frond, she would have a buffer.

Squinting, scenting, she surveys the terrain. A pulse batters her skull, and her thoughts will not align themselves. "Water," she thinks into the void, and a crew of vultures plummets from the sky and hops behind her squealing, "Water! Water!" and when she turns on them they open their wings and lift with improbable grace.

Tornadoes spin behind her eyes. She teeters a few steps and sinks to her knees at the verge of the rattling flames. She remains like that for how long? A minute? An hour? Elapsed time is apparent to her only in the cramping of her joints. When her mind clears enough for her to distinguish the smoke in her head from the smoke outside it, she curls her trunk under her chin, presses her ears against her skull and positions her face above a scallop of flame.

Perhaps because the pain is expected it is not as awful as expected. It is, at last, the piercing of that bullet—what the bullet should have felt like—and then it is cold and quite bearable. Not until she smells herself burning does she lift her head. She comes to her feet and walks away, and near a place where there are no rocks or bones she lowers herself to the ground again.

The burn gathers into itself all her other discomforts, even her thirst, and incinerates them down to nothing, and although she can't bring herself to stand, she feels recovered.

She murmurs a song of thanksgiving:

"Oh, for a faith that will not shrink,
Though pressed by thirst and fear,
That will not tremble on the brink
Of death, though life is dear.

"That will release each care and grief,
Each hurt and doubting call
To Her, the She, the Cow of Cows,
Whose trunk curls round us all."

And then she falls into unconsciousness.

When she awakes she notices, inches from her eyes, a pile of her own dung, the sweet known smell of which is so appetizing she would eat it had she the will to move. Her near vision is superb, and she watches the flies that scramble over the boluses. Wings like slices of blue light. Green gibbous eyes. How nervous they are! They seem to be at their wits' end, maddened by the loss of some necessity they hope to find in her dung, and despite appearing to take no notice of each other they produce a unified buzz that makes for an impression of a single multi-eyed, multi-winged, overwrought creature.

What does this creature call itself? Mind talkers and insects don't communicate, so there is no point asking. And yet she does ask . . . she thinks, "Which breed of speck are you?" and the buzz seems to configure into a sound that says, "Vital."

"Vital," she thinks, amused because all creatures go by such vainglorious names, and because (since it is impossible that the flies answered her) she must have thought up this name herself. She decides that the creature is female. "Hello, cow vital," she thinks.

All the flies rise up and settle back down on the bolus closest to her right eye, and she has the feeling that the entirety of her is too much for them to grasp and that they suppose her eye to be a creature all on its own whom they call the Shine. What is curious is that while it is her mind that is forming this narrative, she is dependent upon the buzzing for inspiration. She hears no words. She hears an oscillation that seems to enter the hole in her head and within that cavity make itself intelligible to her. "In what respect," she thinks, "are you vital?"

"I span The Domain."

"Span The Domain," she repeats, mystified, and then she begins to picture it. One fly buzzes to another, who buzzes to another, who buzzes to another, and so on, each buzz a thread in a fine mesh, and eventually the mesh is a shimmering hum the length and breadth of the world. "How marvellous," she thinks, forgetting that she may be talking to herself.

"I span The Domain," the buzzing says again.

"Yes, I understand."

"I command the panorama."

"Of the whole Domain," she submits.

The flies fail to respond to this, and she is aware again of her tremendous thirst. "Where might I find water?" she thinks.

"That way."

She lifts her head. "Which way?"

"That way."

The flies all face in different directions.

Defeated, she lowers her head and falls into a waking dream in which she is airborne. The landscape is magnificently detailed but colourless. Round hills, like colossal eggs, skim past on her right and left, and for some reason she can see to her left and right simultaneously. Everything is so big and clear. Underneath her, a creature resembling some giant insect scampers by, and that's when she realizes she is seeing with the eyes of a fly in order that she may be directed to a source of water.

She had better pay attention. And make allowances. What might be a great distance to a fly will be nothing to her. She notes by the shadows that she is heading away from and a bit to the left of the sun. She zooms past a chain of those round hills, which must be pebbles, and then over a trail of dark mottled discs the size of ponds. Cattle dung? On her left an escarpment swells into view . . . no, it's a bone, a femur. A little farther along is a ribcage and skull. Of what? A zebra foal? It is hard to identify things whose size has inflated a thousand times.

Cracks in the earth plunge like gorges, masses of humpbacked insects range like buffalo. A wall of webbed tree trunks is either a bush or a tangled ball of shrubbery. She passes termite mounds as enormous as mountains and then there is bare earth for a spell, each granule of dirt a distinct, shivering pebble. The ground dips and she glides over a honeycomb of mauve boulders at the end of which is a dawn of white sand.

The dream ends.

She gets herself to her feet and stands there acquainting herself with her reawakened agonies. Now that she is up off the ground and can no longer even see the flies, her exchange with them strikes her as inconceivable. Nevertheless, she sets off as the dream instructed, with her back to the sun and veering slightly to her left, and in minutes she comes upon the femur and skull and ribcage of a zebra foal. From there, she races. Past termite mounds, over a bank of mauve stones and onto the bed of a dried-up river where, in a delirium of anticipation, she digs.

Chapter Eight

It's not safe to linger at the swamp. Humans are known to return to their slaughters for any feet and tails they may have overlooked, or simply to wander around gloating. Sometimes they carve the corpse into pieces and carry the pieces off, presumably with the intention of eating them elsewhere, but more often they build a fire right at the scene, and their uproarious feasts can carry on for days.

Tusks they always take away immediately after a slaughter. Where the tusks end up and what the humans want with them (or with the feet and tails, for that matter) nobody knows for certain. Torrent says he has come across two human corpses whose necks and forelegs were encircled by narrow bands of ivory and he speculates that these bands demonstrate nostalgia for the days when humans were she-ones. He thinks, as nearly everyone does, that humans also pulverize tusks and inhale the ivory powder in order to heighten their poor sense of smell.

The humans who waged the slaughter at the swamp took every last bit of ivory, even from the calves, but they left all the tails and feet behind. One less atrocity, one more cause for alarm. Even if those humans don't return, members of their family may. She-Snorts, however, refuses to leave.

"Go, if you want," she rumbles indifferently to She-Screams that first morning. "I'm waiting for my daughter."

"If she were coming, she'd be here by now," She-Screams protests, not without reason. "She won't come, not Date Bed, she's too sensible. She won't imagine that *we're* still here." She casts anxious glances at Swamp. "I'm certain She-Scares wouldn't have wanted us to risk our hides like this. And my poor mother wouldn't have wanted it, either, I can tell you that."

With her hind feet She-Snorts kicks more sand over the headless body of She-Drawls-And-Drawls. The kicks undulate her backside in a way so conspicuously carnal that little Bent attempts to mount her thigh. She shakes him off. "Your poor mother is no longer with us," she says. "She-Scares is no longer with us. I am your matriarch, and as your matriarch, I advise you"—she waddles around until she is facing She-Screams—"to do whatever you like."

"Oh, now!" She-Soothes roars, dumbfounded. The two other big cows ignore her.

"Are you banishing me?" She-Screams cries.

"I'm telling you that you are free to go."

But, of course, She-Screams isn't free, and it is a scandal that She-Snorts would suggest such a thing. "She is out of her mind with grief," Mud thinks to account for it. And yet she also thinks that She-Snorts and She-Screams are aunt and niece, not sisters, and aunts and nieces sometimes do separate, each taking along her own calves and perhaps her younger sisters to start a new family. Except that this family is so reduced already, and if She-Screams left, there would only be Swamp to go with her because who else, given the choice, would choose She-Screams? And even Swamp—Mud looks at him where he stands in the blood-brown shallows with Hail Stones, whose side he has not left since last night—even he might abandon his mother.

For the first time that Mud knows of, She-Screams is speechless. She flails her ugly head, the clapping of her ears disturbingly like the approach of a helicopter.

She-Snorts begins to saunter away.

"You are a glutton!" She-Screams finally shrieks.

She-Snorts keeps walking.

"If I were the glutton you are," She-Screams cries, "*I'd* be the biggest cow!" She whirls around and struts off in the opposite direction. Both of them sway their hips, She-Snorts giving an impression of exquisite nonchalance, She-Screams of digestive trauma.

The day hauls itself along. The sun, as it will do whenever a spell of torment or waiting must be endured, enters a heightened state of watchfulness and moves more slowly across the sky, so that what would normally be dusk is only early afternoon, and Mud feels drained from singing hymns and weeping, from pouring sand over the slaughtered and from the pointless, infuriating work of chasing the vultures. She stands in the shade of She-Screams, who leans wheezing against the bank. Throughout the morning She-Screams complained of shortness of breath, although she seemed no more winded than any of them. "I am having a spell!" she kept screeching at Swamp. Now she really does appear to be ailing, but as if to prove to She-Snorts that she is the more heroic one she does not enter the water until She-Soothes roars that she risks heat sleep. It is so hot you can see the stench rising in wavering red streams from the corpses. Every gash, every spill of blood is black with the kind of stinging flies that are an incarnation of ash, and this means either that humans are firing flesh somewhere, beyond scent, or that there are grass fires up on the plain.

Despite the stench and danger, the swamp is not theirs alone. Wildebeests, gazelles, buffalo, hippos, zebras and troops of baboons mill near the shore and bump against the crocodiles, who leap up to snatch ankles and heads and swooping-down birds. Only she-ones and hippos are safe from these attacks, and the hippos show off their immunity by gnawing on the crocodiles' toothy spines. The crocodiles slip beneath the water. There is no sign of their feasting on the carcasses except for a slight rocking of the legs, which stick out of the water like tree stumps. Vultures perch on the legs and some sit in the face cavities, as in nests. Far down into the bellies the vultures poke their blood-coloured skulls and emerge tugging thongs of gore that they tear free with a twist of their beaks.

Turned away from that impossible sight, out in the centre of the swamp, Mud and She-Snorts browse on either side of a clump of sedge. They have the deepest voices, so every few hours one of them wades back to land and sends an infrasonic rumble, first to Date Bed and then to Torrent, and then to Tall Time and finally to the three matriarchs who have been known to bring their families to the swamp. After each call everybody stops feeding and listens for a response. None comes.

The White Bone

The family is unnaturally scattered. She-Soothes and Bent stay in the shallows, and whenever vultures alight on the bodies of the little calves She-Soothes splashes to shore and chases them off. She-Screams feeds alone at the swamp's south end and from there wails at Swamp. At one point she tries to pull him out into the deeper water but he violently jerks himself free, trumpeting, "I am not a newborn!" which is so unlike him—the animation, let alone the anger—that she backs away whimpering.

Swamp is rapt by Hail Stones, who is rapt by the carcass of his aunt, She-Demands. Hail Stones doesn't unduly harass the vultures or crocodiles, it's not that he is devoted to guarding the remains. He drinks and showers, and he suffers Swamp to stroke his hide and to swish the flies from his face, but when anybody urges him to feed, he says he isn't hungry. Twice Mud brings him a swatch of grass only to have him give it to Swamp, who says, "If you're sure," and eats it in his resigned way. The second time she makes her offering, toward the end of the afternoon, she ventures to say, "There must be a reason you were spared."

Hail Stones looks at her. Between them, shadows strain across the swamp. "I expect you are right," he says courteously. "And yet I can't imagine what it might be."

"Not yet you can't. But you will." Although she believes this, she can hear how feeble it sounds.

Swamp sighs. "Only in moments of bliss," he says, "does it become apparent to us why terrible things happen."

Another of his groundless pronouncements, and Mud, in her turn, sighs.

Hail Stones looks toward the shore. Everyone else is there now, standing among the dead. Mud studies Hail Stones' gaunt young face, and what she feels is the prospect of pity, that eventually she will pity him. Now everything she feels must be conserved and directed toward keeping Date Bed safe. For Hail Stones she can only call up something ungraspable, like a half-formed thought. "If I should be killed," Date Bed had said, "who would you talk to?" Him, Mud thinks, but she is unable to imagine it. Hail Stones is not Date Bed, just as She-Scares was not Mud's birth mother, and Mud was not She-Scares' dead newborn.

◆ ◆ ◆

They don't travel in a line with the matriarch at the front and the second-biggest cow bringing up the rear. She-Snorts *is* the one setting the course, but only She-Soothes and Bent follow her. She-Screams, who should be the hindmost cow, pointedly keeps abreast of She-Snorts, twenty or so yards to her left, as if to give the impression that she is equally in charge or that only by coincidence does she happen to be going in the same direction. Every once in a while she turns to scent Swamp and Hail Stones. The two young bulls trail behind, and whenever they go out of sight or smell altogether She-Screams cries, "Stop!" and She-Snorts does but only for the sake of Hail Stones (who is still distressingly thin and whose wound continues to fester). In this way the pace is determined, as is the frequency of infrasonic rumbles because every time there is a halt She-Snorts or Mud calls out to Date Bed. If anything edible is nearby, the stops also allow for a quick feed.

Mud walks alongside She-Soothes and Bent, as far to the right of them as She-Screams is to their left, which is about twice as far away as she would normally position herself. The family has gone back to using her cow name, She-Spurns, and even though she understands that this is inevitable, she feels abolished every time she is addressed.

All three big cows are poor company anyway. The swaggering enthusiasm of She-Soothes—so heartwarming in good times—seems mad out here. Mud has become revolted by her, the stench of her eye wad (a mixture of chewed fevertree bark and hyena dung stuffed into the socket) being the least of it. The nurse cow eats the dung of the other grazers, "drought fruit," she calls it, and exhorts the rest of them to do likewise, and when anybody craves salt she revives her urine-drinking campaign: they could forgo salt licks altogether if they drank each other's liquid waste. Roaring, "Watch She-Soothes!" she curves her trunk under Bent to drink his, and the little calf wobbles on his delicate legs and shows the whites of his eyes.

She-Snorts and She-Screams, when they start in on each other, are no less irritating, She-Screams especially, but shouldn't She-Snorts know better? Much as Mud resents She-Screams for resenting her, she doesn't gloat when She-Snorts mocks or otherwise offends the ridiculous cow. Had Mud any authority she would ask She-Snorts to *pretend* to indulge She-Screams, as She-Sees used to.

It stuns Mud how many matriarchal skills She-Snorts lacks. "Do whatever you want" is her most commonly issued command, and except for Hail Stones she spares little conversation for any of them. Hail Stones she sweet-talks. At Blood Swamp she sweet-talked him into abandoning his vigil at the corpse of She-Demands. This was on the fifth morning after the slaughter. On the fourteenth morning, by which time she had finally accepted that Date Bed was not returning, she sweet-talked him into joining the search, since she feared that, left on his own, he would starve himself. Now, at the end of every day, while She-Soothes is replacing his poultice, she praises him for having kept up with the trek and she tells him stories about his dead relations, stories that celebrate them. She sounds like a mother comforting her calf and a bull seducing a nervous oestrus cow, both, which in itself is strange, but the flattery, from the most vain of cows, is stranger still. Flattery inclines *toward* She-Snorts, that is its principle. To hear it flow the other way is like seeing water stream uphill. Eventually all of them go quiet, listening. For his part Hail Stones rumbles, "Thank you, Matriarch," or "I am honoured, Matriarch," some modest acknowledgement in his gorgeous voice and in the formal timbre.

There is a spell of peace then, an apprehension within each of them of the grandness of their recent loss and of the mystery of their own intactness, or so it seems to Mud because that's what she feels. She also feels in these moments—when the air has cooled and the plain is no longer a pageant of dust devils—almost blithely certain that Date Bed is alive and that they will find her. With She-Snorts in the lead they will find her. Who suspected that self-absorbed She-Snorts was so devoted to her daughter? Mud doubts that even Date Bed had any idea. And who suspected that she could be so single-minded? In the six days since they left the swamp She-Snorts has scented Date Bed five times, which is phenomenal considering how faint and easily adulterated Date Bed's odour is, let alone that the wind sucks the pungency out of everything. One time She-Snorts found a neat ball of indigestible palm fibre that Date Bed had spat out. Twice she located Date Bed's dung and twice she smelled single drops of her blood. At the first discovery of blood, on the node of a log, She-Snorts said, "She is wounded," and She-Soothes bellowed, "Hardly at all!" and their voices, one frightened, one encouraged, described the precise, contracted boundaries of what could be reasonably felt. Not despairing, not yet. Not relieved yet, either.

To Mud's mind the matriarch's shortcomings are forgivable when set alongside her sharp trunk. She is their hope for locating not only Date Bed but clear water. She-Screams will strut to a spot on a dry riverbed where, two or three decades earlier, the family excavated a drinking hole, and as she digs she makes eager self-satisfied noises and then grunts with exasperation and then she screams to Swamp that she is short of breath, whereupon he strolls up to her, sighing, and kicks loose a few clumps, his trunk always swinging back to Hail Stones, and in the end something may ooze out—rank muck or slime—some sludge that She-Screams acts delighted by and tosses on her hide as if all along she was only planning a mud bath. "Help yourselves!" she trills. Why would they? By now they have themselves dug wells at a place She-Snorts has led them to. Eventually She-Screams inserts her warty, slime-coated trunk into one of these wells and drinks and afterwards, shamed and ill tempered, she slaps Swamp or little Bent or even Hail Stones, and then she fawns over whomever she has mistreated, which effusions Swamp and Hail Stones endure and Bent runs squealing from.

If the family does not move on at this point, She-Screams

will typically have one of her spells, and after that she will nestle into a mood of frazzled self-pity. While extravagantly ignoring She-Snorts (who will be browsing or sending infrasonic rumbles . . . and scenting, always scenting), She-Screams will criticize her as if she isn't there. A squabble is inevitable now. It is inevitable at dusk. Sadly and always, She-Screams is the one to smash that collective spell of peace. She starts by flicking her trunk. She taps her face. She says, finally, something to the effect of: "My poor mother would never have— Of course, nobody cares what I think—"

✦ ✦ ✦

It is late afternoon on the sixteenth day. They are discouraged, all of them except Hail Stones, but he is so polite and inscrutable who can tell how he feels? They have yet to meet another she-one family. Rather, every day for the past seven days, they have found a she-one carcass. Early this morning they came upon a slaughter: five amputated cow carcasses belonging to the Second She-S's-And-S's, who are—or were—close relations.

Mid-morning they resumed walking. Already they were exhausted from the burying and mourning, the weeping. They hadn't gone far when She-Snorts turned and led them back the way they'd been going. Many miles later she changed her mind and took up her original route. "You've lost the trail!" She-Screams cried, and from then on she whined to herself but not quite to herself, her peevish voice like crevices breaking through the rock-hard heat to release the day's portion of torment.

The White Bone

There was no luck in the day, no deliverance. Just before noon they arrived at a wire fence and were forced to walk south along its length until they discovered a break in the weave. Returning north, they passed a bad-tempered, one-eyed bull wildebeest, and as if he somehow knew that his affliction was an ill omen he trotted alongside them, grunting, "Ugly, ugly," until She-Soothes chased him off. Moments later an airplane flew low overhead and compelled them to stampede toward an outcrop where Bent nearly stepped on a cobra. Despite the wind and the blasting dust, cow flies held fast to their hides in clusters thick as moss. Mud's bad leg ached. Hail Stones' foot ballooned. When She-Soothes pierced the swelling with a thorn it discharged a foul green sludge that the nurse cow, for all her bluster, had obviously never seen before. Bent slumped on his rickety knees, and to keep him moving She-Soothes had to curl her trunk between his hind legs and half-lift, half-push him along.

Added to all this was the incident with the white bone.

On the day they left the swamp She-Soothes asked if they should keep their eyes open for the "white prize," and She-Snorts said carelessly, "Suit yourselves," which they took to mean that *she* wouldn't be looking. They were wrong. She has been as eager as any of them to search for a flash of white whenever they come upon a circle of boulders or termite mounds, and she is the one who pointed out that their eccentric formation is an advantage in this search because, spread out as they are, they cover a wider territory. Every so often somebody veers off course, and the rest of them wait until the signal comes back—No.

If She-Screams isn't the one who thinks she has spotted something, if she is among the watchers, instead of dropping her trunk in disappointment she cries, "Ha!" Whereas if she is the mistaken one she blames the light, the dust. Once, she said that she rushed away not because she thought she saw the white bone but because she was certain she had smelled Date Bed. She had the gall to say that.

On this day, in the middle of the afternoon, she suddenly goes waddling off in the direction of an outcrop of boulders. Halfway there she stops and picks something up. "I found it!" she trumpets. "The white prize!" The boulders do not form a circle and there are no hills to the east, but the little bone she holds aloft *is* very white. Everybody rushes to her. Sobbing, streaming temporin, she waves the rib above their heads and screeches, "I saw it! I'm the one who saw it!"

"Show it to me," She-Snorts says.

"Be careful!" She-Screams whimpers, and as she lowers her trunk Mud sees that it's not a she-one's rib at all, it's a rhino's.

She-Snorts has already smelled as much. She retracts her trunk and, disgusted, addressing She-Soothes, mutters, "What's wrong with her?"

"What?" She-Screams cries.

Hail Stones and Swamp have just arrived. "Mother," Swamp sighs, "that is obviously from a ghastly."

"It is not!" She-Screams wails.

"A perfectly understandable error," Hail Stones murmurs.

She-Screams brings the rib to her wet eyes. She sniffs the length of it. The mortifying knowledge that it is, after all, from a rhino twitches across her face. Still, she clutches it under her chin and says with an air of dignity so baseless as to be almost splendid, "None of you wants to believe that I found it. You all despise me."

The White Bone

"That's the salt deficiency talking!" She-Soothes roars. "A few swallows of piss and you'll feel as sane as stone!"

"You are grotesque!" She-Screams cries.

She-Snorts, who has been scenting the air, starts moving away.

"Wasn't that exciting?" She-Soothes trumpets cheerfully and she tugs Bent to his feet and beams around at the rest of them through her sighted eye. "Coming?"

Nobody responds. Swamp has unearthed a bouquet of roots and is offering it to Hail Stones. Hail Stones is regarding She-Screams, and the look on his face—pitying, ruminative—gives Mud the impression that he is reminded of some other pathetic cow. How horrid it must be for him, Mud thinks, stuck with the dregs of this family, obliged to accept the peculiar attentions of a doting bull calf and to limp along on a suppurating foot in search of a calf he hardly knew. All this while bearing, in heartbreaking silence, the loss of his entire family. He will leave us as soon as he is strong enough, she thinks, and feels a spasm of euphoria as if it is she who will leave. But then she looks at his bony torso, at his foot, and his escape is inconceivable and she is despairing, although consoled as well. . . . That ignoble feeling is there.

She tosses dirt over her hide and is about to start walking when something white soars at the edge of her vision. She whirls around and sees dust bloating beyond the outcrop.

She-Screams rushes to the spot. "It's pointing that way!" she trumpets, indicating behind herself. "The Safe Place is back there!"

She-Snorts comes to a stop but does not turn. She-Soothes turns slowly. Bent sinks to his knees. She-Screams retrieves the rib and lifts it high so they can all witness how it landed. "Shall I throw it again?"

What can she be thinking? "Oh, I shall!" she cries ecstatically. Like an inebriate* she spins in clumsy loops, shrieking, "I believe! I believe!" and then flinging the bone. It shoots directly at the matriarch and strikes her in the belly.

She-Screams releases a delighted-sounding screech. Mud gasps, and She-Screams gives her an infuriated look that collapses into horror and then she, too, gasps.

Blood dripping from her wound, She-Snorts steps around to face She-Screams. "I harbour a newborn," she rumbles.

"Of course," She-Screams says. She begins to weep. "I . . . I don't know . . . it's so hard for me. . . ." She sobs openmouthed, like a calf. "Swamp!" she wails, flailing for him.

Swamp ducks out of reach.

"Only a flesh cut!" She-Soothes trumpets after a quick investigation of the matriarch's wound.

The matriarch flaps her ears. From her, who hardly ever rages, this is a menacing sign. Bent scuttles under She-Soothes' belly. She-Screams shuts up. In the erotic, hip-rolling fashion of an oestrus cow presenting herself to a bull, She-Snorts turns her back to the rib. She raises one hind foot and stamps down hard. Mud is reminded of She-Demands crushing the body of her newborn and she lets out a distressed sound, which brings from She-Screams a look, both contemptuous and yearning, that says, "It was only a ghastly's rib, you dimwit," and "*Was* it the white bone? *Was* it?"

---

* Certain fruits (such as that of the doum palm) ferment in the stomach and, if eaten in quantity, can cause intoxication.

For the rest of the afternoon Mud's belly rumbles and cramps, and she can't dodge the thought that there really is life in there. The snarls of tenderness that unfurl with the thought horrify her. Her sense is that if she loves even the idea of her newborn, she is doomed to give birth, and if she gives birth, and the calf lives, she will have to stay in this family forever. Two cows on their own (she is imagining herself and Date Bed) have a fair chance of surviving, so she has persuaded herself. A calf with only two young cows to protect it has no chance. She doesn't want the calf to die, what she wants is for it not to be born.

She refrains from telling She-Soothes about the cramps because she suspects that the cure requires the ingestion of something repugnant, and as soon as She-Snorts calls a halt to the day she lies alongside the croton thicket whose unappetizing branches they will feed on during the night. Their normal routine—eating steadily from before dawn until several hours after dark and then sleeping for about five hours—cannot be maintained on a trek. They eat as they walk, drink when they can. In such torrid heat travelling at night would be far easier and safer, but She-Snorts will not risk overscenting any sign of Date Bed, and night is when the ground heaves up the distracting odours of burrowed life: catfish and reptiles, and the musk of regeneration in scorched roots.* By the time the sun is low, everybody is ravenous and they forage most of the night and sleep very little, except for Bent, who falls into brief stupors day and night.

---

* Known as underscents, these odours hover beneath the buoyant smells of dung, leaves, living animals and even slaughter.

She-Snorts locates water in a sandy depression under a grille of fallen thorn branches, and Mud arouses herself to drink and then lies back down, saying that her bad leg needs to rest awhile, which it does. Not that anybody is listening. She-Soothes is investigating Hail Stones' foot. On his other side, She-Snorts kicks for grass roots while murmuring her blandishments: "You must be the most long-suffering bull calf on The Domain. Any other bull calf in your state would have turned into a raving brute by now. . . ." Directly behind him, facing the other way, Swamp also kicks the ground, although with frequent sighs and less vigour. From where Mud lies, the two bulls appear to be joined tail-to-tail—Swamp with his greater height and girth like Hail Stones' distended shadow.

Before the drought Mud asked Swamp, "Does the prospect of leaving the family frighten you?" and he looked at her, for so long that she thought the question had offended him, but finally he said, "On the contrary, it captivates me."

"Why don't you go, in that case?" she asked.

Another long empty look. She guessed that he was wondering whether or not to blame his mother, because She-Screams tells him and everyone else that he is too trusting and dreamy to be on his own yet.

Again Mud was wrong. "I am waiting for the right moment," he said. And then he said, "The right moment is always as apparent as the sunrise."

Now, in the moonlight, Mud watches his spiritless kicks and wonders whether the right moment wasn't the arrival of Hail Stones. Perhaps Swamp was told, by a visionary or in a dream, about a bull calf showing up one day to captivate him. Every few moments he sniffs behind himself as though the nauseating smell that gases out of Hail Stones' foot is, to him, irresistible.

One of the times that he does this, his trunk is snatched midair by She-Screams, who inserts the end of it into her mouth. He draws it back out. Ignoring this slight, she says in a loud voice, "I am so proud of you. Staying with Hail Stones, putting yourself at risk."

She-Snorts falls quiet.

She-Screams swells into the void. "There is no bull calf more generous than you are. No bull calf more comely, either. Or well spoken. Everybody says so."

Swamp sighs.

She-Screams strokes his head. "All I've ever wanted is for you to be safe. We could have been on our way to The Safe Place this very day—"

At this, She-Snorts snorts. She-Screams falters—she knows she has overstepped the bounds—and yet on she goes as if she could persuade their incorruptible memories that her foolishness was really an act of doomed heroism. "Well," she rumbles, "that's the end of the white bone."

Another snort from She-Snorts but, surprisingly, nothing more. She-Screams delivers a few fussy huffs. She will be quiet now, Mud thinks. Surely. And it seems that she will—she snaps off a thorn branch, and the darkness itself seems to unloosen . . . and then she says to Swamp, "*You* are the long-suffering one."

Mud groans.

She-Screams whirls on her. "What do you know?" she cries. "Always wandering off, snubbing everybody, what do you know about this family?" She turns to Hail Stones.

Quavering, brightly courteous, she says, "I don't wish to offend you, Hail Stones, but it is not by choice that you trail behind the rest of us. Swamp has a choice, and he chooses to watch over you even though your wound is an attraction to the flesh-eaters. For your sake he willingly places himself in danger."

"I am very grateful to him," Hail Stones says quietly. "I am grateful to all of you."

"Mother," Swamp moans.

She-Screams smacks him. "Who will stand up for you if I don't?" she trumpets.

There is a hill of boulders to the east, and a high note from her voice rings among them like a particle of reason worth hearing out. When the note dies, She-Snorts rumbles matter-of-factly, "Swamp is a coward."

"Shame!" She-Screams cries.

She-Snorts looks at Swamp. "You *are*," she says, as if she couldn't care less.

"Shame!"

Still addressing Swamp, whom she has never before reproached, not in earnest, She-Snorts says, "You did not join the V formation before the slaughter. You went into the middle with the newborns."

"I was in the grip of a paralysing terror," he says complacently.

"Oh, this is insufferable!" She-Screams trumpets. She turns on She-Snorts. "You slander my calf and here I am almost an invalid, and my skin is cracked, I have extremely tender skin, I shouldn't be out in the sun nearly as much as I am, and by the way"—a swerve of her trunk in She-Soothes' direction—"I require a poultice for my shins. But I do what

I must. I traipse through this wasteland for the sake of finding *your* calf"—whirling back to She-Snorts—"even though she's. . . ."

"She's what?" Mud says.

"Dead," She-Screams mutters. "We all know she's dead."

"No!" She-Soothes trumpets.

"How can she possibly have survived out here on her own?" She-Screams says. "When she's wounded, what's more?"

"A few drops of blood, that's nothing!" She-Soothes roars. "Date Bed is doing fine! You saw her crap heaps! She-Soothes will tell you how she's surviving. By her wits!"

Mud reaches her trunk toward She-Screams. "Are you—?" she rumbles. Her heart swings in her ribs. "Are you hearing anybody's thoughts?"

"No, no." Irritably. "Nothing like that."

Tonight the underscents are especially powerful and as Mud sucks them in, her belly goes still. Either her newborn has withered or it is asleep or, more probably, the underscents have lulled it. Like everyone else, Mud is waiting for She-Snorts' reaction. The matriarch sniffs, deep thirsty breaths, while She-Screams fidgets and sighs and finally rumbles, "I would dearly love to be proven wrong. You all know how fond I am of Date Bed."

She-Snorts keeps scenting. Starlight slides down her swivelling trunk and pools in the dip of her strong tusk, whose shape and glow are precisely the new moon's. The sky is overrun with stars. It is a "memory night," when the sky is recollecting itself, every cow who ever dwelt up there, every shine, retrieved and lit up in a sensational dream. Down here, hares have appeared. Their eyes leap like sparks. Mud's eyes dim, and she feels a burning between them and knows that her third eye is about to open.

The vision is of a place like here, but it is not here. Dust blows by, and tumbleweed, east to west. Mud's third eye starts moving in the opposite direction, across stony earth and stubble and onto sand where a skeletal female impala takes high twitchy steps toward a fever tree. From a branch of the tree a male baboon dangles and drops and then scrambles over to a troop of his own kind. There are at least twenty of them, lean and squalid, spread out on the bank, and in the sand at the feet of every big male is a water hole. A mother baboon with a youngster hanging from her belly approaches one of the holes, and the male who guards it bares his teeth. The mother sits. At the next hole a huge male gnaws at the face of a dead impala calf, whom he holds by the neck and swings while he chews, and the limbs of the calf whip like vines. The male squints toward a pool of muck. In the centre of the pool a crocodile spins. When the spinning stops, the crocodile opens its jaws and out spills a gang of hatchling crocodiles. They wriggle to the far side of the pool, where the first of them is scooped up between another pair of jaws, these belonging to a lizard. Before the lizard repositions the hatchling so that it can be gulped down head-first, the hatchling's miniature jaws snap at a fly.

On Mud's third eye goes, past a running ostrich and along the base of a hill into the wreckage of fallen acacias. A little beyond the logs, lying on the ground, is a cow.

She-Screams. Her skull is crushed, her torso bloated. Her tusks and feet are still there, although she appears to have been dead for some time. A hyena enters the scene and tears at the rump, and a torrent of maggots gushes from under a flap of skin. The hyena devours them. When a lappet-faced vulture alights on the trunk, Mud's eye begins to close. The last thing she sees is the vulture looting gore from the skull.

Chapter Nine

Tall Time is worried. The persistent itch in his right ear, the oryx arriving at the salt lick, the anonymous she-one skeleton, the circle of vacated human "nests"—all proclaimed that the day would be unlucky. Not calamitous, the links were more indifferent than that, their collective message adding up to: Do as little as possible. Or, as his late aunt She-Balks used to say, "Venture nothing, forfeit nothing."

Since quitting the vicinity of the escarpment twenty-one days ago, he has drunk only from mucky seepages, even though the links those days were generally favourable. Why, then, on a day when the links are *not* favourable, has he come across a giant water hole where water never used to be? He rounded the thorn trees and saw, downwind, a circular glare. A female Grant's gazelle stood at the bank, head bent but not drinking. Mesmerized by her reflection, Tall Time thought. Or by the water, its sudden, uncanny arrival.

When she caught Tall Time's odour she hobbled off snorting and he cautiously approached the hole. That the feathers and swill of previous drinkers were on the skin of the water told him the hole at least had a history. Humans dug it, he guessed, judging by the size. And yet in this vicinity there was no smell of humans. And why was the hole not swarming with other creatures?

He drank and showered, sprayed himself with dirt, ate all the tasty grass roots surrounding the hole, scratched his hide on a stump, had a second shower and a dirt bath (taking his time with each activity, slowed down by wonder and suspicion) and then started to feed on the thorn trees.

Late afternoon he is still feeding, still wary, but allowing himself to fall in and out of a memory of yesterday so that he can look for the powerful link he must have missed. He can't find it. Or perhaps what he can't do is identify it. Suppose Torrent was right about the links being infinite? Suppose everything is a link? High above him he hears the creaking of a big bird's wings, and he thinks, "That could be a link," and he reels within the sickening prospect that everything exists for the purpose of pointing to something else.

In his search for the white bone he has travelled long distances without reaching the horizon, and the misgiving has grown in him that even were it possible to hold a perfectly straight course you could walk a hundred years and never arrive at the brink of the world. "Domain without end," he often finds himself thinking, and it sounds like a lyric, an old truth, but it is blasphemous. Thinking it now, he worries that he is cursing himself and he twirls his trunk three times to the left, three times to the right, drops to his foreknees and bellows:

"With gladsome pulse and open throat,
Down on my knees I fall
To thank the She, creator of
The links, both great and small.

"From shades of night She brings the light
And from the ground the grass.
From everywhere Her blessings break
Our praises to amass.

"Full in Her sight we lowly stand
By Her strong tusk defended,
For She whose mercy guides this realm
Our footsteps hath attended."

Thus transported he is oblivious to the upwind approach of the She-B's-And-B's. They are directly behind him when the new matriarch, She-Brags, trumpets, "I *told* you he wouldn't hear us!"

The greetings are far more passionate than they normally are between a bull and his kin. Not since the last Long Rains Massive Gathering has Tall Time run across any member of his birth family, and not since early in the drought has he had news of them. He tells them of coming upon the carcass of She-Bores-And-Bores and they tell him, weeping, that it was a single human with a miniature gun that killed her. He sings "Where Do the Tusks Go?" and, as the last line is fairly optimistic ("And there to float serene, past care, upon The Shoreless Water"), the greetings erupt again, and the evacuations of dung. "You are the same," he gloats. They are not, he can see that. To a cow they are angular, and the calves smell sickly. What he means is, they are not dead.

When the greetings are over, She-Brags rumbles, "Let us drink in proper order." The big cows go first while the younger ones keep the calves—the three who are small enough to risk falling down the water hole—from approaching the perimeter. And then the adolescents drink while the big cows guard the calves, and after the adolescents have had their turn, the big cows fill their trunks again and pour water into the calves' throats and over their bodies. Tall Time resumes browsing on the thorn trees. He waits until the family joins him before asking his adoptive mother, She-Bluffs, in whose sly, glittery eyes he detects a plea that he single her out, "What brings you to this place?"

"What brings *you*?" she says cagily.

"The big water hole," She-Brags answers him. "Naturally."

The trunk of the large tree he has been butting snaps and the tree falls, throwing up a stack of dust. "You have been here before," he says.

"Not at all," She-Brags says. She breaks off one of the tree's branches.

"How did you know that the hole was even here?"

The matriarch wags her ears. All the other occasions on which she has preened in this fashion flutter through his mind, and he prepares for a self-glorifying response, but she says only, "We were told."

"By whom?"

"Me-Me."

"Me-Me?"

"Me-Me the longbody," she says, watching him closely, "told She-Booms."

She-Booms is the family's mind talker and his former calfhood playmate. She has only one tusk and was consequently timid and virtually silent until the first day of her inaugural oestrus. On the morning of that day her squeal swelled into a roar so powerful as to eventually produce in the ears of all the She-B-And-B cows an incessant ringing. Tall Time turns to her and finds her peering at him.

"YOU HAVE NEVER MET A LONGBODY NAMED ME-ME?" she thunders.

"No."

"HE IS TELLING THE TRUTH," she informs She-Brags.

"Me-Me is a notorious liar," declares She-Brags. "I knew she was the instant I smelled her."

"SHE DIDN'T DECEIVE US ABOUT THIS WATER HOLE."

"About its being where she said it would be," She-Broods mutters. "But is it safe? Why are we the only creatures here?"

"If this were a hindlegger's trap," says the stern young nurse cow, She-Betters, "bones and carcasses would be everywhere."

"Hindleggers have been known to remove the evidence," She-Broods says darkly.

The reedy voice of She-Begs, who is a fine scenter, says, "There is no stench of hindlegger in the vicinity. And no ominous signs either, or the Link Bull wouldn't be here." She moves into Tall Time's line of vision and fixes him with her supplicating eyes. "Would he?"

"No," he rumbles, but feels fraudulent and turns to She-Booms. "This longbody. Why would you think I had met her?"

"SHE SAID YOU DID. SHE SAID THAT THE TWO OF YOU CROSSED PATHS WHEN YOU WERE AMONG THE SHE-R'S AND THAT YOU SPOKE TO HER THROUGH THE SHE-R'S MIND TALKER."

"I have never been among the She-R's."

"Didn't I say as much?" rumbles She-Brags. She appeals to the former matriarch, She-Blusters. "Mother, didn't I say that our Tall Time would never mingle with those dreadful She-R's?"

"Well, ah—" sputters the old cow, bits of bark dropping from her mouth. "You may . . . I can't . . . ah . . . you. . . ."

"What did this Me-Me say she and I spoke about?" Tall Time asks She-Booms.

She-Booms' odour turns anxious. Without meeting his eye she thunders, "SHE SAID THAT YOU PROMISED HER OUR NEWBORNS. SHE SAID THE PAIR OF YOU CAME TO AN AGREEMENT THAT IT WAS WORTH SACRIFICING THE NEWBORNS' LIVES IN EXCHANGE FOR—" She stops at a slap on her rump from She-Brags.

"Promised her the newborns!" Tall Time is aghast.

"Naturally I didn't believe her," She-Brags says. "I said, 'That is not possible!' "

"Who am I to promise the lives of newborns to anybody?" He gapes at the smallest of the three tiny calves, her thin rump, her meek flickering presence. "The lives of innocents!" he trumpets. He whirls upon She-Booms. "In exchange for what?"

"Calm down," She-Betters says, as if speaking to a calf. "You are frightening the little ones."

So he is. The smallest now cowers between her mother's hind legs and Tall Time is reminded of his first sight of Mud. Looking past mother and calf, he sees that two ostriches have arrived at the water hole but they do not drink and he is overtaken by a promiscuous alarm, as if the ill omens here are so pervasive as to be undetectable. "Don't linger at this place," he says.

"I believe I know what's best," She-Brags snaps. "As it happens," she says more amicably, "we do *not* intend to linger. We have heard of green browse to the north."

"From whom?"

"Rumours abound," She-Bluffs says slyly.

"The longbody?" Tall Time trumpets. He looks at the matriarch, who looks at She-Broods.

"A shared secret is no secret," She-Broods mutters. "Thus spake the She."

"Whom could he tell?" She-Brags says. Turning to him she says, "Me-Me knows where The Safe Place is."

"I beg your pardon?"

"Somewhere on The Domain there is a place called The Safe Place."

"I know of it."

She-Brags nods. "I thought as much," she says. "When we hadn't heard any news of you, I told myself, he is searching."

"For the white bone!" a bull calf says rapturously.

Tall Time touches the youngster's flank. "Speak of it as the that-way bone. It loses power when spoken of directly." To She-Brags he says, "Does this Me-Me creature know of the that-way bone as well?"

"I am sure she doesn't. She has never spoken of it to She-Booms. We ourselves learned of it from She-Laughs of the She-L's-And-L's. How Me-Me learned of The Safe Place, now . . . well, she knows where almost everything is. Where there is browse, where there is water—"

"But, Matriarch, she lies!" Tall Time trumpets, affronted

that this slanderer should be granted the least credibility.

"It surprises me," She-Brags says, "that you have never heard of Me-Me. No"—she anticipates his interjection—"I am convinced that you haven't. It is only that she is notorious for trailing any number of families since the end of the last Long Rains Massive Gathering."

"How unnatural," he says.

"Oh, she is quite unnatural. Not only does she not respect territorial bounds, she craves the flesh of newborn she-ones. She couldn't bring down a newborn on her own, she has no exceptional physical prowess. She says to the mind talker, Your newborn in exchange for the location of green browse, the location of The Safe Place. She asks for the bulls. She appears to be under the impression that we don't value bull newborns as much as we do cow newborns."

"But you have given her no newborn," Tall Time says.

She-Bluffs smiles at him. "Nor," she says, "have we said that we never will."

"That is abominable!"

She-Bluffs folds a bundle of twigs into her mouth. "It is strategy, my dear."

Tall Time feels the coarse trunk of She-Blusters rasp across his hide. He twists around and she brings her face close to his, her ancient bloodshot eyes fairly howling. "Don't," she growls. "I . . . we . . . all these. . . ."

"SHE'S TRYING TO SAY," She-Booms roars, "THAT THESE ARE TERRIBLE TIMES AND WE DO WHAT WE MUST TO SURVIVE. OF COURSE WE WOULD NEVER GIVE ME-ME ANY OF THE NEWBORNS. BUT WE LED HER TO BELIEVE WE MIGHT IF SHE PROVED HERSELF OUR ALLY."

"It is to her advantage," She-Betters says, "to lead us to soft browse that the newborns can eat so that they remain fit."

"It is to her advantage," She-Broods says morosely, "to tell us where to go so that she knows where to find us."

"OUR HOPE," She-Booms continues, "IS THAT WE COME ACROSS THE . . . THE THAT-WAY BONE, AND THEN WE CAN GO TO THE SAFE PLACE ON OUR OWN AND HAVE NOTHING FURTHER TO DO WITH HER." She opens her ears. "HAVE YOU ANY SUGGESTIONS AS TO WHERE WE SHOULD BE SEARCHING?"

"Torrent said to go to the most barren places and the hills and to look for an extremely large standing feast tree. What were you told?"

"NOTHING LIKE THAT. THE SHE-L'S-AND-L'S SAID IT WILL BE FOUND NEAR A WINDING RIVERBED NORTHWEST OF A RANGE OF HILLS."

Tall Time is taken aback. After a moment he says, "Torrent's information came directly from the Lost Ones."

This creates an uproar and a great many questions and speculations, at the finish of which She-Broods mutters, "We had better widen our range."

"I'll find it," says She-Brags.

"Have you really told us all you know?" She-Bluffs asks Tall Time.

"Dash it all, Mother," he says. Her gleeful refusal ever to take him at his word is the reason (it occurs to him now) that he allows himself to lose touch so completely with the entire family. "Why would I deceive you? If I knew anything more, you would be the first cows to hear of it. And if I find The Safe Place, you will be the first cows I lead there."

The White Bone

"THE SECOND," She-Booms says, apparently without intending to, for she startles and then seems embarrassed to have divulged his thoughts, which were, it is true, that he would go first to Mud. Quickly recovering herself, she asks, "WHICH MUD? FROM WHICH FAMILY?"

The question annoys him. She-Booms is too free with her mind listening, and while he is anxious to learn whether there is any news of the She-S's, he does not want his family—his adoptive mother—to know which Mud is so dear to him. Or even that there *is* a creature outside of his birth family who is so dear to him, although it is probably too late to conceal that. "I will lead you there," he growls. "By my troth."

"It is more likely," She-Brags rumbles, "that *I* will lead *you* there."

Tall Time looks at her, wondering if he can bring himself to ask the unthinkable question.

"What is it?" she says.

He exhales a long breath. "Has any family given the long-body a newborn?"

She-Brags turns her back and says briskly, "Me-Me claims that the She-R's gave her an injured one. In exchange for an island teeming with green grass."

"No!"

"They are a lowly herd. I wouldn't put it past them."

"But there is no such island."

"Don't be so certain. Me-Me's knowledge of The Domain rivals my own."

It is intolerable to him, the admiration in her voice. "How can you trust her?" he trumpets.

"She can't fool me," rumbles She-Bluffs.

"Where and when did you last see her?" he asks.

"Four days ago," She-Brags says, shaking dirt from the roots of the bush she has excavated. "At the huge Rogue's web southeast of here."

He looks at the water hole. The ostriches are gone and a flock of sand grouse hops indecisively at the hole's edge. He is grateful that Mud is at Blood Swamp, where the water never migrates in its entirety and where, for more than twenty years now, the signs have been favourable. He would be there himself were he not searching for the white bone. And from now on he'll be keeping a scent out for that revolting cheetah as well. He tries to picture doddering old She-Sees (he thinks that she is still the matriarch) contending with Me-Me. Considering how well fed the She-S's are, Me-Me is bound to attach herself to them sooner or later. He looks at She-Booms—he is about to ask her which families the cheetah has been harassing—and finds her gaping at him and is overcome by the dissevered feeling of watching himself and therefore knows that he is living a moment already witnessed, days ago or hours ago, by some visionary cow. He knows that the moment is portentous. Later he will even imagine that he knew what She-Booms would say. Which is, "OH, MY DEAR TALL TIME! THE SHE-S'S ARE DEAD!"

◆ ◆ ◆

It is five hours later, and Tall Time is halfway to Blood Swamp. Telling his family only, "I have an obligation," and refusing to linger with them overnight, he set off.

The White Bone

There is a full moon. In its pallid light birds swoop as they do at sunset, and there are shadows holding at lengths suggesting early afternoon. For Tall Time, these "Rogue nights" have always been unsettling. He knows them now to be mad. Profane. Wind-slanted bushes, termite mounds, bones, carcasses lit up and telling him nothing. His faith in the links is suddenly and utterly gone. Thirty years of aligning his every move to what he believed was a world trembling with mystic revelation . . . what was it that sustained such a mountainous delusion? He no longer knows. He is stunned to think that only hours ago he believed. But if it can happen that in a matter of seconds an entire herd of cows is annihilated by a round of gunshot, he supposes it should be no surprise that an entire faith (which, he reminds himself, was wavering anyway) has been annihilated by four words.

All of them? he asked, and She-Booms said yes, according to the She-L's-And-L's all of the She-S's perished in the slaughter, as did all of the She-D's. According to Me-Me, however, some of the She-S's got away, and Tall Time is inclined to believe this version because, plainly, the world has entered an epoch where the liars are to be trusted and the trustworthy are to be doubted.

To abandon your faith in the signs and superstitions is to abandon your faith in the She who made them. Still, Tall Time prays in case the absurdity of faithless prayer is precisely what the times call for. "Let Mud be alive," he says. "Let her be alive."

He interrupts the prayer only to send out infrasonic calls to the She-S's—each of them in turn, since he doesn't know who may have survived—and eventually the sound of his own voice takes on the aspect of an incantation necessary to troll him through the night's clamour. He accepts as simply another unfathomable occurrence that his sense of smell has become fine. Beyond the putrefaction of the carcasses littering the plain he can smell, he would swear, the debacle at Blood Swamp. If Mud is alive and within a day's trek of him, he will pick up her scent.

She has three scents, as all cows do. A regular or she-one scent, a "delirium" scent and a "radiance" scent. Because she has come into oestrus only the one time, he holds just the one memory of her delirium and radiance scents, but he has summoned both to mind so often that he wonders if they haven't been adulterated by too many retrievals. Tonight he fights any thought of them. They compel him to re-enact the mating, and even if he had the heart for that now he hasn't the time.

The scents arrive anyway. Strangely, they don't overtake him. They trail behind the actual odours of the night, and further back than that—behind the memories that those odours generate—so that the memory of the two of them mating fails even to interfere with his prayers, it is too diluted, more like somebody else's recounting of that day when the first pulse of her delirium song released him from the hindquarters of the loathsome She-Wheedles, whom, in the grip of an embarrassing infatuation, he had been attempting to mount.

The song had come from the southwest. From Creaker Pond, he soon ascertained. Between himself and the pond was an expanse of muck that by the middle of the short rains would be Long Water. There was a hard rain falling that day, it pelted the muck into a field of eruptions he felt cheered on by. As he hurried along, his engorged penis bumped splashing on the ground, and believing himself to be experiencing something akin to Mud's lifelong affliction—the dragging along of a dumb, undisciplined limb—he was profoundly moved. He imagined her running in that pathetic kicking-out way of hers from whatever aroused bulls were already there, and this so maddened him that for the rest of the journey he rumbled infrasonic threats, with the result that when he got to the pond he found Mud standing alone at a distance from three bulls who, the instant he arrived, moved even farther away from her.

"Twig-tusks!" he roared, immensely relieved to find himself the largest bull present.

Meanwhile the She-S big cows were crowding around him and trumpeting a wild chorus of "Digger Bull! True Digger!" which cows do when a bull they judge to be of sufficient girth finally appears on the scene. A morsel of reason reminded him of the decorum: he must halt and let each big cow sniff his temporal glands and his penis. This he did, and when the last of them was satisfied they all sang:

"Ready and Ripe? Yes! Yes!
Streaming rank smell? Yes! Yes!
Go then and bore the tunnel wherein
A newborn will dwell! Yes! Yes!"

Mud by now was watching him over her shoulder. He approached her warily. He did not want her to run from him, even flirtatiously.

"I am the biggest bull," he murmured. She did not move. "You glow," he said. "You are as fat as a water-boulder. You are the blue haze that surrounds the sun at dawn."

At last he was close enough that he could reach out his trunk and tap her vulva. He stroked her until she urinated, and even before he brought the liquid of her to his mouth he knew that, just then, just as he had touched her, she had entered her radiance.

If she had bolted he would have let her go and would have waited until she felt herself ready, but she was motionless, and unexpectedly quiet (most cows, once they are in their radiance, babble lascivious encouragement, or "zeal"), and he laid his head upon her back and levered himself onto his hind feet and began to dig.

This part of the memory is vivid enough that his legs tremble and he comes to a stop and thinks, uneasily, that he must be having a shadow memory.*

If you live long enough, your memory leaks right out of you. Before that time, there are ten to fifteen years during which your old memories are almost always shadow memories. Torrent once told him that this is a blessed period because it allows you to look back over your life with a degree of impartiality. "You can't do that," he said, "if every time you fall into a memory you are in the thick of every blessed second of it. You have no hope of standing beside yourself, so to speak."

"What does it matter?" Tall Time said. "Sooner or later you forget everything anyway."

"Not who you are," Torrent said. "Who you are is the one thing you can't forget. It is all you have to take into the hereafter, and if you don't have it, you eventually crumble and

---

* Instead of being virtual re-enactments, shadow memories, similar to most human memories, highlight only the more striking aspects.

become the silt at the bottom of The Eternal Shoreless Water, that's my belief." And in his off-key bass he sang:

"Afloat ten thousand years within
A thought, the only one
That holds the mind and bones
In unison."

It is not unheard of for she-ones to have the occasional shadow memory before the age of fifty, and, in fact, those who do are considered precocious and lucky. But who knows any longer what is lucky? Don't ask Tall Time. To have a shadow memory at his age feels more like a symptom of the chaos in which the hard lines that used to distinguish one thing from another turn out to be shadows themselves. Even *he* conspires in this chaos. Because look at him! Crazed over the fate of a crippled cow who is neither his birth mother nor his matriarch.

Were Mud willing, he would mate with her for life, the way jackals do. He would take her from her family and the two of them plus the newborn would form their own tiny herd. What is to be made of that? Up until today he believed that an inclination so bizarre must have the She's blessing, and he would indulge himself in intoxicating explanations, his most cherished being that Mud's calf tunnel shelters the daughter of the She Herself, "the newborn lovely as light" who, the hymns prophesy, will "silence the screams of night, and cruel hindleggers put to flight," and it is this divine newborn he is meant to safeguard. Oh, he winces to think of this now. Not that he loves

Mud any less for no longer knowing *why* he loves her. The truth is, his love for her is one of the few remorseless certainties left to him.

◆ ◆ ◆

As he approaches Blood Swamp the bleats and whinnies and barks of the creatures there begin to reach him. It is dawn. A huge bull appears on the bank and starts hurrying toward him. Silhouetted against the smoky red hole of the sun the bull looks like a primordial warning, a charred refugee of a carnage older than memory.

It is Torrent.

"I smelled you coming!" he rumbles, out of breath.

So much for Tall Time's own fine sense of smell. For at least an hour his trunk has caught nothing but the stench of the slaughter.

They twine trunks and bang tusks, after which Tall Time respectfully pokes the end of his trunk into Torrent's mouth and tastes rotting molars. The greeting stops at that, with Torrent jerking up his mammoth head and saying, "I warn you, the faces are hacked off."

"Is it the entire family?"

"Which family?"

"The She-S's," Tall Time says, perplexed. And then he understands and says, ashamed to have all but forgotten them, "I scarcely knew the She-D's."

"The She-D's. Yes. Three fell, the last three. They survived the slaughter at the Rogue's web, only to be caught here."

"What slaughter? Which Rogue's web?"

The White Bone

"Ah—" Torrent says heavily. He sweeps his trunk northeast to southwest. "A six-day trek from here, there's a web. Corpses all along it, mostly lunatics, some ribs. Corpses as far as the trunk can scent, every one perished from thirst. But the She-D's, hindleggers got them, the whole family apart from the few who escaped to this cursed place." His breath rattles.

"What about the She-S's?" Tall Time says. "Did any of them survive? Are any of them still here?"

"No, no. They left eight days ago, judging by the dung. I missed them by four days."

"Who? Who are the survivors?"

"She-Snorts." This said with an edge of admiration.

"Who else?"

"Let me think." He touches his trunk to the temporin that runs down his right temple, following the course of a deep furrow, and Tall Time looks beyond him at the arc of the horizon and feels that in that arc a tremendous revelation is suspended.

"These are bad days," Torrent mutters. "All the old matriarchs slaughtered or deranged and the new matriarchs too ignorant to know where the safe drinking is."

"Who else got away?" Tall Time asks again.

"Who got away? That squawker, She-Screams. No sign of her bones here. And the nurse cow, She-Soothes. She's a wide one, I'd know her frame. And her newborn. What's that calf's name?"

"Bent," Tall Time says. With a kind of frigid sadness he thinks, The old patriarch is losing his memory.

"Bent," Torrent says. "That's right. He made it."

"Did Mud get away?"

"Mud?"

"The young cow with the withered hind leg."

Torrent squints into the distance. He looks suddenly exhausted and ancient. "Mud," he says.

"Let's go down to the shore," Tall Time says.

"It's a sorrow," Torrent rumbles. "When you have mounted the She-S cows as many times as I have, and you know the inside of each of them like you know the inside of your own mouth. . . ."

Despite himself, Tall Time scans the terrain for signs that would have warned of the disaster, or that now warn of further danger. There is only the aftermath: the levelled bushes and, gouged into the bank, the parallel tracks of a vehicle. On the bark of a fever tree a bright green slash flares. Tall Time recoils at the unnatural colour of it, and at the thought that vehicle skin scrapes off like that. He races to the edge of the bank and then halts, startled by the sight of so many creatures—hippos, wildebeests, zebras, gazelles, buffalo, baboons, countless flocks of birds and, out in the middle of the swamp, two small families of she-ones whose scent eludes him. He turns to Torrent. "Who are they?"

Torrent is pulling down a fever-tree branch. He gives the branch a twist and it breaks off with a hollow crack like lightning. "They are—" he says. He strips away the dead ant-eaten leaves and uses the naked branch to scratch inside his ear. "The She-N's! And the She-N's-And-N's!"

His roar has all the cows lifting their trunks. A fine scenter (Tall Time guesses it is She-Needles) rumbles, "Steer clear, Tall Time! No one here is in her delirium!"

"I should think not," Tall Time rumbles, faintly insulted that she would presume he wouldn't have smelled oestrus. Besides which, who enters oestrus—or musth for that matter—during a drought? He scans the packed shore for the carcasses. "Why are you still here?" he asks Torrent. Only now has it occurred to him how odd it is that the old bull loiters at this evil swamp when he must know a score of watering places. Places in the hills, for instance, where he should be anyway, searching for the white bone.

"It's the molars," Torrent says. "When I think of leaving the soft browse, I say to myself, one more day." He taps the branch on Tall Time's rump. "Come along, son. I'll guide you through the tragedy."

As they move down the bank, the creatures below start scattering. Torrent has been terrorizing this poor crowd, Tall Time thinks, but he is grateful because with the shore cleared the remains of the slaughtered are conspicuous. At a glance he identifies She-Sees. Her body has been covered with sticks and some of her bones have been pulled loose by the carnivores. These new bones gleam white and release a cruelly sweet smell (Tall Time sniffs her femur) that is indistinguishable from the smell of wilting lilies.

"Now here," Torrent rumbles, "here is . . . uh . . . the one who was always standing over the newborns." Gently, with a forefoot, he nudges the skull. "Wonderful scent she had . . . milky. . . ."

"She-Stammers," Tall Time says. He is weeping.

"She-Stammers, that's it." The old bull's voice cracks. "That's right. Daughter of She-Soothes." From out of the torso he removes a bone as fine as a thorn. "She had a newborn growing in her. I myself dug the tunnel, I believe." He holds the bone close to Tall Time's eye and then carefully puts it back where it was. He scoops up one of the big cow's shoulder blades and rocks it in the crook of his trunk. He replaces this and sniffs her amputated trunk.

It seems that he is prepared to fondle and inspect all of the remains as he must have done at least once and as he no doubt presumes Tall Time will want to do now, but Tall Time is impatient to learn the fate of Mud. He tells Torrent this, and Torrent fixes him with a keen look and rumbles, "Go on, then."

It is short work. When he has inspected all the remains on the shore, lingering to weep over the newborn twins, he walks into the water and feels with his feet the bones and hides on the swamp bottom. He then wades over to Torrent, who is browsing on creepers.

"She got away," Torrent says.

Tall Time doesn't respond. His relief is dazzling but so is his sorrow, and no reaction seems appropriate except that he stay teetering between these two emotions.

"Drink first," Torrent says. "Eat."

"First" meaning before he returns to shore to properly mourn the dead. Tall Time pulls up a slimy rope of tangled roots and as he tucks it into his mouth is gripped by the feeling of having entered somebody's memory of feeding here in the hours before the slaughter—the heat pushing down, the stamped twinkling surface of the water.

"They'll fare all right," Torrent says.

Tall Time is jarred back into the present. "Do you know where they went?"

Torrent shakes his head. "They're nowhere in this vicinity, I can promise you that. But I wouldn't worry. She-Snorts will sniff out the watering places."

"She-Snorts?"

"She'll be the matriarch, with She-Sees and She-Scares gone."

"Upon my soul," Tall Time says, realizing. A cow as flippant and indifferent as She-Snorts taking charge. His fear for Mud flares up.

Torrent is watching him. In a friendly tone he says, "Mud is still a calf, is she not?"

"No, she has had her inaugural delirium. I have mounted her."

"But she wouldn't be in her delirium now."

"Of course not."

"All the same, you intend to search for her."

"I do." He looks hopefully at the old bull. Don't they have this in common? Isn't what he feels for Mud an amplification of what Torrent feels for She-Snorts?

"You may be deranged," Torrent says. "Derangement is a contagion these days."

"But you love She-Snorts—"

"Love!" He glares over his tusks. "What do you take me for? A suckling calf?"

"Forgive me," Tall Time murmurs.

"Why aren't you searching for the white bone?"

"I have been! Throughout this whole drought. I assure you, Torrent, that I have not been idle. And I will not be idle after I leave here. I am entirely capable of searching for the surviving She-S's *and* of keeping a sharp scent out for the that-way bone, as you yourself told me to refer to it. In any event one endeavour does not annul the other. Indeed, I intend, as a matter of record, to be successful in both. And I should also tell you that I have just now come from my birth family, and they heard from the She-L's-And-L's that the that-way bone will be found near a winding riverbed northwest of a range of hills."

"Is that so?"

"I am only reporting what I heard."

The glower is slow to leave Torrent's face but eventually he pulls up a hank of roots and rumbles, "The assumption being that there even is a that-way bone."

"What do you mean?"

"I haven't been idle, either, son." He stuffs the roots into his mouth and gives them only a few soft tamps before swallowing. "You would have thought that some rumour, some trace, would have turned up by now." He glances at the sky. "The darkness is here, you know. It has come."

As tall as he is, Tall Time does not reach Torrent's shoulder, and yet he feels monstrously elongated, adrift in the blue air.

"What do the links tell you?" Torrent asks.

A surprising question from the bull who advised him not to rely on the links. "I have lost all faith in them," Tall Time says. On the soaring columns of his legs he sways. It is a revelation to him that the white bone is itself a link. Obviously it is (it is both a good omen and a powerful sign), but not until Torrent cast doubt on its existence did Tall Time ever think of it as occult. When he abandoned every other link he did not abandon the white bone. It, he took for granted, was as unassailable as a path. You stumble upon it and, willy-nilly, you are led.

The White Bone

"Lost faith?" Torrent says. He sounds puzzled.

"They have failed us all. No link warned of the slaughters! No link warned of the drought! Dash it all, Torrent, what use are the links if they do not warn of such tragedies?"

"No link with which *you* are acquainted warned of such tragedies," Torrent says.

Tall Time tugs free a batch of sedge. Wounded, indignant, up in some airless partition of the ether, he flaps his ears.

Torrent closes his eyes. He seems, briefly, to sleep. Opening his eyes he says, "To forsake all the links because your knowledge of them is wanting is cowardice at best and foolishness at worst. One does not throw away the fruit with the husk."

"But how—" Tall Time says. In his frustration he is on the verge of weeping. "How can we know anything absolutely?"

"We cannot."

"How can we have faith?"

"Faith is not trust in the known."

There is a ruckus in the shallows. A zebra, whom Tall Time earlier recognized from a brief sighting when it was a foal spinning in circles at the edge of a Long Rains Massive Gathering, is again spinning, and viciously kicking out its hind legs.

"Drought crazed," Torrent observes.

"Perhaps that is what I am," Tall Time offers as a show of deference and to redeem himself in Torrent's good opinion. Of course, he isn't—his love for Mud predates the drought by a decade—but the longevity and severity of his craziness, if crazy he is, will never have the old bull's understanding, let alone blessing, that much is now evident.

Torrent gives a noncommittal grunt and points his trunk toward the She-N's. Tall Time points his trunk in the same direction although, unlike Torrent, he cannot scent against the breeze.

Presently, in this atmosphere of companionable despair, Tall Time loses the feeling of being supernaturally tall. He says, "If the that-way bone does not exist, what hope is there for any of us?"

"It may well exist."

"But you said—"

"Don't tell me what I said." His voice is gentle. "I am aware of what I said." He lets his trunk fall. It hits the water with a loud smack, and Tall Time senses, behind them at the shore, a hundred heads snapping around.

Chapter Ten

It is the matriarchs who keep track of the days—how many since the last rainfall, how many until the black plums ripen, how many since a bull was in musth or a cow in oestrus, and so on. Their method is mysterious, even to them. Anyone can come up with the exact number eventually, by counting backwards or forwards day by day. For the matriarch, the calculation is immediate. It is not a skill she learns. She assumes the family's leadership and several hours later if somebody mentions, for instance, the evening a certain calf died, she finds herself thinking, "Four years and forty-seven days ago."

Of all the gifts that aren't Date Bed's, this precise, instantaneous measuring of the passage of time is the one she used to envy the most. As a young calf she tried to train herself to count days at matriarchal speed and when she finally accepted that it couldn't be done she devised a shortcut ("grouping," she calls it) for arriving at a close approximation. Instead of tallying the days, grouping tallies the full moons, which occur every thirty days, give or take a day. Two full moons, or two groups of thirty days, add up to sixty days. Three groups are ninety days. You only have to do the addition once to know forever afterwards how many days or years are in five groups, or thirty-five, or in seventy-three and a half.

Every morning when she chisels another scratch into her left tusk she wonders if her life's remaining days will add up to the three and a half groups that would bring her age to exactly thirteen years. She is not very hopeful. The wound above her right eye has scabbed over, but behind the scab is a buzzing sensation that is only slightly relieved by eating cycad bark. Coming to her feet she reels through a dizzy spell, and several times a day she falls into hallucinations—ravishingly strange, and as sharply visible as if she were looking through Mud's eyes, but disturbing. She is walking in an immense cavern where it is somehow as bright as midday, and on each side of her, in phenomenally straight rows, stacks of strange fruits—sweet-scented and vividly coloured (red, orange, yellow)—glide by; she is on a rise of land and, all around her, tiny white blossoms drift from a frigid sky and sting her skin and settle on the earth like sand.

None of these complaints are necessarily deadly and they do not frighten her. What does is that her memory is leaking. Six mornings ago, a blue lizard scrambled past her face. She could not identify it, although she knew she had studied that breed and added it to her lizard inventory. Since then, half of her memories have been shadow memories: impeccable in parts, in other parts faded or gone altogether.

She prays, despite the fact that she has little faith in prayer and no comprehension of it. How can the circumstances of a preordained life be altered by begging? Her prayers, consequently, are modest. When she prays that the remnants of her family are safe, she is thinking especially of Mud and her mother but does not presume to single anybody out. For herself she asks that she suffer no more than she can bear and that if her fate is to survive she not thwart that fate through foolishness or inattentiveness. She may add that she *hopes* the leaking of her memory will spontaneously stop, as haemorrhaging sometimes does, or that she comes upon a family whose nurse cow knows a remedy. "I would love to see my own family again," she throws in. Instead of pleading to find the white bone, she describes to herself, in prayer-like phrasing, various aspects of The Safe Place: ". . . for in that blessed realm are swamps, where grasses sweet and new. . . ."

It is at dawn, just after she has come to her feet, that she prays. Such is her ambivalence that she can bring herself to petition the She only when she is reeling with dizziness and not quite herself and therefore the She may pardon her impertinence. When the dizziness stops she finds a sharp stone and chisels another scratch in her tusk. One scratch for every day since the slaughter. This is not yet a necessity, it is a precaution. She has no idea how quickly her memory is leaking, but she has met old cows who couldn't tell whether it had been an hour or a year since they'd last spoken with her, and she must prepare herself for becoming that addled. She thinks of the scratches as a kind of net. The apprehension of time going by may fall from her body, but here it will be, caught on her tusk.

✦ ✦ ✦

Barbara Gowdy

On the morning of the twenty-sixth day she fails to find a sharp stone. Every one she picks up feels as smooth as an egg. She is in a croton thicket beside a huge jawbone of rock and is just now appreciating that the face of the rock is abnormally worn, and it strikes her that this must be a sacred vicinity. First it yielded the amazing Thing, and now there is this strange worn rock and these globular stones, which are almost as smooth as the Thing. She was drawn here, she thinks. Yesterday, mid-afternoon, she had stopped on the east side of the rock with the intention of having a brief feed and rest before continuing on to the giant water hole that was her destination. But while she was lying down, a cocky genet lounged in the crook of her trunk and told her that there was water under the ditch on the other side of the rock, and so she shook him off and came to her feet. She had dug eight holes and decided that the genet had deceived her when a mucky trickle seeped up. By this time, night had fallen and she was so parched that she got down on her knees and drank, like a calf, with her mouth.

A hallucination overtook her as she drank. It seemed to her that she was kneeling at the edge of a cliff. Below, luminous in the surrounding darkness, was a looped band upon whose upper surface two lines of bright-eyed creatures skimmed. In one line all the eyes were red and in the other they were white, and the two lines rushed alongside each other but in opposite directions. There was the rank smell of lionesses and this frightened her enough to heave herself up, and the hallucination snuffed out in the vortex of a dizzy spell near the end of which she realized that the lionesses were not in the hallucination but on the rock.

She whirled around, lifted her trunk. By the range and thickness of smell she guessed that there were four of them. The moon was almost full, and she could discern a darker shade of night where they were, and the glimmer of an eye.

"What do you want?" she thought.

They wanted to eat her, that went without saying, but why did they imagine they might? On the second day following the slaughter she had scared off a pack of hyenas by telling them that her blood was venomous, even to the touch. The carcass of a male lion had been nearby and she'd pointed at the bullet wound above her eye and thought, "As soon as he drew blood, he fell." The hyenas exchanged looks and nervous giggles. She asked them how they supposed she had survived on her own, when she was so small. And because there she was, alone and small, the pack loped away and they must have spread the word. Three days later she was approached by a delegation of awe-struck gazelles who'd heard she was an avenger sent by the god of her kind to punish any lions, hyenas or wild dogs who dared assault her. Was it true? She told them it was.

"What if one of us touched you?" the largest gazelle asked.

"I am poisonous only to creatures who would harm me," she answered, marvelling at how effortlessly she lied, and with what zest.

After that she began to feel invulnerable, at least to lions, hyenas and wild dogs. But then, last night, the four lionesses had attacked her. They had never heard the avenger legend, and neither did they fall for it. They laughed indulgently, as you would at the outlandish claims of a calf.

A sluggish feeling overcame her. She thought, "I am going to be killed."

"That's right," the leader said.

"It's painless," another said.

The leader said, "Don't fight us."

But she did fight. The suggestion that she shouldn't was so pernicious that it jolted her awake and she turned and began to run. The lionesses jumped from the rock. They swiped at her hind legs and she spun, trumpeting. Her right foot came down on a stone. She snatched it up. Even in her terror she could feel how unnaturally cold and smooth it was. She swung it, and a pale beam of light flew over the ground. The lionesses stepped back from the beam. She swept the stone again, and the light skimmed their faces.

"Let's go," the leader growled. And while Date Bed continued to trumpet and brandish the stone, her assailants disappeared.

As soon as she could no longer smell them, she examined her weapon. It was no stone. It was too cold and too symmetrical: flat on one side, curved on the other, about the size of an ostrich egg but heavier than that and more elongated; it was like an elongated egg sliced in half. The curved side shone like slime. The flat side shone like water, and like water she could see herself in it . . . if she held it at a certain angle, with the moonlight in her eye, and when she did that her image was so unclouded that she gasped. She pivoted the Thing and waved it where the lionesses had been. The beam appeared. She tried waving the Thing in various directions and at various angles until she realized that the beam was moonlight passing through the Thing and coming back out again. Only then did she detect the faint stench of vehicle. She thought that the vehicle who had carried it must have lost it, because who would deliberately abandon such a treasure? She turned it over and held it up to see her face again.

"The She is good," she said. "The She is great."

She slept lying on it and in her dreams forgot about it, and she forgot about it when she awoke until, during her dizzy spell, she hurt her foot on the edge between its flat and round sides. Appalled to think that the fact of it could have leaked out of her body even for a moment, she picked it up. In the morning light she could see that its curved side was the unnatural blue of a vehicle's skin and she realized that it must have been a feature of the vehicle itself—a kind of gall perhaps or extrusion of bone—and she had a moment of disgust and yet she did not let it go. She swept it back and forth and a stunningly bright flash shot onto the rock. By accident she directed the flash at a warthog, who ran off squealing. She blew dust from the Thing's flat side and held it to her face. Again, she gasped to see her reflection. Look at that—a tick running along a fold under her eye! She couldn't feel the tick or smell it, but there it was. She examined her eyelashes, the veins in her ears, the puckered landscape of her scabbed-over wound. In no body of water, no matter how placid the surface, had she ever seen herself so distinctly. "Are you my spirit twin?" she asked her reflection. With great care she set the Thing on a termite mound and started looking for a sharp stone.

✦ ✦ ✦

She fails to find one, although she makes a wide search. She returns to the Thing and picks it up. Now it is almost too hot to hold. Cradling it in her trunk, she looks at herself. "There is not a single sharp stone in this vicinity," she says. Her eye blinks. The dark circle in the centre contracts to a dot and her sense is that the reason for the contraction is so that the eye may fetch an idea from within itself. And here it comes, the idea, leaping from the image of her eye into her actual eye and from there into her head where she hears, "Use the Thing."

Of course. Use the Thing, its keen edge that hurt her foot. She turns the Thing so that she can draw the edge over her tusk. Back, forth. Just the once and she has her scratch. Day twenty-six.

She holds the Thing to her eye. The dark circle shrinks and plucks from its abyss another idea. "Oh!" she breathes. The idea is so inspired that her heart starts pounding. She nods and repeats what she hears. Without realizing, she speaks in the formal timbre.

As far as she knows, her kind have never doubted that who they see when they see themselves in water *is* themselves. Monkeys don't doubt it either, nor do cats. Of the other creatures who are able to see themselves (plenty aren't; wildebeests, buffalo, warthogs, rhinos, hippos and zebras look into an unruffled pond and see nothing but water) most think that they're catching a glimpse of the spirit of somebody who drowned or was killed at that very spot. With birds, it's hard to know what they think. Some of the bigger birds—hornbills, spoonbills, storks—reportedly laugh or take umbrage if you say, "That's you." They say it's a fish, obviously, or a shadow. The smaller flocking birds can scarcely be talked to at all, they're so high-strung and scatterbrained. Solitary gliders— the eagles, the hawks—have a reputation for being thoughtful and articulate but they're aloof. In the three years that Date Bed has been a mind talker she has spoken with only two hawks and a single martial eagle, or "eminence" as that breed calls itself. This one was sickly and earthbound, and when Date Bed asked if there was anything she could do for him, his startling answer was that she could keep him company.

Perhaps because he was doomed he was unusually forthcoming. He advised her that if her kind were to eat flesh, curb their appetites and flap their ears they might stand a chance of becoming airborne. He then told her about guardians, or spirit twins.

At the hatching of every martial eagle there is the hatching of a spirit twin whose fate determines the eagle's fate. The twin lives underwater and feeds on fish and carcasses, but otherwise the events of his life are identical to the eagle's. When the twin ails, the eagle ails. When the twin mates, the eagle mates, and so on. When the twin dies, the eagle dies. The spirit twin can be heard calling during high winds and storms and can be seen in hundreds of bodies of water, since he moves from lake to river to pond by way of underground aquifers. Frequent sightings of the spirit twin are essential. Without these contacts the twin loses faith in his own existence and begins to wane and act carelessly, and if he should deteriorate, so will the eagle. The clearer the sighting, the more the twin is reassured, the more vigorous he is, and viceversa. So it is that in high winds, when the surfaces of water are turbulent, or during the dry season, when the water isn't there, the eagle's life is imperilled. "I haven't seen my guardian in four days" was how the eagle Date Bed met accounted for his condition.

It never occurred to Date Bed to suggest that his reflection was merely himself. That would have been tactless and pompous and, besides, she was far from certain that his reflection *wasn't* a guardian. Or even that *her* reflection isn't a guardian. After her talk with him she would sometimes peer at her face in Blood Swamp, just in case. To tell the truth, it has crossed her mind that she owes her survival, in some measure anyway, to the fact that a few hours before the slaughter she had studied herself in the flat water within the sedge-grass beds.

And now that she has the Thing to see herself in, she must admit that she feels . . . not recovered, far from that, but pluckier.

She looks at herself again, at her liquid eye, which alerts her to her thirst, and she sets the Thing down and kneels at the pit she dug last night and tusks the bottom until water seeps up. She drinks, comes to her feet, has a dizzy spell, tosses dirt over her back, then feeds on the thicket and the tufts of dead grass between the bushes. She would prefer to continue to feed and then, a little later, to sleep, to always feed and sleep during the day and travel by night, out of the sun. But since the slaughter she has a terror of night, every blurry shape transfiguring into a human, and she never moves from a safe spot after dark. Today, before setting off, she climbs onto the rock and sends her infrasonic rumbles. There is no response, there is never a response. She curls the Thing into her trunk and rumbles, "The She is nigh,"* and starts walking.

The inspired idea depends on her attracting the attention of a martial eagle. She will try to do that while she walks, but

---

* Said when approaching or leaving a sacred place.

her priority is to get to the giant water hole she was on her way to yesterday, before this place enticed her to stop. She heard about the hole from a gerenuk who claimed to have seen fresh she-one boluses in the water hole's vicinity. It was news Date Bed wept to hear. In twenty-five days, twenty-six now, she hasn't once come across the dung of her own kind. Their bones are what she comes across, their carcasses. Even though there is little likelihood that the she-ones are still at the water hole (the gerenuk disparaged the nearby forage and said that the hole itself, while it yielded fresh water, was eerily deserted) she would make the trip ten times over simply for the dung. For evidence that she is not the last of her kind.

The land she walks through is one great burn. Black ground, scorched black thorn trees, black boulders, black ash that she flings over her back and between her legs. Without slowing her pace she sends the Thing's light into the sky where, as she had anticipated, it attracts birds. Not an eagle, unfortunately, but kites, who swoop down and scream, "What is that?" and flare up before she can answer. Hooded vultures drop hissing from the trees and jump in front of her and bob their obscene heads.

She follows a course she remembers from when this was all new grass and She-Sees was leading the family to a soda lake. She and Mud were calves then. They were so devoted to each other that they walked with Date Bed grasping Mud's tail, and they said "we" instead of "I"—"we are tired," "we want," "we can't"—as if they were a single calf. When She-Screams slapped Mud, it was Date Bed who squealed.

The burn ends at the lake, which is now an arid pan. Date

Bed puts down the Thing and kicks loose a chunk of salt, crushes the chunk to granules and grasps these with the tips of her trunk. As she drops them into her mouth she falls into a clear memory of the shine of the water that was here and the thousands of flamingos, her first acquaintance with them. Because she took for granted that no large creature could be that spectral colour, she saw the blur of birds as an exotic reed bed and thought that their twanging call must be some deployment of the air.

Why is it, she asks herself now, coming out of the memory, that she recalls some things perfectly while others are hazy or lost to her entirely? By what criteria is the selection made? To relive a moment from seven years ago, lovely as the moment was, is a luxury when what she needs is to remember the journeys that would tell her where she is in proximity to Blood Swamp. Whenever she tries to link up those journeys, however, her mind races along until it skids to a stop at a place of nothingness.

She envies birds their sharp eyes and panoramas. She wishes she could seduce one into scouting the landscape on her behalf but she has a hard enough time getting one to talk to her. Even the normally friendly nightjars keep their distance. She blames the drought. There is a gloom to the light, and little charity in creatures. She has resigned herself to being an unwelcome presence to all birds who don't think of her as food.

She *had* resigned herself.

She picks the Thing up and holds it to her face. She is black from the ash she threw over herself. In its sooty surroundings her eye has a spooky aspect. She turns the Thing and a white disc bolts over the plain. She continues on her way, throwing light into the sky.

✦ ✦ ✦

She smells fresh water but not fresh dung nor any kind of creature. She hears, far off to the west, the cry of geese, nothing else. The gerenuk warned her, but she didn't really believe him, she thought he might merely have regretted telling her about such a valuable find.

It is the same day, high noon, when even the foulest of water holes are swarming with birds and grazers. Only humans can vacate a place so absolutely, and yet there is no smell of them here. She sets the Thing down and sniffs the dirt, which is weirdly empty of dung, even vulture dung. The dirt vents a smell of date palms. How can that be, when there are no date palms in the vicinity? She picks the Thing up and consults her eye. The thought within it seems to be that she has come all this way, she may as well investigate.

Slowly she moves forward. To her left, a ball of dead shrubbery tumbles by. A good sign. She picks up her pace. The water hole is beyond a tumult of toppled thorn trees, and as she approaches, the thin odour of old dung wafts her way. Ostrich and patas-monkey dung. She-one dung!

She hurries to the source of the craved smell. There! And there! Piles of dark, dried-out, trod-on boluses between the logs. Dropping the Thing, she greedily sniffs. It is She-B-And-B dung. She-Brags, She-Bluffs, She-Booms, She-Bluffs again. A fine family, the She-B's-And-B's, Tall Time's birth family. The boluses have been polluted by flies and raided by beetles but she eats several anyway, she wants the taste of them at the back of her throat.

She-Broods, She-Betters . . . all She-B-And-B dung. Every bolus summons memories of its cow, and despite the menacing queerness of this place she lets herself swoon into the memories, some of them shadowy, some clear. She weaves among the logs. She is at the far side of them when she comes upon the boluses of Tall Time.

She lifts her head, alert again. So he was here. She sees the glint of the water hole and thinks that if the Link Bull foraged at this place, there can be no ill omens, or at least there weren't four or five days ago. His fragrance, his regular bull fragrance, has a quality she associates with perfect safety, and she eats one of the boluses and has a clear, happy memory of meeting him for the first time. She emerges from the memory weeping and with the timbre of his voice caught in her ears and then the thought of the Thing jolts her and she rushes back and retrieves it and returns to the far side of the logs and stands there.

The dark surface of the hole indicates a depth that may account for the hole's existence in a drought: a source far underground constantly replenishing the migrating higher levels. She shifts the Thing under her chin and starts forward, scenting, ears tensed. Here also the ground is empty of dung and even of sticks and crevices and it vents a fruity odour incompatible with the landscape. The water is like a hallucination. She has not drunk since this morning. She has not smelled water so fresh in hundreds of days. At the edge of the hole she confers with herself in the Thing but her eye has a stranded, don't-ask-me look. She sets the Thing down and drinks, little sips at first, then trunkfuls. She showers and coats herself with dust, after which she squints about and inhales the unfitting odours. Should she stay to eat and sleep or should she leave? If she leaves, where will she go?

She picks up the Thing and points it at the white crater of the sun and almost instantly a half-dozen oxpeckers arrive and flutter above her, chattering in the embryonic language of their species: "That! It! What! Look! Where!"

"Scat!" she trumpets and they zoom away. What use are those imbeciles to her? An eagle would be a stroke of luck, but she has failed to attract one so far and now she simply wants to talk to some reasonable creature. Find out whether she is safe here, and why there is no evidence that Tall Time or any of the She-B's-And-B's drank.

Her belly growls. Even if she decides to leave she will have to eat. She goes over to the logs, wedges the Thing in the fork of a branch and tears free a bunch of roots. Thorn-tree roots are, for her, a duty food: their saltiness calms her stomach but she despises the aftertaste. She eats them now only until her belly settles and then she peels a strip of bark and rolls it into her mouth . . . and hears munching. So much about this place is out of kilter that her first thought is that the sound of what she is doing must have jumped ahead of the act of her doing it, that while she munches she will hear swallowing and while she swallows she will hear herself ripping another piece of bark and so on. A moment later, however, the smell of a black rhino reaches her and she squints downwind and a dark mass is there.

Date Bed has a soft spot for rhinos because of their weak

eyes and fabulous ugliness, and because of how rare they are. When she was a calf, there was always at least one black rhino mother and calf at Blood Swamp. In the last five years none has shown up, so many have been slaughtered by humans, and in fact it is very odd that one should be here, close to a water hole but not *at* it and nowhere near a mud wallow. The munching grows implausibly loud. For a reason nobody understands, you can hear rhinos eating a hundred yards away and sometimes, such as now, the sound seems to issue from your own throat. As she starts walking forward, Date Bed thinks about her theory that the sound is transmitted from the rhino's "tusks" by some means having to do with the peculiar placement of the "tusks" on the snout. "Hello, bull peerless," she thinks, forcefully to be heard above the chewing. "What an honour and surprise it is to come upon a peerless in this wasteland."

Snorting, the rhino bustles over to her. It is only a few feet away before Date Bed scents that it is not a male. So here is another oddity: a lone female. Like herself. "I beg your pardon," she thinks. "Cow peerless."

The rhino turns sideways and as if addressing somebody off to the west squeals, "Go away! Scat! Are you crazy? Are you a crazy defective half-wit?"

"Certainly not—"

"Then get away from here!" She jabs the air with her horns. "Why did you come?" She puffs and trots around in a circle and when she is facing Date Bed, squeals, "You must be a stupid crazy simpleton!"

"I apologize for trespassing," Date Bed thinks, flattening her ears and hunching so that she appears less of a threat. "I came for the water, and because I was told that my kind had recently been here."

The rhino goes still. Her hog-like ears twitch.

"I am separated from my kind," Date Bed thinks. "From my family."

The rhino steps right up to Date Bed's forelegs. Date Bed lowers her trunk and smells the expiration of pure misery. She can't say what comes over her—compassion, loneliness, or perhaps she is simply reckless with curiosity—but she touches the rhino's back, the scored skin there, the wrinkle of an old wound, and the rhino stands still and lets herself be dabbed, which is stranger than what Date Bed is doing, and in the midst of this unlikely moment, the rhino grunts, "Poor witless ignoramuses. They have been killed."

Date Bed draws up her trunk. "Who have been killed?"

"Your kind." She steps back and cocks her head. "They were here. Yes, yes, they were. A small meagre herd of ten or fifteen, and they were killed."

"All of them?"

"All? Yes, yes, I think so. Well, perhaps not all. I don't know, I don't know. But that is what happens at this place. Know-nothing demented dunderheads come to drink, and vicious brutal hindleggers come to slaughter them. Why do you imagine there is a huge enormous water hole in the middle of nowhere? Who do you imagine dug it?"

Date Bed sways on the verge of fainting. "There is no blood, no scent of—"

"They cover their tracks." She snorts the ground, all at once distraught again. "Go away!" she squeals. She squats, and urine fans out behind her. "Don't be a stupid raving numskull!"

The sharp smell of the urine brings Date Bed out of her dizziness. "When?" she thinks, meaning when were her kind slaughtered.

"Immediately! Straight away! At once!"

"But you are here."

"I can't leave!"

"Why not?" Date Bed is weeping.

The rhino goes still again. "They killed my calf."

"No."

"Yes, yes, they killed him, slaughtered him, butchered him, and took him away."

"Oh, how dreadful."

"I am waiting for his breath."

Date Bed has heard about this, how rhinos believe that after an interval of anywhere from ten to thirty days the breath returns from wherever the spirit has gone. For an hour or so it lingers above the place where the death occurred, and if a female rhino happens to inhale the breath she will one day give birth to a calf in whom some portion of the spirit of the deceased is preserved.

Date Bed thinks, "Aren't you afraid that the hindleggers will kill *you*?" but far enough back in her mind that the rhino won't hear. It is not for her to question the rituals and compromises by which somebody stumbles through monstrous loss. "Thank you for the information," she thinks at audible range. She gives a brisk nod and heads back to the water hole.

"Not that way!" the rhino calls after her. "Dolt-head lunatic moron!"

At the water hole Date Bed has a drink and a shower and collects the Thing. She looks at herself in it. Red, witless eye.

Lunatic moronic dolt-head eye. Against whom, against what breadth of experience, can she measure herself out here? She throws dust over herself and starts off with "Get away from here," the only directive in her head.

It could be that she has travelled across this landscape before but she doesn't remember. She prays, out loud and immoderately. All these slaughters have been conceived of and are now being remembered by the She, who is not vindictive or mad—unless She is, in which case She might be bargained with, but Date Bed does not believe this. If the One in whose image all she-ones were created is mad, then they themselves are piecemeal madness. And they aren't, not yet. Date Bed will not accept that the living, however many remain (all the thousands of them or all ten of them), are mad. But enough suffering may drive them mad, and if that happens, if all of Her best creations go mad, it will be the reshaping of Her. The maddening of *Her*. Which, of course, She knows. Praying, "In the name of mercy, let Tall Time be alive," Date Bed has only the tiniest hope that she can influence what has already taken place.

She loves Tall Time, she can say that now. She can admit to herself that she wanted him to dig her inaugural calf tunnel and that she has always been a little jealous of his adoration of Mud, although she understood it from the start. It has much to do with *why* she loves him. At the Long Rains Massive Gathering when he said to Mud, "We are alike," she thought, "No, *we* are alike, you and I," and wondered, purely baffled, how somebody as observant as he could fail to recognize whom he resembled. Like her, he is inquisitive and fastidious and lean. They both categorize information, they gather facts that nobody else can be bothered with. They both have a fondness for the old language . . . she its inflections, he its turns of phrase. They both love unnaturally. The thought of him dead is terrifying because she loves him but also because what he knows should have protected him. If the Link Bull can be caught off guard, who is safe?

A high wind flames the dust. She walks straight into it, eyes shut against the grit, smelling and hearing her way, which is no way, no direction. Where there is forage she eats. Roots, twigs, they taste like dirt to her. She trumpets prayers, mutters to herself and feels ancient and crazy. She sings hymns:

"Blind unbelief is sure to err
And scan Her work in vain;
She is Her own interpreter,
And She shall make it plain."

And:

"To us a Calf of hope will come,
To us a Daughter soon.
She shall the hindleggers destroy,
And send them to their doom."

That she is carrying the Thing she forgets until she sets it down to feed and then she thinks fretfully, "I mustn't go off without it," and she never does although every time she puts it on the ground she can never remember having picked it up again. She ambles through hallucinations: the interior of a cave, straight white walls, green stone floor as shiny and flat as a still pond, miniature suns in the roof of the cave spreading a cool white light. Another wall, twice as high as she is and three times her width, it stands alone on a web of silver sticks, and life unfolds against it in jerks and flashes as if it were the shifting scene of someone else's memory. And this: a male human holding bunches of aromatic yellow fruits in his forefeet and offering them to Date Bed while saying something that her mind cannot translate. But the sound of his voice—a throaty cooing such as a dove makes—is soothing.

✦ ✦ ✦

Four days later she finds herself under the shade of a huge acacia close to the bank of what was once a river. No other trees still stand, only this solitary giant with its splintered trunk that holds most of its bark and supports a miraculous crown of foliage, withered however, crackling in the wind, and in any event too high for her to reach. From almost every branch forsaken weaver-bird nests dangle like a moribund harvest, and farther up is the immense dish of a vulture's nest but it, too, looks vacated and the splats of white dung on the ground directly underneath smell old.

She has excavated a seepage in the riverbed and has eaten three strips of bark. Now she lies on her side and gazes at herself in the Thing. "Don't fret, spirit twin," she says several times. "I am here." Presently, from her eye's dark circle, she feels prodded to recall her inspired idea. "I haven't forgotten," she says, but as she considers the idea she begins to tinker with it.

The idea is this: she will attract an eagle, and as soon as he (or she) is hovering close enough to hear her mind she will say that his spirit twin, his guardian, is resting in "this oasis of impenetrable water" and yearns for a glimpse of him. He will be curious enough to drift lower, he may even land on a bush or a termite mound, and when he does she will show him not only the clearest image of himself he has ever seen but in all likelihood the *only* image he has seen in many days. He will be riveted.

She will offer him a bribe.

In exchange for glimpses of his guardian he must patrol the land for the white bone. She will direct him to concentrate his search to the west of hill ranges and to pay particular attention to any boulders and termite mounds that form a circle.

Initially the plan also involved getting him to hunt for others of her kind, and she will still ask for sightings, but if the sighting is farther away than a two-day trek and the cows aren't She-S's, she won't pursue it. In a drought, nobody stays in one place very long unless the place is a body of water, and except for Blood Swamp and the evil water hole, most bodies of water seem to be gone. She has decided not to imperil herself by returning to Blood Swamp even though it is her sacred duty to mourn the bones. Her family, those of them who returned to the swamp, probably won't be there now anyway. They will be on the move, as she is, looking for a white bone, looking for her. If her mother hasn't died, she will be the new matriarch and the one leading the search.

At the thought of She-Snorts trying to locate her, scenting the air with her sensitive trunk, Date Bed's eyes well up. In the Thing she watches the warping of herself, and a part of her mind wonders whether tears seep up from under the lower lid or from minuscule holes in the eyeball itself. It is only now occurring to her that in order to help her mother, the best thing she can do is to stay put in one spot for a while.

This is as good a spot as any. Near a riverbed, plenty of bark on this tree, scrub thorns. She inhales and squints in all directions. Overhead she spies a bird. Probably a vulture, but seconds later she is overcome by acute self-awareness and realizes that she is living a moment already experienced by a visionary, which means that it is a moment of consequence. With the sense that she is being directed by a need more distressed even than her own she angles the Thing at the sun.

Chapter Eleven

A great numbness hits Mud's heart. She peers through the darkness, sniffing. Except for Bent, who now lies beneath his mother, everyone is scraping the ground for roots.

She-Screams stands near Swamp and doesn't seem upset, and that can only mean that while Mud was lost in her vision, nothing happened. She-Snorts must have held her peace. Why? Why would she after She-Screams had declared Date Bed a lost cause? There were all those inhalations of the calming underscents, but Mud can't believe that they alone would have stopped She-Snorts from reacting to what must be the most unforgivable thing She-Screams has ever come out with.

Mud goes over to the matriarch and brushes her rump. As if Mud wasn't there She-Snorts continues to pull on a root cord, and Mud can't bring herself to speak. She moves beside She-Screams and starts to tusk at the earth while weeping silently over the image of She-Screams dead—her crushed skull, her bloated torso. She-Screams, smelling her sorrow (and no doubt considering it, whatever its source, less justified than her own), lets out irritated breaths, and this strikes Mud as almost cruelly pathetic—that She-Screams, in ignorance of her fate, should behave exactly as she always has.

After several hours, without a word to any of them, She-Snorts kicks the ground to make a bed. At the outset of their journey they slept, as they always have, in a clump. Now, sixteen days later, their habit is to sleep in a line—She-Screams at one end, next to Swamp, then Hail Stones, She-Snorts, Bent and She-Soothes. Mud is at the other end, next to She-Soothes, and the space she leaves between the two of them is not, as she suspects everyone thinks, more evidence of her aloofness, or even of her repulsion to the nurse cow's obnoxious-smelling eye wad. That space is where Date Bed would sleep if she was here. Where she will sleep when she returns.

The big cows seldom snore. Tonight they do—they are a ruined choir featuring She-Screams. Starting at an excessively high note, She-Screams' exhalation quavers downward as though toppling from a cliff, and Mud thinks, "Every breath is precious for her now." She can't imagine telling She-Screams about the vision (". . . trunk-necks fed from your skull"). She can't imagine telling anyone. If She-Snorts knew, she might find it easier to take She-Screams in stride, but Mud can't face the possibility that She-Snorts will be relieved. No, that's not the whole truth. She can't face the possibility that if she witnesses relief in the matriarch, she will locate it in herself.

There is nothing to guide her. This is her first vision of a dead family member, and when She-Sees had such visions they weren't spoken of, not in front of the calves. It isn't as though telling anybody what she saw will prevent it from happening. This much Mud is certain of, and she wonders why, in that case, the future allows itself to be glimpsed. Are the affected parties meant simply to brace themselves? If so, she *ought* to tell She-Screams.

But she won't, she knows she won't. And she won't sleep. She lies there wondering things. How soon She-Screams will die. (Judging by the look of her—her tusks, her emaciation—it won't be long.) She wonders why She-Snorts didn't scold She-Screams for saying that Date Bed couldn't be alive, and whether beyond the limits of the vision there were more carcasses. Every once in a while in a ritual as regular and unconscious as scanning the horizon she draws her thoughts together until they are the shape and scent of Date Bed, not any particular memory of her but an impeccable likeness that she then releases from her mind as an inspiration from which Date Bed herself may take heart.

✦ ✦ ✦

She does sleep, straight through until dawn. When she wakes up, the others are already on their feet.

There is an odour of anxiety, thick as smoke. "I don't smell her," She-Snorts says. Faced away from everyone, she shakes dirt from a bunch of roots.

"What nonsense!" She-Screams trills.

"I don't hear her," She-Snorts says.

A forced laugh from She-Soothes. "How can you not hear the cow?"

"Her words are wind." She-Snorts looks over her shoulder, directly at She-Screams. "*She* is the dead one."

Mud thinks, "She heard my mind, she knows that She-Screams is doomed." But even before the thought is formed she realizes that it can't be. If She-Snorts is hearing minds, then Date Bed is dead, and if Date Bed was dead, She-Snorts would be wailing on her knees.

"Blasphemy!" She-Screams cries.

She-Snorts chews, flicks her tail.

"Are you banishing her?" She-Soothes roars.

"Banishing whom?" She-Snorts asks incuriously.

"She-Screams!"

"There is no She-Screams."

The nurse cow gives She-Screams a bewildered glance.

"Yes, there is," Bent says in a worried voice. He touches She-Screams' leg. "She's right here."

She-Snorts snorts. "That," she says, "is a memory."

Swamp grunts, an amused sound, and his mother swats him across the head. "It would suit you fine," she shrieks, "if I were a memory! Then you and your darling here"—a thrash of her trunk toward Hail Stones—"could wander off without me to worry about, be your own merry little bachelor herd." She starts to weep. "Well, I am *not* a memory! I will *not* be banished!" She turns on Mud. "This is your fault!"

"Mine?"

"You were the one who made me say it." She puts on a low, doltish voice—her imitation of Mud: " 'She's what? What? What were you going to say about Date Bed?' "

Swamp sighs. "Don't exaggerate, Mother."

"You are an interloper!" She-Screams trumpets at Mud.

"No, no!" She-Soothes bellows. "Enough now!" She curls her trunk around She-Screams' trunk.

She-Screams wrenches away. "If anybody should be banished, it is her." She gazes over Mud's head. "There is no She-Spurns!" she announces.

"Enough of this crap!" the nurse cow roars. She looks from She-Snorts, who peacefully tusks the ground, to She-Screams, to Mud.

"There is no She-Spurns," She-Screams repeats in an official way, and swinging her hips she goes to the other side of the croton thicket.

"This will blow over!" She-Soothes roars. "We'll all come through this!" She strokes Mud's head. "She-Soothes is hungry! Aren't you?"

Mud looks at the nurse cow—her kind expectant face, her eye socket with its rank stuffing, her sighted eye . . . wide open, guileless—and she shakes her head. Yes, she is hungry, but no, it won't blow over. They won't come through this, not all of them.

"*I* am hungry," Bent says tearfully.

"Up on your feet," She-Soothes says and pulls him off his knees and stretches out her foreleg so that he may suckle.

The light this morning is misty and fraudulent. To the east are lakes of light Mud would swear were water. They are a favourable sign, such lakes. Feeling invulnerable, she walks some distance to a shelf of stone and sends an infrasonic call to Date Bed. She waits a moment, and then decides to test Date Bed's theory about severe droughts leeching the earth of too much moisture for infrasonic rumbles to get through, and she sends a rumble to She-Snorts. The matriarch doesn't react, but Mud suspects that the failure may have something to do with the short transmission distance.

She stands there for a while looking at her family. They seem like acquaintances, no more known to her than Hail Stones is. Whereas to themselves (Hail Stones is excluded from this impression) they appear complete and alike in some way that she can't hope to insinuate herself into.

"I *am* an interloper," she thinks, mildly astonished that it was She-Screams, of all cows, who enlightened her. She-Screams, who is banished to death. As they all are one day, Mud doesn't need reminding, but she has not envisioned any other deaths and she cannot imagine them. Only to She-Screams does she grant the kind of unobscured perspective she supposes must occasionally be the prerogative of even the unwitting and silly among the soon-to-be lifeless.

✦ ✦ ✦

The laws of banishment are not, it turns out, inflexible. In better times they may well be, who knows? (She-Soothes says that this is the family's first experience of banishment.) But when the land itself is so hard, everything and everyone upon it sacrifices a little rigour.

If She-Screams cries "Stop!" because the bulls have fallen too far back, She-Snorts calls a halt. If, however, She-Screams cries "Stop!" because she is having one of her spells, the matriarch, once she has established the reason for the cry, keeps going, and since she *is* the matriarch the rest of them follow. When She-Screams talks, naturally they all hear her, but only Bent, in his innocence, appears to listen, and nobody answers her questions. "We must all respect the matriarch!" She-Soothes will bellow. "What the big cows say, the smaller cows obey!" Something along those lines to let She-Screams know that she would acknowledge her if she could. She-Screams cries, "Nonsense!" She accuses everyone, including the nurse cow, of being only too delighted to have an excuse to ignore her. "Oh, now!" She-Soothes blurts, then she slaps her own face, abashed at her direct response. And yet she continues to examine She-Screams' cracked hide and to rumble, as if to herself, that cracked hides should be rubbed with the flesh of acacia galls, that vulture dung toughens the soles of feet.

Mud, having been banished by She-Screams, is never addressed by her and is not expected to speak up, would get no thanks from the older cow if she did. Which is too bad. Ever since envisioning She-Screams dead, Mud is more apt to make allowances for her querulousness and her ridiculous antics and to want to take her side. For the first time in her life she almost admires She-Screams, pities and admires her, and these feelings have little to do with the fact that the older cow's days are numbered. It is She-Screams' uneasy place in the family that moves her, and She-Screams' refusal to accept that place, although refusal means constantly having to perform an ungainly dance that attracts not even ridicule. She-Screams looks one way and there is Mud, whom she pretends is not there. She looks another and there is the matriarch, pretending the same about her. She grasps her son's trunk and he doesn't even pull away, so disincarnate is she. She orders Hail Stones, who as a young bull and a family guest owes her deference, to answer her question, and he dips his head in an apologetic gesture. She sprays dirt in his face. Swamp blows the dirt away. She weeps and begs Hail Stones' forgiveness. She wiggles her ears at Bent. He laughs, and she screeches, "My darling calf!" which frightens him. She strolls off, head up, trunk up, feigning nonchalance and contempt and then comes racing back when water is found. "I'm next!" she squalls. So she is. If there is just the one hole, first the matriarch drinks and then the second-biggest cow, regardless (it would seem) of whether or not she exists. She lies down, her trunk extended toward her son, murmuring into the darkness, "I am here, Swamp. Mother is right here."

What makes it worse for her is that her banishment of Mud is recognized only by herself. "Don't speak to her!" she orders Swamp and Bent and Hail Stones. "Don't touch her!" But they do. She-Screams is not the one who makes the rules. She becomes hysterical. "Look at Hail Stones," she cries, "talking to nobody!" She steps into Mud's shadow and says, "Isn't this peculiar! The shadow of a cow when there is no cow!" She shrieks with laughter. Overhead, vultures circle. Rabbits sheer off onto the plain.

✦ ✦ ✦

On the thirty-sixth day of the trek, after three days of following the thinnest strand of scent, She-Snorts discovers a dung ball no bigger than a beetle. Date Bed's dung. It is thirty-five days old.

"This calls for a celebration!" roars She-Soothes and she regurgitates a foul stew that begins to cook on the hard hot ground and that she starts sucking back into her trunk, inviting everyone to join "the banquet," and so scanty have their feeds been these past days that Swamp rumbles, "It can't be as nauseating as drought fruit," and helps himself to a mouthful.

The dung doesn't call for a celebration. True, it is the first visible evidence in thirty days of Date Bed's existence, but it is also, apparently, the end of this particular scent trail. After sniffing the air and earth around a perimeter at least a quarter of a mile wide, She-Snorts says, "I've lost her," and picks up the piece of dung and puts it in her mouth. Temporin oozes down her face and lures flies. Her scent is pure dejection.

"Are you weeping, Matriarch?" Bent asks.

"Don't be brash!" She-Soothes roars.

Bent starts to wail. She-Soothes positions herself over him and he tugs at her left breast, her right, her left again, and then falls to his knees and squeals, "Where's my milk?"

Mud weeps, too, not to herself but producing tears, although it is foolish to waste fluids. Her newborn seethes. It is like digestion, and she feels a reluctant gratitude that at least *something* stirs in her belly. She-Snorts no longer speaks of her condition, and Mud wonders whether this is because she fears the worst. The matriarch has already suffered two stillbirths, one eight years ago and another three years later. "Let mine perish for hers," Mud thinks, shocking herself a little. "Should a choice be necessary," she appends, and as if in retribution for that unholy prayer her left ear is stabbed by She-Screams screaming, "What do we do now?"

Silence, except for the bleating of Bent.

"Well?" She-Screams cries, looking from She-Snorts to She-Soothes so that you would think a response was her incontestable due. "Find water, I suppose," she finally mutters.

"But where? Look at all these useless pits," and she indicates the long line of holes that were presumably dug by Date Bed.

The family is on the floor of a departed river—Jaw-Log River, so called for the crocodiles that once milled in dense packs just under the surface. All that's left of them are coils of rib and racks of teeth tossed into heaps. Up on the banks among the fallen trees, bleached bones bristle out of the earth like some miserable species of thicket.

The trees are giant ebony and Phoenix palms. Most have been knocked down and stripped of bark. The bit of bark that remains is the only decent forage in the vicinity. To the west is a land of black boulders known as The Spill, on the far side of which is Feed Swamp. Getting to the swamp takes five days according to Torrent, who is the only living she-one known to have made the journey. With the water gone from Jaw-Log River, nobody would have cause to come here.

And yet Date Bed came.

"Why?" She-Screams asks. While everyone digs for water, She-Screams carries on a bitter conversation with herself: "I'll tell you why. Some lunatic told her to!" (Date Bed's reliance on other creatures to guide her to food and water is taken for granted.) "Some lunatic said, 'There is still plenty of water at Jaw-Log River!' and Date Bed believed it! Either that, or she was . . . well. . . ." She waves her trunk. "Never mind," she mutters.

Either that or Date Bed was suffering from "heat sleep." Who among them hasn't entertained the awful prospect of Date Bed wandering in a stupor?

"Smell this," She-Snorts rumbles from downstream, or what was downstream before the river departed.

"Water!" She-Screams cries, shoving into the lead.

Yes, water, bubbling out of the sand. What the matriarch is pointing out, however, is a plug of compacted brush and dirt and dung. "This was in here," she says, holding out the plug.

"Date Bed!" Mud exclaims. The dung is Date Bed's.

"What's it doing in the hole?" Bent asks.

"Date Bed stuck it there!" his mother bellows. "What has She-Soothes been saying all along! Date Bed's mind is as sharp as a thorn. You dig a water hole, you plug it up so that the water is still there when you return!"

"But why would she return?" Mud asks.

"Why? Why? Because. . . ." Confusion plays over the nurse cow's face.

"Because she dug the hole?" From Bent.

"Because she dug the damn hole!" She-Soothes roars.

The matriarch is looking thoughtfully at She-Screams, who is taking advantage of the preoccupation over the plug to drink before her turn. (Or taking advantage of her banishment—if she does not exist, how can she be reprimanded?) "Perhaps Date Bed knew we would come here," She-Snorts rumbles at last.

"How could she know that?" Mud says.

"I have no idea. But she could have made a plug with only saliva and dirt. And yet she rolled a bit of her dung into it."

"To preserve it from scavengers!" She-Soothes bellows.

"To let us know she was here," Mud says. Her throat seizes.

"The urge to leave a trail is at the root of all inventiveness," Swamp declares languidly.

"Matriarch, may I speak?" It is Hail Stones, using, as he does when addressing She-Snorts, the formal timbre.

"Of course."

"I would only like to suggest that she may be on the trail of the white prize."

"The white bone?" cries She-Screams, water spraying from her trunk.

"She said white bone!" Bent squeals. "You're not supposed to say it!"

"Since there is no other reason for her to have come here," Hail Stones says, "it could be that she learned from some creature that the white prize might be found on The Spill."

She-Snorts looks toward the black boulders, and everyone except She-Screams does the same. In the mid-afternoon light each boulder is the precise size of its shadow. Here and there, on the highest, vultures perch, backs humped to the wind. "How I would love to think that she has gone to The Safe Place," She-Snorts says.

She-Screams sprays herself with water. "If she has, I would expect her to turn right around and start searching for us for a change. When I think of everything we've suffered for *her* sake."

"I'm thirsty," Bent whispers. She-Soothes nudges him, and he drops to his knees and sips with his mouth.

"Matriarch," Hail Stones says, "may I presume that it is your intention to cross The Spill?" He knows, as they all do from Torrent, that to the north lies a barren plain and then a desert, and to the south is a mighty wire fence beyond which is a large aggregation of humans.

She-Snorts looks at him.

"At the very least," he says, "you may find that not all the water has migrated from Feed Swamp."

"Take your drink now," she says.

"Ahead of the matriarch?" She-Screams trumpets.

"I am content to wait," Hail Stones says.

"Go on," She-Snorts says. "Take your drink."

So he does.

She-Screams expels her breath in exasperated blasts.

For her part, Mud moves away. She rumbles her litany of infrasonic calls and while waiting for the responses that never come pulls a tangled ball of dead shrubbery and tucks it into her mouth. How will they survive a five-day trek across those boulders? she wonders. How will her leg hold up? And what will they eat out there? She-Soothes is not producing enough milk, and Hail Stones . . . his wound has scabbed over but he limps badly and is so emaciated that it hurts him to lie down. When he sleeps he remains standing and leans against Swamp, who, for his friend's sake, sleeps standing as well.

◆ ◆ ◆

Night finds the She-S's still on the riverbed. They have cleared a lying-down place, the bones that were in the way now deposited in a stack against the bank. Every once in a while the stack creaks or snaps . . . the bones settling, Mud assumes, but a little later she decides that a snake or a lizard has entered the stack and is wondering what monstrosity once claimed such a skeleton—the mess of ribcages, the multiple jaws.

Sleep, for Mud, has become the brink of a trap. As soon as she starts drifting off, she jolts awake from a feeling that something terrible is about to happen, and so she takes this as a sign and tries to keep her eyes open. Her writhing newborn feels as if it had scales. What if she is carrying a crocodile? A fish? These are ruthless times, and perverse. Everything seems to have fled for good: water, food, reason. Why should the laws of procreation be excluded from the exodus?

"Please," she thinks. In the face of so much to pray for, her prayers have dwindled to the one word. The darkness deepens but not by much. It is a bright, cold night. A three-quarter moon in the northern sky, in the south a gauze of stars. "None of those dull shines belongs to anyone from the slaughter" is Mud's bleak thought. She-Sees, She-Scares, She-Demands and all the rest, instead of living in bliss among the sky cows, float oblivious and tuskless upon The Eternal Shoreless Water.

> Now on this holy water
> Our blessed dead ones keep.
> No scent remains of slaughter,
> No sound afflicts their sleep.

And no fear, either, Mud thinks after the last line of the verse has run through her mind, no fear afflicts their sleep. It is such a peaceful prospect that she closes her eyes. When she opens them, it is near dawn. She lifts her head, alarmed to have let down her guard. She hears a soft clatter and twists around.

Swamp and Hail Stones. They are walking away.

She pulls herself to her knees. They have reached the bank. Hail Stones goes first as Swamp nudges him up the incline. At the top, Swamp takes the lead, and Hail Stones starts to follow but then he stops and looks around.

Mud lifts her trunk. Hail Stones does the same, and in that small moment before he turns again she knows he is imagining what she is: their mating. So vivid is the image that she almost has the sensation of falling into a memory, and she is struck by the thought that what could have happened one day—but won't now (strangely, she is certain of this)—was somehow substantial enough for the very possibility of it to generate a memory.

She lowers her trunk, suddenly shy. Swamp emits a low rumble and Hail Stones turns. Off they go eastward, back over the plain.

At the point when Mud can no longer smell them, She-Snorts comes to her feet. Mud stands as well, and the matriarch hears her and swivels her trunk behind herself and then goes to the bank, moving over the bones as quietly as the bulls did.

Mud joins her. "Did they tell you they were leaving, Matriarch?" she murmurs.

She-Snorts doesn't answer. She is scenting, she can still smell them. Presently she drops her trunk and rumbles, "No, but I knew. Hail Stones wouldn't have been able to manage even half a day on The Spill."

"Where do you think they are headed?"

"One of the hill ranges, perhaps." She lowers her head.

She is weeping, Mud guesses. Weeping not for Swamp, who is her blood relation, but for Hail Stones. Mud begins to weep as well, tearlessly and in silence.

"Hail Stones has trunk," the matriarch says.

Yes, Mud thinks. He does. What other bull calf ever mourned the death of his matriarch so deeply and reverently? Or walked over a thousand miles, without complaint—without flinching!—on a septic foot? Hail Stones has trunk. He is soulful and valorous. Whereas Swamp is anything but. Still, Swamp recognizes trunk and is drawn to it, unlike many who are threatened by trunk in other bulls of their approximate age and size.

"Have you envisioned the death of either of them?" She-Snorts asks.

"No," Mud says, startled. Her thoughts go to She-Screams, who sleeps in innocence of her own doom and her son's departure. She says, "She-Screams will be frantic when she wakes up and finds—" She stops, realizing that she has spoken the banished cow's name.

She-Snorts doesn't seem to be listening. She is scenting toward The Spill. Mud lifts her trunk. Vulture dung, carrion . . . Mud picks up nothing worth lingering over.

"A longbody is out there," She-Snorts says.

Mud still can't detect it.

"It has been following us for two days, staying just out of scent." She gives a self-congratulatory snort. "Or so it thinks."

"How very odd," Mud says. Cheetahs have limited ranges, none as large as a two-day trek.

"I suspect it is Me-Me," She-Snorts says.

Instantly Mud's mind is back at Blood Swamp on the day of the slaughter . . . She-Demands saying that Me-Me may know where The Safe Place is. "Why do you think so?" she asks.

"Because longbodies don't track she-ones."

"What does she want?" Mud asks.

The matriarch shakes her head.

"She knows where The Safe Place is," Mud says.

"She *may* know."

"Or may not," Mud concedes. How weary she is of ambiguities. She says, "I wonder if she was here when Date Bed was. Date Bed could have mind talked with her."

"I've thought of that."

"Do you suppose Hail Stones was right? That Date Bed came here looking for the white prize?"

"It is possible. It is possible she came here aimlessly. Hail Stones is a good bull. He says the comforting thing."

"I shall miss him," Mud says, and the image—the memory?—of the two of them mating returns to her and she waves her ears, abashed.

She-Snorts is quiet. Presently she says, "I have been mounted by all of the living She-D bulls and four who are now dead, and except for Torrent there isn't a bull in any other family to compare with them. *I* know what Hail Stones might have been had he not been lamed."

"He won't lose the limp?" This hadn't occurred to Mud.

"She-Soothes says there is no hope of that."

"He'll be like me," Mud says pityingly, but in some abysmal part of herself she is comforted.

"Fortunately he has Swamp to take care of him."

"Swamp," Mud says doubtfully.

"Swamp is fit, and more resourceful than he lets on."

Mud tries to picture somnolent Swamp felling trees, scenting danger. She guesses that as far as water goes, the two of them will avail themselves of the holes She-Snorts excavated.

She-Snorts lets out a rueful chuckle. "Swamp the heartbreaker," she says in her old deadpan, "impervious to my charms."

Not since before the slaughter has She-Snorts talked this

easily and at such length with any of them. Mud looks at her. In the transparent pre-dawn her skin is glossy and her tusks beam white, as Mud's don't. Mud's and everyone else's tusks have gone dull and stained, but the matriarch's hoard their white, and the nodular peak of her head and the thick base of her trunk are the same as they ever were. She is thin, they all are, and yet she does not appear diminished by her thinness, and to Mud this seems like a display of mettle, as if for her to have kept her beauty were a feat. In a kind of infatuation she finds herself leaning against the bigger cow. She-Snorts permits the intimacy, and as soon as Mud realizes this, she is self-conscious, and the feeling of being a stranger in the family, of being honoured by rather than entitled to the intimacy, returns. She doesn't pull away. It would be an impertinence to do so. The thought occurs to her that in She-Snorts' mind, and in this fragile moment, she could be Date Bed, and so she breathes more quickly, the way Date Bed does, and she lowers her eyes, whose green light is not Date Bed's. They stand like that, the two of them, while the last of the darkness lifts. A bird starts up a piercing song and they move apart to brace for the scream that comes a moment later.

Mud turns. She-Snorts does not.

She-Screams is charging up and down the riverbed, pulverizing bones.

She-Soothes and Bent scramble to their feet. "Where did they go?" She-Soothes bellows in Mud's direction.

"Back over the plain."

"Swamp!" She-Screams gallops up to the bank. "They went this way!"

Nobody moves.

She-Screams whirls around. "They're only calves!"

Silence.

"Are you going to abandon them?"

She-Snorts sniffs the ground. Bent cowers under She-Soothes, who gapes from the matriarch to She-Screams and sways one forefoot irresolutely. Up on the bank She-Screams tosses her head. Mud longs to tell her what She-Snorts said about Swamp being more resourceful than he lets on, but She-Screams would pretend not to hear. And wouldn't believe it anyway.

"Cowards!" She-Screams cries. Behind her the sky blazes gold and orange. She looms above them. She looks threatening, magnificent even. "Traitors!" she cries.

And she turns and is gone.

"Shall She-Soothes fetch her back?" the nurse cow roars.

She-Snorts ambles to the water hole and removes the plug. She holds it daintily in the tip of her trunk and appears to study it.

"She'll track them!" She-Soothes roars finally. "If she stops to send out a grounder, they'll know she's coming." She nods, convincing herself. "She'll catch up with them soon enough."

She won't, Mud thinks. It strikes her that the reason She-Screams was alone in the vision was that she will be alone when she dies. She steps over to the bank and climbs it and lifts her trunk.

There is no wind. There are footprints . . . three sets, and above them a virtually motionless ridge of dust stretching to the horizon. Beyond the dust She-Screams is not visible but her scent is still strong. And so too, now, is another scent, evil and cloying, drifting from The Spill.

Chapter Twelve

Tall Time plods northwest. Just before dawn he spotted an ostrich running in that direction and now, the farther he goes, the more tracks and dung he comes across. Jackal, hyena, oryx, giraffe, lioness.

It would appear that he is headed for water.

Although not necessarily. The loud scraping of a grasshopper, which pesters his right ear, advertises water not to the northwest but to the northeast. If you pay attention to such things. Tall Time can't pretend he doesn't. He is no longer driven to act, that's the difference. For him the links have become like an ancient matriarch in her final, addled days—your first instinct is to obey her, and sometimes she's worth listening to. Almost always she isn't.

The last time he drank was yesterday morning, taking a mad risk at a water hole near a circle of human dwellings. Before that he was dry for two days. Since entering the desert he has eaten only the spines of date-palm fronds. How (he keeps asking himself) did Torrent survive this terrain? Tall

Time can't imagine the old bull surviving it now, in his deteriorated state. Given which, Tall Time wonders if he isn't a fool to be trusting Torrent's directions.

He has not planned for failure. He reminds himself that when Torrent first spoke of how to find the Lost Ones, his memory was not yet demolished, and back then he mentioned—as he did again at Blood Swamp—a northern desert that took four days to cross. Well, this is a desert, the *only* northern desert as far as Tall Time knows. And he has been crossing it for three and a half days now.

Already, so early in the morning, the soles of his feet burn. No relief comes from spraying himself with sand as hot as this. Flies buzz at his anus, in his ears, in front of his eyes, colossal ticks rummage through the cuts on his skin. To fend off thirst he sucks on a stone. He hums nonsense songs, hymns, they are the same to him. He keeps his eyes on the ostrich track, which seems to tow him along. When it suddenly ends he flinches as if the ground itself gave way.

A scuffle has taken place here between the ostrich and a lioness. The lioness's tracks approach from the north. The blood has the odour of both creatures and is only now beginning to coagulate. Whatever the lioness's wounds may be, they cannot be very serious because she has dragged the ostrich away, and in so doing has made a wide path that blots out her prints. Down the centre of the path the smeared trail of blood is a pink ribbon.

The path leads northwest, and Tall Time follows it. The landscape undulates. At the top of every crest Tall Time expects to see, in the gully below, the lioness, and perhaps several members of her family, eating the big bird. But on the path goes, incredibly. For any lioness, let alone an injured one, a grown ostrich would be no small burden to lug up and down these hills.

What he does finally see is so unexpected that he growls.

The ostrich turns to look at him. It is alive, and upright. The lioness is the one who is dead, sprawled before the ostrich who is . . . mourning the corpse? That crazy explanation seems to be the only one available to Tall Time until he is a few yards from the pair and sees that the ostrich's left foot is embedded in the lioness's chest, and then he realizes that the ostrich must have kicked its attacker with a blow that cut straight through the ribcage and probably caused instant death. But the foot remained snared.

"You dragged her all this way," Tall Time says, flabbergasted at such a display of strength.

The ostrich, who of course doesn't understand, gazes up with its heavy-lidded eyes, apparently too exhausted to be frightened.

"I may be able to help," Tall Time says.

The ostrich opens its beak and lets out a dreary whistle.

"I shall try not to hurt you," Tall Time says. He side-steps splats of blood. When he is close enough, he twines his trunk around the rosy strip below the ostrich's knee. The skin there is loose and ringed, the leg itself a twig. The miracle now is that the ostrich is allowing this to happen. "Here we go," Tall Time murmurs and gives a tug.

Simultaneous with the snap is a lion-like boom. Tall Time releases the leg and gapes at the carcass, but it is the ostrich who boomed. And does so again, while desperately pecking at Tall Time's shin.

"Forgive me!" Tall Time says, aghast. The foot is still stuck but now the leg is broken.

The ostrich booms and flaps its useless wings.

Tall Time turns and runs . . . northeast, where the grasshopper advised he should go, although he is scarcely aware of direction other than that he must have been going the wrong way if it led to such a calamity. "I've killed it" is his one thought, and it's true, he has. Even if the ostrich frees its foot, as a cripple it won't live another day. Weeping, Tall Time lumbers up the sandy hills, slides down on his haunches and feels the gist of existence in this enterprise: the slog, the respite, the slog. The relentlessness. The end . . . at midday, the sun drilling straight down, and his leg throbbing where it was pecked, his body like a boulder that will roll no farther, his throat a charred crater, and his mind falling into memories, slipping from one to another down through his life by way of holes that at the time were pauses and mysteries and misapprehensions.

He believes that he is experiencing the descent into "heat sleep," and he is resigned, but when he comes to the memory of his first meeting with Mud he fights himself into the present and to his feet.

When he left Blood Swamp twenty-eight days ago, his hunch was that the She-S's had gone to one of several remote watering places known to their extended family. The dung trail was so dry and reduced he was unable to detect any individual scents. There was only the bittersweet She-S scent, which ended after some fifty miles, but he thought he knew where it led. He was wrong. And then wrong again, and again. Wherever he went, not only were the She-S's not there, nobody was, and what signs of she-one life he came across—denuded and fallen trees, trampled thickets—were never recent. At least once an hour he sent out infrasonic calls. None was answered.

Where is everybody? Dead, yes, hundreds are dead, in Tall Time's estimation as many from the drought as from slaughter. You can tell the drought deaths by the absence of bullet holes in the hide, or by the presence of feet and tusks, or (since humans are scavengers) by the absence of bullets among the bones. Still, the number of corpses doesn't add up to annihilation. Either all the remaining families have found their way to The Safe Place—and there is no evidence of such a mass exodus in any single direction—or they have scattered in every direction to wait out the era of darkness at the fringes of the world.

It would seem that among his kind he is alone in having chosen this particular route. Which is as he would expect. Only the mad try to cross deserts during a drought. If he makes it to the other side and locates a family of Lost Ones he is not even certain what he wants of them. Naturally he'll ask about the white bone, but will they be able to tell him more than Torrent already has? At the least, they'll know where *not* to look. And perhaps they'll advise him about how to find the She-S's. An entire race of master trackers should have a few tricks he's never heard of. It is possible, in fact likely, that they will elude him. It is possible that they have found the white bone and gone to The Safe Place and are being stared at by the entranced humans. In either event he will have their forest to feed on while he plans what to do next.

The thought of the browse starts him walking. Not northeast, which is too great a diversion from his original destination, and not northwest, he won't go that way again. He heads due north. By attending to where the sun hits his skin, he holds a steady course. Eventually he is aware of his shadow leaking out from his feet to his right. Of the world growing. He dreams and hallucinates, and the fierce patch of heat creeps across his back. When the air cools and a breeze comes up he thinks he imagines these comforts. When the landscape begins to change he ignores it for miles. He see the rocks, the clumps of bush, he hears within the bush the rustling of tiny creatures. What memory is this? He has to stroke the rough brown trunk of an acacia before he accepts that he is in the present. Awed and suspicious, he peels free a piece of the bark and puts it into his mouth and then spits it out because his mouth is too dry to swallow.

He is in a grove of acacias. Ghostly, most of them, their bark torn away. None is particularly large . . . the white bone won't be found here. But water will be. He smells it. That silver glare through the trees is a pond bed then, and that darkness beyond the bed is not the horizon. It is a forested hill so high he cannot see the summit.

He hurries to the bed and in the depressed centre he digs. Not too far down there is water, and as the seepage gurgles up he sobs and gives thanks to the doomed ostrich, because if not for the ostrich kicking the lioness and if not for his breaking the ostrich's leg, he would have kept going northwest.

Within the acacia grove is a line of termite mounds. They are no longer visible from where he is but he saw them as he came here: four mounds ascending in size from the southernmost to the northernmost. "Hasten to the hill" is their arcane message, and although he wants to feed on the acacia bark and although the message irritates him with its self-important urgency, he hastens—after he has drunk himself into a mildly nauseated state and then drenched and dusted his hide—to the hill.

Why? He can't say. Obscurely he feels that to heed a message he no longer respects is to submit to the same capricious luck that doomed the ostrich and is therefore penance for his clumsy intervention. As he walks, the water sloshes in his belly. He swipes his trunk along the trees but resists stopping to feed.

The woods thicken, the wind becomes erratic. There is dead calm and then a brief blast, and on one of these blasts the odour of she-one calves reaches him. He halts and swivels his trunk, opens his ears. The smell is gone. Heart galloping, he keeps going. Another gust carries the heavier odour of an adult cow, and this time the smell stays long enough for him to locate it, and he starts to run, skirting huge multi-spurred termite mounds and red boulders, dried vegetation crackling under his feet.

They are about a third of the way up the hill. A small bull calf, a smaller cow calf and a newborn. And a cow, lying head-first on her side, and behind her the path she made as she fell—toppled trees and long swaths of pinkish dirt smoothed to a sheen, like exposed muscle. The youngsters look at him with the glittering green eyes of visionaries.

"Hello," Tall Time rumbles. Despite the obvious tragedy, he is exhilarated to be addressing Lost Ones. "I am Tall Time the Link Bull of the She-B's-And-B's."

The three are silent.

"I am a friend of Torrent's, Torrent the Trunk Bull. You may have heard of him."

"We know who you are," the bull calf says, the gruff timbre of his voice adding a good three years to the eight that Tall Time had guessed as his age.

"You envisioned me, I dare say."

Silence.

"Are you We-F's?"

"Lower your voice," the bull calf says.

The impudence startles Tall Time. And then, alarmed, he opens his ears and rumbles in an undertone, "Are hindleggers nearby?"

"No longer."

"Is the cow your mother?"

"Yes." The bull calf looks at her. "I cannot get her to stand."

By the improbable twist of the cow's neck Tall Time suspects that she is dead, and yet, curiously, there is no death fetor. "I'll come help you," he says. He scans the hill. It is treacherously steep.

The bull calf points to Tall Time's left. "Go over there."

Tall Time moves along the gully at the foot of the hill to the cleft of a departed waterfall whose bed provides a series of steps he is able to climb without too much trouble. When he is level with the calves he walks gingerly toward them along a narrow lip. The lip broadens until it is the ledge where the falling cow came to a stop.

Her green eyes are riveted and unlit. Here, Tall Time can smell the fetor, but it is remarkably faint. He looks at the bull calf, and the calf stares at him a moment and then drops his head and says with quiet ferocity, "I thought she might only be stunned."

The newborn whimpers. She has been trying to suckle from the corpse and now she whips her trunk in frustration. She whips the legs of the cow calf, who appears to be in the thrall of a petrifying memory—her eyelids flutter, temporin exudes from her temples—and yet there is no point arousing her to the horror of the present, so Tall Time studies the mother. A moment later the cow calf says, "I hear his mind!" and ogles him, open-eared, as if his thoughts were revolting, whereas all he was asking himself was how the accident could have happened.

"You have become the mind talker," the bull calf growls.

The cow calf turns her stricken face to him.

Tall Time understands now. The cow calf has assumed the cow's gift of mind talking and it is this—the irrevocable proof that her mother is dead—that has distressed her. How small the mother is! But judging by the fabulous length of the tusks, and taking into account that Lost One tusks are said to be deceptively long, he puts her age at thirty years. "How did she fall?" he asks the bull calf.

No answer. He's weeping, Tall Time thinks, and he weeps as well. He touches one of the cow's tusks.

"She tripped," the cow calf says.

"Tripped?" Lost Ones are supposed to be as sure-footed as mountain antelopes.

"She stepped in a grunt hole. We were running. We smelled the hindleggers' little smoke."

Tall Time scents the air.

"Not here," the bull calf says scornfully.

"Up on the ridge," the female says.

Her ears are spread, her radiant heartbroken eyes skewer through Tall Time's skull. It will take her some time yet to learn the art of mind listening while seeming not to. "What are your names?" he asks her.

"Our mother is I-Fret"—(so they *are* We-F's!)—"and I am Rain, and he is Sink Hole."

"And the newborn?"

"Grief."

"Grief," he says. The little calf looks up expectantly. He touches her ear . . . smooth and cool as a new leaf. To Rain he says, "Where is the rest of your family?"

"Back at the cave."

"Why did your mother bring you here?"

"She was afraid of the dark."

"She was not afraid," Sink Hole says angrily. He swats the flies that nuzzle the corners of his mother's eyes. "She couldn't breathe in that cave. If she had stayed there another day she would have become deranged."

"Is your family hiding?"

"From the hindleggers," Rain says in a haunted voice. She starts weeping again and drops to her knees, and Grief drops down with her, precariously close to the brink of the ledge, Tall Time scarcely has time to register the danger when Sink Hole curves his trunk around the newborn's belly, plucks her off her feet, turns her in the air and places her between himself and the corpse.

It is a fluid manoeuvre, quicker than thought and requiring enormous strength. "Upon my soul!" Tall Time says. He blows out several astonished snorts. "Upon my soul!"

Sink Hole looks at him. "Leave us now."

Tall Time is taken aback. "No, no, I won't leave you on your own. I shall accompany you, make certain you arrive safely. I assume you plan on returning to the cave."

"We haven't mourned yet," Sink Hole says.

The White Bone

"Oh, you want me to leave you while you *mourn*. Very well." He tries turning. The ledge is too narrow. He starts backing away.

"We'll meet you on top," Sink Hole says.

Tall Time looks up.

"He thinks he might fall," Rain tells her brother.

"Go back to the cleft," Sink Hole says. "When it starts to steepen you'll come to another ledge. Go west along that. The hill levels out." He sounds not surly now but profoundly tired.

The hill does level out, moderately. The climb is still perilous (how will Grief manage it?), and only by grasping tree trunks and root cords is Tall Time able to gain the summit, a flat expanse of sparse grasses and scattered terminalia trees. Tall Time's stomach heaves from hunger, but rather than starting to eat he peers back down the hill. He feels uncomfortable that he hasn't properly paid his respects to the corpse. He clears his throat and in a soft rumble sings:

"Ascend! Ascend! unto the home
Wherein the happy cows
Whose Island days are over roam
In sweet and luscious browse."

He pauses. There are two hundred and seventy-three verses to the hymn and he is thinking that he should skip the majority when he hears a loud keening. It sounds like a high wind, coming from . . . where? Everywhere, and yet the air is still. He looks at the calves. Their trunks are aloft, their mouths open. It can't be them. It is! It *is* them, he hears a melody now, desolate and meandering. But beautiful, he realizes after a few moments. And strangely insinuating, as if in the absence of words the long slides and surges of the melody itself speak a language.

✦ ✦ ✦

By the time the calves join him on the summit it is dark and frosty and he is lying on a bed of mulch. Not since early in the drought has he eaten this well, and for the first hour or so that he lay here his gut whined and groaned an oddly rhythmic accompaniment to the mourning dirge. And then he dozed... lightly, he thought, and yet he failed to perceive the calves' approach. Suddenly they are beside him, their green eyes paired holes in the blackness.

He comes to his feet. "Are you hungry?" he asks.

"No," Sink Hole says. "Let's go." He turns, and his sisters quickly fall in behind him, Rain grasping his tail, Grief grasping hers.

Their pace is vigorous. Tall Time keeps expecting Grief to protest or to release Rain's tail, but she doesn't. She is like a warthog, they all are, small and sturdy, miraculously nimble. Even going down steep inclines into utter blackness their footing is sure, their vision keen. All visionaries have sharp eyes but these three could be cats. At one point Sink Hole halts and says, "I don't like the look of those," and Tall Time scents and squints ahead of himself and says, "What?"

"Those two humps," Rain says. "There."

All Tall Time can see are shades of murkiness so imperceptible he may be imagining them. "Why?" he asks as Sink Hole detours into thick sage bush.

"Two single-peaked humps close together are unlucky," Rain says. "Don't you know that?"

"I dare say I don't." It occurs to Tall Time that the Lost Ones must have a host of signs and superstitions known only to themselves and that this is what Torrent meant when he said the links may be infinite. If not infinite, Tall Time thinks now, so abundant as to be finally ambiguous. In his doctrine of links, two single-peaked termite mounds indicate ancient she-one bones in the vicinity.

"Yes, there are," Rain says. "Buried right under us."

She is not only listening to his mind, she is presuming to respond to whatever she hears there. Unlike mind talkers from his part of The Domain, she doesn't have to be facing him to penetrate his skull, and he finds himself trying to suppress the thoughts he'd prefer she not know. He answers her questions out loud so that Sink Hole won't feel excluded, but except for a few derisive grunts, Sink Hole is silent. One of these grunts comes when Rain says she had her first vision of Tall Time earlier in the day—"Yanking a big fly's leg"—and then, divining that he had broken the leg, says, "Sink Hole, he killed the big fly."

She tells him that they knew who he was because he has been seen in the visions of their matriarch, I-Flounder.

"Visions?" he thinks. "More than one?"

"Five."

"What was I doing?"

"Nobody tells Matriarch's visions." She sounds appalled.

"I beg your pardon."

"Only she can tell her visions."

"Tell me about the cave, then."

She says that the family has been hiding for a hundred and forty-seven days, and during that time has had no contact or communication with any other Lost Ones, although at one point or another everybody has envisioned some distant family member. (Bulls, cows, calves, all Lost Ones are rampant visionaries.) Like the We-F's, most other families have taken to dwelling in caves. In their cave the We-F's hide from before sunrise until after sunset, when they go out to forage but not until I-Flirt, the finest scenter, has given the all-clear. Inside they talk softly. Inside and out, they sing, throwing their voices so that humans can't identify the source, and in any event confident that when they sing they sound like birds. ("You sound like wind!" Tall Time says. "No, we don't," Rain says, and he entertains the possibility of there being winds and birds here with which he is unfamiliar.) Close to the mouth of the cave is a salt lick, and a rivulet of water falls down the rear wall. Three cows and one calf remain. The family was eight before I-Fret and the three of them left, which they did despite the misgivings of the matriarch, I-Flounder, who had envisioned I-Fret's death.

"And yet your mother still left," Tall Time says.

"She thought it was a sham vision."

"Is there such a thing?"

"Of course. Everybody has them. Don't you?"

"I don't have visions at all. Very few of my kind are visionaries. Bulls never are."

"Oh." She appears to find this information distasteful. After a moment she says, "That saves you from having sham visions. The only time you can be certain you're not having a sham vision is if you have one of the that-way bone, but nobody ever has a vision of the that-way bone."

Sink Hole comes to such a sudden halt that Rain bumps into him and Grief bumps into her and falls.

"But he already knows of it," Rain says, divining the reason for the stop. She turns and helps Grief to her feet.

Sink Hole turns, and his eyes, which flash a deeper green than they did earlier, ascend to Tall Time. "It is not for us to speak of," he says sternly and starts walking.

"Quite right," Tall Time says. He will speak of it with the matriarch.

They have been walking for several hours now and are deep into the hills. The underscents here are intoxicating; they lull Tall Time into a state of calm wariness that he has little experience of. Wary he always is. Calm, hardly ever. The atmosphere rings with queer forces, and its own silence. He smells plenty of creatures: monkey, antelope, giraffe, warthog . . . and lion somewhere overhead, those exotic tree-climbing lions from the old songs. And yet there are no cries, no grunts. There is stealthy movement, that's all, the dead foliage snapping. He thinks of Torrent saying that the type of prodigal slaughter practised by humans is a new horror here and he guesses this accounts for the quiet creeping around.

Near midnight they enter an arid riverbed in a crevice between massive boulders. Wind sweeps down from the cliffs, and on an especially strong blast Tall Time hears snatches of the same melody that the calves were keening at the corpse of their mother.

"They know," Sink Hole says.

"Who?" Tall Time says.

"The big cows," Rain says. "They know our mother is dead."

As before, Tall Time is unable to locate the source of the song—the sound both rebounds off the rock and tolls within it. "Are we almost at the cave?" he asks.

"It's up there," Rain says. She gestures ahead and to the right. "On the other side of High Hill."

"That peak?"

"On the other side. We have to climb over."

It seems impossible.

"You're afraid," she says.

"I'm concerned."

"Nobody is forcing you to follow us," Sink Hole says.

✦ ✦ ✦

From a plateau at the mouth of the cave the We-F cows and calves watch them descend. The eyes of the three cows are so brilliant that they produce funnels of light, casting upon the precipitous slope a swampy luminescence without which Tall Time has no idea how he would have picked his way down. He had made his way *up* by clinging to roots and trees, but he had slipped and scraped his shin where the ostrich had pecked it.

Rain, Sink Hole and Grief trot down. "The earth tilts to meet their footfalls" is Tall Time's wistful thought. Suddenly his little guides are lost to him. No, he is lost to them, it's as if he's not there. The family surrounds the three in what is clearly a reunion ceremony, hushed and exacting, unlike anything Tall Time knows. From what he can see, the calves take turns inserting their trunks into each of the cows' mouths and then into the mouth of the one other calf. Meanwhile the cows sway their hips in unison, a honeyed musk seeping from their hides. Two of them have stunningly long, straight tusks. The third has only one tusk, and it is the length of one of his, although much thinner.

When the swaying stops, the matriarch starts bellowing a mourning song—this one with words—about courage and hardship and death and boundless mystery. There is a chorus, everybody joining in, and after some three hundred verses, Tall Time joins in as well. "Fear not!" he roars. "The She conceived it thus! Oh, be ye not dismayed!"

Immediately and without consulting each other or acknowledging him, the cows fall silent and move out of the circle. He has ruined something, or transgressed some protocol. "I beg your pardon," he rumbles, mortified.

The matriarch steps briskly up to him. She is as small as an adolescent calf but the largest of the three cows, and her tusks are almost the length of her trunk. The green wands from her eyes skim over his body, up to his face, obliging him to squint. "Hello, Tall Time the Link Bull," she says tersely. "I am I-Flounder."

"Hello, Matriarch," he says in the formal timbre. "I do apologize."

"No need. It is our custom to sing until disturbed by an unpleasant noise or scent. I-Fret was my sister, and had you not interrupted I would have sung until dawn."

If she is weeping to herself, he can't tell. He can't imagine that a creature so contained and direct would ever flounder. He is shattered that she would refer to his singing as unpleasant.

The rest of the family are now behind her. She gives a curt nod and the two cows introduce themselves. They are I-Flirt (who suckles Grief from one breast and her own newborn from another), and the single-tusked nurse cow, I-Fix.

"You are bleeding," I-Fix rumbles. For some reason she sounds outraged.

"There is not much darkness left," I-Flounder says. "We shall retire to the cave, and I-Fix will attend to you."

◆ ◆ ◆

The cave is spacious and high. At a cow's glance, lengths of rock flare up, and Tall Time is able to glimpse what he smells—the little mounds of hyraxes that sleep in the creases between floor and wall. The fruit bats. He leans against the west wall as I-Fix deftly applies a lobelia poultice to his leg. It is obvious she resents the task. "I was saving this," she fumes, referring to the lobelia. The instant she is done she rushes away from him, and he goes to the rear of the cave and drinks from the rivulet.

He feels huge and awkward among these tiny cows. That his welcome has been so cool perplexes him, and he is wondering how he should proceed when he realizes by the corona of light surrounding his shadow that the We-F's are looking his way.

"We await you," I-Flounder says.

He hurries to where they are gathered along the east wall. By the salt lick, he assumes.

"For two days now," I-Flounder says, "I have been envisioning you. But not until I envisioned you in the company of our calves did I know we would meet. Prior to our meeting

Torrent the Trunk Bull, no Lost One had envisioned any of your kind. We had heard stories of dull, unsightly giants but we had thought that they no longer lived on The Domain—if they ever lived at all. I-Fix's visions of Torrent preceded his visit by mere hours."

"Not all of my kind are dull and unsightly," Tall Time rumbles quietly. He is more offended than he cares to let on.

I-Flounder makes a dismissive gesture with her trunk. "We have something we must show you," she says.

Must show him. At last he is being granted a degree of consequence. He sniffs from one cow to the next, expecting to be presented with a fragment peculiar to his region of the world, a type of nut perhaps, or a small animal skeleton, to which they have attached significance.

But prompted by a signal beyond his senses they all turn and face the wall, illuminating it.

"Look there," I-Flounder says. "At those marks."

He touches the scored, green-lit expanse. The marks have obviously been made by tusks. He brings his trunk to his mouth and expects to taste salt. When he doesn't he grunts, surprised.

"Do you see the likeness?" I-Flounder asks.

"What likeness?"

"A Lost One cow. That is her head, her rump, her trunk and tusks." She is pointing at the marks. "Those are her legs. Behind her is a bull hindlegger. His head, his forelegs. He grips a hack, here, between his forefeet. Do you see?"

Tall Time slowly nods. Briefly he does see, and then doesn't, and then does again. It requires a trick of mind, as when you discern a likeness in some contour of landscape.

"Think of silhouettes. Imagine it is near dusk or just after dawn and you are looking toward the She-eye."

He tries this, and instantly the shapes pop out of the rock. "Did you make them?" he asks, amazed.

"We did not."

"Who, then?"

"One of our kind."

"Surely more than one," he says, because of the varying heights of the marks. But why are they here at all? He brings particles of dirt to his mouth again. There is nothing worth digging out of this rock, nothing that he can taste.

"They were not thoughtlessly produced," I-Flounder says. A faint strain of emotion has entered her voice. "They are the deliberate creation of a single cow intent on preserving her visions."

"No," he says. That a cow would intentionally carve likenesses into rock, that she would conceive of such an enterprise, let alone possess the dexterity to execute it, is more incredible to him than that randomly made scratches could so closely resemble real creatures.

I-Flounder turns away. "There are three more," she says. She and the others move along the wall and halt before a new dispersion of marks.

He tells himself that he is looking at shapes on the horizon, and the scene reveals itself. Two Lost One cows and a calf lie on their sides. The cows have cavities where their faces should be. Nobody has tusks, feet or tails. "A slaughter," he says. He touches the outline of the calf, and he could be stroking a corpse. He begins to weep, but without tears. "How is it possible?" he asks.

"The marks are very sacred," I-Flounder says. "And very old. Look here now, at the third one." She walks along the wall, and her family and Tall Time follow.

This likeness is of a large flying bird. "A sky-diver?" Tall Time asks.

I-Flounder nods.

In its beak the eagle holds what appears to be a curved twig. Tall Time runs the tip of his trunk over the eagle's outline.

"That's right," I-Flounder says. "Keep touching."

The marks seem to suck his trunk along their lengths, a queer sensation. He feels himself sinking into a memory and tries to pull himself out but the memory has already surrounded him and yet is not familiar, and he concludes that he has fallen asleep. Except that there is nothing dream-like about the perfection and clarity of the blue sky and how it fails to warp into something else as he looks at it. A martial eagle cuts through the blue and idles inches from his eyes. Teetering, it scours the ground. When it dives, Tall Time's gaze dives likewise. He cannot smell the bird. His sense of smell is absent but his sense of sight is fantastically sharp. He sees the small brilliant white rib in the hollow between two boulders. He watches as the eagle grasps the rib in its talons and flies off. "The white bone!" Tall Time calls and finds himself looking at the cave wall.

He turns to face the cows. "I dreamt—" he rumbles.

"It was no dream," I-Flounder says. "It was a vision."

"Bulls of my kind don't have visions."

"Nevertheless you did. If you match it against any dream you have ever had you shall find there is little resemblance."

She is unerring and his superior. If she tells him that despite everything he knows he had a vision, he must believe her. "But I am incapable of having visions," he says weakly.

"The likeness inspired your vision. Away from these likenesses it is doubtful you shall ever have another."

He is grateful that she did not urge him to envision the slaughter. "I had a vision," he rumbles, relinquishing himself to wonder. "I saw the white bone."

"The that-way bone," I-Flounder says sharply.

"The that-way bone. Quite right."

"It loses power when it is spoken of directly."

"Yes, of course. Forgive me. I must say I'm concerned about how much power it has already lost. In my part of The Domain alone, I suspect that quite a few families know of it."

"Are all your kind as careless as you?"

"Among my kind I am considered unwholesomely cautious," he says apologetically.

She is quiet, and then her eyes flash, and all the We-F's lower their heads. Guessing that some observance is under way, he lowers his head as well. At the back of the cave the rivulet ticks out an agitated rhythm. The sound is like that of two small bones tapping together, and he finds himself thinking of the delicacy with which Torrent fondled the bones of the She-S calves at Blood Swamp. He glances at I-Flounder.

Her eyes are burning centrums. "Pardon my absence, Tall Time. I, too, had a vision." She says this kindly. She sounds like somebody else entirely.

"Of what?" he asks.

Her gaze veers to the wall. "There is one more likeness."

"Was it of me?" Her manner has given him the idea that she saw him in peril.

"The visions of the matriarch are confidential," she says, brisk again, "unless she herself chooses to divulge them."

He looks at Rain, who is looking at I-Flounder and plainly hearing her thoughts. In the gloom the little calf's expression is indecipherable. He sniffs the air for some prevailing emotion, but the musk of the cows is muffling their more subtle odours.

"In this likeness is one of your kind," I-Flounder says. "A cow calf."

"How's that?" He whirls around to face the wall.

"The tusks are stunted." She points to the marks. "The ears are oversized."

His fear relaxes to wonder. "How curious."

"More curious still is that it will not yield. When we touch it, we fail to enter a vision. As you can see, the calf is holding the that-way bone from the third likeness."

He traces the tip of his trunk along the mark that is the calf's rump. To enter a vision of this scene would be to take in the location. And to take in the location would be, with luck, to find it. But will the calf and the white bone still be there, waiting to be found? Apparently the We-F's think so. Apparently they have been hoping that the likeness will yield to one of the calf's own kind. So far he feels nothing of the sucking sensation he felt from the third likeness. He moves his trunk to the enormous acacia the calf is standing under. "This is certainly very large," he says.

"We wondered if it was common to your part of The Domain," I-Flounder says.

"I have never seen one this size," he says.

"It is grotesque," I-Fix says with mystifying passion.

"I do not find it so," I-Flirt says, looking at him. "I am partial to bigness."

I-Flounder says, "Every day we touch this likeness and hope it will yield. Searching aimlessly for the that-way bone seems foolish when the answer to its location is right here. I imagine that the calf is in the midst of throwing the that-way bone. If, in a vision, one witnesses how it lands, then one can find the way to The Second Safe Place."

"Yes, I understand," Tall Time says, and now he does. The We-F's aren't depending on finding the calf or the white bone. They need only determine where that acacia is and in which direction the white bone lands once the calf throws it. They are the masters of the master trackers. From a single indication they will be able to find The Safe Place, or The Second Safe Place, as they call it. Provided that the calf really *is* in the midst of throwing the white bone and that there really *is* a Safe Place. He tells them about Torrent's doubts.

"Torrent the Trunk Bull," Sink Hole says contemptuously.

I-Flounder slaps the calf hard across his rump. "There is but one Torrent the Trunk Bull," she says. Which surprises Tall Time, this defence of a member of his kind. Turning to him, she says, "We have none of us envisioned The Second Safe Place. To our knowledge no Lost One has. Has any of your kind?"

"Not that I've learned."

She nods, and he suspects that this failure on the part of his kind relieves her. "Nevertheless," she says, "we have envisioned the making of these likenesses by the last white cow on The Domain. We have heard her sing that when the hindleggers had annihilated and crushed the bones of all of her kind except for herself and her newborn, she offered the newborn to a longbody in order to preserve the rib that, in future eras of darkness, would lead she-ones to a—" And she lifts her head and booms:

"Refuge where no
Breath of slaughter
Stains the breeze, where
On the water
Blessings rain."

"Torrent the Trunk Bull," she finishes, "has not heard this."
"I dare say he has not," Tall Time rumbles.
She gestures at the wall. "Keep touching the marks."
Tall Time hears her brittle voice behind a cacophonous twittering. Another voice—a familiar one—says, "The white bone." He is drifting into a vision and wants to tell I-Flounder but he cannot speak. He is looking at the dead foliage of the huge acacia from the fourth likeness. It swarms with derelict weaver-bird nests, they swing in the wind. He is unable to direct his gaze downward. He feels, as he did not the first time, that he is seeing through an eye in the centre of his forehead. With torturous slowness the eye travels to the horizon—a range of low blue hills—and then back to the base of the tree and a pile of she-one dung. Past the tree is a jumping mongoose, more mongooses, all of them jumping and twittering. And now a she-one's foot, a suppurating shin. His gaze draws back. It is Date Bed. He hardly recognizes her, she is so emaciated. Where are the rest of the She-S's? Where is Mud? "Mud!" he bellows within his head, and it seems that Date

Bed hears. She turns to face him and he sees her pitifully narrow skull and the purple wound above her eye. She sways. In her trunk she clutches something. The white bone! She has it! She curls her trunk under her chin, twists as if to look over her shoulder and then jerks forward, flinging her trunk open, releasing the bone. Where it hits the ground dust sprouts and arcs off and his third eye closes in on a single speck. The speck sails, and his eye rides it for miles, for days, over the blue hills and then along a riverbed to a plain and across the plain to an escarpment, across the escarpment, down the far side to a swamp, and surrounding the swamp the land is all green. Grass, papyrus. A delirium of green. . . .

The eyes of the We-F's are aimed low to protect him from the glare. He says that he was gone for a long time and I-Flounder tells him, No, only moments. Did the calf throw the that-way bone? she asks. Yes, he answers, she did. Did he mark how it landed? No. No? But—listen to him—he saw The Safe Place itself, he was led to it from the spot where the that-way bone landed! Is he certain? As certain as he can be, if he indeed had a vision and not a dream. You had a vision, I-Flounder says. Very well then, he says, he saw The Safe Place. What is it like? Green, green. Could he locate the vicinity where the that-way bone was thrown, where the calf is? He believes so. He is an inferior tracker, is he not? Not a master, it is true, but no, not inferior. Is it far away, this vicinity? Ten days away. Beyond the desert.

Silence.

"Ah, the newborns," he says as it dawns how treacherous it would be for the small calves, doughty as they are but forest dwellers, after all, to try to cross the desert, let alone the plain.

I-Flounder says, "If we set out and find that the journey proves too arduous, we shall return and await the rains. The Safe Place won't disappear before then." She glances behind her at the white mouth of the cave. "We shall leave tomorrow evening. Now let us drink and weep for my sister. And then we shall rest while you describe the vision in all its particulars so that we ourselves may imagine the route."

✦ ✦ ✦

There are beds of mulch at the rear of the cave. His is large and fresh . . . evidently it awaited him. The calves and I-Fix lie in a row at his tail end, Sink Hole and I-Fix pressed against the wall as if to keep as much distance as possible between themselves and him. I-Flirt's bed is next to his, and once he is settled she lowers herself down, sighing, grunting, shifting and finally going still with her rump against his back, a most provocative and inappropriate position, but he fears offending her and doesn't move away.

On his other side I-Flounder lies facing him. During his recounting of the vision she frequently interrupts to ask about bird calls, the shape of the horizon, the exact placement of bushes, rocks, the texture and incline of the ground, the light. She does the same as he is describing how to get from here to the blue hills. He says that at some point during their journey, if dung or any other practical sign indicates that Mud and the She-S's are in another direction, he may be the one to part company. He confesses that he is sorely worried to have found Date Bed alone in the vision, and I-Fix says harshly, "Your Mud is not dead."

He cannot speak, he is so overcome. Why did he not think to ask if any of them had envisioned the She-S's? That they had envisioned only himself and Torrent he took for granted.

"The big cows call her She-Spurns," I-Fix says, as if no name was more odious.

"Is she well?" he asks.

"She is lame. She is gaunt."

Her tone implies that these afflictions are self-imposed, but he is too full of emotion to retreat from her bewildering hostility, and he asks, "Where is she?"

"She *was* in a region of black boulders. Five hundred miles south of here, judging by the shadows and the light."

"The Spill," he says. "When do you think this was?"

"I had the vision five days ago. I was seeing the near future. I cannot be more precise."

"How many cows were with her?"

"Three. And only the one calf, the newborn. There was a longbody stretching and meowing nearby. It was exceedingly strange."

"Me-Me," he says, alarmed. "It must be her. She is nefarious. A longbody who craves the flesh of she-one newborns." A startling thought occurs to him. "I wonder if she is descended from the longbody who ate the newborn white one?"

"We know nothing of this longbody," I-Flounder says. The light in her eyes deepens. "Is it your intention to go directly to The Spill?" she asks.

"Yes, Matriarch."

"I caution you against it. I caution you to go first to The Safe Place."

"Why?"

"Once you are there and have gathered your strength, you will be better able to resume your search."

"I am strong already," he says, but he understands that her answer is an evasion. He is shaken again by the thought that she has envisioned him in peril . . . perhaps dead. If so, it doesn't matter where he goes; his fate will prevail regardless. Why, then, is she warning him? Is she able to envision what *might* be? Or has she seen not a vision at all but some powerful Lost One omen? In either event, he finds that he isn't brave enough—or mad enough—to oppose her.

"Very well," he says finally.

She closes her eyes. Within seconds all of them do. The cave amplifies into blackness.

Chapter Thirteen

The cheetah must see that they are watching her—certainly she can't doubt that they have caught her odour—and yet she creeps between the boulders in a crouch, as if she is stalking them.

"The damned thing's deranged," She-Soothes bellows.

The cheetah freezes mid-stride. When she starts moving again, Mud says, "Matriarch, how close are we going to let her come?"

"As close as she dares," says She-Snorts.

They stand on the bank of Jaw-Log River where only moments ago She-Screams stood and called them cowards, traitors. It is dawn. Cold and no wind. More out of habit than caution (a cheetah is scarcely a threat to three cows) they have formed a truncated V formation: She-Snorts at the apex, She-Soothes at her left shoulder, Mud at her right. Bent lies in the crux.

"She-Soothes wants to charge," the nurse cow trumpets. The cheetah is now so close that her nauseatingly sweet odour obliges them to squeeze the tips of their trunks together.

"No," She-Snorts rumbles.

The cheetah sits. She lifts her right paw and appears to study it. She extends it toward them, and they all swivel their trunks to scent behind themselves. Mud also peers over her shoulder. Nothing, there's nothing that way. The cheetah stops pointing and licks her other paw and rubs the black lines of "mock head drool"* that run from each of her eyes.

She-Snorts says smugly, "She is not as calm as she pretends to be."

The cheetah drops her paw and begins to chirp.

"She's appealing to our mind talker," She-Snorts says.

"Date Bed's not here!" She-Soothes roars.

The cheetah stops chirping.

"That's right!" She-Soothes trumpets. "Shut your stinking hole!"

"How can we know if it's Me-Me?" Mud asks.

"Me-Me?" She-Soothes bellows.

"Who else would it be?" the matriarch says.

"Well," She-Soothes roars, "if it's Me-Me, She-Soothes will tell you what she's pointing at! She's pointing at The Safe Place!"

She-Snorts shakes her head. "No, I don't think that's it."

As if her attention has been captured by something over The Spill, Me-Me looks west. She starts circling toward Mud while still faced away, and the three cows step to the right so

---

* When Rogue was making cheetahs He intended for them to have orifices that would release temporin, but in His careless fashion He settled for the easier solution of permanent lines.

that the apex of their V remains fixed on her. She halts. When she resumes her approach, she makes no pretence of her ambition. Shoulders bulked, she zigzags her head to catch glimpses of Bent.

"Be off!" She-Soothes trumpets. Me-Me goes still but holds her ground.

She-Soothes rushes her, and Me-Me makes a leisurely swing around and lopes between the boulders. When She-Soothes pulls up, Me-Me turns and sits. She studies her right paw again. Again points it their way. Since they are now faced northwest (the first time she pointed, they were faced due west), she can't be indicating the way to The Safe Place.

"It's as if she is saying, 'You,' " Mud rumbles. " 'You are the ones.' "

"Which ones?" She-Soothes bellows, trotting back to them.

She-Snorts says, "There is a second odour." Her eyes are shut, she is scenting hard. "It's very insistent but faint. Something she has brushed against, I would imagine. I can't quite catch it. It is too corrupted by *her* odour."

"She-Soothes could chase her out of scent completely!" the nurse cow roars.

"She'll only come back," She-Snorts says.

"What does she want with Bent, anyhow?" She-Soothes rumbles. "Longbodies don't eat she-ones."

"Not normally," She-Snorts says. She opens her eyes. "We'll keep our trunks on her while we browse."

The heat on The Spill will be terrible in a few hours, impossible for Bent to walk in, so the plan is to wait until dusk before setting off for Feed Swamp. Mud asks about the underscents. (If they travel by night there is the risk of under-

The White Bone

scents masking any odours leading to Date Bed.) But She-Snorts doesn't think they'll be very strong out there, it's too barren.

"What about Me-Me?" She-Soothes roars.

"She'll follow us," She-Snorts says.

"Follow us!"

"I would imagine so."

"*Follow* us!" the nurse cow roars again. She picks up a log and hurls it.

"She-Measures advised us to indulge her," She-Snorts rumbles. "Indulge her we shall. For now."

She sounds exhausted suddenly. Defeated, even. Mud thinks, Why wouldn't she be? In only a few hours the family has dwindled from seven (including Hail Stones) to four, one of them a calf with rickety knees and no stamina. Five days it took Torrent to cross The Spill. How long will it take the four of them to cross, half-starved as they are? How is it possible that Date Bed made the trek? Probably she didn't. But since she somehow found her way here, and since there is no sign of her anywhere to the east, and since to the north is desert and to the south a vast wire fence and a huge aggregation of humans, what alternative do they have except to head west?

They start to forage, alert to Me-Me, who sits facing them. They scour the savaged ebony trees and Phoenix palms for strips of bark. They tusk the riverbank to unearth roots. Mud has the guilty thought that it is just as well that Hail Stones and Swamp and She-Screams went away, there's little enough to eat here as it is. And yet she already misses Hail Stones: her fellow interloper and cripple, her would-be and longed-for suitor. She frets for him, and for Swamp, too. Not for She-Screams, who may already be dead and in any event is past saving. "Poor She-Screams," she thinks, to muster pity, but the silence in the wake of the big cow's absence is such a relief that she can't pretend to miss her. She looks east, half-expecting to see the dust squall that would signal one of them returning. She-Soothes and She-Snorts occasionally scent that way. Nobody mentions the departed. For an hour or so She-Soothes mutters about the perils of family rifts, but then she roars, "What's done is done!" and beams at Mud and She-Snorts as if this conclusion, her habitual one, were a great revelation and a great relief.

A little later, the water hole that Date Bed excavated dries up, and She-Snorts digs another, whose weak seepage requires them to kneel and drink with their mouths, as Bent does. Bent stays close to his mother and glances wild-eyed at Me-Me. Once, he turns to Me-Me, opens his ears and bleats a feeble "Be off!" and Me-Me responds with a curiously tender chirp that terrifies him. He ducks under She-Soothes and tugs on her breasts, but she has had no milk for three days now, so she pulls away and prepares to feed him the contents of her stomach. It is nothing anybody wants to witness. As her shrivelled hide sucks at her ribcage, she yanks up his trunk and puts her mouth as close to his as she can, but most of the vomit lands on his face. Today he refuses to swallow. Breathing hard in the awful heat, She-Soothes doesn't scold him. She showers him with dirt. Showers herself. The flies lift as the dirt falls. The flies fall back down, thick as the dirt.

From where they are, against the relatively cooler south bank of the river, Me-Me is in their sights. Far more tolerant of the heat than they are, she lolls and stretches. Mid-afternoon she takes off north and returns dragging a still-living warthog. She eats it languorously and playfully, pretending to catch it anew, lunging at it, throwing the trotters into the air and batting them down, all this while barely using her right paw. She-Snorts speculates that the paw is injured.

As if hearing her, Me-Me points the paw toward them, and She-Soothes bellows, "Damned if she doesn't want She-Soothes to attend to it," and She-Snorts rumbles, "I've caught the second odour again, what is it?" and she snorts, frustrated.

✦ ✦ ✦

The sunset that day is particularly vivid and symmetrical. Three straight bands of equal width and brilliance—purple on top, then red, then orange—across the whole of the western horizon.

"She-Soothes wonders who she was," She-Soothes bellows. (You get a sunset like that only when a matriarch has been slaughtered.)

She-Measures, Mud thinks because of the symmetry, but she doesn't say so. She doesn't want the thought confirmed.

They have already set off. Normally Mud would place herself abreast of She-Soothes, but to travel in a line is easier through this maze of boulders and she walks behind the big cow. To their left, Me-Me's small head, lit up in the low sun, sails between the rocks like a moon. Whenever she begins to veer closer, She-Soothes trumpets and she angles back to where she was.

Despite the impossibility of holding to a straight path, they manage a brisk enough pace with She-Soothes nudging Bent along ahead of her. Scents are scarce. There is the ashy smell of the boulders themselves, the blood-sweet smell of Me-Me, the stench of vultures and the prickly fragrances of smaller creatures: of jackal, barbet, lizard. Each of these odours hovers in discrete ribbons above the underscents, which, as She-Snorts predicted, scarcely arrive.

The moon arrives not at all. Aside from the winking of fireflies the night is black. Mud nevertheless scans for the white bone because it is possible that the bone's fabled gleam defies darkness and because who can tell which boulders, among so many, form part of a larger circle? She is alert to the shape of what she steps on. A stick is not a rib. She moves silently. They all do, Me-Me as well. The five of them are a grim thought moving through an immense mind—so Mud imagines. Or she imagines that she is alone, the odour of the others being merely what lingers of them. She herself, in all her booming pain, feels conspicuous. Her withered leg throbs. It doesn't seize, though . . . there is that blessing. Her belly is what seizes, from hunger or the newborn, and she strokes the rungs of her ribs and wonders whether the newborn feels it. She feels the newborn's heart pulsing two beats to her one. She counts the heartbeats, her footsteps—she is able to count up to three things at once. After some ten thousand steps She-Snorts says, "Stop."

They have come to a teclea thicket, and since it would be mad to pass up anything digestible in this wilderness, they begin to forage. South of them, Me-Me paces and yelps.

"Shut your stinking hole!" She-Soothes trumpets, and Me-Me does, but only for a moment. Twice she darts closer and She-Soothes charges her.

Both times She-Snorts smells that elusive odour but fails to identify it. She says to She-Soothes, "Don't chase her off next time. I want to get a better whiff of her."

Before resuming the trek, while She-Soothes is eating gazelle dung (a brand of her so-called drought fruit), She-Snorts and Mud move to a slight rise of land and from there transmit a series of infrasonic rumbles, to Date Bed, Torrent, Tall Time and then to Hail Stones and Swamp. When no responses come, Mud says, "I was hoping that at least Hail Stones or Swamp would answer."

"They are being assailed by somebody else's grounders," She-Snorts says.

By She-Screams, in other words. "I had a vision of She-Screams dead," Mud says.

She-Snorts expels a slow breath.

"She was alone." Already Mud knows that she has made a bad mistake, mentioning the banished cow. "She was at the bottom of a hill," she says quickly, hoping that the details will somehow absolve her. In her anxiety she uses the formal timbre. "Near a pool of muck. Nothing of the place was familiar."

Silence.

"Her hide was clean." She is weeping now. "There weren't any sting holes. She looked as though she had been lying there for several days."

Silence.

"I think it was the near future," she says in a final pitch of anguish.

"Did she have her tusks?" She-Snorts asks. Her voice is without inflection.

"Yes! Yes, she had her tusks!"

She-Snorts turns and ambles back to the thicket.

Barbara Gowdy

✦ ✦ ✦

They have been walking about an hour when a large pack of spotted hyenas shows up and cavorts close behind them. Mud moves beside She-Soothes and fights hard not to fall into her memory of the hyena that stalked her on the night of her birth. "Ignore them," She-Snorts tells She-Soothes, whose bellows of "Be off!" only provoke manic cackles. Are we so reduced that they think they can get to Bent? Mud wonders. Or perhaps it's Me-Me they want. Mud has never heard of hyenas bringing down a grown cheetah, but in this devious landscape no behaviour seems fantastic. When the hyenas cackle, Me-Me hisses and discharges a bitter odour like bullets. Toward morning she runs away south, and the hyenas give up their pursuit and fall back out of scent.

"She'll return," She-Snorts says.

The sun rises. They are nowhere near water and so they keep walking and after several hours arrive at a salt lick. A little beyond the lick She-Snorts finds a cavity she has only to prod with her foot before a small fountain gushes up. "Jubilation!" she trumpets. They all twine trunks and defecate and then they drink and spray each other, exhilarated not only because the digger might have been Date Bed (although there aren't any signs of her) but because their expectations of locating clear water on The Spill had been so dismal.

They eat the desiccated brush and shreds of grass surrounding the lick, and when that is gone they tusk the ground for roots. When there are no more roots, they eat salt and earth and then they lie in the shade of giant termite mounds, and while everyone else sleeps, Mud worries about having divulged her vision . . . although how could she have guessed that even *it* would not penetrate the banishment? She prays her one-word prayer—"Please"—and shapes her thoughts into a Date Bed spirit. (She has come to believe that provided it is perfectly imagined—that as long as it is *capable* of being perfectly imagined—the spirit not only sustains Date Bed, it is the proof that she lives.) She keeps her eyes open, watches the shade ebbing from the bodies of the others and falls into memories of shade sliding off skin, of sun-grilled corpses. At intervals she says, "We'd better move out of the She-eye," and they all get up and drink and spray themselves with water and dirt and scratch their hides on the mounds before lying down again. Every few hours She-Snorts sends infrasonic calls and Mud makes a careful scan of the horizon, especially to the north, which is directly upwind and on which dust tornadoes sit like the smoke from a line of fires. Wavering shapes that could be Me-Me turn out to be ostriches, oryxes. No shape as big as a she-one materializes, and nothing, certainly no bone, is blinding white.

Mid-afternoon She-Soothes wanders off to collect hyena dung for her eye wad, and Mud says to She-Snorts, "I am sorry, Matriarch."

She-Snorts glances at her. "It matters less that you spoke about a banished cow, She-Spurns, than that you spoke of your vision. A death vision is the burden of the visionary alone. Never again tell me about such a vision."

"I won't," Mud vows in the formal timbre.

"Unless," She-Snorts says, "it is of Date Bed."

They travel through another black night, this one uneventful and quiet. Just after dawn they arrive at a parched streambed in which they dig six holes before striking a seepage of muddy water. It will have to do. Long, dry thatch grass crackles in narrow rows along the banks. So much untouched grazing, while it is a find, is not good news—no one has been here since before the drought.

"There's more than one way to peel a tree!" declares She-Soothes. In other words, Date Bed might have veered north or south of this place and still held a course leading to Feed Swamp.

She-Snorts breathes in short puffs that blow the dust from the grass. "I am so tired," she says finally, and her scent plummets to bleakness.

"Take a whiff at all the browse!" roars She-Soothes, as if they have only this moment arrived.

She-Snorts suddenly raises her trunk. She points it behind herself.

Mud, She-Soothes and Bent do the same.

"What?" She-Soothes bellows.

All of them turn around. Perk their ears.

"Is it that stinking longbody?" She-Soothes bellows.

No answer. Presently Mud sees the huge disturbance of dust on the eastern horizon. A she-one, it must be.

"Well, what do you know," She-Snorts murmurs, dropping her trunk.

From her tone—scornful, disappointed—Mud guesses who it is. A moment later she catches the odour.

"Jubilation!" She-Soothes trumpets. Wheezing and weeping, she dashes up to She-Screams and the two big cows twine trunks and clang tusks, and then She-Screams tries to go after Bent, but he quails under She-Soothes' belly. Mud is utterly ignored, although she lifts her trunk toward She-Screams in a hesitant salute.

"She-Soothes knew you would return!" She-Soothes hollers. "Matriarch—" She looks over her shoulder and only now appears to grasp that the matriarch isn't taking part in the greeting, and she steps back from She-Screams and shakes her head, flummoxed, or protesting the matriarch's behaviour, probably both.

She-Screams, meanwhile, has rushed past all of them to the water hole. She lowers herself to her knees and drinks. Drinks until the seepage goes dry. "I'll dig another!" she cries, hauling herself to her feet. "No, no!" she cries, as if one of them had demurred. "I'll dig it. All my scents are sharper. I have been blessed with a tremendous bloating of my intellect. I don't suppose anybody has noticed how much larger my skull is."

They look at her, even She-Snorts throws her a glance. Her head does seem a bit bigger, but that may be because her body, like theirs, is shrunken from hunger. In her self-adoring way, eyes fluttering, rump swaying, she sprays her rutted hide with muck, after which she returns to the bank and pulls up a hank of grass by the roots and stuffs it into her mouth, dirt and all, and says, "You won't believe what I've been through since . . . was it only yesterday that I left? So much has happened to me. I don't suppose anybody cares to hear what."

Nevertheless she tells them.

Late morning she lost the trail of the bulls, who, ten miles or so east of Jaw-Log River, headed southwest into a terrain of flat rock that she suspects was once a She-D thoroughfare, familiar to Hail Stones. She also suspects that at this point the bulls began to eat their dung and bury their urine in order to vanquish their scent ("Hail Stones' idea, I have no doubt"). She decided to veer west, but there was no sign of them that way, either, so she roamed aimlessly for a while, moving in and out of The Spill. A wire fence obliged her to head north again and almost straight into a cluster of inhabited human dwellings. She raced northwest and, just as she was feeling relatively safe, came upon a shambles: the tuskless skeletons of the She-A's-And-A's, nine bodies and therefore the last of the line. She weeps out loud as she describes her solitary mourning of that notoriously clever family of riddle solvers and philosophers, how she sang all seventy-five verses of "The She Is My Matriarch," all three hundred of "Oblivion! Oblivion!" and in so doing attracted vultures, "packs of them, and they were very quiet, I could tell they were deeply touched by the expression and gravity I bring to a hymn." (Mud wonders, Is she altogether deluded? And yet Mud weeps out loud, too, as does She-Soothes, notwithstanding that if She-Screams is banished, they aren't supposed to have heard the tragic news.)

It was dark by the time She-Screams had finished mourning the She-A's-And-A's and she was so tired and distraught that she began to have a series of her spells. "I was ten heartbeats from death," she declares. When the spells passed she made a fruitless search for water and then returned to the scene of the carnage, where she dozed on her feet. Every so often she roused herself to send infrasonic rumbles to Swamp, but there was no response. All night she remained in the one spot, and when the light arrived so did the conviction that, while she had stood there, her skull had grown to accommodate an expanded intellect. Why had this happened? Because (the answer leapt into her big head right away), as a reward for her brave, lengthy vigil among the She-A's-And-A's, the She had bequeathed her a measure of that family's cleverness. Her second thought was that even if she found the bulls—and with her big new head she was bound to—they would flee again. And where would that leave her, a cow on her own, a cow who, for all her increased powers of mind, was nearly an invalid? She must give up the chase.

She searched again for water and quickly located a seepage under a ditch. After drinking and showering she set off into The Spill, heading west. The entire way she rumbled infrasonically to both She-Soothes and She-Snorts. "Why didn't you respond?" she demands.

From She-Soothes' expression it is obvious that she longs to blurt out a host of things, among them that they never heard the rumbles. Behind her, She-Snorts has stopped feeding, and Mud bends her trunk the matriarch's way (to make it plain that she is not answering She-Screams) and mentions Date Bed's postulation about hard earth blocking infrasonic messages.

She-Snorts lifts her head, she appears to be considering this, but before she can speak, She-Screams says, "Well, I'm here now. It's going to be a sore trial for me, with Swamp gone. You can't imagine what I've suffered." She whirls at She-Snorts, who, Mud now notices, is scenting urgently, trunk straight out, ears open. "Is it Swamp?" She-Screams cries, raising her own trunk.

Mud spies the hump of dust on the horizon.

"It smells like a longbody!" She-Screams cries.

Me-Me, then. Mud still hasn't detected the cheetah's odour. That She-Screams has astounds her, and she glances at She-Screams' head and this time it definitely does seem larger.

"Me-Me!" She-Soothes trumpets as the scent reaches her. She hustles Bent under her belly. "What is that sack of crap coming back for?"

"Me-Me?" She-Screams shrieks. By now, Me-Me is easy to see, trotting between the boulders. She-Screams cries, "Did she tell you where The Safe Place is?" She answers the question herself. "How could she have, when there is no mind talker? Let's all keep calm. Everybody keep calm." A severe look at the nurse cow. "If we drive this Me-Me creature away, we'll never find out anything."

"How do we communicate with her?" Mud says helplessly, and gets a warning snort from the matriarch. But She-Screams' big smart head is too extraordinary to ignore. Mud wants to say, "Matriarch, this is not the cow you banished."

"Oh, look!" She-Screams cries. "She sat down. She's pointing! What's she pointing to?" She scents behind herself. "She's standing! Here she comes!"

She-Soothes growls.

"No," She-Snorts murmurs, and she leans into the nurse cow to arrest her charge.

The cheetah moves cautiously now. Her spots ride the roll of her shoulders. Her head makes slow sweeps back and forth.

"There it is," She-Snorts murmurs, "that other scent."

"I smell it!" She-Screams cries. "What is it?"

Me-Me sits and extends her right paw and begins to chirp.

"Shut your stinking hole!" She-Soothes roars.

"Let her be," She-Snorts says.

For several moments they are all silent, Me-Me as well. And then this impatient observation from She-Screams: "She wants us to sniff the paw. It couldn't be more obvious. That scent is on her paw."

"Let her sniff She-Soothes' hind hole!" She-Soothes bellows and goes into a flustered shuffle over having responded to She-Screams. But She-Snorts, by the agitated twirling of her trunk, is also responding to the banished cow. Mud, too. . . . Mud breathes, "Of course."

"Go back a ways," She-Snorts tells She-Soothes. "You and Bent." The nurse cow hesitates. "Go on!" She-Snorts snaps, and She-Soothes tucks her trunk under Bent and hauls him five, six paces. With small jogs of her head Me-Me tracks his retreat but otherwise doesn't move.

"Everybody else keep still," She-Snorts rumbles. By everybody, she means She-Screams, who has taken a step forward. Ears flattened, trunk drooped, She-Snorts strolls toward the cheetah. "That's right, Me-Me," she calls in the alluring rumble she last used with Hail Stones, "I won't harm you. You stay right there." Me-Me's tail whacks the ground.

When She-Snorts is about two feet away, Me-Me offers her paw. The matriarch sniffs and instantly whips her trunk back under her chin. "It's Date Bed," she says with tight matter-of-factness. "The smell of her dung."

"Let me scent!" She-Screams cries, and she rushes past She-Snorts to Me-Me, who straightens alertly. "Your paw, your right paw!" She indicates with her trunk. Me-Me extends the paw. She-Screams sniffs. "It's Date Bed, all right!" she cries.

"But what does it mean?" Mud asks. She feels light-headed.

"She stepped in Date Bed's crap!" She-Soothes trumpets, and the cheetah slinks backwards several yards. "At Jaw-Log River!"

"No, she had the scent before then," She-Snorts rumbles.

"How did she know it was Date Bed's?" Mud says desperately. "And why did she want us to know? How did she know we'd *want* to know?"

"Date Bed has the She-S odour!" She-Soothes points out.

"Of course she does," She-Screams says. "*Date Bed* is a She-S." (As opposed, the emphasis suggests, to Mud, who isn't.) "The moment Me-Me picked up our scent, she realized that Date Bed was a member of our family and had become separated from us."

"But how would she know to preserve Date Bed's scent in the first place?" Mud asks. "How could she know she'd eventually come across us?"

She-Screams won't answer. She looks at She-Soothes, as if to say, "*You* tell her," but the nurse cow only roars, "Good question!"

"What question is that?" She-Screams asks politely.

She-Soothes can't repeat it, not in front of the matriarch. It is Bent who ends the deadlock by offering, "Perhaps she's clever."

"She *didn't* know!" She-Screams cries. "She couldn't have! Some of Date Bed's dung got lodged in her pads, and not long after that it so happened she picked up our scent!"

"She wants to eat Bent," Mud mentions in case She-Screams hasn't already figured this out and because the doomed cow's slights have no power to wound her and because the various banishments and grudges require a dexterity of mind she hasn't the capacity for right now.

Me-Me is standing. She stares at Bent a moment and then looks to her left. They all scent that way. Nothing is there. She starts creeping forward, muscle by muscle in small halting increments more suggestive of stillness than motion. They allow her to go past She-Screams, to come abreast of She-Snorts. But when she passes She-Snorts, Bent squeals and She-Soothes charges and Me-Me spins around and lopes about forty yards out, then turns and sits, the low morning sun drafting her in a gold mist.

"That was not called for!" She-Screams cries as the nurse cow comes ambling back. "Do you really think she was going to try to bring Bent down with us all gawking at her?"

She-Soothes casts troubled glances at She-Snorts, who looks at Me-Me and reveals nothing.

"Me-Me may know where The Safe Place is," She-Screams reminds them in a lofty, lecturing tone (she must fancy herself a sermonizer now, what with her new sermonizer-size head). "For wretches like ourselves, *may* is good enough. Undoubtedly she has chatted with enough mind talkers to understand how badly we all want to go there. Well, here she is, the famous guide. Who, naturally, has her price. That's all she was trying to tell us just now: that she has her price. A rumble would have been sufficient to discourage her from getting closer."

The nurse cow grunts.

"But we are different from other families," She-Screams continues. "We have become separated from a cow calf, and finding her is more important to us than finding The Safe Place." Her voice leaps to a sarcastic screech. "It is no secret how greatly we all prize our *cow* calves!"

A crew of vultures waddles with outspread wings to boulders farther flung, and She-Screams pauses to collect herself—which she does, as she could never have done before her head expanded, almost instantly. "Me-Me," she goes on, "stepped in the dung of our precious cow calf. She can lead us to the dung. Or at least to where the dung was. What she asks in return is that we *indulge* her. We tolerate her mingling with us. And then we let down our guard for a moment so she can kill Bent."

"What?" She-Soothes roars.

"Kill *me?*" Bent squeals.

"Of course she could simply wait for him to collapse," She-Screams says. "That's the other possibility. One way or another, she has the advantage of being fit. While we all wither away to vines."

"Kill Bent?" She-Soothes bellows, clearly past realizing that she shouldn't be responding.

She-Screams sighs. "I'm not proposing that we let that happen. We *indulge* her, as She-Measures told us to. We indulge her not only until we find Date Bed, either, but until we find out how to get to The Safe Place."

There is a dissenting rumble. It comes from She-Snorts, whose trunk and eyes remain on Me-Me. "We cannot let her think that we will give her Bent," she says quietly. "It is too dangerous."

"Why else would she help us?" She-Screams cries.

"When I drop my newborn"—her gaze swings to She-Soothes, as if she were the one who had asked the question—"she can have it."

"No!" the nurse cow roars.

"Now *that's* an idea," She-Screams says, evidently surprised neither at the dreadful proposal nor at the matriarch's appearing to have a conversation with her, however oblique. "There remains the question of *putting* it to her."

"We let her *think* she can have the newborn!" She-Soothes bellows. "We only let her *think* so. Is that it, She-Spurns?" She nudges Mud, and Mud nods uncertainly and the nurse cow brightens. "We throw the longbody a hollow pod!"* she bellows. "Is that it?"

She-Screams uproots a tuft of grass. "All this mind work takes a lot out of me," she says. "If I'm to be doing all the thinking, I'll need at least twice as much browse as I've been getting."

✦   ✦   ✦

After an hour or so of grazing, She-Screams says, "Time to find out," and struts toward Me-Me. The cheetah runs. "Stay where you are!" She-Screams orders. Me-Me halts, glances over her shoulder. "Stay! Stay! Stay!" She-Screams squawks. Me-Me sits. When She-Screams is close enough, Me-Me holds out her paw. Directly above this scene, against florid ribbings of sunlight, vultures loop in anticipation of disaster.

"No, none of that!" She-Screams pushes away the paw. "Now pay attention!" And she launches into a succession of gestures and noises so explicit and spirited that Bent bleats, "Who is she?" Who, indeed? She touches her stomach, groans,

---

* An expression akin to "pulling the wool over somebody's eyes"; hoodwinking.

points to She-Snorts, squats, grunts, squeals like a calf, taps the cheetah's right paw, points at the four horizons, stamps her foot, points again at She-Snorts and then repeats the sequence. If they doubted her story about inheriting the talent of the She-A's-And-A's they can do so no longer, because it was with such performances that certain non-telepathic members of that family established rudimentary communication with other creatures. In a virtuoso exhibition of her own, Me-Me instantly tracks the gestures. When they end she comes to her feet, shakes her paw three times, makes a staccato churring noise and begins trotting away.

"Stop!" She-Screams cries.

Me-Me stops.

She-Screams turns around. "She accepts the bargain!" she calls. "The place she wants to take us to is a pan three days from here. When should I tell her we'll be setting off?"

And even now, from what reserve of toughness or wrath Mud can't imagine, the matriarch won't answer.

"Well?" She-Screams demands.

The matriarch glances westward.

"At dusk," She-Screams calls, as definitely as if She-Snorts had rumbled the words. "That suits *me*. It's a fire plain out here!"

◆ ◆ ◆

Me-Me heads north-northeast. If she can be trusted (and she probably can, at least as far as knowing where it was that she stepped in Date Bed's dung), she has spared them a futile journey to the other side of The Spill. This alone makes her company worth bearing—even for She-Soothes, who, every time they stop to give Bent a rest, tolerates her trotting back as though to determine the reason for the delay. But Me-Me's lust for calf flesh is no less perceptible than her stench, and they are not fooled. Neither is Mud's newborn. When Me-Me comes close, Mud's belly goes into an uproar and she gets it into her head that it is *her* newborn, not the matriarch's, who has been offered in the bargain, and the thought panics her, for all that she has said this prayer: Let mine perish for hers.

While they are on the move Me-Me positions herself out front by some twenty yards. Now and then her torso is visible flowing between the boulders, but her stench is what guides them, and it is an odd and exhausting experience to be drawn by an odour you flinch from. Mud walks behind She-Soothes and Bent, who are behind She-Snorts. She-Screams walks, as previously, abreast of and about twenty yards to the left of the matriarch. But whereas before she whined and slumped, now she is quiet and her trunk is up. She frequently glances around . . . on the lookout for anything white, Mud imagines, and wonders whether she plans to go on pretending that the rhino rib she found was the white bone. She wonders, jealously, how much sharper She-Screams' eyesight has become. Can she see, as clearly as Mud can, the spectacle overhead? From horizon to horizon are the thousands of brilliant stars that declare this a "memory night."

On the ground is an atmosphere that may be some answering deference, it is so silent. Mud's impression is of moving through the night in innocence, she and Bent and the cows, like first creatures who with their sighs and stomach growls, their soft rumbles, are concocting a repertoire of night noises that will eventually issue from creatures not yet made. They pass no forage and, apart from those short recesses for Bent's sake, walk steadily until shortly before sunrise, when She-Screams says that she must fortify herself. She summons Me-Me and breaks into another seizure of gestures and grunts, at the finish of which Me-Me slaps her tail on the ground and points in several directions, and She-Screams turns to them and reports that forage is north of here, a grove of acacias, and that there is water, too, under a ditch.

This translation, like the first, seems impossibly detailed to Mud. She asks the nurse cow to ask She-Screams if she is hearing the cheetah's mind. A little later, during one of their rests, when the matriarch wanders off to scratch her hide on a termite mound, She-Soothes puts the question to She-Screams. And is assailed with: "Dimwit! Don't you think I'd tell you if I was? Do you think I'd torture myself hunting for some sign of a calf who no longer even lives!"

It is not a *grove* of acacias, it is four stunted trees in a clearing formed when somebody, it must have been a human, pushed a dozen or so boulders into a pile. Still, the trees *are* acacia, not entirely stripped of bark, and under them is an unfamiliar species of dead grass that She-Soothes eats a blade of and proclaims safe and tasty.

"How would *you* know what is tasty?" She-Screams says, folding a swatch into her mouth. "It is not inedible," she allows after swallowing. She grabs a second swatch and is chewing this when she spies the matriarch scenting the ditch that runs through the clearing. Shrieking, "*I'll* find water!" she hurries to the ditch and begins to dig. She excavates five holes before she locates a seepage. "Matriarch first!" she cries happily when the cavity has filled.

She-Snorts sways a little, her bony hips creak like trees. She moves onto a small rise of land in order to transmit her infrasonic calls to Date Bed . . . or so Mud presumes. But like Mud herself the matriarch appears to have abandoned that chore. What's the point, if the calls sent by She-Screams—who wasn't even that far away—failed to get through? Head and trunk lowerered, She-Snorts simply stands there until all of them have taken their drink, and then she comes back and takes hers. At least she *acknowledges* the water hole, which was no certainty considering that a cow who is not supposed to exist located it.

By late morning, the browse is gone. Grass, roots, bark, branches, they have eaten it all. They retire, still famished, to the rim of shade on the west side of the boulder pile. Me-Me lolls on the ground as if the awesome heat and the flies and the black blowing grit were exactly her element. She doesn't need water, Mud thinks, astonished, but as soon as everyone lies down the cheetah creeps to the hole and has a long drink. She then sits and begins to lick her left paw as if she intends to settle there.

"Too close!" She-Soothes trumpets.

Me-Me chirps imploringly.

She-Screams comes to her feet. From where she is, she turns in a circle, points and flaps her ears, and Me-Me attends to all this with a cocked head and then moves off to perch on a boulder and scan for prey. Over the course of the afternoon she catches a lizard and two guineafowls. The smell venting from the opened guts is what advertises the nature of the kill, although Mud is able to see the corpses as well. So is She-Screams. In an entertained tone she reports on the capture—"She bit the head off, she's tossing up the torso. There! That's the torso!"

Near dusk, just as they are setting out, a raging warthog charges toward them. It trots right by Me-Me, close enough for her to touch it. She watches it sidelong with an attitude of remote curiosity. Squealing at an insanely hysterical pitch, the warthog bolts between She-Screams and She-Snorts and keeps going. Deranged it so obviously is, nobody mentions that. Nobody mentions the other obvious thing, either. They all know the saying: "The three unluckiest things you can come upon: a three-legged she-he, a one-eyed lunatic, a crazy grunt."

Less than an hour into the trek The Spill starts giving way to populated scrub and night noises—hoots, cackles, barks—and the odour of slaughter and rotting carcasses. Me-Me tries to pick up the pace, but with Bent scarcely able to stand, speed is out of the question. And so she races back to walk between and only a few yards ahead of She-Snorts and She-Screams, and She-Snorts allows this. At such close quarters her smell is a terror to Mud's newborn, who starts kicking at the belly walls for a way out, that's how it feels.

Tonight the destination is a pair of baobabs. Me-Me has communicated to She-Screams that the trees were still standing fifteen days ago and that water was in a pool nearby. Because of the mad warthog, Mud has no expectation that they will find either and is surprised when, stamped against the rising sun, she discerns the shapes of the beloved trees. That the pool turns out to be bone dry is the bad warthog luck, so She-Soothes assures everybody, the beginning and end of it.

One tree is completely hollowed out, but the other only partly. They postpone scenting for water and tusk into the pulp, the matriarch and She-Screams going first, Mud and She-Soothes snatching up whatever is dropped and taking quick turns every time the two bigger cows pause to chew. Some pulp is still left in the cavity when She-Snorts begins to search the pool bed for the scent of water. After a quarter of an hour she declares the bed parched. She-Screams then scents and fares no better. She confers with Me-Me and announces that they probably won't be drinking again until dawn tomorrow, by which time they should have reached a small freshwater basin. "I don't know how I'll last until then," she wails.

How will Bent last? Without water in her belly, She-Soothes is unable to regurgitate any swill. Her milk has dried up, but Bent still tugs at her shrivelled breasts. She feeds him chewed baobab pulp. He coughs it out. He can tolerate nothing except liquids. She dribbles saliva into his mouth, and when her mouth goes dry Mud contributes what saliva she can and sees that his lips foam. To restore her milk She-Soothes needs papyrus or sansevieria. Throughout the afternoon she throws incoherent bellows over the plain as if she could call back the swamps and rivers, and Me-Me, sitting on a crocodile carcass, appears to understand that this fury is not directed at her and stays where she is.

The trek that night takes them along one of the gravel trails favoured by vehicles. They follow it because it is an easy walk, level and empty of rocks, but when She-Screams hears a distant roar they turn west and go in that direction for a mile before resuming their northeasterly course. They meet a small herd of buffalo too listless to do more than shuffle a few steps out of their way. Passing an old bull, Mud is grazed, shoulder to rump, by the tip of his horn. She feels not transgressed but taken account of: she has a certain shape and length, she moves. She lives.

She sleepwalks and dreams. Or these aren't dreams, they are visions that exhaustion loosens into dreams. All are of debacles. Carcasses, skeletons. Gunshots, and the cows that have been hit dropping with that almost comical suddenness. She falls into a memory of the slaughter at Blood Swamp. Her trumpets halt the trek. She-Soothes persuades her to eat cold grass ash, and it is immediately effective, securing her for several hours in the desolate present.

Tonight they produce as much noise as any other creatures. Bent whimpers, and She-Screams is back to her old practice of wailing grievances. She claims to be having her spells, but her stride is strong, her head and trunk up. Twice she rushes off to investigate circular boulder formations barely visible to Mud's eyes, and miles before even the matriarch appears to have caught the scent she announces the proximity of lions and hyenas. Lions she scents almost simultaneously with Me-Me, who fears them above all other carnivores. "We'll protect you!" She-Screams cries as if Me-Me were their comrade rather than a murderous exploiter. She warns that their slow pace may provoke Me-Me into giving up on them, but when She-Soothes begins to stumble from exhaustion Mud is the one who offers to take over nudging Bent along. She has to curl her trunk between his hind legs and half-push him, half-lift him. It is the most strenuous thing she has ever done. She can't imagine how even stalwart She-Soothes kept it up over so many miles. This is love, she thinks, She-Soothes' sensible brand: ferocious while it is required, abandoned the moment it stops serving any purpose. As the hours pass and she and Bent are still paired, she begins to believe that the choice between ferocious attachment and abandonment is the essential choice. You haul the calf or you abandon it. You stay with your dead sister's newborn under the gutted baobab, or you suckle it one last time and run.

It occurs to her that it is madness for four cows and a calf to be risking themselves in an almost hopeless search for a single calf. The thought comes and goes in an instant. But it comes.

Just before dawn She-Soothes relieves her of Bent. By now Mud has lost all sensation in her trunk and it remains curled for several moments and then floats up on its own like something airborne. Her bad leg is past feeling and past straightening. "We are almost there," she tells herself. They aren't. They keep going, continuing on from the miniature basin at which they were supposed to drink. It isn't that Me-Me deceived them. Water was there only days ago, they smell the vestige of it and see it in the wilted frill of new grass whiskering the basin's lip. And yet the holes they dig are dry.

The sun climbs. Egrets appear and alight on the raw skin of their spines. Every movement of those little feet feels like stabbing thorns. The wind awakens and sucks the dust into coils that crash into their legs as if with malignant intent. Where the heat has opened the earth, down in several of the widest seams, are heaps of bones, and She-Snorts stops and rummages in one of the seams and lifts out a tiny monkey skull whose odour, like Date Bed's, is frail and pleasant and ambiguous. She-Snorts fondles the skull. She hangs it on the end of one tusk and studies it from that angle. Then she smashes it against a boulder.

The sun is almost overhead by the time they arrive at the place where Me-Me stepped in Date Bed's dung—a small pan surrounded by bleached logs. In the centre of the pan are five Grant's gazelles who come snorting to their feet. A cheetah wouldn't ordinarily frighten them but they are little more than the bones of their ordinary selves, and when Me-Me sinks to her stalking crouch they turn and bound away. Now, where they were, can be seen the fly-swaddled corpse of a newborn fawn.

"I smell water!" She-Screams cries. She hurries past the corpse, which Me-Me is already starting to drag to the logs.

Passing cheetah and fawn, She-Snorts growls but keeps walking. She is scenting hard. She goes to the other side of the pan and out onto the plain, and Mud, She-Soothes and Bent follow. At a deserted ostrich scrape she stops and picks something up.

A hard, blackened morsel of dung.

"How old is it?" Mud says.

"Thirty-five days," She-Snorts murmurs. "Perhaps more."

They smell the morsel in dumb wonder. It is so precious and so paltry. She-Screams, who has already excavated a seepage, comes over and pokes her trunk in among everybody else's. "Thirty-seven days exactly" is her exasperated judgement.

She-Snorts brings the morsel up to her eye. Puts it in her mouth. She declines to drink and begins scenting the terrain for a clue to where Date Bed went from here.

"I'll do that later!" She-Screams yells. "I can do that!"

Me-Me is the one who turns around.

"I'm not talking to you!" She-Screams yells, sounding almost fond.

With a jerk of her head Me-Me fixes on Bent.

"What are you gawking at!" She-Soothes roars.

Me-Me resumes ripping apart the fawn. Out on the plain the gazelles watch.

"Thirty-seven days!" She-Screams cries, as all of them except She-Snorts head back to the centre of the pan. "I wish somebody would explain to me what use we will be to Date Bed if we are corpses by the time we find her!" She glances at the matriarch and lowers her voice. "*If* we find her. We have been searching for forty-two days. Do you realize that? Forty-two days, wandering like lost newborns." At the hole she has a long drink and then says, "I don't know why you stand for it, She-Soothes. Watching Bent suffer."

"Date Bed is lost," the nurse cow mutters. Both she and Mud have excavated their own holes and are waiting for them to fill.

"Oh!" She-Screams lets out a high, crazy laugh. "And we're not?" She drinks again and showers. "When my skull grew," she says, squirting water between her legs, "it split open my skin." She inclines her head to show the nurse cow her crown. "See there? I need one of your water-glory poultices, but what hope is there of that? In my opinion, the wisest course"—she has switched to her sermonizer's voice—"the only course, as our matriarch will eventually realize provided she doesn't die first, is to stop the search right now and have Me-Me lead us to The Safe Place."

"Suppose Me-Me doesn't know where The Safe Place is?" Mud asks.

"At The Safe Place," She-Screams continues as though Mud has not spoken, "we can regain our strength and then go out and search again if we must. For all we know, Date Bed may already be at The Safe Place."

"Suppose Me-Me doesn't know where The Safe Place is?" She-Soothes rumbles without betraying, by her tone, that the question has already been asked.

"She knows," She-Screams answers distantly, and an odd, harsh smell leaks from her hide.

◆ ◆ ◆

She-Snorts finds only a single scent trail. It either approaches from the northeast or heads off that way.

"She must have left more than one trail," She-Screams says, but after a quick search complains that she never knew a calf to have such a thin odour. "What was she doing here, anyway? There's no browse. Not a speck of shade." She turns to the matriarch. "What's the plan? I hope it's not to keep going northeast." Quoting Torrent, she says, "There's only empty plain and more empty plain and at the end of it all is a desert." She starts tapping the warts on her face. "We don't even know if that's the way Date Bed went. It may just as easily be the way she came."

She-Snorts keeps drinking. She is so lean that in the workings of her throat and belly it is possible to track the descent of the water. Her belly is bloated, from hunger or the newborn, Mud can't tell. She is red. They all are. They have coated themselves in the pan's red sand. They are another species, Mud thinks—baked and spiny, frail as insects.

"Are we going northeast?" She-Screams persists.

No answer.

She-Screams nods. They are going northeast, she has concluded. She turns to She-Soothes. "It is the worst drought in living memory," she says. Her measured tone suggests that she and the nurse cow see eye to eye. "And the plan is to head for a desert."

She-Soothes looks at She-Snorts. "Is there spike weed in that desert?" she bellows. Spike-weed oil stimulates the flow of milk.

"I would not go to The Safe Place," She-Snorts says, "knowing that Date Bed might still be alive and lost."

"Nor would I," Mud says. In her shame she weeps. The matriarch's allegiance to Date Bed is steadfast while hers has wavered.

She-Screams whirls on She-Soothes. "And what do *you* have to say?" she cries.

"Is there spike weed in that desert?" the nurse cow rumbles.

❖ ❖ ❖

Behind them, to the southwest, the land smoulders in the low red sun. Ahead is a clarity squandered on so much nothingness. No bushes are visible northeast, no trees except for two poisonous candelabrums. Is this the right direction? As if she can't believe it, Me-Me keeps glancing around. She roosts on termite mounds to wait for them, her gaze on Bent. She is not the leader anymore, and yet she walks out in front.

They haven't chased her off because She-Screams has convinced them that she is their best hope of arriving at The

Safe Place, whether they make use of her now or wait until they find Date Bed. Before quitting the pan She-Screams gyrated through another consultation with the cheetah and afterwards told them she had led Me-Me to believe that the bargain (She-Snorts' newborn in exchange for the location of Date Bed's dung) would be honoured. "But," she said, "in exchange for taking us to The Safe Place, I had to strike a second bargain. So I promised her She-Spurns' newborn."

The matriarch, who hadn't betrayed that she'd been listening, now looked at Mud.

"Our newborns may drop before we arrive at The Safe Place," was all Mud said. The possibility had to be mentioned, she felt, that they could actually be forced to honour their bargains or else lose Me-Me and almost all hope of finding The Safe Place. Hearing her own calm voice, in which no objection to the bargains themselves was perceptible, Mud understood that she had declared her position—between Date Bed and her own newborn she chose Date Bed—and she felt vindicated and worthy, and she felt immeasurably vile.

"Bent is not to be bargained with!" She-Soothes warned.

"Don't worry," She-Screams rumbled.

For what remained of the afternoon they rested. She-Soothes, Bent and She-Snorts slept. Mud lay on her right side and watched Me-Me. Having eaten the gazelle fawn, she was spraying certain logs with her urine. Choosing a log and a spot on the log seemed to require much deliberation and uneasy sniffing. Here? *Here?* On the burning plain the fawn's family waited . . . for an opportunity to mourn the bones, Mud presumed.

She-Screams, who also lay facing the cheetah, whined continuously but at muted volume. Occasionally she glanced at Mud and each time seemed incensed to find her awake, as if Mud were eavesdropping on her torment. She whined about being famished, scorned, sickly, despised, burdened and smarter than everyone else. She said that she was tired of the struggle. "How much longer?" she asked once, and imagining that she was wondering when she would be relieved of this life, Mud silently told her, "Soon."

Late afternoon, with only water and dirt in their bellies, they left the pan. The matriarch set a slow pace for the sake of Bent and She-Soothes. For the sake of all of them. To keep her mind occupied, Mud counted steps. Now, as the light leaves, she finds herself nodding off. At any sudden sound she jerks awake, amazed that while she dozed she did not veer from the course. Lions are nearby, and wild dogs. When a pride passes on their left flank, Me-Me moves back between She-Snorts and She-Screams. The dogs come in close and look around with their twinkling eyes. Dogs tend a low fire in their skulls.

Fires are on the ground, set by fireflies (She-Snorts suspects) because neither she nor She-Screams can smell humans, although it is difficult to pick up scents through the smoke. Like a thousand fallen blossoms the scattered flames flutter wherever the stubble of some despicable vegetation has survived. Between the flames, gangs of hornbills run. "They drive me mad!" She-Screams shrieks, it is not clear why. The hornbills pursue the scorched insects whose odour (She-Screams alone is able to distinguish it from the overall smell of the smoke) also drives her mad. The heat drives her mad. She wails that it is more than she can bear. Later, when the fires are behind them, the cold is more than she can bear. "My feet!" she wails. You would think she'd welcome the rest stops, but when they are called she cries, "Again? Already?"

After the seventh stop, in the middle of the night, Mud offers to carry Bent for a while. She is hauling him up when She-Screams trumpets that she has caught the scent of tubers. Everybody waits while she investigates. Mud falls asleep. And awakens to find Bent trying to suckle her. She pushes him away and, as she does, smells milk. She touches the nipple and brings the wetness to her lips. "I have milk!" she trumpets. Bent latches onto the other nipple.

She-Soothes and She-Snorts hurry to her. They nuzzle her breasts.

"Early milk!" the nurse cow roars.

She-Screams, chewing tubers, comes over but does not touch Mud and does not speak.

"How is it possible?" the matriarch says. She squeezes a breast, and milk jets out.

"It's early milk!" the nurse cow trumpets. "Early milk! You heard She-Cures speak of it." She rears up on her hind legs (and Me-Me, who has crept closer, scuttles away). "Early milk!" She spins in a circle. She is beside herself. "Early milk!"

"Yes, but during a drought," She-Snorts says.

"The She has blessed us!" She-Soothes trumpets. "The She is good. The She is great. Jubilation! She-Spurns is the saviour!"

"I wouldn't go that far," the matriarch says with some of her former drollery. She drops her trunk on Mud's head. "But it is true you have saved *him*."

"Little Bent," Mud says. The tugging sensation, which extends far into her chest, doesn't feel unpleasant, but it doesn't feel entirely harmless, either. She is being drained, after all. It is only milk, she tells herself. It isn't blood. It isn't memory.

✦ ✦ ✦

The sun and moon are warring, although that is not yet known. When a great blessing and a great tragedy happen within hours of each other, then you know. In battles between the holy Mother and Her dissolute son these extreme occurrences are the incidental consequences, the smithereens.

So far this night there have been only blessings. The milk. The tubers, enough to ease their hunger cramps. Later, after they have walked another five thousand steps (with She-Soothes hauling Bent because when Mud takes over he tries to feed), the ground softens and in a sandy ditch they dig water holes. While Mud waits for hers to fill, Bent nurses. Already, by the strength of his tugs, she can feel that he is hardier.

Patches of bitter but edible fire grass are in the vicinity, and the matriarch calls an early halt to the night's trek so that they can forage and celebrate. They sing as they eat. "The Bursting Breast Song" and a hymn of thanksgiving: "Come, Thou Fount of every blessing! Fill my trunk to blare Thy grace. . . ." Strangely, She-Screams, whose off-key shriek usually dominates any chorus, doesn't join in. She feeds apart from them, on thorn bushes, and she talks to herself in an unintelligible whimper. Not far from her Me-Me sits and makes a sound in her throat like breaking twigs.

The fire grass is a sedative, a potent one for cows as debilitated as they are, and Mud, She-Soothes and She-Snorts are obliged to lie down while it is still dark and they are still famished. Bent lies between Mud's legs with his trunk resting on her right teat. She-Screams continues to feed on the thorn bushes. She'll keep a scent on Me-Me, Mud thinks and yet is uneasy and rumbles to She-Snorts, "Matriarch, I'm going to try to stay awake."

"I've got that feeling behind my eyes," She-Snorts murmurs.

Mud recalls Hail Stones telling them—only hours before the slaughter—that She-Demands had a feeling behind her eyes. "That warning feeling?" she asks.

"Yes."

"What does it mean?"

But the matriarch is already snoring.

Alarmed, Mud hauls herself back onto her feet, determined now to fight sleep. She drifts off anyway. She dreams about Date Bed: She and Date Bed are wading among water lettuces in a swamp that transforms into a meadow of consimilis grass, and Date Bed says in her earnest way, "You must understand, we aren't where we think we are," and when she turns, Mud sees that she has no trunk, and out of the cavity where the trunk should be a wind blasts, and a newborn cries, "Mama!"

She wakes up. Bent is gone. A vagrant wind blows, it scatters his cries, which come from the north, then the west, then the northeast.

"Bent!" she trumpets.

She-Soothes and She-Snorts awaken.

"Bent!" the nurse cow roars.

"Where is She-Screams?" She-Snorts says.

Mud is so surprised at the matriarch's mentioning the banished cow's name that it takes her a moment to realize

She-Screams isn't here. She squints into the darkness. "Where is Me-Me?"

She-Soothes starts racing north. They hurry after her, side-stepping guineafowl flushed into the open by her bellows. Bent's odour and calls now arrive from all directions. The wind moans. How can She-Soothes know which way to go? By some grace granted terrified mothers, she does. She goes straight to him.

He sits on his haunches near the edge of an escarpment. "She-Screams is down there!" he cries, shrugging himself free of their trunks.

"What?" the nurse cow roars.

Mud moves to the brink and looks over. The bottom, all blackness, is a long way down. Her vision of She-Screams returns to her. "She *fell*," she thinks, finally understanding the reason for the crushed skull.

"She walked over!" Bent cries.

"Walked over?" the nurse cow roars.

"She may still be alive," Mud says. That her vision could actually have been fulfilled horrifies her, as if she had wished it. She-Screams' new big head . . . shattered. "Is there a path down?" she wonders out loud.

"Bent, what do you mean, 'walked over'?" She-Snorts says.

The drop is sheer, the face of the escarpment one great slab, Mud can discern that much.

"She did it on purpose!" Bent wails and begins to sob, and the wind shifts and throws up a breath of She-Screams' odour in which the fetor of death is detectable.

"Ah, she's gone," Mud says.

Chapter Fourteen

By Date Bed's twenty-third day in the vicinity of the huge acacia she has scratched fifty-three marks on her tusks (forty on the left, thirteen on the right) and made bargains with three martial eagles, three males. Two of the eagles showed up for the first time on the same day—day nineteen. The third arrived only this morning and has already returned twice.

They are enthralled by the Thing, far more so than she could have wished. All three tried to negotiate unlimited daily looks, but that would have restricted the breadth of their search and she held firm to a single look every second day. They tell her that there are no humans or vehicles or other she-ones in their territories and she says, "Go beyond your territories." If humans are headed her way, she wants to know. For a sighting, provided they bring back proof (dung or "skin"* or clutter from the humans; from the she-ones, dung or a message) they will be granted daily looks. The

---
* Clothing

reward for finding and delivering the white bone is the Thing itself.

They perch either on a large boulder or on an abandoned termite mound, and while they study their reflections she holds the Thing and studies them. She can see, this close, how their pupils contract at certain sounds—other birds, and any noise from the dwarf mongooses whose den is in the mound. They have hooded, yellow eyes, empty of expression, and no emotion vents from their bodies, but how they feel is evident by how they stand. One keeps glancing around, and his wings are never still. One sways a little, he seems to swoon into what he sees. The third is transfixed except for his tongue, which flutters in his open bill. This one has a mob of black spots on his belly. The nervous one has hardly any spots, and his right foot turns slightly inwards.

From inches away they are individuals. From more than a yard away they are identical in her dim eyes. It is by their scents that she initially identifies them. The transfixed one, the one she lured this morning, has the most revolting odour. Privately, she calls him Stench. The swooner smells like a stagnant swamp. She can hardly call him Swamp (although, like Swamp, he moves slowly, flying off on sluggish wings), so he is Swoon. The nervous one is Sour.

She could probably attract more than three but she worries about a gang conspiring to steal the Thing. Five or six martial eagles against one sickly calf—she knows who'd win. And too many gazers might weaken the sharpness of the reflections. If speaking of the white bone by name reduces its powers, who's to say that looking into the Thing won't have a similar effect? She herself looks into it no more than twice a day and only if she is especially frightened or dispirited. She holds it up to her stronger left eye and addresses the eye in the formal timbre, saying, "What do you think?" and "Help," saying, "Are you there?"

She is careful to tuck the Thing under her belly whenever she lies down. While teetering through her dizzy spells she tries to keep it within the barricade of her legs, and she wedges it into a bole of the acacia before wandering away to drink or eat or send infrasonic rumbles. She has decided that the earth is almost certainly blocking infrasonic rumbles and yet she continues to send them anyway, two or three a day. Mostly, during the day, she keeps to the acacia's dense shade.

She works at retrieving her memory. Her method is to select a certain shadow memory and pluck from it every part she is certain of—the odour of cattle dung and bruised lilies, a cool dry southwesterly breeze and so on. She then dwells on the parts in turn and allows herself to fall into the other memories that the parts invoke. Sometimes, in the midst of one of these other memories—even if it, too, is incomplete—she recalls a lost fragment of the original shadow memory.

It is a painstaking enterprise, and it won't save her. While she is recapturing one fragment, a thousand others are escaping. To make the effort more worthwhile she tells herself that a recaptured piece of memory is equivalent to an hour of life. She tells herself (and this doesn't seem arbitrary; this, she feels, stands to reason) that you never forget the things you alone witnessed. She means the things outside of yourself. But not a shadow or a tree or rock, because though you may have experienced any of these from a perspective peculiar to you alone, they have also been perceived by others . . . various notions of them exist regardless of you. Not a cry, either, or a clap of thunder or any sound that countless other creatures will have taken account of. Not even an ant climbing a rock, since the ant itself will have recorded a version of that small event. The fluttering of a new leaf is the kind of phenomenon she is thinking of. The dull snap of a wet twig in which no worm resides. At the end of a long life you forget everything except who you are. But who is that? What is left to you? When she had an impeccable memory and the prospect of a long life, she might have said that you are the measure of what your cow name has come to signify. She can imagine (although not recall) having thought something along those lines. Now her hunch is that you are the sum of those incidents only you can testify to, whose existence, without you, would have no earthly acknowledgement.

She has stopped appealing to the She, but she gives thanks and she sings hymns for the pleasure of being able to. No lyric has yet abandoned her. Her singing brings the mongooses. They climb onto her, if she is reclining. If she is standing, they gather at her ankles and scuttle and hop, all of them except for the biggest female, who sits on the summit of the termite mound and scouts for predators. They tell her that the vibration of her singing voice temporarily relieves their skin irritations, but they enjoy the lyrics, too. Incredibly, they understand lyrics. Like other creatures with whom she mind talks, they find her thoughts comprehensible and her speech gibberish. Why they should understand *sung* words, she has no idea. Their explanation, sufficient for them, is that it is because the words are sung. Imparting any kind of general information, they tend to chorus out loud, everybody delivering roughly the same phrase and starting and stopping at roughly the same moment. Their speech is a twittering in which words are repeated two and three times: "Sing, sing, sing the song, song about, the song about the hot, the hot, hot, hot fight, fight, fight." ("Though Hot the Fight" is a hymn promoting faith in the face of insufferable hardship, but they think it glorifies territorial battles.)

They and the martial eagles couldn't express themselves more differently. Thinking and speaking, the eagles use as few words as possible. "There." "How long?" They prefer to gesture. "Bad, bad, bad," the mongooses initially growled at her for deliberately attracting an eagle (they are under the impression that all three eagles are the same one) but within a few days they were clasping her legs and twittering, "Sorry, sorry." The eagles are so hungry to see themselves in the Thing that they ignore the mongooses, as Date Bed promised would be the case. And they fly away the instant the Thing is withdrawn. If any other large birds arrive with the object of hunting, Date Bed trumpets and thrashes her trunk and they fly off as well.

The mongooses are dear to her. They are what she is not: quick, thriving, fierce, part of a family. Well after sunrise they emerge from their den. "Big, Big, Big, Big," the twittering starts. "Big" is their name for both her kind and her individually. Usually she is lying down, and they climb on her and eat her ticks. They are excessively careful, moving as weightlessly as flies and skirting her infected burns. The worst burns cause them to peep sympathetically or screech in alarm. They like to strum their toes along the notches on her tusks where she marks the days. In the crook of her trunk an elderly male sits grooming himself and telling her the story of his life, which is one vicious territorial battle and one riotous mating session after another. He has no name, none of them do. Their name for themselves as a species is "flawless." "This flawless" means I or me, "that flawless" means any other mongoose. Pronouns are used sparingly. "This flawless, this flawless," the old male twitters, "mounted, mounted, mounted that flawless, that flawless, flawless, flawless one hundred, one hundred and nineteen, and, and nineteen times, times, times. . . ."

Finally somebody jumps off to start digging for beetle larvae, and it seems to Date Bed that every morning the whole clan forgets why they came out of the den until one of them remembers and starts doing it, at which point they all leap to the ground and begin a manic search as if to compensate for lost time.

Her own earnest feeding time begins at dusk, after the mongooses have retired. As soon as the last of them is in the termite mound she peels a narrow strip of bark from the acacia, having calculated that by restricting herself to a single short, thin strip per day she will be able to eat sweet bark forty days all together. For the rest of the night she consigns herself to the tasteless, disfigured scrub.

The nights are quiet, and cold. But some nights are not so cold and this is when the fireflies rise from the ground. Thousands of them, flickering in perfect synchrony, a green nebular light in which, for an instant, the silhouette of the acacia erupts, and then blackness again. And then the light. Slow alternating pulses of light, black, light—as if the days are passing in a matter of seconds.

Other nights she is overtaken by hallucinations.

Her fabulous hallucinations, she welcomes them. The wonders she has seen! Corridors flanked by soaring slabs of rock upon whose smooth faces, ground to sky, rows of identical squares are aligned, the squares radiating a white light as if the rock impounds a sublime fire. A conical green tree bristling with short thorns and laden in what appear to be sparkling fruits or flowers of every shape and hue but are actually miniature antelopes, miniature humans (not living, and yet not rotten or ravaged), and the sky around suddenly darkens and the tree is swarming with tiny blue smokeless flames that don't spread beyond themselves.

Has anybody ever witnessed these sights, or even dreamed them? She has begun to think that they must be connected with the seeping of her memory. The lost memories of a creature from a place unknown and unimagined have drifted over the plain and found temporary refuge in the cavities created by her seepage. Her own memories . . . supposedly they linger outside herself until they evaporate, but if it is true that she shelters an exotic's memories, then perhaps *her* memories have entered the body of some strange, doomed creature who, like her, is enthralled by the scenes unfolding in its mind.

Not that the creature would be ceaselessly enthralled. It would be frightened by some of its hallucinations, it would have to be. Terrified. Plenty of what Date Bed has forgotten is nothing she would ever willingly recall.

❖ ❖ ❖

On her twenty-fifth morning under the acacia her odour becomes stronger and muskier. Throughout the rest of the morning and early afternoon she falls into daydreams about Tall Time mounting her. Standing, she is inclined to sway her rump.

Mid-afternoon Sour swoops down and drops before her feet a ball of fresh dung belonging to She-Slanders of the She-S's-And-S's.

The She-S's-And-S's are her closest relations outside of her immediate family. She picks up the ball and the pieces that have fallen away from it, and he perches on the termite mound and says, "Show me."

"In a moment," she thinks. Weeping, she wedges the dung into a crevice of the mound.

He rocks from foot to foot, one eye on the Thing.

"How many in the family?" she thinks.

"Four."

"How many calves?"

"Four cows."

"Ah," she says, breathless with grief. Not a calf left. Her wound buzzes, and she presses it with the knuckle of her trunk. "How did the cows seem to you? Were any sickly?"

"Bony." He tips his head to look at her.

"Did you speak with the mind talker?" Before the drought that would have been She-Scoffs.

A jerk of the head to one side.

"Why not?"

"They have no mind talker."

No mind talker. How odd . . . another family who has become separated from its mind talker. "Where are they?"

He looks southwest.

"How long did it take you to get here?"

He sweeps a wing at the sky, indicating the movement of the sun from mid-morning to now.

"Did you fly fast?"

He flaps his wings, as if to demonstrate. "Show me," he says.

She forces him to wait a little longer. She wants to know exactly where the She-S's-And-S's are, in what kind of place. In a riverbed, he says, among trees. Standing trees? A nod. What breed? Yellow bark. How many? Many.

She decides to make the journey. She can't imagine anybody quitting fever-tree browse in a hurry. A distance that took him five hours to fly, with the wind at his back, will take her three full nights to walk, at least that. She will set off at dusk. Maintaining a straight course will not be as easy for her as it is for him and she asks for geographical markers, although she risks either forgetting them or not seeing them. Another bargain is struck: in exchange for two more daily glimpses of himself, he will track her and correct any deviations. Tomorrow while she rests, just in case the She-S's-And-S's do decide to move elsewhere, he will fly ahead to confirm their location.

So much promised work earns him a lengthy look at himself. When he finally soars away, Stench shows up for his look, and by the time he leaves there are only a few hours to go before dusk. She covers herself in water and dirt and begins to forage. Apparently there is a baobab a third of the way to the riverbed. If she maintains a brisk pace, she should be feeding from that tree by sunrise. There is, moreover, a range of hills east of here, close enough that Sour was surprised when she admitted she couldn't see them. All this time, then, she has been in a vicinity where the white bone is likely to be dropped, even though Sour said that on this side of the hills he has come across no circular formations of termite mounds or boulders. Still, as she walks she will keep an eye out.

The mongooses return and she tells them that she is leaving for at least six days, perhaps longer, perhaps forever, and they clasp her legs and each other and screech, "Danger! Danger! Danger! Peril! Peril! Danger! Danger!" Over the din she tries to reassure them: the eagles have reported that the land is almost free of carnivores and, anyway, a rumour is afoot that she is inedible, poisonous. She swings the Thing and skims a beam of light over the ground and tells them of how the beam scared off the lionesses. They hiss and bristle. They themselves are frightened of the Thing. "Sing, sing, sing, sing," they twitter, and she gives them a few verses of "Oft in Danger, Oft in Woe." Soothed, they start disappearing into their den, the last of them, a muscular female, lingering long enough to twitter, "Big's, Big's scent, Big's scent, scent is, is, is different, is different, different."

It is true, then. All day she has been telling herself that her symptoms aren't really there, that her ungovernable mind has taken it upon itself to delude her. She is too sickly to enter her inaugural oestrus. Too small, too skeletal. She picks up the Thing and looks at her good left eye. "But Tall Time is gone," she says, and tears distort her reflection. She takes it for granted that if she really is in oestrus, then staring at her spirit twin explains how her body gathered the strength to bring the oestrus on. Why, though? Why go into oestrus? Tall Time died at the big water hole, and even if she wanted the attentions of another bull, there aren't any close enough to smell her, much less hear her calling. Thinking of Tall Time as he was when he mounted Mud, she begins to rumble "zeal," that lascivious babble she had assumed, before now, was voluntary.

She walks in circles, rumbling, and so transported that she loses all sense of where she is until swatted in the face by a light. She stops and squints around and spies a big bird flying low over the plain, weighted down by what he carries.

❖ ❖ ❖

The lingering scent is Sour's. "You have cursed yourself!" she thinks to the dissolving blur of him. He keeps flying. She trumpets, and the mongooses re-emerge. Learning what has happened, they hiss, "These flawlesses, these flawlesses will, will rip, rip the stinkard's, the stinkard's wings, wings, wings off, off, claw, claw the stinkard's, the stinkard's guts, the stinkard's guts, guts, guts out, out," and she is touched and pretends to believe that they will stand by their threats and makes them promise not to do anything rash.

Once they are back in the den she takes a long drink. She can't not go. After hours of imagining what it would be like to touch and smell the She-S-And-S cows, the thought of staying is intolerable. She determines precisely where southwest is and sets off, chanting the directions rhythmically, and then working them into rhymes, adding a melody.

> Southwest.
> A burn to my left.
> Dry pond bed, next comes
> A passable cleft.

> Rogue's web.
> Along my right flank.
> Bad trees, a streambed,
> With stones on the bank.

So far the trick has worked. Here is the streambed, here is the stony bank, here she is alive and unmolested. But feeling the absence of the Thing more severely by the hour. The Thing steadied her. Without it she is anxious. The reek of lionesses clings to these stones. Could she defend herself? She is far weaker than she had counted on, having lost the habit of walking, and being driven, during voluptuous states of mind, to strut and to peer coquettishly over her shoulder.

She digs three holes that come up dry. Not wanting to waste any more time, she points herself southwest (verifying her position by the moon and the prevailing west wind, now fallen to a light breeze) and starts walking.

> Rock path.
> A straight narrow burn.
> Fissured brown earth past
> A stink tree upturned. . . .

She reaches the baobab after sunrise. It is so thoroughly gutted she wonders how it can still be standing—her last thought before she falls asleep on her feet. When she opens her eyes the sun is past its meridian. She kicks loose a mound of dirt, throws it over her back. Aside from the tree's smell, the odours here are thin: jackals, and a cobra, but they are old smells. She sniffs for a source of water and in the end excavates enough tubers to slake her thirst and allow her to eat the bit of pulp she is able to prise from the baobab's cavity. She finds a sharp stone and chisels a mark into her tusk. Day fifty-six.

She sleeps again and awakens into darkness. How many hours has she lost? At least five. Anxious, staggering, she hurries away. "Thorn scrub," she sings, "all trampled and ruined, a raised path, a pan, egg-shaped. . . ."

Then what? Something that rhymes with "ruined." Nothing does. But here, underfoot, is the thorn scrub, trampled and ruined. "A pan, egg-shaped. . . ."

It's no good. The rest of that verse is lost. "Southwest," she tells herself. That's all she needs to know. Southwest.

The other verses are similarly butchered. She sings what she can remember and hums what she can't. She fights the fall into hallucinations and memories. Alertness is essential. Somewhere in this vicinity there are human dwellings: ". . . hindlegger nests on a circular ridge. . . ."

Midway through in the night her right hind leg develops a wobble. It may be from the strain of all that carnal hip-swaying, but it's possible she has been bitten by a snake and, if so, she needs sausage-tree fruit or palm fruit, the antidotes. A little farther on, as she is threading through a colony of termite mounds, she hears a snort. Terrified, she stops and scents. It is a giraffe. Two giraffes, a female and a calf. "Masters!" she thinks joyfully. They will tell her where she is, where water is! She moves blindly toward them. They gallop off. Through the pall of dust she smells palm hearts. But it is a memory of smell.

The madness starts there. For the next three days she is lost in memories. They aren't even shadow memories, they are a mixture of the remaining fragments, a corrupt redisposition. She is wading in a pond and surely it should be Mud who is with her, not Swamp, and Swamp says something that was said, yes, but never by him. A helpless part of her *knows*.

When she emerges into the present—and she does, briefly, every few hours—she discovers that she is otherwise behaving rationally. Lying in the shade. Drinking. While her mind was looping through its shambles she must have sniffed out water and dug a hole! She wonders if her practical mind operates more cunningly when she is unaware of it. She has obviously decided she should return to the acacia. Every time she finds herself on the move, she is labouring along (no longer strutting, her oestrus has passed) in a northeasterly direction.

On the second night, there she is having an apparently cordial conversation with five wild dogs.

"Or is it only yourself?" a big male is asking.

She blinks at him, trying to imagine the question and finally answering, "Not only myself," because of safety in numbers.

He backs away. "The smell is evil," he growls, and she guesses that he is referring to her leg and that his question concerned the rumour that she is poisonous.

On her right hind shin is a putrid sore. If she was, after all, bitten by a snake, no snake she has ever heard of would leave such a mark and provoke the kind of derangement she is suffering. She tells herself that once she is back at the tree she will start to heal. She is not without hope that Sour will feel cursed by his thievery and return the Thing and she will be able to look into her eye again and locate her sanity.

✦ ✦ ✦

She is lying under the acacia, breathing in its ancient, elaborate odour, and the mongooses are scuttling up and down her body and twittering, "Reek, reek, reek."

She touches her trunk to the ones she can reach, their quivering little bodies, and in the bliss of being among them again she urinates and streams temporin, and the mongooses near her skull dab at the exudant and twitter, "Sticky, sticky."

"Flow-stick bite," she thinks to explain the foul smell, and they growl and spit and say how, if they'd been there, they'd have "chewed, chewed the, the stinkard's, stinkard's, stinkard's head, head, head" and beaten the stinkard against a rock and so on.

"How long was I away?" she asks.

"Four, four, four days, days, four days."

"Get off me now," she thinks, all of a sudden conscious of her enormous thirst.

In the riverbed she digs a water hole at a spot they recommend. As she waits for the hole to fill, and then as she drinks, they are strangely quiet. It isn't until she begins to shower that they chorus that yesterday a lone female cheetah showed up and ate two of their young ("that new flawless and that new flawless"). Date Bed staggers and they dash away from her feet. She can't believe how hideous she feels, as if the infants belonged to her own family. She begins to weep. The mongooses don't. They become enraged, remembering. They slam their hips into each other and describe how they lunged at the cheetah and tried to bite her. They perform a re-enactment, finishing with a chorus of "Killed! Killed! Killed!" and then they abruptly calm down and advise her to feed herself. Still weeping, she dislodges a length of bark from the acacia. While she eats they tell her that on the morning after her departure, the martial eagle (they continue to believe there is only the one) returned many times and perched on the termite mound. Did he have the Thing? she asks. "No, no, no, no!" they screech, alarmed because of their fear of it, but then they swear that had they seen it they would have retrieved it for her by "biting, biting, biting the, the, the stinkard's, the stinkard's wings, wings" and various other tactics.

She falls into memories.

When she resurfaces, the sun is overhead. She is on her feet, and the mongooses forage nearby. Squinting, she discerns them scurrying beneath the scrub. Everything shimmers in the heat. No wind, the insects sending out their long lines of sound. She chews bark. She is light-headed, but the stench of her shin wound has diluted and for that she credits the bark. She sings a hymn of thanksgiving: "Blessed be the trees we uproot at our will," and the mongooses come trotting back and are assembling around her ankles when one of them, the lookout, screams, "Wings!" and they all race to the termite mound.

Date Bed cocks her head at the sky. The bird must still be way up there. Or perhaps it is an airplane, she can hear an airplane's roar. She closes her eyes to scent hard, and something drops on the ground behind her.

She turns. Even from this distance, even though dust shrouds it, she sees the sheen, and it is not a light. It is not the Thing.

The mongooses are already there, twittering, "White! White! White!"

She picks it up. It smells faintly of Sour and nothing else. She holds it to her eye.

"Whose, whose is, is, is that bone, that bone, bone, bone?"

She fondles and tastes it. She weeps. The mongooses scream and throw themselves up in the air and against her legs. "Whose, whose is, is that, that, that bone, bone?"

"The white bone," she says out loud. They don't understand and keep screaming. "It is a newborn's rib," she finally thinks. "From one of my kind. It is magical." She curls it under her chin, twists her head around, then jerks forward, flinging her trunk open.

Its landing is obscured by dust. She hurries to it and in sudden exhaustion lowers herself to her knees. The tapered end points southeast. "That way!" she says, amazed, but any direction would have amazed her. The mongooses hop and twitter, wanting to know what she's doing. She gets herself standing, and the mongooses spring from her feet as she toddles through a dizzy spell. When her head has cleared she picks up the bone and throws it a second time and staggers over to the sprouting of dust. Southeast.

She cherishes the bone against her throat. "Good-bye," she thinks ecstatically to the mongooses, and starts walking off. "Danger! Danger! Peril! Peril! Peril!" they scream. Their voices and the heat and her breathlessness and all the places on her body that hurt drift out into the passing landscape, no concern of hers. Even as she falls, she believes herself to be walking, and on either side of her the brutal plain slides by.

◆ ◆ ◆

She is lying under the tree. In the strong breeze the weaverbird nests sway and disassemble and bits of yellow grass flock down. Behind her the mongooses forage. She cannot move her legs or her torso, but at the same time every part of her twitches in agony. She waves her trunk across the ground. Lifts her head and squints about, drops her head back down. If the white bone is anywhere nearby, she can't see it.

She thinks, "I am dying."

The acacia smells unusually strong. "Tree," she thinks in a kind of last inventory. "Dung," she thinks, "wound, poison," each of these scents seeming to burst up, to offer itself as a phenomenon no less sublime and yearned for than the white bone itself. She arches her neck and squints toward the plain. "Dust," she thinks, "bush," and as her vision closes into herself—"stone, dirt, me, Date Bed."

She can't remember (perhaps she never knew) but she suspects that you don't become a sky cow unless you have been designated a She. Twisting her head so that she is looking at the sun, she says, "From this day forward and forevermore, Date Bed shall be She-Soothes-And-Soothes."

Nothing happens. There is no change in the strength of the breeze, no branch falls from the tree. The big cows would now say, "The She approves."

Date Bed says, "So be it," and closes her eyes.

Chapter Fifteen

Only hours after promising I-Flounder that he will be able to lead the We-F's to the spot where the white bone was thrown, Tall Time is forced to confess that he has never been anywhere near that region. By now he has fallen into a memory of the blue hills he saw, just once, ten years earlier; he has studied their profile and compared them to the profile of the hills in his vision, and even making allowances for perspective and distance, there is no pretending they are the same range.

"We shall find them" is I-Flounder's response.

"How?"

"From your descriptions of the landscape it was immediately apparent to us where they were."

He is dumbfounded. Humiliated. "Where?"

"Our method of calibrating location would not be comprehensible to you."

"I'd be interested in hearing it, all the same."

"You are ashamed," she says crisply. "Don't be. You cannot be expected to know what is beyond your capacity to know."

The White Bone

Once the trek is under way, his shame is not so crushing. The Lost Ones outmatch him when it comes to scenting water and hazards and moving rapidly through the darkness, which they do grasping tails and thundering song, rods of green light sweeping from their eyes like celestial antennae. But all of them except for the melancholy Sink Hole are jittery, too easily alarmed. At the smell of lions they run. At the sound of aircraft they stop dead. They don't have his endurance either, or his tolerance for heat. Most of the day, under a coating of sand, he sleeps. Not them. Almost buried in sand they pant and burn and drift in and out of visions, none of which they tell. At the end of the second day the skin of the calves is so severely blistered that I-Flounder makes the decision to return to the cave and await the rains. Without consulting him, it is decided that Sink Hole, whose skin remained relatively unscorched, will remain behind as his guide and his charge. Once the two of them arrive at the blue hills, Tall Time will retrace the route revealed to him in his vision and Sink Hole will "correct any blunders."

"Between the two of you," I-Flounder says, "there is but the one tracker."

A tracker who, it turns out, is every bit as masterful as I-Flounder herself. He steers the course away from ominous scents and sounds, if there is browse he finds it. More than I-Flounder appeared to, he takes account of omens and signs. Should Tall Time mention what a feature of the terrain signifies according to *his* prognosticators—and out of some despairing urge to instruct, he often does—Sink Hole snorts or ignores him, which wounds Tall Time only a little. Let Sink Hole snort at the old lore, it's not as if Tall Time hasn't. For the record (Tall Time can't help keeping one) both varieties of signs have so far been accurate. Proof of nothing. Proof of coincidence.

They travel, the pair of them, with Sink Hole out front, silent and not singing. There is no hint that Tall Time should hold the bull calf's tail. As soon as they were alone together Tall Time awaited the twitch that would say, "Grasp." He felt obliged in those first moments to make conversation: "Just you and I, a bachelor herd of two." "When I first set off on my own, I was scarcely ten years old, which is younger than you are, I'll warrant." Sink Hole moved farther away from him. Now when they are on the move Tall Time talks under his breath. Occasionally he sings . . . hymns, prayers for Mud's safety and songs about being astonished—"Well, I'll Be!" or "Incredible, Inedible." Here he is, trotting blindly behind a calf he hardly knows, who himself blindly obeys what can hardly be known, since the omens are infinite and contradictory. The calf turns, Tall Time turns. The calf stops, Tall Time stops.

The stops are frequent because Sink Hole needs to catch his breath. The Lost One cows also took plenty of rests. To Tall Time's suggestion that they walk more slowly, I-Flounder said, "There is but the one pace." This was in the desert. Here in the plain—which he and Sink Hole entered on their second day together—he can forage during the halts. He tusks for grass roots and devours the bitter shrub. Sink Hole, who eats remarkably little, pants and watches him, and under those molten eyes Tall Time snaps into his instructor's role and cracks into the earth as he believes you should, with many sharp pokes rather than with the steady prising that risks breaking off the tip of the tusk.

The White Bone

They are heading southeast into flat, rocky terrain. It is no use asking Sink Hole where they are going, or even when they will be stopping for the day, such questions invariably being met with an odour of disapproval so powerful it burns the inside of Tall Time's trunk. When they make a rest stop, Sink Hole lies down at least ten feet away from Tall Time, and he refuses to drink at the seepages Tall Time excavates. He digs his own . . . slow, tiring work for somebody so small. As Tall Time fills his trunk and throws water over his back he watches this pointless enterprise with pity and irritation and bafflement.

Several hours before dusk on their fourth day together they stop at a grove of dead cordia ovalis trees. A herd of impalas loiters nearby, probably because the smell of water vents from a nearby ditch. It takes Tall Time almost an hour of tusking through layers of shale, however, before he hits the aquifer. Sink Hole carries on digging for another quarter of an hour or so, then gives up and goes over to the trees.

"You must drink," Tall Time says.

Sink Hole lies down. "I will continue digging after I sleep."

Tall Time tosses his trunk toward the impalas. "If you don't drain this hole, they will."

"They are welcome to it," Sink Hole says and closes his eyes.

Tall Time moves between the two tallest trees and starts scraping away the top layers of dirt and then decides to doze on his feet. While he waits for sleep he scents toward Sink Hole and wonders how anyone so young can be so proud and uncivil. Well, it is not as though Sink Hole is an oddity among the We-F's, Tall Time has to allow the bull calf that much.

I-Flounder is scarcely an exemplar of courtesy. And I-Fix . . . her antagonism veers on derangement.

He remembers Torrent saying that the Lost Ones are vain, and that this is why they prefix their individual names with "I" and their family names with "We." But as Tall Time starts nodding off he wonders whether it isn't the other way around: they are vain *because* of their names. It strikes him as not improbable that cows who constantly hear themselves being called I, in families who know themselves as We, may form the impression that beyond their own skin the worth of the world dwindles.

He wakes up at dawn. Sink Hole is still asleep. Since the sun will soon be hot, Tall Time walks over to the bull and sprays him with dirt. Sink Hole opens his eyes. Their green blaze is so strong that Tall Time takes a step back.

"I had a vision of your birth family," Sink Hole says.

"Just now?"

"Before you arrived at High Hill."

"Yes?"

"They were at a big water hole. You had been there earlier in the day and had told them to leave the place."

Tall Time's heart starts booming. "That's right," he says.

"The big cows were arguing about whether or not to take your advice. The matriarch wanted to go, but another cow, your mother, wanted to stay."

"My adoptive mother," Tall Time says softly.

Sink Hole comes to his feet. "They spoke of that longbody, Me-Me."

Tall Time only now hears how strange Sink Hole's voice sounds. Moodless and far away, almost identical, in fact, to an infrasonic rumble.

"She had told them about green browse to the north," Sink Hole says.

"What did the cows decide?"

Sink Hole looks at him, looks away. "As soon as they started talking about the longbody," he says, "I felt a foreboding, and the next instant I heard the shots. Three very quickly. The matriarch fell. After that, there were many shots. I didn't see the hindleggers. My third eye stayed with the family. I saw everybody fall. They all fell."

Tall Time looks out over the plain. The upper ridges of every bush and termite mound are rimmed orange. A myriad horizons. A myriad infinities. He says, "Why do you tell me this now?"

"I was instructed to in a dream."

"Instructed by whom?"

"That is not for you to ask."

Tall Time walks back to the two tall trees. "Go away," he says.

"I was ordered to stay with you."

"Go away. Leave me alone." He lies down, his rump to the calf. He should have warned She-Brags. He *did* warn her! But he should have been more forceful, more frightened. He should have known what was coming. He falls into a memory.

✦ ✦ ✦

He didn't expect the calf to do what he said! The calf never did what he said!

No, let him be honest. He knew that Sink Hole would go. Knew he was going, heard him—at the verges of the memory—trotting off, that sour odour thinning to a wisp.

There are footprints and a scent trail heading north. Tall Time follows them. The footprints are so small. What chance will Sink Hole have against the hyenas that are everywhere? He'll avoid them, as he has done so far. But can he? Avoid every pack, and the lionesses as well? The humans? "Between the two of you, there is but the one tracker," Tall Time says out loud, to reassure himself. To punish himself.

A master tracker, if he doesn't want to be pursued by his own kind, won't be, and after several hundred yards the trails veer east, then south, then they disappear, as if Sink Hole lifted off into the sky.

It is early afternoon. Cones of dust race like a suggestion of manic scrambling Tall Time has the panic for but not the stamina. Where would Sink Hole have gone? Tall Time can't imagine a calf as proud and self-reliant as Sink Hole returning to his family, but perhaps among Lost Ones there is no shame in a young bull running back to the herd. Should Tall Time go after him, cross the desert a third time for the sake of satisfying himself that Sink Hole is safe? What if he gets there and learns that Sink Hole never turned up? What will the withering I-Flounder have to say to that?

He decides that Sink Hole is headed for the blue hills. And it dawns on him that without Sink Hole he has no hope of finding the blue hills or The Safe Place, and he thinks he will have to return to High Hill after all and plead with the Lost One cows for directions, and the prospect of doing that is so discouraging that he finds himself scanning his surroundings for some counsel.

Not far to his left a marabou stork sits rattling its bill on a log. Tall Time trumpets and the stork takes off, circling

The White Bone

east once it is level. East, then. He should go east, as he has been going all along, toward Blood Swamp. So says the stork sign. Which cannot be trusted. And therefore he should not go east.

But he does.

✦ ✦ ✦

The fever trees are uprooted and stripped and covered with hooded vultures, who sit in crammed lines and monitor the shore. The shore is likewise crammed. Wildebeests, hartebeests, topis, zebras, gazelles, impalas, baboons, crocodiles and more creatures than these, many more than when Tall Time was last here. Queerly still and silent, all of them, like spellbound spectators of Torrent's dreadful performance.

In the centre of the swamp, or what *was* the swamp, the old bull throws clods of muck and bellows a deranged version of "The Mounting Song"—"Jump on the kind eggs, don't call quack" instead of "Up on the hindlegs, don't fall back." He is the only she-one here.

"The Trunk Bull!" Tall Time trumpets. The bellowing doesn't let up, but the vultures Tall Time is next to shunt farther along their log, and he kicks out at them and they halfheartedly hobble away.

He descends the bank and clatters over the turmoil of bones. As the throng parts before him, he sees the carcasses—nothing but anonymous hides draped over bones by now. At a water hole guarded by a baboon he lowers his trunk. The baboon hops to one side, grunting and slapping the ground. Tall Time removes the mat of she-one skin that covers the hole and drinks. He watches Torrent, who still hasn't noticed him.

"... When you make that sound! And she's lean and round...."

Where does he get the vigour to roar like that? No soft browse is left, he probably isn't eating at all. From here, Tall Time can see the spine pushing against the hide. He enters a memory of Torrent when they were last together and emerges from it weeping at the defection of so much flesh and knowledge in only forty days.

"The Trunk Bull!" he trumpets again. This time the roaring stops. As he heads into the basin his feet smash through crust to ooze, and then there is only ooze and rotting catfish and submerged crocodiles whose steep, toothy jaws thrash up out of nowhere. Next to Torrent a crocodile executes slow rolls. Just as Tall Time reaches out his trunk in greeting, Torrent's attention is caught by this disturbance at his knees.

"They do that," he rumbles, "and then they die."

"How odd," Tall Time says, his spirits lifting a little. The old patriarch's mind is not completely gone.

Torrent turns to him. "What do you want?"

"Torrent, it's Tall Time." He touches the bull's mouth. "Tall Time the Link Bull."

Torrent pokes his trunk right into Tall Time's mouth and grips his molars. Withdrawing, he mutters, "Can't tell the smell." His own scent is sickly sweet.

"We are friends," Tall Time says.

Torrent's eyes fade into the smoke of his dreams. He looks ancient, the cracked mud on his skin magnifying the ornate webwork of wrinkles underneath. Conscious now that his own skin is unprotected, Tall Time lowers himself to his knees and onto his side and rocks back and forth until he is coated in muck. When he is standing again, he squirts fresh muck on Torrent, who fixes him with a ferocious look and roars, "Where's the browse?"

"Gone," Tall Time says carefully, in the formal timbre. "You have to go up onto the bank, but what remains is woody, I'm afraid. Difficult to chew."

"Difficult to chew!" Torrent roars. He tosses his head, and Tall Time lurches out of the way. "Difficult to spew," Torrent mutters. He hangs his trunk over his left tusk. "A sheet of heat."

"I am Tall Time," Tall Time tries again. "Son of She-Bellows-And-Bellows of the She-B's-And-B's. Tall Time the Link Bull."

"They do that," Torrent says, "and then they die."

There is no breeze, not down here, and the odours of rot and mud hover in separate, motionless layers. Tall Time turns in a circle. Hundreds of days of searching to end up in this cursed, familiar place. Not that it makes any difference to him but the signs are neither threatening nor promising. Nothing will happen, the signs say, nothing that isn't happening already. It is as safe to stay as it is to go.

Go where?

"Have the She-S's been here?" he asks. "Since I left?"

Torrent looks toward the shore.

"The She-S's. Did they return?"

Wisps of what smells like fresh sadness vent from Torrent's hide, and Tall Time notices that where the crocodile was rolling, the muck has smoothed over. He searches with his foot and finds the corpse and shoves it out of the way so that he can stand there and give Torrent his shade. He is desperate to eat but doesn't want to leave the old bull's side, not yet. Later, toward dusk, Torrent may be agreeable to going up onto the bank and even accepting chewed browse, although that's unlikely because it's demeaning and a mountain of browse won't save anybody so sapped of memory. What remains to him? Tall Time wonders. What thoughts and smells, what names? Or are there only sensations and a clutter of incompatible words?

"She-Snorts," he says, testing.

Torrent looks down at the muck.

"I met the Lost Ones." Another test, but also he longs to broadcast it—his big news.

Torrent closes his eyes.

"I had a vision," Tall Time says. "A true vision. I saw the that-way bone." He waits. "The white bone," he says loudly.

"The light moan," Torrent mutters.

"I met the Lost Ones," Tall Time says again, and tells the whole story, from coming upon the We-F calves to seeing the likenesses on the wall of the Lost Ones' cave to setting out with the We-F's and finally parting ways with Sink Hole. Torrent's eyes stay closed. It isn't quite like talking to nobody. Even if Torrent is asleep, he hears . . . the words drift into his skull and roam the scoured cavity of his body, and it would seem to Tall Time that some of them must stick. "There is but one Torrent the Trunk Bull," he says when there is nothing more to tell, repeating this pronouncement from I-Flounder because if "who you are" is all you take to your death, then perhaps words that flatter stand a chance of being grasped.

Torrent opens his eyes. "Those blue hills," he says. "I know where they are."

"I beg your pardon?"

Torrent glances at him, a look of perfect lucidity. "There's a giant feast tree to the west of them."

Tall Time nods.

Torrent points his trunk southwest. "Exactly there. A five-day trek."

Tall Time goes on nodding.

"You doubt me?"

"No, no." Shaking his head now.

Torrent points again.

"You will accompany me," Tall Time says.

Torrent looks away.

"I'll help you," Tall Time says, not knowing how, but prepared to do whatever he must. Torrent obviously contains more memory than Tall Time had at first thought. He scans the old bull's flanks, and his optimism dies. Torrent wouldn't even survive the trek to the blue hills, let alone to The Safe Place; it would be cruel to persuade him to leave. "Of course," he murmurs, "it is for you to decide."

Torrent squints at him. "Where did you come from?"

"Most recently?" Tall Time asks, confused.

The old bull glares sidelong, showing the whites of his eyes.

"Most recently, from High Hill. The We-F's cave. Truthfully, Torrent. I crossed the desert—"

"Lunatic!" Torrent roars. Temporin slides down his face. His penis dribbles urine. He seems, suddenly, to have gone into musth. "Twig-tusk!"

Tall Time starts stepping backwards, not far enough. Torrent charges him. He chases him all the way to the bank and then returns in a tusk-thrashing, hip-swinging saunter to the centre of the swamp and starts throwing clods of muck and bellowing his mad rendition of "The Mounting Song"—"when you skin your shank, and you're pink and rank"—and Tall Time finds himself laughing at how marvellous it is that the old bull can still muster so much power and lust. But as the singing persists, the same tune, the preposterous lyrics, it isn't funny. It isn't even tragic. It's a marvel of a different order—an old bull dying the way the old bulls are meant to die, as they died before the drought and slaughters.

◆ ◆ ◆

He has decided to leave. Tusking for roots on the bank, out of sight of the patriarch, he feels an urgency to go to the blue hills. Date Bed will no longer be there, of course (he imagines her fattening up in The Safe Place), but it is not unlikely that the She-S's will have tracked her, either to the hills or beyond. If he discovers no sign of them he will continue on to The Safe Place with the hope of finding that they have arrived ahead of him. At the very least Date Bed may know something of Mud's fate. And one day, when this dark era has passed, he will return and properly mourn Torrent's bones.

He eats enough to sustain him until morning and then descends the bank for a drink. The bellowing has ebbed to a passionate groaning, but Torrent himself, in the moonlight, looks like his former huge, forbidding self. Tall Time is grateful that this—and not the mud-slinging cadaver—should be his last sight of the old bull. "Good-bye!" he trumpets and is ignored.

The White Bone

He walks up the bank and out onto the plain, where he is surprised by a feeling of euphoria having to do with his own strength and escape. The farther he goes the wider the feeling. The world is before him, infinity drops away at his back. For all that he is following the directions of a deranged bull, he has no doubt that he is going exactly the right way. Not once, in thirty years of being guided by the speechless messages of his surroundings, did he ever feel this certain. There is a membrane of moonlight on the ground, bats flare up, terrible omens he strides through as if in defiance of a natural law.

He hears the helicopter but keeps walking until a cone of white light drops from the helicopter's belly. He halts. The light finds him. He runs, the light keeping pace. Gunshot pits the earth at his feet, and he spins around into the fog of his own dust.

The shots that pelt his hide feel as light as rain. It is bewildering to be brought down under their little weight.

Chapter Sixteen

From what Bent tells them, and from what they can gather, it seems that when he opened his eyes She-Screams was above him, whispering that she thought she had spotted the white bone but wasn't sure. She didn't want to disturb the cows until she was sure. Would he come take a look?

She lifted him to his feet and tucked her trunk between his hinds legs as they hurried away. He had been having a dream about She-Snorts saying that the white bone was a bird, and now he asked, "Did it have wings?" No answer. He smelled Me-Me and said that the cheetah was following them, and she said, "You shouldn't have to die slowly. I won't let you die slowly." This frightened him. So did her nervous scent and Me-Me's odour and he told her he wanted to go back to his mother. "Your mother can't help you," she said. Whereas she could, he took her to mean. They had reached the edge of the escarpment. "Is it down there?" he asked, peering over. "Don't move," she said and rushed off, and he supposed she was dealing with Me-Me. But the smell of the cheetah grew thicker not thinner and when he looked around, Me-Me was behind him. He started to run. Me-Me caught him and grasped him around the neck. He was unable to scream. She licked his ear. The next thing he knew, She-Screams was there. She kicked out and Me-Me flew off his back and raced away bleating. She-Screams walked past him. "Where are you going?" he cried. At the edge of the escarpment she didn't even pause.

"Why did she do that?" he asks now as She-Soothes, Mud and She-Snorts scan his hide for injuries. They don't answer, thus revealing to each other that they suspect the same thing: She-Screams lured him to Me-Me and then had a calamitous attack of remorse.

"Not a single gash," She-Soothes says, surprised.

"Why *did* she?" Bent persists.

"Because—" She-Soothes sighs, and Mud thinks she is about to tell him the truth but the sigh is because she is about to deceive him. "She had heat sleep," she says. "She thought she could float. Cows suffering from heat sleep often walk over cliffs. It is not a bad way to die."

He is too young to pick up the tinge of deviousness in her scent. "She kicked Me-Me," he says, awed.

"Yes, she saved you."

"What about the white— What about the white prize?" he says, worried again.

"She didn't really see it. Heat sleep plays tricks with your vision." She nudges Mud to lift her leg so that he can suckle.

They remain at the brink of the escarpment, and while Bent sleeps they forage on the roots that loop out of the ground like the half-buried ribs of small animals. Although they are exhausted from having eaten the fire grass, there is no question of them closing their eyes. Every once in a while the wind throws up a waft of She-Screams' cow scent entwined with her death fetor. The scent of Me-Me is gone. It is a cold night and Mud sees an orange ring around the moon. When she tells the others, She-Snorts observes that the She and Rogue must have been battling.

"You had that feeling behind your eyes," Mud says, "before you fell asleep."

"What feeling?" She-Soothes wants to know.

"That feeling that something terrible was going to happen," She-Snorts answers.

"And so it did," She-Soothes says.

"But I still have that feeling," She-Snorts says.

"Is it about Bent?" She-Soothes roars.

"No," She-Snorts says weakly. "I don't know. Don't wake him."

"Well," She-Soothes rumbles. A little later she mutters, "She told She-Soothes not to worry," referring to the assurance She-Screams gave her, only yesterday, that Bent wouldn't be bargained with.

The wind dies. In the grey dawn light, Mud looks over the escarpment. Mist, and the sheer, mauve cliff face. She and the matriarch search for a way down and finally settle on a zigzagging breach about thirty yards along the crest. A wedge of geese comes flying and honking across the canyon, and Bent wakes up. Mud suckles him and then the four of them set off. It is a slow descent, what with Bent's feeble knees and her bad leg. When they are halfway down, a troop of baboons tumbles past them and they have a moment of panic before they realize that the baboons aren't boulders.

At the bottom is a ditch and the wreckage of the fallen acacias Mud saw in her vision. The body is visible from here, and as they get closer to it Mud is surprised by sadness. Last night there was only incomprehension and horror and an older sensation of relief, which she finally felt entitled to. The skull is clearly smaller, not only because it is smashed, and they guess that the faculties She-Screams inherited from the She-A's-And-A's must have slipped out through the fractures.

"That damn head is what undid her," She-Soothes growls. "She wasn't fit to lug around such a big head."

There are no scavengers, not yet, and no signs of Me-Me. How will they get to The Safe Place without the cheetah? Mud feels unprepared to ask this question, even of herself. She passes one hind foot over the body and urges all her thoughts toward releasing the spirit. Only Bent weeps obviously, but when She-Snorts starts up the hymn ("Joy Abounding," an odd selection for such an occasion), She-Soothes begins to blubber. Both Mud and She-Snorts look at her in astonishment—you would think she'd be the least forgiving—and she shakes her head, helpless in her grief until the end of the hymn. Then she blinks and sniffs the air and rumbles, "She-Soothes is parched."

They drink at the water holes Mud saw in her vision. As they enter the pool of muck, the resident crocodile thrashes to the opposite shore and poses sidelong, steam rising in curls from her checkered back. Thorny grass grows in the ditch, and after their wallow they forage on that. She-Soothes also eats impala dung and drinks Bent's urine, which she declares much tastier now that Mud is nursing him. By the time they head out onto the plain the dust is spinning.

For three days they plod northeast on a filament of hope that Date Bed set off from the pan in that direction. Early afternoon on that first day they arrive at a range of blue hills running north-south several miles to their left.

The matriarch halts.

"We are on the wrong side of those!" the nurse cow roars.

If they are to find the white bone they should be west of any hills they come across, but it is not a white flash that has arrested She-Snorts, it is an odour. She lifts her trunk and points it toward the hills and shuts her eyes to scent hard, and Mud and She-Soothes lift their trunks likewise but smell nothing. Presently She-Snorts drops her trunk and resumes walking.

"What was it?" the nurse cow roars.

"I'm not certain," She-Snorts murmurs.

"Do you still have that feeling behind your eyes?" Mud asks her.

"Yes."

"The terrible thing hasn't happened," Mud prompts.

"Not yet."

"What do you think it might be?"

She-Snorts shakes her head. She doesn't know.

Bent is stronger and can walk on his own provided that he suckles every few hours and that the pace is moderate. They expect the terrain to become sandier—they are supposedly heading toward a desert—but it remains much the same as it has been since the escarpment: flat, stony, the difference being the profusion of wire fences. Of the fences that bar their way they are able to trample only two. The rest are too powerful, or they burn, and to get past them they have to travel along their length until a gap is found or the fence veers off in another direction. Once through, they cut forward at an angle that eventually brings them back on course, moving more quickly than they want to because human and vehicle tracks are usually somewhere in the vicinity. Hearing the clanging "wattles" of the Masai cattle near noon on the second day, they start to run. Although black grazing humans are said to be harmless, there was a time several generations ago when they weren't.

The following morning, soon after setting off, they arrive at the carcass of an airplane. Smashed snout, broken wings, cracked eyes, shiny impervious guts strewn everywhere, and gathered in and around the torso a pack of wild dogs. As She-Snorts leads them through the scene, two of the dogs, a male and female, urinate right in front of them, the male up on his forefeet, and She-Snorts charges but the damage is done. Farther on, Mud's leg begins to seize. Another bad omen.

Late afternoon finds them on a road banded with the shadows of denuded cycad trees. They smell lions and hyenas and a few moments later hear fighting. About ten yards up the road a large male hyena reels out of the trees. She-Snorts hesitates. She-Soothes moves up beside her. Mud steps back. Blood flies from the hyena's belly as he whirls in a circle, snapping at himself, and when he finally stops it is to begin jerking out his own intestines and devouring them.

They avert their trunks going by. He snarls as if they would rob him of his feast. He is not a bad omen, unless an obscure one, but he is hardly an encouraging spectacle, especially in light of Mud's seizures and the wild dog urinating up on his forefeet, and they continue on in silence. Placing her feet in the footprints of the matriarch, Mud feels a dread that is almost thrilling for being insuperable. They stride hypnotically toward some doom is her impression, and when they halt for the day and She-Snorts rumbles dully, "It's not here," her first thought is that the doom has eluded them.

They are at a streambed among black thorns that fan out of the ground like petrified spray. An outcrop is some fifteen yards to the west and in its shadow they crowd together. "Before," She-Snorts says, "even when there was no sign of her, I never entirely despaired because there was always something in the atmosphere, a quivering. . . ."

"A scent!" the nurse cow booms.

"Not a scent. An urging onward."

The nurse cow nods, uncomprehending. "If She-Soothes knows Date Bed—"

"You don't. You can't, not any longer. None of us are who we were."

This She-Soothes appears to understand, and to lament. She releases a gusty sigh. "Where do we go next, then?" she asks.

"I don't know."

"Don't know!" The nurse cow's face bursts into perplexed alarm and stays like that an instant before squirming for the ray of hope. Mud thinks, She-Soothes is not who she was. In that she used to have an eye where a stinking plug of hyena dung now lodges, in that she used to be sturdy and was never one to sigh, no, she isn't who she was. Otherwise, she seems the same. As for the matriarch, she was once fat and nonchalant and now she is cadaverous and grave, though still clever and a fine scenter and even occasionally droll. The possibility occurs to Mud that, being an outsider, she herself may never have known either cow in the first place. So whatever essential thing about them has changed would not be evident to her.

In which case she never knew Date Bed, either.

It offers itself, this prospect, like an escape route. Her deliverance. If Date Bed is somebody she never really knew, then Date Bed can be lost and the loss will be no more painful than all the other losses have been.

Her next thought startles her, since it isn't hers. But she assumes it is, she takes it for a sudden memory of the matriarch saying, "You're not scenting hard enough, you're too distracted, what about over there?" And yet the words evoke nothing and their ring is strange. As they keep coming—". . . perhaps we should go back to the pan . . ."—and are reflected in the matriarch's face and the motion of her trunk, Mud feels the truth break over her and she says, with light astonishment, "I hear your mind."

✦ ✦ ✦

She feels nothing of the rupturing misery she thought she would. Once the surprise has passed, what she writhes with is anxiety. All this time searching for a doomed calf when they could have been searching for the white bone.

It is the middle of the night, and she and the nurse cow browse on the thorn bushes. For an hour or so She-Soothes sobbed on her knees and hurled every stone in the vicinity. Now she appears completely recovered, although concerned about the matriarch, who hasn't budged or spoken since Mud's revelation. The scent that pulses from She-Snorts is not only grief, it is shame and something porous. Surrender? More likely she languishes in memories. She seems stunned. Twice she has allowed She-Soothes to squirt water into her mouth, and a few moments ago, when She-Soothes bellowed, "You're frightening She-Soothes," her struggling thought was simply, "She-Soothes."

It somehow leaked out, that thought. Both cows are blocking their thoughts as cows will do when they are especially distressed. All Mud picks up from either of them is a low moan. Beneath her, Bent sleeps between bouts of suckling, and *his* thoughts are as distinct as if she had her ear to his throat. Milk, Mud, sore, dead, there, She-Screams, cold, itch, sand . . . he thinks in single panted words except when he is remembering. "Me-Me licked Bent's ear," he thinks once, talking about himself—in the way his mother talks about herself—as if he were somebody else.

Not until mid-morning does the matriarch emerge from her daze. "Perhaps a drink," she rumbles in a sociable tone and commences excavating a hole. A little later a small group of impalas arrive to avail themselves of the water, and She-Soothes wants to chase them off because the streambed is short and shallow. But She-Snorts won't let her. "Be kind," she says, a surprising instruction from her, and unfair considering that She-Soothes has been the kinder one all their lives.

Day becomes night becomes the next day. "What are we still doing here?" Mud complains to She-Soothes.

"She-Soothes will talk to her," the nurse cow says and goes and leans against the matriarch and roars, "Time to think of setting off!"

"Where to?" She-Snorts asks with a lilt of curiosity.

"We've got to find Date Bed! We've got to mourn her bones!"

"How do we find her?"

"We search!"

"In which direction?"

She-Soothes blinks. Don't ask *her*, exclaims her face. *She* isn't the fine scenter.

As their water holes empty they move down the streambed and dig others, and they eat the bordering black thorn. More impalas arrive to drink, also giraffes and oryxes. Today, whenever they look at her, Mud can hear their thoughts. They are apprehensive and thirsty, weary, suffering . . . and grateful, at least the oryxes and impalas are. The giraffes are haughty. "We have every right," they think. They call Mud and her kind snouts, whereas the impalas and oryxes call them fats. What they call themselves Mud doesn't know, she never bothered to ask Date Bed, and not knowing, she can't conceive of addressing them. Besides, why would she?

She asks herself this because they fascinate the matriarch, who frequently sniffs in their direction and several times walks around them and studies them from various vantages. If She-Snorts is not who she was before the slaughter, neither is she who she was before yesterday. She peers at insects and stones, as Date Bed herself did. Without coaxing, she joins She-Soothes in eating oryx dung. She eats dirt. She has no plans.

As an example to her, or from a core of deathless optimism, She-Soothes continues trying to pick up Date Bed's fetor. While she's at it she hunts for the white bone. Even though there are no termite mounds or boulders in the vicinity, Mud hunts as well and can determine at a glance whether the whiteness that has caught She-Soothes' eye is worth investigating. Always it isn't, and yet She-Soothes strolls off and collects the stick or stone anyway. "Close enough!" she roars, seemingly heartened by what aren't even near misses.

The next day dawns. Instead of browsing, She-Snorts occupies herself scraping out a perfect bed on the northwest side of the outcrop. She removes every stick and pebble and she tamps the earth with her feet. The task seems like lunacy to Mud. It is forbidden to listen to the mind of the matriarch but Mud nevertheless tries, and hears only the low moan. Finally she says, "Matriarch, how much longer—"

She-Snorts gives her a blinking, interested look.

"—until we set off?" Mud finishes, jarred. That look is Date Bed's. "Shouldn't we be searching for the white prize?" she presses on. "There's always the possibility that while we're searching we will stumble on . . . on Date Bed's. . . ."

"Carcass," She-Snorts furnishes.

"Yes." She feels upbraided and resents it. She has not wept, not even to herself, she has displayed no grief and she knows she must appear hard-hearted. Well, what if she is? One of them had better be. They are starving. There is a place where they won't starve or be slaughtered, and either they find that place and live, or they die. How will grieving and loitering, how will kindness to impalas, help them? She feels a hundred years older than these two cows, one perpetually baffled, the other sinking into some soft-headed delusion of herself.

"She-Spurns," the matriarch says, in her new, tender voice, "even were I agreeable to wandering aimlessly, we can't leave yet."

"Why?"

She begins to dribble urine. Twisting around to smell it, she says, "Because I am about to drop my newborn."

✦ ✦ ✦

In two days Mud has not once thought about her own newborn, let alone the matriarch's. The commotion in her belly, which used to be the ceaseless reminder, is gone, and suckling Bent requires so little of her that she has stopped thinking about why she produces the milk. She sniffs the matriarch's urine and smells the birth aroma and is horrified at the prospect of the search for the white bone being impaired by a newborn.

The labour drags on. She-Snorts squats, straightens, browses and throws stones until assaulted by another pain, squats again, sometimes rolling onto her side. Meanwhile She-Soothes rumbles encouragement and, when She-Snorts is standing, herds her into the shade and leans against her to take her weight. She tastes the urine but says nothing. If the urine was clear she would bellow that news, clear urine indicating no complications.

Mid-morning, unannounced by a pain, the newborn shoots out and lands rump-first in the bed She-Snorts prepared. She-Soothes quickly tusks open the foetal sac and pulls at the cord wrapped around the newborn's chest. Mud comes closer. It's a male, as She-Scares predicted. He doesn't move. Mud swallows to push down an ache in her throat. "Up you get," She-Soothes rumbles savagely and nudges the tiny brown body with her foot. She-Snorts sniffs his skull, withdraws her trunk, makes a graceful pivot and walks to the other side of the outcrop. She-Soothes thrashes her head. The slap of her ears wakes up Bent, who squeals, "Is it here?" and shunts on his knees toward the corpse, but before he reaches it She-Soothes snatches him by the tail and hauls him back. She-Snorts emerges from the other side of the outcrop. "He shall be Drought," she says as if she only went away to think of a name. Looking off, she sprays him with dirt. She-Soothes and Mud add more dirt, also sticks, and when he is covered, She-Snorts stands over him. Vultures pour down from the empty sky. Hour after hour She-Soothes charges them. Finally She-Snorts says with dreamy unconcern, "Let them be," and then the nurse cow seems suddenly to apprehend her own exhaustion and, with a look of puzzlement, sinks to the ground. The vultures take position on a single thorn bush whose branches bow back like an opening flower.

Mud stands apart from the two cows, upwind to be out of scent. Bent doesn't matter, he wouldn't recognize the relief she vents. To give way to sorrow would be easy, but to be glad—for Drought's sake as much as anyone's—requires a tightening of the mind and breath and blood. When Bent comes up on his knees and suckles, she can't quite believe that anything still flows out of her. She forages on roots and watches the vultures. If one of them should glance in her direction, eyeing Bent, she is able to hear snatches of its gory thoughts, and against these she tests her invincibility. Eventually they begin to sicken her, and she is about to turn her back when one of a pair who is looking at Bent thinks, "Smells like the carcass beyond the blue hills," and its neighbour thinks, "Sweeter."

For a dizzying moment Mud perceives that carcass as they first did: at sunset from above. The purple scent cloud, the particulate clarity, the body in its tensed death pose, head thrown back. The flash of the tusks. That the tusks are there pierces her tempered heart. She goes to the cows and tells them.

"It's Date Bed," she says, and She-Snorts says placidly, "I *thought* I smelled something at those hills."

"She is under a very large feast tree. I can't imagine that we would fail to find her."

"I suppose we could set off at dusk," She-Snorts says.

"Why not now?" Mud says.

She-Snorts cocks her head.

"The sooner we get to her," Mud says bluntly, "the more of her there will be to mourn." She doesn't add, although it is her foremost thought, that the sooner they get to the west of those hills the better their chances of finding the white bone.

"What about this one?" She-Soothes bellows. She touches her trunk to Drought.

The matriarch glances down, glances away. "Forever in oblivion," she sings softly, " 'tis immortality," and the three of them surround the corpse in the outward-facing mourning formation and sing all one hundred and three verses and then take a last drink and leave. Behind them, the vultures shriek. To Mud that sound is outrage and repossession, as if what should never have slipped into the world were being snatched back. Only Bent turns to look.

They hardly make a beeline. Anything that captures the matriarch's attention—an ostrich nest, a bit of blown fur—she wanders over to and sniffs. She stops at a teclea bush and breaks off a twig, holds it to her eye. "All the tiny furrows," she murmurs, and She-Soothes seizes a stick and holds it to *her* eye and roars, "Look at them all!"

Once they are walking again, Mud moves up beside the nurse cow and mutters, "You had better take the lead."

She-Soothes recoils.

"We haven't even travelled a mile," Mud says.

"She's searching for the white—"

"Nothing she has picked up is white," Mud snaps.

"You never know," She-Soothes rumbles unhappily.

"I do," Mud says. "I know."

She-Soothes looks at her. "Has your head grown?" she asks.

The question brings Mud to a stop. "What nonsense," she says as the implication dawns. She stomps away . . . and there goes the matriarch to investigate a wildebeest skeleton, so she stomps past her as well.

Her surprise when she hears the two cows falling in behind her soon stiffens to resentment. She has no illusions that she is the new matriarch. Being the one in front is simply another burden on her shoulders, and a danger, what's more. She keeps an eye out for hyenas, also for termite mounds and boulders despite the unlikelihood of finding the white bone on this side of the hills. She urges a fast pace, which still must be torturously slow to accommodate Bent. Mid-afternoon the wind rises and dust crashes across the plain in swirling pillars and

Bent drops to his knees, screaming he can't, he can't. She-Soothes charges over, but Mud already has her trunk between his hind legs.

"I've got him," she says.

"You're not strong enough!" the nurse cow roars.

"I'm not?" Mud rages and starts to shove the whimpering calf forward. "*I'm* not strong enough?"

Dimly she knows she isn't. Her withered leg cramps, every breath scalds. She would leave her body behind, if she could. Like this ruined family and the newborn within her ribs, her body is what she lugs, out of no choice. She feels the pounding in her temples as her mind clamouring to escape, and she entertains the prospect that she really did inherit the cleverness that leaked out of She-Screams. She touches her head to feel whether it's bigger. Hard to tell.

By sunset, with the wind down, Bent can walk on his own. Since the matriarch is no longer trying to detect Date Bed's dung, the underscents are no longer a concern, and Mud decides that they should keep going until dawn. In the middle of the night a gang of hyenas attends them on all sides, and neither She-Soothes nor She-Snorts cares. But Mud, annoyed at the hyenas' presumption and thrilling at her own absence of fear, drives them off.

"Ten couldn't bring down a she-one," she crows to Bent.

"I know," he says.

"Well," she says, brusquely. Of course he knew, even Bent knew. "*I* didn't."

Dawn arrives, the sun climbs. Mud wants to press on until at least noon but the matriarch begins to stagger and she herself is limping badly and fighting the treacherous descent into memories of Date Bed, treacherous for how they may unbrace her, and she calls a halt on the shore of a pan. That her head is indeed bigger seems confirmed when she is the first to excavate a water hole. After drinking and showering she lies apart from the cows, whose grief she finds stifling. Behind her a pair of plovers calls in that loud irritating way they have that is like two stones being knocked together, and she is on the verge of getting up and charging them when she feels her third eye opening.

It is a vision of the near future. Dawn. A smoky yellow light. Transecting hippo paths, all muck, tiny green leaves on the thorn bushes. Five hippos walk in a line. Their backs bristle with oxpeckers. The screech of queleas, thousands of them . . . and here they are, rising from a swamp as if sucked by a funnel of wind. In the air they form a square mat that shifts this way, that way. The hippos arrive at the swamp. Sighing, they slip into the papyrus. The crocodiles sink down. The separate cries of the queleas attenuate to a single, rapidly fading creak. Mud doesn't recognize this place. She doesn't recognize the voice. "I envisioned the lilies," it says and sounds like a bull calf but can't be, bulls don't have visions. It is, though. A little bull calf. Outlandishly long tusks, small ears. With the certainty visions provide, she knows that he is a Lost One. Behind him are two big cows of her kind and behind them is a newborn whose tail is in the grip of its mother's trunk. The cows are strangers to Mud. Her eye lifts and sweeps over more of them—cows, calves, newborns. From this height they are like stepping stones. The plain glints with the green of new grass. On her eye goes, along a road pocked with water pools, off the road to a resting vehicle. Perched in the vehicle's back cavity is a human. It stares toward the swamp. If humans feel emotions she would say that this one feels amusement. When its head turns in her direction, her third eye closes.

She comes to her feet. "Let's go," she says.

"Where?" Bent says.

To The Safe Place . . . but the words don't reach her mouth. Where? she thinks.

"What's the matter?" Bent says.

"Quiet. It's all right. I had a vision."

"Oh." He goes still and reverent.

"I don't know the way," she says miserably.

"Was it a bad vision?"

She glances down. What a doomed little creature he seems. "No," she says. "It had rained."

"Here?"

"There."

"Where?"

"I don't know. I don't know."

She sleeps standing. When she awakens it is late afternoon, and She-Snorts has moved onto the pan and is scenting to the south. Mud sees the approaching shape and the shadow streaking eastward. "Me-Me!" she exclaims.

The matriarch starts walking back. "I was dreaming about her," she says in wonderment, vaguely mystified.

"Bent!" The nurse cow is scrambling to her feet. Bent rushes to her. "Be off!" she trumpets over the plain.

"Are you mad?" Mud cries.

"She-Soothes wants to charge!" the nurse cow roars.

Mud slaps the bigger cow, who rears back, stunned. "You

listen to me," Mud rages. "I have envisioned The Safe Place and she is going to take us there."

She-Soothes gapes down at her.

"I will warn her to stay away from Bent," Mud says.

"She is lame," the matriarch observes mildly.

Mud whirls around to see. So she is: a buckling of the right foreleg, the result, no doubt, of being kicked by She-Screams. About fifteen yards away she stops and sits. Mud casts a warning glare at the nurse cow and starts forward. The cheetah rises. "I won't hurt you," Mud thinks.

Me-Me dangles her foreleg reproachfully.

"Yes," Mud thinks. "That's a shame."

"Where is the one with the warts?" Although she chirps, in Mud's mind her voice is a peevish sing-song.

"She died," Mud thinks.

"The bull calf is Me-Me's." She twitches her small head, seeking out Bent.

"He is not. He never was. The one with the warts had no right to offer him."

"That one gave birth." Staring now at She-Snorts.

"Yesterday. A stillborn."

Her tail slaps the ground. She looks toward Mud's hind legs. "You haven't given birth."

"Not yet."

"It's Me-Me's."

Mud's belly seizes. "That's the bargain," she says.

Me-Me gazes west. In her orange eyes are suns. "Me-Me knows where to go," she says gloatingly but not dishonestly. For the first time Mud appreciates that a claim made in the mind cannot be false. All she hears of cunning is that until the newborn is born the route will be indirect to prevent them from guessing it.

"You'll lead us there," Mud thinks, "whether my newborn drops before we arrive or after."

"This way," the cheetah says, turning east.

"No, this way," Mud thinks reluctantly. She nods toward the southwest. "First we must mourn one of our dead."

✦ ✦ ✦

"What's done is done," Mud thinks.

They encircle and fondle the carcass, stinking and eyeless though it is, smeared with vulture dung and gouted with flies and spilling over with maggots though it is. Behind them, Me-Me dozes at the termite mound into which, when they arrived, a horde of mongooses fled.

The tusks have almost fallen out of their sockets. The narrow skull is unrecognizable under its rag of skin. "Afloat upon The Eternal Shoreless Water," the nurse cow said when they arrived, and Mud's throat clenched. Poor Date Bed, dying too young to ascend to the family of the She. Mud would have wept had She-Soothes not burst out with, "What's done is done!" and despite all the times she has bellowed it and the inevitability of her bellowing it now, Mud was struck as if by a transcendent, authorizing truth. "So it is," she said, seeing the nurse cow in an elevated light.

"What's done is done. What's done is done." Chanting this to herself, Mud wards off memory and therefore grief. It is so simple. The matriarch turns her back to the corpse and starts up a hymn. Mud turns and plants her eyes and trunk on Me-Me, who is their salvation. And whose facile heartlessness Mud suddenly envies. By what misguided arrangement were she-ones made swollen with memory rather than sleek with appetite?

It is dusk when they finish mourning. They browse and drink and then lie close enough to Date Bed to protect what's left of her from predators. Now that Me-Me is back, Bent has resumed sleeping next to his mother, and She-Soothes has instructed him to wake her if he wants to go to Mud and suckle. As for Me-Me, she hasn't budged from the termite mound. That the mongooses are trapped is Mud's last thought before she drops into her first sleep in two days.

A fierce belly cramp wakes her several hours later. She comes to her feet—disturbing only Me-Me, who looks around with shining eyes—and walks to the nearest thorn bush. The stones still hold the heat of the day. The crickets circumscribe the darkness. She suspects she has entered labour but isn't certain until she urinates. It is not only the unmistakable odour that tells her, it is the great volume. Me-Me slinks forward.

"Stay away," Mud thinks.

"It's Me-Me's."

"I'm in pain. I could hurt you without intending to."

"You could kick Me-Me." Self-pityingly.

"Go on!" She tosses her head and Me-Me scuttles to the mound. The cramp eases. She lies on her side but another cramp twists through her abdomen, and she hauls herself up to a squat and begins to dribble urine.

"I thought it would be tonight," says the voice of the matriarch. She awakens the nurse cow, and the two of them and Bent come closer.

She-Soothes tastes the urine. "Clear!" she announces happily. "Clear," the matriarch echoes, wistful.

Mud straightens. Teeters. She recalls how in the moments after she was born, her mother teetered, and she plunges deeply into that memory and emerges from it sobbing, to her alarm. Both cows prod their trunks at her mouth. She pulls away. Her urine tasting clear is *not* happy news. A live newborn will be so much harder to surrender, and yet this witless pair obviously hopes for a live one and she realizes that they may try to thwart the bargain with Me-Me. "Go back to sleep," she says as a stupendous pain brings her up on her toes, and she falls against She-Soothes and loses consciousness.

Opening her eyes, she finds herself supported between the two cows. "Why won't it drop?" she wails.

"Kneel," the matriarch says, and she and the nurse cow help lower her. "Strain," the matriarch says. Mud strains. The matriarch strokes her rump. The nurse cow strokes her vulva.

"It's not time," the nurse cow rumbles. "Lie down, She-Spurns."

Mud lies down. The two cows soar above her, irresistible, suffocating. Under the nurse cow's belly Bent hunkers. Me-Me paces at the termite mound. The shine of her eyes shafts through to Mud's belly, to the newborn, piercing it. She-Snorts steps to one side, and now the precise distance between her legs and She-Soothes' legs draws Mud into another birth memory of looking through those other legs that, during her entrapment, were the bearings of the known world.

Again she sobs. It doesn't matter. Like a calf she sucks at the matriarch's trunk. She sleeps. Sleeps for hours, it turns out. When a cramp wakes her, the darkness is lifting but the cows have not moved. The cramp heaves her to her feet. The cows assist her as she sinks back to the ground. Another cramp, and she is helped up by She-Soothes, whose eye plug drops out and is stepped on by She-Snorts. The matriarch raises her foot. "Leave it be!" She-Soothes bellows. "She-Soothes doesn't care!" Down comes the foot. Down from the eye socket comes a dreadful stench. Mud vomits. She-Soothes kicks dirt over the gleaming pool. Mud strains and feels her entire birth canal disgorging and sees a blue shimmer she thinks is escort to the agony.

"Lightning," the matriarch says.

"Here she comes!" She-Soothes bellows.

The force of the expulsion propels Mud onto her rump. Frantic, she scrambles to her feet.

There it is. Alive. Running in slow motion. Female, as predicted. Mud smells the head, which is still encased in the foetal sac. She pulls the sac free and steps aside.

"That was a bolt of lightning," the matriarch says, looking off.

"Name her Bolt!" the nurse cow trumpets. She nudges the tiny thing with one foot.

"Bolt," Mud whispers.

"She shall be Bolt!" the nurse cow trumpets.

Mud is aware of the cheetah creeping toward them and yet somehow can't determine the peril, or who presents it. When Me-Me gets too close, the nurse cow roars and the cheetah runs back to the mound. "Don't look at her," Mud tells herself, as if not hearing Me-Me's mind is the solution.

From Bolt's mind come faint peeps. She is trying to stand. Finally she does and locates the nipple, and then Mud hears a humming, which must be pleasure although Mud suspects it is also the sound of another kind of satisfaction: that of having an urgent notion confirmed. But from where in that memoryless body could a notion have arisen?

The matriarch points east. "Look," she says. Along the dawn horizon is a range of pink clouds.

"Jubilation!" the nurse cow trumpets.

"Jubilation," the matriarch says thoughtfully. She and She-Soothes and Bent walk about twenty yards onto the plain. In this burnt light, from Mud's vantage point, their thinness is accentuated and yet they seem not diminished but refined to a more intricate and essential anatomy. Behind Mud, the cheetah creeps closer. There is no sound, there is only the thickening of her nauseating stench. It is all Mud can do not to fall into a birth memory of the hyena. "I could lie down," she thought that night, and she thinks it now, the impossible decision being, should she lie beside her newborn or on top of her? She looks over her shoulder.

Me-Me is not three yards away. "Tell them it's Me-Me's," she is thinking.

Mud thinks nothing.

"You are the leader."

"I'm not."

"Me-Me knows where to go."

"The Safe Place," Mud thinks stupidly. The cleverness she inherited from She-Screams has deserted her.

"Walk over there." Me-Me points to the termite mound.

"No."

"It's Me-Me's. It's Me-Me's."

As if won over by such conviction, Bolt starts toddling toward the cheetah. Twice she falls but gets herself back up and keeps going. She is crumpled, tiny, hairy and, to Mud's eyes, alien, belonging to nobody. Nothing could be more inevitable than her woebegone little journey. Me-Me creeps closer. She is reaching out one paw when the matriarch's foot catches her under the chin and stretches her up on her hind feet. Bolt rushes back to Mud. The second kick gets the cheetah in the ribs. The third, in the side of the skull, throws her limply against the tree. Immediately the vultures hop down to the lower branches.

"You killed Me-Me," says Bent. He gapes at the matriarch, at her murderous foot.

"Good riddance," the nurse cow growls, but she, too, is astounded.

She-Snorts strolls to the tree and picks up bits of straw that have fallen from the weaverbird's nest and scatters these on the cheetah. She goes to where Mud and Bolt are and inserts her trunk into the newborn's mouth. "You'd have done the same to save mine," she says as if Mud had thanked her. Her voice is impassive, but temporin slides down her face and her odour of wrath still fumes.

Mud begins to sob. "Date Bed," she says, this beloved name a requiem for every loss of her life, from her birth mother to her birth name to Date Bed to the brief, dream-like loss of herself. Bolt screams to nurse, and Mud nuzzles her and is suddenly terror-stricken and thrashes her head around, searching for the perils that could be anywhere.

"Stop that," She-Snorts says quietly. She pulls on Mud's trunk, and after a moment Mud goes still.

"Lift your leg," the nurse cow says.

Mud does. Almost immediately Bolt finds the nipple, and

Bent rushes over and latches onto Mud's other breast, and the two calves root her to the spot so that although she sways she doesn't fall.

And now, from out of the termite mound, the mongooses emerge. There are dozens of them. They growl and hiss. They gallop over to the cheetah. Some lunge at her and some bounce on the spot, spectacular leaps as high as Bent. All at once they stop and sit on their haunches and regard their audience.

"Big, Big, Big, Big," Mud hears from their minds. She rubs her eyes with the knuckle of her trunk. "What is big?" she thinks.

A swivelling of every head in her direction. "Big, Big, Big killed, killed, killed the, the stinker, killed the stinker," they twitter out loud. They look from Mud to She-Soothes to She-Snorts, back to Mud.

"Ask them if they mind talked with Date Bed," the matriarch rumbles.

There go the heads, all turning to her now. "Sing, sing, sing the song, song about, the song about the hot, the hot, hot, hot fight, fight, fight," they twitter.

"Did the dead she-one sing?" Mud thinks, and they start screeching and jumping and falling on their backs.

"What's the matter with them?" the nurse cow bellows.

"I don't know," Mud says. She can't decipher the screeches. She pulls away from the calves and walks toward the mongooses, who suddenly sit up on their haunches. She points at Date Bed. "We came to mourn her."

"Dead! Dead! Dead!" the mongooses twitter with great distress.

"Do they know how she died?" the matriarch asks. Her voice is steady.

"Poison, poison bite, bite, poison bite," the mongooses twitter, as if they heard.

"She was struck by a flow-stick," Mud tells the cows and begins again to weep. Her birth mother and Date Bed both killed by snakes. For the third time that day she falls into her birth memory, and when she comes out of it the mongooses are gathered around her feet, twittering urgently about the white bone.

"That, that way, way!" They gesture and leap toward the southeast. "That way! That way!"

◆ ◆ ◆

The pace is slow and not only because of the calves. As always happens before the rains, spears of grass have pushed through the earth, still too fine and short to be properly grazed, but for the bliss of tasting green they walk pecking like birds.

On the second day the matriarch discovers a clod of Tall Time's dung. It is, she judges, fourteen to sixteen days old.

"He may have taken this same route!" the nurse cow trumpets.

"Perhaps," She-Snorts says.

Who they will meet at The Safe Place consumes the two big cows. Torrent, certainly—She-Snorts has no doubt that he'll have found his way. Swamp and Hail Stones . . . if they linked up with Torrent or another master tracker, there is a chance that they'll have made it. And Tall Time. Barring disaster, they can't imagine why the Link Bull wouldn't be there.

Mud doesn't tell them about her vision, in which she recognized nobody. She saw, after all, only a small corner of The Safe Place and hardly anyone up close. Neither does she speculate. She nurses her calf, and Bent. She plucks the new grass. She does things delicately, out of contrition and because she is weak with love. At least once an hour she falls into a memory and sometimes, coming out of it, she mistakes the smell of Bolt for whomever the memory featured. Bolt is Date Bed, or Hail Stones. Bolt is Tall Time in musth.

Bolt walks under her, She-Snorts in front of her, She-Soothes and Bent follow. Before them are the blue hills, and directly overhead white wads of cloud speed by, going the other way. If you look back, as Mud keeps doing, you can see the dust raised by their passage rolling out as far as the horizon, and the entire plain washed in light.

Acknowledgements

Many books proved helpful to me during my research. Among these are: *The Eye of the Elephant* by Delia and Mark Owens, *The Last Elephant* by Jeremy Gavron, *Green Hills of Africa* by Ernest Hemingway, *I Dreamed of Africa* by Kuki Gallmann, *In the Presence of Elephants* by Peter Beagle and Pat Derby, *Elephants: Majestic Creatures of the Wild* edited by Jeheskel Shoshani, *Elephants: The Deciding Decade* edited by Ronald Orenstein, *Elephants* by S. K. Eltringham, *Safari: Experiencing the Wild* by Neil Leifer and Lance Morrow, *Elephants* by Reinhard Künkel, and *The Natural History of the African Elephant* by Sylvia K. Sikes, this last a rather chilling text for how often the author shot in the head "a fine and healthy specimen" so that she might study its corpse. Various field guides, especially those published by Collins and by the National Audubon Society, were constantly consulted, as was a remarkably comprehensive and fascinating treasure called *The Behavior Guide to African Mammals* by Richard Despard Estes.

In addition to the above are three books I could not have done without, all written by people who have spent the better part of their

Acknowledgements

adult lives in Africa studying the elephant and tirelessly fighting for its safety. The fight is an uphill one because of the pressures of the ivory trade, which encourages poaching, and the disappearance of habitat. These books are: *Echo of the Elephants* by Cynthia Moss and Martyn Colbeck, *Coming of Age with Elephants* by Joyce Poole, and *Among the Elephants* by Iain and Oria Douglas-Hamilton.

I am indebted as well to Christopher Dewdney and Jan Whitford for commenting on an early version of the manuscript, and I am forever grateful to Beth Kirkwood not only for her editiorial suggestions but for helping me find my way to the Masai Mara so that I might see the African elephant in its natural home.

Thanks to the Canada Council, the Ontario Arts Council and the Toronto Arts Council for financial support. And a special thanks to my editors: Iris Tupholme at HarperCollins Canada for her foresight and unwavering faith, and Sara Bershtel at Metropolitan Books in New York for her acuity and devotion.